THE CARNAL
PRAYER MAT

THE CARNAL PRAYER MAT

(ROU PUTUAN)

LI YU

*TRANSLATED, WITH AN INTRODUCTION
AND NOTES, BY PATRICK HANAN*

AVAILABLE
PRESS

BALLANTINE BOOKS · NEW YORK

An Available Press Book
Published by Ballantine Books

Translation, notes, and introduction
copyright © 1990 by Patrick Hanan

Library of Congress Catalog Card Number: 89-91506

ISBN: 0-345-36508-9

Text design by Holly Johnson
Cover design by James R. Harris
Cover illustration: *Whiling Away the Summer* by Yin Chi,
one of twelve album leaves, 19th century.
Courtesy of Sydney L. Moss Ltd.

Manufactured in the United States of America

*I*NTRODUCTION

What first attracted me to Li Yu was his love of comic invention. "Broadly speaking," he once wrote to a friend, "everything I have ever written was intended to make people laugh." He was never content, as other writers were, to make minor variations upon the standard literary themes. Instead he submitted those themes to a drastic overhaul and created a new comedy of his own, claiming all the while that his version of reality was the true one and that everybody else was deluded. He thus belongs to that rare breed of comic writer—rare in any culture—who discovers or invents the terms of his own reality.[1]

Let me give two obvious examples, both of them discoveries rather than inventions. In its most general outline a Chinese romantic comedy consisted of a handsome youth with brilliant literary gifts falling in love with a beautiful and talented girl and, after overcoming a number of vicissitudes, marrying her. By the seventeenth century countless stories and plays, some of them masterpieces, had been written to this formula. But Li Yu would have none of it. In his first play (or opera, both terms apply), *Lianxiang ban*, a title freely translatable as *Women in Love*, he adapted the formula and applied it—for the first, and perhaps only, time in the history of Chinese literature—to a love affair between two women. Eventually the lovers are united as wives to the same man—the only solution open to them. Similarly, in Li Yu's *Silent Operas (Wusheng xi)* collection, there is a story about a love affair between two men that derives its comic power from the way it parallels a perfect heterosexual marriage, all the way from courtship to widowhood. Examples of comic discovery and invention abound also in his novel, *The Carnal Prayer Mat (Rou putuan)*.

---

1. Li Yu thought he had been born in 1611, but the clan genealogy says 1610. He died early in 1680.

Invention and discovery, together with the implied virtue of originality, were stressed more by Li Yu than by any writer before him. "Newness is a term of approbation for everything in the world," he wrote, "but above all for literature." Copying is taboo, of course, even from the ancients, but so is echoing other writers, and not merely other writers but ourselves; we are not permitted even to echo ourselves—an impossible ideal, and one that Li Yu himself did not come close to realizing.

His passion for invention carried over from literature to life. He was a designer and practical inventor as well as a writer, and his essays ring with the (slightly self-mocking) refrain: "Is it not strange that the world had to wait for Li Yu to invent this?" A version of the refrain occurs in Chapter Ten of the novel, too, after Vesperus has shown his savoir-faire with pillows: "The general principle is known to all, but . . . that particular formula has never been understood before." So strong was Li Yu's passion for novelty that he was also quite capable of shocking his readers for sensational effect.

A second unique quality is his voice or persona. Strictly speaking, he had not one voice but a range of them, mostly humorous, that he employed in his fiction and essays. The narrator in the traditional Chinese novel had always been a strong vocal presence anyway, in vague simulation of an oral storyteller, and Li Yu exploits that convention—openly manipulating the narrative, commenting on the action, addressing his readers as if they were an audience, and even answering questions posed by a fictitious member of that audience. A passage in Chapter One of his novel exemplifies this last convention:

"Storyteller, since you want people to suppress their lecherous desires, why not write a tract promoting morality?"

"Gentle readers [or audience], there is something
of which you are evidently unaware . . ."

The difference is that Li Yu is substituting a voice of his own
for the voice of the traditional narrator. Every Chinese novelist had to make some accommodation with the figure of the
traditional narrator—a history of the genre could be written
in terms of their accommodations—but Li Yu's solution was
the most personal, and perhaps the most satisfying. He was a
noted wit and pundit in life, and I suggest that he managed
to create in the voice of his fictional narrator a perfect literary
correlative for his oral wit and punditry.

Few people realize that a lively tradition of erotic fiction
existed in China, particularly in the sixteenth and seventeenth
centuries. It was a superior tradition, in my opinion, to its
somewhat later counterparts in England and France. Granted,
Fanny Hill is a small miracle, but it seems a miracle precisely
because it is isolated; and Sade's novels, *as fiction*, are second-
rate at best—full of philosophizing as well as ludicrous cruel-
ties and blasphemies. In China, by contrast, several novels of
undeniable power were written. The *Jin Ping Mei (The Golden
Lotus)* is only a partial member of the genre, being much else
besides. If there is a classic example of the Chinese erotic novel,
it is surely Li Yu's *Carnal Prayer Mat.*

It is in the nature of erotic fiction to seek out forbidden
territory to explore. In China that was likely to mean adultery,
not defloration as in the corresponding European genre. (In
Europe adultery was left to the bourgeois novel.) The reason
is clear enough: adultery violated the husband-wife ethic, one
of the key Confucian social obligations. In a family-centered
morality, it was a natural choice as the crucial sin, but for
precisely the same reason, it also posed an intolerable threat to

society. The libertine's adulterous adventures may enthrall the reader with their glimpse of forbidden pleasure, but *ultimately they must fail*. Sexuality for the Chinese writer, unlike Western apostles of eroticism from Sade to Lawrence, was a drive that had to lose when it collided with social values. That is why Chinese libertines are generally the objects of satire—as they certainly are in *Prayer Mat*. And it also explains why the Chinese novels can end only with the libertine's punishment and repentance.

But although the libertine adventure may be headed for disaster, the erotic novels obviously cannot be taken at their face value as the dire warnings they profess to be. For all its obsessiveness, the libertine adventure is presented to us with so much gusto that we are surely meant to enjoy it. I suggest that there is an inevitable—and artistically quite justifiable—tension in much visual and literary art on erotic subject matter. In Chinese fiction at least, the reader plays voyeur as well as judge as he watches the tale unfold, observing, with both pleasure and foreboding, its exploration of forbidden territory and its inescapable end.

The agency of punishment varies from novel to novel. A common one is retribution according to the doctrine of karma—that is to say, punishment in the next life for sins committed in this one. In Chapter Two of *Prayer Mat*, Li Yu takes the extraordinary step of introducing the Buddhist priest Lone Peak to explain this notion to us. The priest calls it "otherworldly" retribution and pairs it with a "thisworldly" retribution by which one's sins are repaid in this life. The second kind of retribution is an age-old, popular notion unrelated to Buddhism proper. (The novel's views are eclectic, embracing Heaven, the Principle of Heaven, the Creator, and the ancient sages, as well as Buddha.) The priest goes on to quote the adage "If I don't seduce other men's wives, my wife won't be seduced by others," and then erects it into a general principle by which an adulterer's wives and daughters are condemned to "redeem" his sins with their own—a characteristic Li Yu twist to an old idea.

The retribution plot fascinated the Chinese novelist, and one can see why; it allowed him to work human experience into newer and more meaningful shapes. He did not need to believe in the actual possibility of metaphysical retribution, for both he and his readers accepted it as part of the machinery of causation in fiction. But although Li Yu himself adopts the retribution plot gratefully enough in *Prayer Mat*, he cannot suppress his skepticism about it, as witness the debate between hero and priest in Chapter Two. The possibility of self-mockery must always be kept in mind while reading Li Yu.

The typical qualities of the erotic novel are almost all to be found in *Prayer Mat*, often in exaggerated form: the relentless quantification of sex, a feature perhaps derived from the sex manuals; the fascination with women's sexuality; the emphasis on penis size, in which Li Yu's idea of the animal implant outdoes all other novels; the trivial games, petty jealousies, and revenges that preoccupy the characters; and even the orgy, in which Li Yu's wine-and-cards party again outdoes all others.

At the same time *Prayer Mat* gives a far more prominent place to warnings against libertinism; Chapter Two is taken up with the libertine's debate with the priest, and Chapter Twenty with the former's repentance and redemption. Li Yu is using Buddhism as the ascetic alternative to libertinism—and also as a handy means of atonement. In comparison with the other novels, too, his language is not lubricious; he tends more to ribaldry than sensuality. Nor are the sexual techniques he describes particularly eye-opening by the standards of other novels.

His prime values of novelty and structural ingenuity are everywhere apparent, and there is no need to detail them here.

In any case they have been adequately described in the critiques. (The critiques are short passages that follow each chapter and assess its moral implications and literary technique.) But one quality that must be stressed is his discursiveness, which the critique to Chapter Five singles out for special mention. Although other novelists may use discourse in their prologues, we are told, they abandon it once the narrative begins, lest the reader become confused. Li Yu, however, continues to alternate discourse and narrative throughout his novel, to the reader's delight. The critique is correctly pointing to discursiveness as one of the most striking features of the novel. Li Yu not only gives up his whole first chapter to a discussion of sex in society, together with an account of the aims and methods of his book, he also constantly intervenes as narrator to explain a principle or give a reason, often conducting a simulated dialogue with his readers to do so. Sometimes the interventions are intended to tease the reader, particularly when they occur just before or during a sexual encounter. But more often they spring from Li Yu's irrepressible, inventive punditry. The opinions are his own, not those of some generalized narrator; some of them actually resemble the ideas we find in his sharp, witty, highly personal essays.

Chapter One is an extraordinary innovation, for in it Li Yu offers us a personal approach to sex. This is Li Yu the essayist speaking, as he offers us a reasonable, if reductive— love is not mentioned once— approach that prepares us for the two contrasting attitudes presented in the next chapter: Vesperus's libertinism and the priest's asceticism. Li Yu's reasonable views thus dominate the novel, even though its narrative ends on an ascetic note. But does Li Yu claim to have resolved the tension between erotic desire and social and moral values? Not at all. The epilogue to his last chapter makes it clear that he regards such tension as a permanent part of the human condition.

However, *Prayer Mat*'s greatest difference from other erotic novels lies in its wholehearted comic spirit. The other works often leave room for ribaldry, even in their most intense moments, and at least one of them is told in a wry, semihumorous tone, but none is as obviously comic as *Prayer Mat*, which is why I have labeled it a sexual comedy. Admittedly, some of the humor is facetious; Li Yu was always reluctant to pass up a comic idea, and some of his ideas worked better than others. As the final critique remarks, "This is a book that mocks *everything*!" But the novel as a whole—by turns humorous, witty, outrageous, vulgar, shocking—remains the ultimate comedy on that forbidden subject: unrestrained sexual desire at large in society.

Prayer Mat was written at the beginning of 1657 and, like most Chinese novels, was published under a pseudonym. (For this book, perhaps because of its controversial nature, Li Yu chose a fresh pseudonym.) He was in Hangzhou at the time, making a living as a writer. His plays or operas, with their audacious brand of social comedy, had caused a great stir, and his stories—a second volume of *Silent Operas* had appeared—were also extremely popular, so popular, indeed, that they were soon pirated.

Over the next three centuries *Prayer Mat* was banned many times, but seldom with much success. A dozen editions survive from the eighteenth and nineteenth centuries alone, some in only one copy; it seems likely, therefore, that still more editions once existed. The novel has circulated freely in Japan ever since an abridged (but unexpurgated) version, adapted for Japanese readers, was published there in 1705. *Prayer Mat* circulates now in several Chinese-speaking countries, but not in China itself, where it is deemed unsuitable, not merely for the general reader but even for the scholar. The earlier generation of Chinese scholars, who *were* able to read the novel, recognized its literary merits even if they deplored its subject matter.

The first edition has not survived, but we know a good deal about it from a manuscript copy and from the other editions. Like the first editions of Li Yu's stories, it must have been a fine woodblock edition with illustrations by a leading illustrator. The title-page attributed the authorship of the novel to a certain Master "Secrets of Passion." The preface, with a date corresponding to 1657, was written by a Hangzhou friend using a Buddhist pseudonym, Layman "Eternal Absolute." Curiously the table of contents and the first page of text, places where the author's name is customarily repeated, give a different pseudonym:

Composed by the Man of the [Buddhist] Way Who,
    After Being Crazed with Passion, Returned to the
    True Path
Commented upon by a Society Friend Who, After
    Dying of Passion, Was Restored to Life

Society Friend means a fellow member of the same literary society. It is possible that the commentator was Sun Zhi, a Hangzhou writer and close friend, who wrote prefaces to some of Li Yu's plays, in one of which he signed himself Society Brother.

Like some other Chinese novels published at the time, *Prayer Mat* carried its own commentary, in fact, two kinds of commentary: the critiques that are mentioned above, as well as upper-margin notes that comment on particular expressions or passages, often in a flippant or humorous way. The notes do not survive in the editions, only in the manuscript. Since I have not included them in my translation, I shall give a few examples here:

In Chapter Three, when the narrator explains that a

woman's feet without their leggings on look like flowers with no leaves about them, the note runs, "The author must be considered the leading romantic of all time. Others who talk about sex are like Yiyang actors performing Kun opera. All you hear is the drumbeat." Yiyang was a raucous popular form of opera, much despised by Li Yu and other writers of the more artistic and melodious Kun form.

In Chapter Five, when the narrator remarks that a painting—like a woman's beauty—is worthless if it lacks power, the note runs, "The insight of a romantic genius!"

In Chapter Six, when the woman whom we later know as Fragrance is described as not wearing heels, the note runs, "These days women with big feet have to use raised heels in order to hide their defect. Not wearing heels is a way of flaunting small feet."

Again in Chapter Six, when Vesperus needles the Knave by suggesting that he finds poor people easier to take advantage of, the note runs, "Brilliant provocation!" And soon afterward, when Vesperus boasts of his sexual prowess by using the analogy of a banquet, a matching note runs, "Fine hyperbole!"

In Chapter Twelve, when Cloud explains to Vesperus her jealous feelings toward her "sisters," the note runs, "If anyone tries to tell me there has ever been a better novel than *The Carnal Prayer Mat*, I shall spit in his face!"

Finally, in Chapter Seventeen, when Flora explains how she and her husband used to involve the maids in their lovemaking, the note runs, "If this method were applied generally, there would be no jealous wives left in the world."

Although the Society Friend was nominally responsible for all of the critiques and notes, it is highly likely, judging from their nature and tone, that some of them were written by Li Yu himself.

The novel shares the familiar features of the traditional

Chinese novel. Each chapter begins with a pair of matched headings that hint at its contents. Next comes a poem or lyric (a different poetic genre with lines of irregular length) that reflects on the chapter's theme. Here and there within the chapter are poems, lyrics, and set pieces (unrhymed passages of strict parallelism) that comment on the action or describe a scene. The chapter closes with some anticipatory remarks. Li Yu's chapters characteristically end with an epilogue that reflects humorously on the novel's progress.

There is no good text of the novel; all of the reasonably well-edited editions prove to be abridgments. The fullest text is a manuscript preserved in the Institute of Oriental Culture of Tokyo University. It is the only one to contain either the 1657 date or the upper-margin notes and, for that reason among others, I believe that its copyist utilized a manuscript copy of Li Yu's original edition. In making my translation, I have relied on this manuscript and also on the fullest printed edition, one that is best identified by its page format (ten columns of twenty-five characters each). The Harvard-Yenching Library at Harvard University has two of several surviving copies.

THE CARNAL
PRAYER MAT

CHAPTER *ONE*

Make use of lechery in putting a stop to lechery;
Start off with sex in treating the subject of sex.

Lyric:
    Raven hair so quickly gray,
    Ruddy cheeks soon past.
    Man's unlike the ageless pine—
    His fame and fortune, e'er in flux,
    Gone in the flower-destroying blast.
    How sad if youth is deprived of joy!
    (From the courts of love the old are cast.)
    So once you hear the siren song,
    Young masters,
    Rush to enjoy the flowers' throng.

    True paradise on earth,
    All things considered well,

Is found in bedroom bliss.
Unlike the realm of fame and glory,
Here joy begins and troubles cease.
Each day is spent in slippered ease, each night
In drunken slumber till the morning bell.
So open your eyes, take this to heart:
All the world's
A vast erotic work of art.

This lyric, to the tune of "Fragrance Filling the Courtyard," points out that our lives would be so filled with toil and worry as to leave no room for pleasure—had not the Sage who separated Heaven from Earth created in us the desire for sexual intercourse to alleviate our toil and worry and save us from despair.

In the parlance of our Confucian sticklers for morality, a woman's loins are the entrance through which we come into the world and also the exit by which we leave it. But the way wise men see these things is that, without those loins, our hair might go white a few years sooner than otherwise, and our deaths occur a few years sooner too. If you doubt their word, consider how few priests there are whose hair has not turned white by the age of forty or fifty, and whose bodies have not succumbed entirely by seventy or eighty. Of course the objection might be raised that, although priests have joined the order, they still have a way open to them, either through adultery or by having relations with their disciples, and that they may be no more apt to preserve their vital energies than the laity, all of which would explain their failure to live to a ripe old age.

But if that is true, consider the case of the eunuchs in the capital, who, far from committing adultery, have lost even the basic equipment for it and who, far from having relations with their disciples, lack even a handle on such things. In theory they ought to retain their delicate, youthful looks over a lifetime of several centuries. Why, then, do they have even more wrinkles than anybody else? And why does their hair go white even sooner? *Granddad* may be our name for them, but the truth is they look far more like grannies.[2] Plaques are put up in the capital to honor ordinary folk who have lived to a great age, but no centenary arch has ever been erected to commemorate a eunuch.

It would thus appear that the activity we call sex is not harmful to mankind. However, because the *Materia Medica* failed to include it, we lack a definitive explanation.[3] One view holds that it is good for us, another that it does us harm. But if we compare both views in the light of the above argument, we must conclude that sex is beneficial. In fact its medicinal effects closely resemble those of ginseng and aconite, two substances with which it can be used interchangeably. But there is a point to be noted here. Potent tonics as they are, ginseng and aconite should be taken only in small doses and over long periods of time. In other words they should be treated as medicine, not as food. When swallowed indiscriminately, without regard to dosage or frequency, they can prove fatal.

Now, sex has precisely the same advantages and disadvantages. Long-term use results in the mutual reinforcement of yin and yang, whereas excessive use brings the water and fire elements into conflict.[4] When treated as medicine, sex relieves

---

2. *Gonggong* was a term of address for a eunuch and also for a grandfather.

3. The *Bencao gangmu* of Li Shizhen, first published in 1593.

4. The kidneys (and the sex functions) are related to the water element, the heart to fire.

us from pent-up emotion, but when treated as food it gravely depletes our semen and blood.

If people knew how to treat it as a medicine, they would behave toward it with a degree of detachment, liking it, but well short of addiction. Before first engaging in it, they would reflect, "This is a medicine, not a poison. Why be afraid of it?" And after engaging in it, they would reflect, "That was a medicine, not a food. Why become addicted to it?" If they did this, their yang would not be too exuberant nor their yin too depressed. No one would die an early death, and what is more, no girls would be left without husbands nor men without wives, a development that would contribute substantially to the institution of Royal Government.[5]

But there is one further point to consider. The properties of sex as a medicine are the same as those of ginseng and aconite in every respect save the location in which it occurs and the criteria by which it is selected; in both of those respects there are contrasting features of which users should be apprised. In the case of ginseng and aconite, the *genuine* variety is the superior one, while the *local* product brings no benefit;[6] whereas with sexual activity, it is the local variety that is superior and the genuine one that not only brings no benefit but can even do harm.

What do I mean by *local product* and *genuine variety*? The term *local product* refers to the women you already possess, your own wives and concubines; you have no need to look further afield or to spend your money; you simply take what is at hand. There is no one to stop you, no matter how you

---

5. The ideal political system advocated by the philosopher Mencius.

6. Li Yu is apparently speaking of ginseng rather than aconite. The best ginseng grew in Manchuria and the next best in Korea. The better varieties were known as *daodi*, that is, genuine.

choose to sleep, nor any need for alarm, no matter who knocks on your door. Sex under such circumstances does no damage to your vital energies; it even benefits your ancestral shrine. If a single encounter results in such physical harmony, surely we can agree that sex does us good!

Genuine variety refers to the dazzling looks and glamour that are found only in the boudoirs of rich men's houses. Just as the bland domestic fowl lacks the refreshing tang of the game bird, so our wives' faded looks can hardly compare with the youth and glamour of these fledglings of the boudoir. When you set eyes on a girl of this kind, you dream about her; you strive to win her at all costs; you make advances, then follow them up with presents; and you scale walls to get to secret assignations or clamber through tunnels to declare your passion. But no matter how emboldened you are by lust, you'll still be as terrified as a mouse; even if no one has seen you, you'll always think someone is coming; you'll sweat more from fear than from love, and semen will seep from every pore. The desire for love exceeds the heroic spirit; when you're taken in adultery, you'll lose your beard and eyebrows. A plunge into the abyss will result in a frightful disaster. In the other world you'll have destroyed your moral credit; in this world you'll have broken the law and will be put to death. Since there is no one left to pay for your crime, your wife will have to live on and develop her own desires, engaging in unchaste behavior and doing all kinds of harm—an unbearable tragedy. In the case of sex it is obvious that people must on no account sacrifice the near in favor of the far, the coarse in favor of the fine, or spurn the commonplace in order to seek what is rare.

The author of this novel has been motivated solely by compassion in his desire to expound the doctrine. His hope is to persuade people to suppress their desires, not indulge them; his aim is to keep lechery hidden rather than to publicize it.

Gentle readers, you must on no account misconstrue these intentions of his.

Storyteller, since you want people to suppress their lecherous desires, why not write a tract to promote morality? Why write a romantic novel instead?[7]

Gentle readers, there is something of which you are evidently unaware. Any successful method of changing the current mores must resemble the way in which Yu the Great controlled the floods: channeling current trends into a safe direction is the only way to get a hearing. People these days are reluctant to read the canonical texts, but they love fiction. Not all fiction, mind you, for they are sick of exemplary themes and far prefer the obscene and the fantastic. How low contemporary morals have sunk! Anyone concerned about public morality will want to retrieve the situation. But if you write a moral tract exhorting people to virtue, not only will you get no one to buy it; even if you were to print it and bind it and distribute it free along with a complimentary card, the way philanthropists bestow Buddhist scriptures on the public, people would just tear the book apart for use in covering their winepots or in lighting their pipes and refuse to bestow a single glance upon its contents.

A far better solution is to captivate your readers with erotic material and then wait for some moment of absorbing interest before suddenly dropping in an admonitory remark or two to make them grow fearful and sigh, "Since sexual pleasure can be so delightful, surely we ought to reserve our

---

7. I have used italics to mark passages of simulated address by the audience to the storyteller/narrator. Simple questions from the audience are not italicized.

pleasure-loving bodies for long-term enjoyment instead of turning into ghosts beneath the peony blossoms,[8] sacrificing the reality of pleasure for its mere name?" You then wait for the point at which retribution is manifested and gently slip in a hortatory word or two designed to provoke the revelation "Since adultery is always repaid like this, surely we ought to reserve our wives and concubines for our own enjoyment instead of trying to shoot a sparrow with the priceless pearl,[9] repaying worthless loans with real money?" Having reached this conclusion, readers will not stray, and if they don't stray, they will naturally cherish their wives, who will in turn respect them. The moral education offered by the Zhounan and Shaonan songs[10] is really nothing more than this: the method of "fitting the action to the case and the treatment to the man." It is a practice incumbent not only upon fiction writers; indeed, some of the sages were the first to employ it, in their classical texts.

If you doubt me, look at how Mencius in Warring States times addressed King Xuan of Qi on the subject of Royal Government.[11] The king was immersed in sensual pleasures

---

8. The victims of amorous excess.

9. The allusion is to the *Zhuang Zi*. See Burton Watson, trans., *The Complete Works of Chuang Tzu* (New York: Columbia University Press, 1968), p. 313: "Now suppose there were a man here who took the priceless pearl of the Marquis of Sui and used it as a pellet to shoot at a sparrow a thousand yards up in the air—the world would certainly laugh at him."

10. These are the titles of the first two sections of the "Songs of the States" in the *Poetry Classic* (*Book of Songs*). They stand for the "Songs" as a whole, many of which are about love.

11. For this passage, see D. C. Lau, trans., *Mencius* (London: Penguin Books, 1970), pp. 65–66. King Tai's flight was a migration to a new settlement. Note that the words Li Yu puts into the puritan's mouth parody Mencius's lecturing style.

and the pursuit of wealth, and Royal Government did not figure among his interests, and so to Mencius's speech he returned only a perfunctory word of praise: "Well said." To which Mencius replied, "If Your Majesty approves of my advice, why not follow it?" "I have an affliction," said the king. "I love wealth." To whet his interest, Mencius told him the story of Liu the Duke's love of wealth, which is on the theme of frugal management. But the king then said, "I have another affliction. I love sex." By this remark he meant that he was interested in becoming another King Jie or Zhou.[12] It was tantamount to sending Mencius a formal note rejecting the whole idea of Royal Government.

Now, if a puritan had been there in Mencius's place, he would have remonstrated sternly with the king along these lines: "Rulers from time immemorial have admonished us against sexual license. If the ordinary folk love sex, they will lose their lives; if the great officers love sex, they will lose their positions; if the feudal lords love sex, they will lose their states; and if the Son of Heaven loves sex, he will lose the empire." To which King Xuan, even though he might not actually have voiced the sentiment, would certainly have replied mentally along these lines: "In that case, my affliction has penetrated so deep that it is incurable, and I have no further use for you."

Mencius, however, did not reply like that. Instead he used the romantic tale of King Tai's love of sex to gain the king's interest and get him so excited that he could hardly wait to start. From the fact that King Tai, although fleeing on horseback, still took his beautiful consort along with him, he deduced that the king's lifelong love of sex made him loath to be parted from his women for a moment. Such a

---

12. The last rulers of the Xia and Shang dynasties, respectively, who were famous for their gargantuan debaucheries.

dissolute ruler ought surely to have lost both his life and his kingdom, but this king practiced a love of sex that allowed all the men in his country to bring their women with them in their flight, and while he was making merry with his consort, his men were able to make merry with their women. It was a case of moral influence exerted by a king who "brought springtime with him wherever he went and was unselfish in all things." Everyone was moved to praise him and none dared criticize.

Naturally from this point on, King Xuan was perfectly willing to practice Royal Government and made no further *I have an affliction* excuses. Otherwise he might well have demurred again with trite excuses such as *I love wine* or *I have a bad temper.* Mencius's ploy may truly be said to have made a "lotus emerge from the flames"[13]—a technique from which the author of this novel drew his inspiration. If only the entire reading public would buy this book and treat it as a classic or as a history rather than as fiction! Its addresses to the reader are all either admonitory or hortatory, and close attention should be paid to their underlying purpose. Its descriptions of copulation, of the pleasures of the bedchamber, do indeed come close to indecency, but they are all designed to lure people into reading on until they reach the dénouement, at which point they will understand the meaning of retribution and take heed. Without these passages the book would be nothing but an olive that, for all its aftertaste, would be too sour for anyone to chew and hence useless.[14] My passages of sexual description should be looked upon as the date wrapped around the olive that induces people to keep on eating until

---

13. A reference to the Buddhist parable of the burning house (*Lotus Sutra*).

14. The olive, with its bitter taste, stands for a salutary lesson.

they reach the aftertaste. But please pardon the tedium of this opening; the story proper will begin in the next chapter.

CRITIQUE

How enticing this novel sounds! I am sure that when it is finished, the entire reading public will buy it and read it. The only people who may not are the puritans. The genuine puritans will; only that species of false puritan, those who try to deceive people with their righteousness, will not dare. On the other hand, it has been suggested that, although the false puritans will not dare buy it themselves, they just may get someone else to buy it for them, and although they won't dare read it openly, they just may do so on the sly.

CHAPTER *TWO*

An old monk opens his leather bag in vain,
As a young layman prefers the carnal prayer mat.

Poem:

> Though the Sea of Desire seems not so deep,
> Like Weakness Water, it cannot be crossed.[15]
> You may skim as light as a dragonfly's flight,
> But touch a wave and you're surely lost.

Our story tells how in the Peaceful Government era of the
Yuan dynasty there lived on Mount Guacang a monk whose

---

15. A legendary body of water. Although shallow, it is uncrossable;
even a feather will sink.

religious name was Correct And Single and whose monastic name was Lone Peak. Before becoming a monk, he had distinguished himself as a licentiate in the Chuzhou prefectural school. However, he had also shown early signs of a propensity for the religious life. While only one month old and still in swaddling clothes, he would babble on and on like a schoolboy reciting his lessons, to the bewilderment of his parents. An itinerant priest came begging to the door, caught sight of the infant half-crying and half-laughing in a maidservant's arms, and after listening intently, declared, "It's the *Surangama Sutra* the child is reciting! He must be the reincarnation of some famous priest." He pleaded with the parents to let him have the baby as his disciple, but the parents dismissed his talk as nonsense.

As the child grew, his parents made him study for the examinations, but although he could absorb several lines at a glance, his heart was not set on worldly success, and on several occasions he forsook Confucian for Buddhist studies and had to be severely disciplined by his parents before returning. Forced to take the examinations, he graduated as a licentiate while still a boy, and afterward used his stipend to help others. When his parents died, he completed the three years of mourning and then distributed the whole of the valuable family property among his relatives. For himself he made only a large bag to hold his wooden fish, a copy of the *Sutrapitaka*, and a few other things, then took the tonsure and lived the life of a recluse while practicing the Buddhist virtues. Enlightened people called him Abbot Lone Peak; others called him Priest Leather Bag.

He differed from other priests in abstaining not only from wine, meat, lust, and depravity but also from three staple activities of the priestly life. Which activities were they, do you suppose?

Asking for alms
Explicating the scriptures
Residing on a famous mountain[16]

When people inquired as to why he didn't ask for alms, he would reply, "In general one must approach Buddhism through self-denial, striving to wear oneself out physically and stinting on one's food in order to make starvation and cold an ever-increasing threat. Once that is achieved, lustful thoughts will not arise, and if they do not arise, impurity will gradually give way to purity, and in the fullness of time one will naturally become a buddha. It is not necessary to recite scriptures or chant mantras. If, on the other hand, you choose neither to plow your own fields nor to weave your own cloth but rely instead on benefactors for your food and clothing, once you're well fed and warmly clad, you'll want to stroll about at your ease and sleep in a soft bed. As you stroll about, your eyes will light on objects of desire, and while you're sleeping in your soft bed, you'll have dreams and fantasies. Not only will you be unable to study Buddhism with any success, all kinds of damning temptation will come unbidden to your door. That is why I live off the fruits of my own labor and abstain from asking for alms."

When asked why he did not explicate the scriptures, he replied, "The language of the scriptures comes from the mouth of Buddha himself, and he is the only one who can explain it. All attempts at popular explication are like the ramblings of an idiot, with each layer of exegesis merely adding another layer of distortion. Long ago Tao Yuanming chose not to seek

---

16. There were eight or nine sacred mountains.

a detailed explanation in reading texts.[17] Now, if a Chinese does not dare seek a detailed explanation in reading a Chinese text, how can he be so reckless as to try interpreting a foreign one? I do not presume to be Buddha's right-hand man; all I hope is to escape his condemnation. That is why I keep my ignorance to myself and abstain from explicating the scriptures."

When they asked him why he chose not to live on some famous mountain, he replied, "A practicing Buddhist must not set eyes on any object of desire, lest it throw his thoughts into turmoil. Now, objects of desire are not confined to carnal pleasure and money. A cool and pleasant breeze, an enchanting moon, melodious birdsong, even succulent fernshoots—anything that charms or enraptures and makes us unwilling to give it up is an object of desire.

"Once you start living in some scenic place, the spirits of mountain and stream will be there to tempt you to poetry, so that you can never put your writing aside. And the nymphs of wind and moon will disturb your meditations and make you fidget endlessly on the midnight prayer mat. That is why those who go up famous mountains to pursue their examination studies never finish them, and also why those who go there to master the doctrine find it so hard to purge their senses. Moreover, on every famous mountain there are women who come to pray and gentlemen who come to celebrate. The affair between the priest Moonbright and the girl Liu Cui is a warning of what can happen.[18] That is why I have spurned

---

17. The poet Tao Qian (A.D. 365–427). See his "Biography of Mr. Five Willows."

18. See the story "The Priest Moonbright Saves Liu Cui" in *Gujin xiaoshuo, Stories Old and New*, published about 1621.

famous mountains and come to live here in this desolate place, my sole purpose being to ensure that nothing I see or hear will block my progress."

His questioners were greatly impressed with his answers, which, they felt, contained insights never before expressed by an eminent priest.

By virtue of these three abstentions, he became famous despite himself. But although visitors flocked there from all quarters to join the order, he would not accept them easily. Before giving applicants the tonsure, he insisted on examining them to ensure that they had a good moral basis and had renounced all worldly desires, and if he felt the slightest doubt, he would reject them out of hand. For this reason, despite the many years he had been in the order, he had very few disciples. He lived alone beside a mountain stream in a small thatched hut that he had built with his own hands, eating the food he grew himself and drinking the water from his stream. He wrote out a pair of scrolls, which he stuck on the uprights in his hut. They read,

No ease or comfort is to be found in the study of
    Buddhism; through all eighteen hells you must
    make your way.
It is no simple matter to understand Zen; how many
    thousand prayer mats have you worn out?

Even in these scrolls one can see his lifelong mortification of the flesh.

One day of dismal autumn wind, when the trees were shedding their leaves and the drone of insects filled the air, the priest rose early in the morning, swept the leaves from his door, changed the pure water before the image of Buddha, inserted the incense, and then, placing a prayer mat in the center room, sat down cross-legged upon it to meditate. By chance he had forgotten to shut the door, and suddenly a young student attended by two pages came walking in. In appearance:

> An expression like autumn water,
> A form like a spring cloud.
> A face like Pan An's,
> A waist like Shen Yue's.
> An unpowdered complexion pale as any woman's,
> Unrouged lips rosy as any maiden's.
> Eyebrows so long as to meet his eyes,
> A form so delicate as hardly to bear his clothes.
> A jet-black crepe-silk cap he had,
> Matching his face like a crown of jade.
> Bright red tapestry-silk shoes he wore,
> And stepped as lightly as if walking on clouds.

These lines describe the grace and charm of his whole person, and yet they give only the most general of accounts. If you were to try describing the various parts of his body one by one, you could write dozens of rhapsodies and hundreds of eulogies and still not do them justice. But with the single exception of his eyes, his features, fine as they were, were not greatly superior to other people's. His eyes, however, were quite extraordinary. Extraordinary in what way, you ask. A lyric to the tune "Moon Over West River" supplies the answer:

> Crevices fine as delicate jade,
> Pupils frozen-crystal clear.
> Their black and white too bold a clash,
> Flames forever on the move.
> At sight of man, they're white,
> At sight of woman, black.

In contrast, Ruan Ji's eyes were short on passion;[19]
No mirror they, of pretty girls.

Eyes of this type are what are commonly known as lustful
eyes. People who have them generally prefer the covert glance
to the direct gaze, and reserve it for their specialty, which is
peeping at women. They do not need to be at close range,
either. Even when hundreds of feet away, they need flash only
a single glance at a girl to tell if she is pretty or not. If she
is pretty, they'll send her a wink. If she is a proper, highly
principled girl and passes by with her head lowered, not glancing at the man's face, the wink has fallen on stony ground. But
if they meet a woman with lustful eyes, one who shares their
own weakness, then winks will pass back and forth, a whole
love letter will be exchanged through their eyes, and they'll
be inextricably involved. That is why, for both men and
women, it is by no means a blessing to be born with such eyes,
for they lead only to the loss of honor and reputation. If your
honorable eyes are of this kind, gentle reader, you must exer-
cise the greatest care.

On this occasion the student came in and bowed four times
before the image of Buddha and another four times before the
priest. He then straightened up and stood to one side, stock-still
and bolt upright. The priest, having already begun his meditations, was unable to return his greeting. Only when he had
finished his duties did he leave the prayer mat and give four
deep bows in return. Then, inviting his visitor to sit down, he
asked him his name.

---

19. The poet, who lived from A.D. 210 to 263. White (contracted)
pupils signify disdain, black (dilated) pupils signify approval and pleasure.
We are told in his biography (*Jin History* 49) that Ruan revealed his mood
by purposely making his eyes white or black.

"Your disciple," said the student, "has come from a long way off to pursue his studies in Zhejiang. My sobriquet is Scholar Vesperus. Hearing that the master is the most eminent priest of the age and a living buddha between Heaven and Earth, I have fasted and observed the proscriptions, and I come here to do him reverence."

Storyteller, when you told us just now that the priest asked him his name, why didn't he give his family and personal names instead of a sobriquet?

Gentle reader, you should understand that the intellectuals at the end of the Yuan dynasty held to certain rather unusual practices. Educated men were reluctant to use their family and personal names and addressed each other by their sobriquets instead. Thus everybody had a sobriquet. Some called themselves Scholar This, some called themselves Savant That, while others called themselves Master Whatever. In general, the young men used the word *Scholar*, the middle-aged *Savant*, and the elderly *Master*. The characters that formed the sobriquet all had their various connotations, signifying some passion or predeliction. The only requirement in choosing your characters was that their meaning be apparent to you; it was not necessary that it be apparent to everybody else.

Since the student was preoccupied with sex and favored the nighttime over the daytime and the earlier part of the night over the later part, he had, on seeing the lines "What of the night? Vesper's still the hour" in the *Poetry Classic*, plucked a character or two out of context and taken the name Scholar Vesperus.[20]

---

20. See the poem "Ting liao" in the *Poetry Classic*. It is translated by Arthur Waley in *The Book of Songs* (New York: Grove Press, 1987), p. 191.

Embarrassed by the young man's effusive greeting, the priest replied with a few modest phrases.

By this time the vegetables in the priest's earthenware pot were ready to eat. Since his visitor had come such a long way, the priest thought he must be famished and asked him to stay and share the morning meal. Then, sitting there opposite each other, they began to discuss Zen, in which their wits proved to be evenly matched. The reason for this was that Vesperus, in addition to being highly intelligent, had not only prepared himself thoroughly in his examination subjects, he had also ranged through the texts of all the various religions and philosophies. Zen subtleties that others would not have understood even after long explanations he grasped completely as soon as the priest touched on them. Although the latter did not voice the thought, he could not help musing, What a fine intelligence the man has! But the Creator is at fault for giving him this physical form. Why match a heart that was meant for the study of Buddha with a face that will lead to damnable deeds? In his looks and demeanor I see all the signs of a notorious satyr who, should I fail to get him into my leather bag, will wreak havoc in the women's quarters with his clandestine amours. Goodness knows how many women throughout the world will be ruined by him! If I'd never met this troublemaker, I could have ignored him, but I would be offending against the principle of compassion if I did not try for mankind's sake to stop him. Even if the root of evil should prove too firmly planted, I will at least have done my best!

"Ever since I set my heart on the salvation of mankind," he said to Vesperus, "these eyes of mine have observed countless people. Those stupid husbands and wives who refuse to turn to goodness we can ignore. But even the scholars who come here to study Zen, like the officials who come to hear the doctrine, are rank novices. In general it takes a different kind of intelligence to understand Zen than to understand doctrine, Zen being much the harder. People who understand ten times as much as they are taught in Confucianism can expect to understand only twice as much on turning to Buddhism. So I am pleasantly surprised at your perceptiveness, worthy lay brother. If you were to apply it to Zen, you could expect to attain perfect understanding within just a few years. For a human born into an earthly existence, attaining physical form is the easy part, attaining a soul the difficult. Mere time is easy to endure, it's an eon that is hard. Having the innate capacity to become a buddha, you must not take the demons' road. Why not seize this moment, in the bloom of your youth, to rid yourself of sexual desire and take your vows as a monk? Common clay though I am, I may still serve to bring out better things in you. If you will take this pledge and secure the fruits of enlightenment, after your death you will not only share sacrificial benefits with other priests, you will also escape the rule of the demons in Hell. Well, layman, what do you say?"

"Your disciple has long aspired to join the order," said Vesperus, "and at some point in the future I shall certainly turn to it. But I have two unfulfilled desires that I cannot rid myself of. I intend to return and fulfill them while I'm still young, enjoying a few years of pleasure and ensuring that my life has not been lived in vain. There will be time enough afterward for ordination."

"May I inquire what your two desires are?" asked the priest. "Can I assume that you want to do justice to your studies by gaining an appointment in some prosperous place and also to repay the Court by winning glory in foreign parts?"

Vesperus shook his head. "It's not fame and glory that I seek. Although all educated men are expected to try, those certain to succeed are far outnumbered by those destined for failure. Even Liu Fen was failed by the examiners, even Li Bai never succeeded.[21] Your talents may seem certain to bring you success, but you still need the right destiny, and I can hardly arrange *that* for myself! Glory and high achievement are dependent on fate, and if Heaven denies you the opportunity for glory and men the chance of achievement, even if you have the loyalty of Yue Fei and the integrity of Guan Yu, you'll still just be beating your brains out and sacrificing your life with no guarantee of ever making a contribution to your country![22] I know how fame and fortune work, and what I am seeking is not to be found among such things."

"In that case, what *do* your desires consist of?"

"What I seek are rewards I can achieve through my own efforts, things I can count on. They are no pipe dreams, nor are they particularly difficult to obtain. To make no bones about it, master, your disciple's memory for texts, his grasp of doctrine, and the quality of his prose style are all absolutely first-rate. Our present-day men of letters are reduced to quoting texts from memory and shuffling them about so as to produce a few school exercises that they then publish in a volume of prose or poetry, after which they set themselves up as original geniuses and indulge their idiosyncrasies for the rest of their lives. If you ask me, their works are nothing but pastiche. If you want to be a truly great writer, you have no choice but to read every rare and remarkable book in existence, make the acquaintance of all the exceptional men of the age,

---

21. Liu Fen, a Tang candidate, was failed by the examiners for criticizing current policies. Li Bai is the famous poet (whose name is usually written Li Po).

22. Yue Fei and Guan Yu personified patriotism and personal honor, respectively.

and visit every famous mountain. Only after that should you withdraw into your study and set down your thoughts for posterity. If you are fortunate enough to succeed in the examinations, you may also make a contribution to the Court. But if you are out of luck, and spend your life in some humble position, you will still have earned yourself an immortal reputation. Therefore I cherish two secret desires in my heart: First, to be the most brilliant poet in the world . . ."

"That is your first wish," said the priest, "but what is your second?"

Vesperus had opened his mouth to speak but then choked back the words as if afraid that the priest would laugh at him.

"Since you're afraid to mention it," said the priest, "let me say it for you."

"How could my master know what I have in my mind?"

"Let me try. If I'm wrong, I'll take the consequences, but if I'm right, you must not deny it."

"If my master were to guess correctly, he would be an immortal as well as a bodhisattva, and I'd beseech him to point out to me the error of my ways. I would never dream of denying it."

Slowly and deliberately the priest intoned, "Second, to marry the most beautiful girl in the world."

Vesperus was struck dumb. After a long pause he managed a smile.

"Master, you truly are a wizard! I repeat those two wishes to myself all day long. You guessed it the first time, just as if you had overheard me."

"Have you never heard the saying, 'The whispering of men on Earth echoes in Heaven like a roll of thunder'?"

"By rights," said Vesperus, "I ought not to discuss matters of sexual passion in your presence. But since you have brought this up, master, I can only reply truthfully. To be candid with you, my religious vocation is still quite undeveloped, whereas my desires are at their peak. The two terms *beautiful girl* and *brilliant poet* have always been inseparable. For every brilliant poet there has to be a beautiful girl somewhere to form a pair, and vice versa. But so far I have never seen a truly outstanding beauty. All the women with any claims to attractiveness are already married to the ugliest of men and cannot help but secretly regret it. Now, my poetic gifts go without saying, but my looks are flawless too. I often gaze at myself in the mirror, and if Pan An and Wei Jie were alive today, I would not concede very much to them.[23] Since Heaven has given birth to someone like me, it must also have given birth to a girl fit to be my mate. If there's no such girl alive today, that is too bad. But if she does exist, your disciple will be the one to seek her hand in marriage. That is why at twenty I am still unmarried—I want to do full justice to my genius and my looks. Let me go back, find a beautiful girl, marry her, and have a son to continue the ancestral sacrifices. By then my desires will have been fulfilled and I will have no further ambitions. Not only will I repent my ways, I will also urge my wife to seek salvation along with me. What do you think, master?"

The priest said nothing at first, but then gave a sardonic chuckle and finally replied. "At first sight, your idea seems irreproachable. The only trouble is that the Lord of Heaven, who created all men, blundered dreadfully in your case. Had he given you an ugly body, your luminous soul might have attained the fruits of enlightenment, for the same reason that so many people crippled by leprosy or epilepsy have become immortals and buddhas by suffering Heaven's punishment. But when the Lord of Heaven endowed you with physical form,

___
23. Pan An and Wei Jie personified male beauty.

he was a little too indulgent. He acted like those doting parents who cannot bear to spank or scold their child lest he be physically or psychologically harmed by the experience. By the time the boy grows up, he is convinced that his body and nature were given him by Heaven and Earth and nurtured by his father and mother so that no harm will ever befall him, and he does any wicked thing that enters his head. Only after he has committed a crime and been sentenced by the judge to a beating or by the Court to execution does he resent the fact that his parents' excessive indulgence has brought him to this state. That soft flesh and pampered nature of yours are not a good sign. Layman, because of your looks, and because you are a brilliant poet, you wish to seek out the most beautiful girl. Whether you find a beauty or not is one thing, but supposing you do, I don't imagine that she'll have NUMBER ONE inscribed on her temples, and when you see someone better, you'll want to change your mind. But the second one, supposing she shares your nature, will be very particular about whom she marries and will want to wait for the most brilliant poet. Will you be able to obtain her as a concubine? And what if she already has a husband, how will you deal with that? If you give up this wild idea of yours, you will not have married the most beautiful girl, true, but if you persist in carrying it out by any and every means, your actions will have consequences that will condemn you to Hell. Layman, would you rather go to Hell or to Heaven? If you're prepared to go to Hell, just continue your search for the most beautiful girl. But if you wish to go to Heaven, I beseech you to put this wild idea out of your mind and join me in the order."

"What the master said before, I found extremely interesting. But terms like *Heaven* and *Hell* are rather banal, hardly the sort of thing one expects from an eminent priest. The way to understand Zen is simply to realize one's own origin in order to place oneself outside birth and death and so become a buddha. There's no such place as Heaven for us to ascend to! Even if one commits a few sins of the flesh, they will offend against Confucian doctrine only. There's no such place as Hell for us to descend to!"

" 'Those who do good go to Heaven; those who do evil go to Hell.' You're right, those are banalities," said the priest. "But you intellectuals can avoid the banal in every sphere of life save that of personal morality, where it is absolutely inescapable. Disregard for a moment the irrefutable evidence for the existence of Heaven and Hell. Even if Heaven did not exist, we should still need the concept of Heaven as an induce-ment to virtue. Similarly, even if Hell did not exist, we should still need the concept of Hell as a deterrent to vice. Since you're so tired of banalities, I'll skip the matter of other-worldly retribution, which will take place in the hereafter, and deal only with the thisworldly retribution of the present. But in order to discuss it, I shall need to start off with another banality, an adage that runs, 'If I don't seduce other men's wives, my wife won't be seduced by others.'

"Now, I grant you, this adage is the hoariest of all banali-ties, but the lecher has not been born who has escaped its consequences. Those who have seduced other men's wives have had their own wives seduced; those who have defiled other men's daughters have had their own daughters defiled. The only way of escaping the banality is to stop your adultery and defilement. If you persist, it will inevitably come to apply to you. Do you want to escape it or not? If not, go right on searching for the most beautiful girl in the world. If you want to escape it, I beseech you to put these wild ideas out of your mind and join me in the order."

"You've given a very thorough exposition, master. The trouble is that, when expounding the doctrine to ignorant people, you have to put things dramatically enough to make their flesh creep if you want them to heed your warnings. But when you're reasoning with people like me, there's no need for any of that. The Lord of Heaven lays down strict rules, but he is always merciful about applying them. Although many adulterers and seducers do receive retribution, a considerable number receive none. If the Lord of Heaven goes from door to door checking on adultery and making the seducer's wives and daughters pay for his seductions, what a prurient mind he must have! In general terms, of course, the principles of cyclic movement and of retribution are infallible, and wrongdoers have to be apprised of them; that is the main theme of moral education. But why must you be so literal-minded?"

"Am I to understand from what you say," said the priest, "that there are cases of adultery and seduction that receive no retribution? I seriously doubt that the Lord of Heaven, having once laid down the rules, has ever allowed anyone to escape his net. Perhaps your loyalty and generosity have so affected your observation that you tend to see people escaping. But so far as my observation goes, no one has ever seduced another man's wife or daughter and failed to receive retribution for it. The cases in both the oral tradition and the written record number in the thousands and tens of thousands. As one who has joined the order and accepted the commandments, I have trouble speaking about such matters, but just think for a moment. Seducing another man's wife or daughter means taking advantage of him, and so the seducer is ready to talk about it and many people come to know. But having your own wife or daughter seduced means suffering a loss, so you are reluctant to talk about it and few people get to know. There are cases, too, of wives and daughters keeping their husbands and fathers in the dark, so that the men are ignorant and think there has been no retribution for their adultery and seduction. Not until the coffin lids close over their heads do they start to believe in the ancient adage, by which time it is too late to tell anyone of their discovery. Not only will your wife and daughters have to repay your debts of seduction and adultery, but the thought of adultery and seduction will no sooner have entered your mind than your wife and daughters will automatically start thinking licentious thoughts themselves. For instance, if you have an ugly wife who does not greatly excite you during intercourse and you get your pleasure by imagining her as the pretty girl you saw that day, how do you know that at that very moment your wife isn't just as put off by your ugliness and isn't getting *her* pleasure by imagining you as that handsome young fellow she saw the same day? This sort of thing is universal, of course, but although no one's chastity has been compromised, damage has been done to even the stoutest heart and, in its way, that damage is also retribution for lechery. If even your thoughts are repaid like this, think how much worse is the crime you commit when you enter a woman's chamber, press yourself upon her, and, unseen by ghosts and spirits and beyond the Creator's censure, deprive someone's wife of her chastity! What I'm telling you, layman, is no banality. Wouldn't you agree?"

"Again, you've given a very logical exposition," said Vesperus, "but there's one question I'd like to raise with you, master. The man with a wife and daughter who seduces other men's womenfolk has his own wife and daughter to repay his debts. But if he's a bachelor, without wife or concubine, sons or daughters, how are *his* debts going to be repaid? This is a case to which the Lord of Heaven's rules don't apply. And there is a further argument. A man's womenfolk are limited in number, whereas there is an infinite supply of feminine beauty in the world. For example, if you have just one wife or concubine, plus a child or two, and you seduce an infinite number of women, even if your wife and daughter go wrong, you will still have made a huge profit on the transaction. How does the Lord of Heaven deal with that?"

When the priest heard him make this argument, he realized that he was dealing with a stubborn stone indeed, one who could not be swayed.[24] His only recourse was to suggest a compromise that would give Vesperus a measure of freedom.

"Layman," he remarked, "your debating skills are so sharp that I'm afraid I'm no match for you. Since my words have failed to convince you, you'll have to experience these things yourself before you grasp the principle involved. By all means go back, marry a beautiful girl, and gain your enlightenment on the carnal prayer mat; then you'll discover the truth. I'll stop my prattling, but I have one last thing to add. Layman, you have the attributes of a sage among men, you have the capacity to attain the heights, and I cannot bear to give you up. When you have seen the light, if you wish to come and ask me about the road back to salvation, don't be too embarrassed and cut yourself off from me just because my advice has been all too correct. From now on I shall spend each day waiting anxiously for your return."

So saying, he cut off a piece of paper, picked up his brush, and wrote a four-line gāthā on it. The gāthā ran,

> Pray cast aside the leathern bag
> And on the carnal prayer mat wait.
> While still alive you must repent,
> Not cry: "The coffin's shut—too late!"

He then folded the paper several times and gave it to Vesperus. "I am a thick-witted priest who knows nothing of decorum. The gāthā is too drastic, I know, but I assure you it is prompted

---

24. The reference is to the legend of a Buddhist priest whose sermons were so powerful that they moved the surrounding rocks or stones to nod their heads.

only by compassion. Keep it with you, and one day it will prove me right."

With that, he stood up as if to see Vesperus on his way. Vesperus realized he was being dismissed and felt it impossible to stay. But he respected the older man too much as an eminent priest to take an ill-mannered departure, so he bowed his head and apologized. "Your disciple is too stupid and pigheaded to accept your instruction, but he still hopes you will forgive him, master. When one day he returns, he will respectfully beseech you to take him in."

He knelt down again and bowed four times. The priest responded in like manner and then saw his visitor out of the gate, where he repeated his warnings before parting.

With this sentence the priest's debut is concluded. We shall proceed to tell of Vesperus's obsession with sex but without further mention of Lone Peak. If you wish to learn what becomes of him, you will have to keep on reading until the final chapter, in which he reappears.

CRITIQUE

Vesperus is the male lead of a play in which Lone Peak is a supporting character. If anyone else had been writing this novel, he would certainly have begun with Vesperus and brought in Lone Peak as his visitor; that is the orthodox method of fiction writing. This novel, however, begins by telling of Lone Peak in such inordinate detail as to make the reader suspect that the priest may later on behave immorally himself. To our surprise, he does nothing of the sort. Only when, engrossed in his Zen meditations, he forgets to shut the door does the true intent of the novel emerge and give the reader pause. This is a variant technique in fiction, an instance of the author's complete rejection of conventional practice. Even if another writer were to try it, he would be bound to confuse the theme and jumble the plot lines, leaving the reader unable to tell who is the main character and who the secondary. In this novel, by contrast, they are as distinct as eyes and eyebrows, so that when the reader reaches the opening of the theme, everything is clear to him.

The remarks at the end of the chapter also clarify the plot, relieving the reader of any difficulties. This author is a master of the art whose equal has never been seen outside of the author of the *Shuihu*.[25] There are those who say he is a younger brother of the author of the *Jin Ping Mei*.[26] If so, might this not be a case of the younger outshining the elder?

_____

25. See Sidney Shapiro, trans., *Outlaws of the Marsh* (Peking: Foreign Languages Press; and Bloomington: Indiana University Press, 1981). The novel probably dates back to the fourteenth century, but reached its present form in the sixteenth.

26. See Clement Egerton, trans., *The Golden Lotus* (New York: Paragon Book Gallery, 1972). A famous erotic novel, it probably was written in the late sixteenth century.

CHAPTER *THREE*

*A puritanical father errs in taking a libertine as
    son-in-law,
And a proper young lady falls for a faithless rake.*

Poem:

　　Though woman's nature has ever been prone to sin,
　　From herself alone no evil thoughts arise.
　　Without the pillow talk of Yingying's fall,[27]
　　Who'd pluck Zhuo's lyre beyond the wall?[28]
　　So mind you stage no plays of love at home,
　　Nor murmur languorous songs in your lady's bower.

---

27. Heroine of the best-known Chinese romantic play, *The West
Chamber* (*Xixiang ji*), written at the end of the thirteenth century.
　　28. Zhuo Wenjun, who eloped with the Han poet Sima Xiangru in
a romance that was much celebrated in later poetry and drama.

And novels corrupt her virtue, people hold;
One day you'll find that every word is gold.

Let us tell how Vesperus, after parting from Lone Peak, spent the entire journey grumbling to himself, "What a colossal bore! Here am I in my twenties, a bud that's just in bloom, and I'm supposed to have my head shaved and start on a course of self-denial and mortification of the flesh! I've never heard of anybody so unreasonable as this priest! My only thought in coming here was that, as a noted intellectual who had joined the Buddhist order, he was bound to hold some unusual views, and I wanted to understand some of his Zen subtleties as an aid in my own writing. What I got instead was one insult after another! The carping was bad enough, but when he gave me that cuckold's gāthā, it was simply too much to bear!

"Any manly, self-respecting husband who becomes an official is going to have to govern the people of the empire. Surely he wouldn't be given any job at all if he couldn't even govern his own wife? Anyway, I'm going to take him up on this. If I don't meet any suitable girls, never mind; but if I do, I certainly won't let the opportunity slip. I'll commit a few sins of the flesh while controlling my own women's quarters as strictly as possible, and then we'll see who comes to collect *my* debts! Far be it from me to boast, but when a woman marries a man as handsome as I am, I doubt that she'll be attracted by any would-be seducer, let alone lose her chastity to him! By rights I ought to have torn that gāthā of his into shreds and thrown it right back at him. But I shall need it to prove my point when we meet again, to stop up that wicked mouth of his. When I show it to him, we'll see whether he'll admit he was wrong." Having reached this decision, he crumpled up the poem and stuffed it in his pocket.

Arriving home, he sent servants out in all directions to

notify matchmakers that he was conducting a search for the most beautiful girl in the world. Since he came from a distinguished family and was blessed with the looks of a Pan An and the literary gifts of a Cao Zhi,[29] there was no father unwilling to accept him as a son-in-law and no girl unwilling to have him as a husband. Every day following the notification brought several matchmakers to his door with marriages to propose. Humble families allowed him to go to their houses and look their daughters over from head to toe, while great families, if they were concerned about appearances, would arrange a meeting at a temple or in the countryside. Both parties knew the meeting was contrived, but they pretended it was accidental. In any case they got a good look at each other, and many were the girls who went home badly smitten. None of them, however, appealed to Vesperus in the slightest.

"It looks as if no one will meet your standards," remarked one of the matchmakers, "except Master Iron Door's daughter, Jade Scent. The problem with her is that her father is an ultraconservative who will never let anyone view his daughter, while you would insist upon it. So I'm afraid that's hopeless, too."

"Why is he called Master Iron Door?" asked Vesperus. "And how do you know she is beautiful? And if she is so beautiful, why won't he let anyone see her?"

"He's the most celebrated old schoolman in the county, and terribly eccentric. He owns lots of property but holds himself quite aloof—never had a single friend his whole life. He just sits at home immersed in his studies and won't open his door to visitors, no matter who they are. There was one very distinguished visitor who was a great admirer of his and came a long way to see him, but despite knocking at the door

29. The famous poet (A.D. 192–232).

for ages, he got no response, let alone a welcome. All he could do was write a poem on the door, part of which ran,

> I know that righteous eremites have huts of matting
> made,
> But I never thought that you, sir, would have an iron
> door.

When the old man noticed these lines, he said, 'Iron Door—I find that quite original, and rather apt too.' And then and there he adopted it as his sobriquet and called himself Master Iron Door.

"He has no son, just a daughter who is as fair as jade and as pretty as a flower. Matchmakers like me see thousands of girls, but none of us has ever seen one to surpass her. What's more, she's studied a lot, with her father as tutor, and she can pick up her brush and write you any kind of poem you please. But the door to her chambers is always securely guarded. She never goes to temples to burn incense or out into the street to watch processions. In fact in all her fifteen years she has never once shown her face in public. As for women visitors such as nuns and the like, it goes without saying—they couldn't get inside the house even if they grew wings.

"But on one occasion the old man caught sight of me from his doorway as I was going by and stopped me. 'Are you a matchmaker, by any chance?' he asked me. 'Yes,' I replied. Then he took me inside and pointed to Jade Scent: 'This is my daughter. I want to find a presentable son-in-law who will be a son to me and look after me in my old age. You might give some thought to finding me one.' I mentioned your name, and he made the comment: 'I've heard of his literary reputation, but I wonder what his morals are like?' 'He has a wise head on young shoulders,' I replied, 'and his conduct is irreproachable. The only problem is that he insists on viewing the girl himself before agreeing to marriage. Since your daughter is so beautiful, naturally she'll appeal to him. I wonder if you'd be willing to let him visit?' When he heard me say that, his face darkened. 'Preposterous!' he said. 'Only the lean ponies they raise in Yangzhou will let you view them.[30] No respectable girl would ever consent to meet with a man!' Faced with this reaction, I could hardly pursue the matter, so I came away. But that is how I know the marriage is hopeless."

Vesperus pondered: I'm quite alone in the world, without parents or brothers, and when I do marry, I'll have no one to supervise my wife. I can't play the custodian myself all the time, because there are bound to be occasions when I'm away from home. In view of the old man's disposition, I can well imagine what his domestic regime will be like. If I were to marry into his family, I'd have no need to keep watch—his daughter would be well and truly supervised. In fact it wouldn't matter if I was *never* at home. What a piece of luck! The only thing that worries me is having to do without a viewing. How can I trust anything a matchmaker says?

"The match *sounds* very suitable indeed," he said. "But I do beg you to find some way for me to get a glimpse of her. So long as you're essentially right about her, I'll be satisfied."

"Absolutely impossible!" said the matchmaker. "If you don't believe what I say, you'd better consult the spirits and take their advice as to what to do. You certainly won't get through that iron door of his."

"*Good idea!* I have a friend who summons immortals to settle questions like this, and the answers are very reliable. I'll get him to help, and then I'll be in touch with you again."

The matchmaker assented and left.

---

30. The expression *lean ponies* refers to girls on sale in Yangzhou, a well-known marketplace for concubines.

Next day, after fasting and purification, Vesperus invited the friend to his house, where he burned incense and kowtowed and then whispered the following prayer:

"Thy disciple wishes to ask about Master Iron Door's daughter, Jade Scent. I have heard that she is supremely beautiful and I would like to marry her. But my information is only hearsay, since I have not set eyes on her myself, and that is why I am asking thy bidding, O Great Immortal. What concerns me is not her virtue, nor her accomplishments. And as to whether she will bear any sons, that is a matter of destiny, anyway, and I don't need to know it in advance. All I'm asking about is her beauty. If she is really as beautiful as they say, I'll marry her, but if she falls even slightly short, I'll decline. I humbly beseech thee, Great Immortal, to be clear and straightforward in thy guidance. Do not, I pray thee, leave me with some vague message that I cannot understand."

His prayer over, he made four obeisances, then rose, and grasping the crosspiece, let the stick trace its message. Sure enough, it traced out a poem:

Among all lovely women she is first;
No need for baseless fears by night or day,
Fear only lest her beauty to adultery lead;
In times of moral crisis, ask the way.
                                —Poem Number One

"So her looks are fine," thought Vesperus. "However, the last two lines clearly state that her beauty will lead to adultery. Surely the girl can't have lost her maidenhead already? But since the poem has Number One at the end, there must be more to come. Let's see what the stick writes next."

After pausing a moment, the stick proceeded to write another poem:

Whether woman's good or bad is not the point,
One needs a man who runs his household right.
If he shuts his door and lets no green flies in,
How can any smut on his jade alight?
                                        —Poem Number Two
(Inscribed by The One Who Returned to the Way)

Vesperus knew that The One Who Returned to the Way was the sobriquet of Lü Dongbin, and he was thrilled.[31] That worthy is an expert on wine and women if ever there was one, he thought. If he approves of her, she must be good. What's more, the second poem removes any doubts I may have had about her chastity. Clearly the girl's still intact and he just wants me to keep a close eye on her. But with such a stickler of a father-in-law to supervise her, I shouldn't have any trouble in that regard. The last two lines—"If he shuts his door and lets no green flies in, How can any smut on his jade alight?"—clearly state that nobody can penetrate his iron door. I needn't hesitate a moment longer.

Facing the heavens, he bowed in gratitude to Lü Dongbin, then told a servant to summon the matchmaker.

"The immortal's poem gave a very favorable judgment," he told her, "and I no longer feel it necessary to hold a viewing. Kindly go ahead and arrange the match."

The matchmaker went gleefully off to Master Iron Door's house, where she reported Vesperus's desire to marry.

"He insisted before on coming for a viewing," said the Master, "which shows that he places beauty above virtue in a

---

31. Lü was one of the Eight Immortals of Taoism.

woman. He's obviously a frivolous young man. What I want is a son-in-law with character, not some popinjay."

In her anxiety to secure the commission, the matchmaker was driven to try any means, no matter how devious, so she came to Vesperus's defense with the ingenious argument that his desire for a viewing had nothing to do with beauty but sprang solely from a concern that the daughter might be flighty and have inauspicious features and prove in the long run not to be a good wife. "But lately he has heard how strict her upbringing has been and what a paragon of the feminine virtues she is, and that is why he has changed his mind and sent me here with this proposal."

Convinced by her reasoning, the Master agreed to the match and chose an auspicious date for the wedding. Despite the matchmaker's report and the immortal's poem, Vesperus still felt some qualms, not having seen Jade Scent himself. Not until the wedding night, when, after exchanging their bows, they entered the bridal chamber and he got a close-up view of her, did he exult in his good fortune.

What was the bride's beauty like? Here is a new lyric testifying to it:

Winsome is she,
And her person full of charms,
Full of charms.
Her tearful face, how easy to caress,
But how hard to imitate, her frown!

Unfit to play the bride, he fears,
Too slight she is, to fold into his arms,
Into his arms.
She's soft as though of flesh alone,
And he'll rest this night on a bed of down.
(To the tune "Remembering the Maid of Qin")

What was the new couple's pleasure like as they joined together in marriage? Here is another new lyric:

Tight shut her eyes, for she's too shy to look;
Two crimson petals on the pillow lie.
Lips that were pursed to keep her fragrance in
Are quickly breached at the tongue's first try.

Her cries have ceased, but passion has no end;
Her breast lies soaked in lovers' sweat.
As opened eyes explore each other's depths,
Their hearts flare hot, and hotter yet.
(To the tune "Spring in the Jade Bower")

Jade Scent's looks were indeed unrivaled anywhere in the world—on that score Vesperus had nothing to complain of. But he did have one grave disappointment. Abundant as her beauty was, she fell short in terms of passion and failed to please her husband to the full. Due to her father's strict upbringing and the severe example set by her mother, she had never been exposed to any of the more licentious aspects of life. Her reading, in particular, had been confined to *The Lives of Virtuous Women* and *The Girls' Classic of Filial Piety*,[32] both of which were full of strictures against the very acts that Vesperus had in mind. As a result there was a good deal of her father in her speech and attitudes, for which her husband dubbed her "the puritan maid." As soon as he said anything in the least suggestive, she would blush furiously and leave the room.

Vesperus happened to be particularly fond of daytime sex,

---

32. Respectively, the *Lienü zhuan* by Liu Xiang (79–6 B.C.) and the *Nü Xiao jing* of the Tang dynasty.

because the sight of his partner's genitals added to his own excitement, but on the several occasions he tried to pull down his wife's trousers, she screamed at the top of her lungs as if he were trying to rape her, and he was forced to desist. As for nighttime sex, although she acquiesced, she conveyed the distinct impression that she did so only because she had no choice. Her distress affected his enjoyment too. Because she was unwilling to try any novel or exotic techniques, Vesperus found himself able to practice only the Doctrine of the Mean.[33] When he proposed Fetching the Fire from the Other Side of the Mountain,[34] she protested that it violated the taboo on a wife's turning her back on her husband, and when he suggested Dousing the Candle,[35] she objected that it inverted the principle of the husband's superiority.

If he did manage, much against her will, to hoist her legs over his shoulders and then, by herculean efforts, to reach a climax of pleasure, she would refuse even to call out "dearest" or "darling," almost as if she lacked the power of speech—let alone beg for mercy so as to enhance his powers. Vesperus was greatly upset, and reflected to himself, What a shame such a strikingly beautiful girl should so entirely lack the pleasure of active participation and lie there like a statue! Where's the pleasure in that? There's nothing else for it; I'll just have to put in some time educating her out of this behavior.

Visiting the art dealer's, he bought an album of exquisite spring-palace pictures by the hand of Academician Zhao Mengfu of the Yuan dynasty.[36] There were thirty-six pictures

---

33. One of the *Four Books* of Confucianism, here used in a punning sense to mean *middle of the road, routine*.

34. Vaginal intercourse with the man on his side behind the woman.

35. Vaginal intercourse with the woman on top of the man.

36. The famous artist and poet (1254–1322).

in all, after the line in the Tang poem, "In the thirty-six palaces all is spring." He brought them home and put them in her bedroom, meaning to look through them with her and get her to understand that sexual intercourse is not a single entity but takes a multitude of forms for our enjoyment. "It is obvious from this book that those techniques I showed you were not invented by me but were practiced long ago by the ancients. I've brought you these model examination answers to prove my point."

As she took the album from him, Jade Scent had no idea of its subject matter, but assumed it contained landscapes or flower paintings. On opening the album, she saw that the two opening pages bore a title in large script: PICTURES FROM THE HAN PALACE. There were many virtuous women in the Han Palace, she thought, and these must be their portraits; let me see what they looked like, to have been able to do the virtuous things they did.

But when she turned to the third page and saw a man and a woman copulating stark naked on top of an ornamental rock, her face flushed and she lost her temper:

"Where did you *get* such pernicious stuff? Just having it here is enough to pollute a lady's chamber. Have the maid take it out at once and burn it!"

Vesperus put out a hand to restrain her. "This is a rare item worth a hundred taels that I borrowed from a friend. If you can afford to repay him, go ahead and burn it. If you can't, kindly put it down and let me enjoy it for a day or two before I have to give it back."

"If you want to improve your mind, do it by looking at famous paintings or calligraphy! What's the point of looking at *this* sort of frivolous stuff?"

"If this were a frivolous thing," said Vesperus, "the artist wouldn't have painted it, nor the collector have paid a large sum to buy it. It is precisely because it is the most serious subject since the Creation itself that literary men have chosen to paint it, mount it on silk, put it on sale in the art shops, and preserve it in libraries—all for the purpose of advising posterity on the right models of behavior. Otherwise, in the course of time, all knowledge of the mutual reinforcement of yin and yang would gradually be lost, husbands and wives would spurn each other, reproduction would cease, and humankind would eventually become extinct. The reason I borrowed it was not just to look at it myself, but to let you understand that this principle is what makes it possible to conceive and give birth, and also to prevent you from being misled by a puritanical father into never bearing any children. Why get so upset?"

"I simply don't believe this behavior is respectable. If it were, why didn't the ancients who established our code of ethics have people practice it openly by daylight in front of others? Why did they insist on its being done secretly at dead of night in dark places as if we were burglars? That *shows* it's not respectable."

Vesperus laughed. "You can't be blamed for these opinions. It's all your father's fault, for keeping you locked up inside the house without an experienced woman friend to tell you about sex. That's why you're so abysmally ignorant. You think I'm the only man in the world who's romantically inclined, and that all the women in the world are as puritanical as you are and never do it in the daytime but insist on waiting until night. You don't realize that every couple does it in the daytime and that every time they do so, they're open and aboveboard about it and let people know. Tell me this: if men and women didn't do it in the daytime, how did the artist learn about these techniques? How did he paint the figures so marvelously, getting them so lifelike that it excites us just to look at them?"

"Well, my parents are husband and wife, too. Why don't they do it in the daytime?"

"Tell me, how do you know they don't?"

"If they did, I would surely have come upon them while they were doing it. How do you explain the fact that in all my fifteen years I've never once done so? I've neither seen them nor heard them."

Vesperus laughed uproariously. "You poor, benighted soul! Children are the *only* ones who don't see and hear what's going on. There's not a single maid or servant who's unaware of it! When your parents want to do it, they just wait until you're somewhere else before they bolt their door and set to. They're afraid that if you see them at it, your sexual desires will be stimulated and you'll start pining for a lover and fall into a state of depression; that's why they deceive you. If you don't believe me, just ask your mother's personal maid whether they do it in the daytime or not."

Jade Scent thought for a moment. "They do often shut their door during the day and take a nap, and I suppose they might be doing it then. But the very idea is so embarrassing! You looking at me, me looking at you—how could we ever do it like that?"

"It's ten times more enjoyable in the daytime, and the wonderful thing is that it's precisely *when* we're looking at each other that we get really excited. There are only two kinds of couples who ought never to perform in the daytime; but apart from them *everyone* should."

"Which are they?"

"An ugly husband married to a beautiful wife and an ugly wife married to a handsome husband."

"And why can't *they* do it in the daytime?"

"Our enjoyment depends on your loving me and my

loving you, as well as on the interaction of our vital forces and blood vessels. If the wife has snow-white skin that is soft and delicate, skin like jade polished to perfection, when her husband takes off her clothes and clasps her to his chest, he will be looking at her all the while and naturally his excitement will be increased tenfold, and that thing in his loins will automatically get harder, stiffer, thicker, and longer. But suppose the wife sees her husband looking like an ogre, with dark, coarse skin. While he has his clothes on, she won't have noticed, but now that he is undressed, his ugliness will be fully visible. In fact it can't be hidden. Moreover it forms such a contrast with her own snow-white skin that what would have seemed merely ugly now looks hideous. Don't you imagine she'll react with disgust? Her disgust will show in her voice and in her face, and when her husband notices, his hardness and stiffness will automatically soften and his thickness and length shrink. Far from gaining any enjoyment, he will feel humiliated. He'd have been much better off having intercourse at night, when he could have hidden his defects.

"So much for the beautiful wife married to an ugly husband. A handsome husband sleeping with an ugly wife violates the same rule, and we don't need to discuss it. Anyway that's why I say there are only two kinds of couples who ought not to do it in the daytime. But in the case of couples like you and me—equally white, pink, soft, and delicate—if we don't take our pleasure in the daylight and show our bodies to one another, but burrow under the bedclothes and grope about in the dark, aren't we hiding our talents the whole of our lives, exactly like the ugly couples? If you don't believe me, let's try it together and see how it compares with the nighttime for enjoyment?"

By this time Jade Scent was half-convinced, even though she was unwilling to admit it. However, a pinkish glow suffused her cheeks and a sensual glint appeared in her eye.

She's beginning to show a little interest, thought Vesperus. I was planning to start at once, but this is the first time her desires have been aroused and her appetite is still quite undeveloped. If I give her a taste of it now, she'll be like a starving man at the sight of food—she'll bolt it down without savoring it and so miss the true rapture; I think I'll tantalize her a little before mounting the stage.

Pulling up an easy chair, he sat down and drew her onto his lap, then opened the album and showed it to her picture by picture. This album differed from others in that the first page of each leaf contained the erotic picture and the second page a comment on it. The first part of the comment explained the activity depicted, while the rest praised the artist's skill. All the comments were in the hand of famous writers.

Vesperus told Jade Scent to try to imagine herself in the place of the people depicted and to concentrate on their expressions so that she could imitate them later on. While she looked at the pictures, he read out the comments:

Picture Number One. The Releasing the Butterfly in Search of Fragrance position. The woman sits on the Lake Tai rock with her legs apart while the man sends his jade whisk into her vagina and moves it from side to side seeking the heart of the flower. At the moment depicted, the pair are just beginning and have not reached the rapturous stage, so their eyes are wide open and their expressions not much different from normal.

Picture Number Two. The Letting the Bee Make Honey position. The woman is lying on her back on the brocade quilt, bracing herself on the bed with her hands and raising her legs aloft to meet the jade whisk and let the man know the location of the heart of the flower so that he will not thrust at random. At the moment depicted, the woman's expression is almost ravenous, while the man seems so nervous that the observer feels anxiety on his behalf. Supreme art at its most mischievous.

Picture Number Three. The Lost Bird Returns to the Wood position. The woman leans back on the embroidered couch with her legs in the air, grasping the man's thighs and driving them directly downward. She appears to have entered the state of rapture and is afraid of losing her way. The couple are just at the moment of greatest exertion and show extraordinary vitality. This scene has the marvelous quality of "flying brush and dancing ink."

Picture Number Four. The Starving Horse Races to the Trough position. The woman lies flat on the couch with her arms wrapped around the man as if to restrict his movements. While he supports her legs on his shoulders, the whole of the jade whisk enters the vagina, leaving not a trace behind. At the moment depicted, they are on the point of spending; they are about to shut their eyes and swallow each other's tongues, and their expressions are identical. Supreme art indeed.

Picture Number Five. The Two Dragons Who Fight Till They Drop position. The woman's head rests beside the pillow and her hands droop in defeat, as soft as cotton floss. The man's head rests beside her neck, and his whole body droops too, also as soft as cotton floss. She has spent, and her soul is about to depart on dreams of the future. This is a state of calm after furious activity. Only her feet, which have not been lowered but still rest on the man's shoulders, convey any trace of vitality. Otherwise, he and she would resemble a pair of corpses, which leads the observer to understand their rapture and think of lovers entombed together.

By the time Jade Scent reached this page, her sexual desires were fully aroused and could no longer be held in check. Vesperus turned the page and was about to show her the next picture when she pushed the book away and stood up.

"A fine book this is!" she exclaimed. "It makes one uncomfortable just to look at it. Read it yourself if you want to. I'm going to lie down."

Vesperus caught her in his arms. "Dear heart, there are more good ones. Let's look at them together and then go to bed."

"Don't you have any time tomorrow? Why do you have to finish today?"

Vesperus knew she was agitated, and he put his arms around her and kissed her. When kissing her before, he had tried to insert his tongue in her mouth but her tightly clenched teeth always prevented him. As a result, she was still unacquainted with his tongue after more than a month of marriage. But on this occasion he had no sooner touched her lips than that sharp, soft tongue of his had somehow slipped past her teeth and entered her mouth.

"Dear heart," said Vesperus, "there's no need to use the bed. Why don't we take this easy chair as our rock and try to imitate the picture in the album. What do you say?"

Jade Scent pretended to be angry. "People don't *do* things like that!"

"You're right," said Vesperus, "people don't do them. Immortals do! Let's be immortals for a little while." He put out his hand and undid her belt. Jade Scent's heart was willing, even if her words were not, and she simply hung on his shoulder and offered no resistance. Taking off her trousers, Vesperus noticed a large damp patch in the seat caused by her secretions while she was looking at the pictures.

Vesperus took off his own trousers and pulled her over to the chair, where he made her sit with her legs apart. He then inserted his jade whisk into her vagina before removing the clothes from her upper body.

Why did he not start at the top and work his way down instead of taking off her trousers first, you ask. You must realize that Vesperus was an experienced lover. Had he taken her top off first, despite all the agitation in her heart she would still have felt shy and indulged in all kinds of coy pretense. He chose instead to seize the key position first and let the rest of the territory fall into his hands later, a strategy that corresponds in military terms to seizing the rebel leader and destroying his stronghold. In fact Jade Scent put up no resistance, but let him loosen her gold bracelets, undo her silk sash, and strip off all her other clothes, including her underwear and breastband, everything but her leggings.

Why did he take off all her other clothes but leave her leggings on? You must understand that everything a woman is wearing can be removed except her leggings. Why is that? Because inside the leggings are the foot-bindings, and when women are binding their feet, they see that the lower part looks neat but leave the upper part untidy and hence unattractive. Moreover, in the last resort tiny feet need a pair of dainty little leggings above them if they are going to appeal. Without leggings, they would be as unsightly as a flower with no leaves around it, and that was why Vesperus shrewdly left the leggings on.

After undressing her, he took off every stitch of his own clothing and then, in full battle array, parted her tiny feet and, placing them over the sides of the chair, thrust his jade whisk forward and began to drive to left and right inside her vagina, searching for the heart of the flower as shown in the first picture. After he had done this for a while, Jade Scent stretched out her arms and pressed down on the chair, gradually forcing her vulva upward to meet the thrust of the jade whisk. If the whisk went to the left, she moved left to receive it; if it went to the right, she did likewise. Suddenly it reached a place where it gave her a rather different sensation, something between a sharp pain and a tantalizing itch, a sensation that she could neither endure nor forgo.

"Just keep it there," she said to Vesperus. "Don't go thrusting all over the place, or you'll stab me to death."

Vesperus knew he had reached the heart of the flower and did as she asked, concentrating his forces and attacking in just that one place. He ceased his diversionary tactics and gradually brought all of his techniques into play, thrusting faster and deeper than before. After a few hundred strokes, he noticed her hands moving instinctively behind him to grasp his thighs and drive them directly downward with a strength she summoned from goodness knows where. Before, she had been consciously imitating the erotic picture, but this development was an unintentional reaction of which she was quite unaware. Apparently it was something beyond even the album's powers to depict.

To get on even terms, Vesperus stretched his arms out and pulled her thighs toward him. He was surprised to find them drenched in the surging seas, as slippery as oil and impossible to grasp.

Her excitement is just at its peak, he thought. By rights I ought to make things hard for her now, but since this is the first time she has broken her vegetarian fast, I must let her eat her fill and acquire a taste for meat before I start to apply my falcon-training methods.

Lifting her feet and placing them over his shoulders, Vesperus put his arms around her slender waist and plunged in to the hilt. This time the jade whisk seemed larger than ever, cramming the vagina full and leaving not the slightest gap. After several hundred more thrusts, he noticed her starry eyes glazing over and her cloud-puffs in disarray. She looked as if she were falling asleep. He tapped her twice.

"Dear heart, I know you are about to spend, but this chair *is* rather awkward. Let's finish up on the bed."

Jade Scent, who was just at the critical stage, feared that if they moved he would have to take out the jade whisk and her pleasure would be short-lived. In addition, her limbs felt so sore and weak she could not have moved anyway, even to walk to the bed. When she heard his suggestion, she shut her eyes and shook her head.

"Dear heart, is it because you can't move?"

She nodded.

"I can't bear to part with you either. Let me carry you over."

He locked his arms securely around her waist and picked her up with her tongue still in his mouth and his jade whisk still in her vagina. Then, thrusting as he went, doing a Looking at the Flowers from Horseback routine, he walked her to the bed and deposited her across it.

He then reached for a pillow to place under her middle, propped up her legs, and began again. After several hundred more thrusts, Jade Scent suddenly cried, "Dearest, I'm done for!" Clutching him tightly, she began mumbling incoherently, like a dying man in his last throes. Vesperus knew that her essence had come and he set the jade whisk against her flower's heart and, with her legs trailing in the air, kneaded it with all his might until he ejaculated together with her.

After they had slept in each other's arms a short while, Jade Scent awoke.

"Dearest, I died just now. Did you know?"

"How could I help knowing? But it's not called dying; it's called spending."

"Why is it called spending?"

"Men have male essence and women female essence, and when they reach the height of pleasure, their essence comes out. But just before it does, your whole body—including your skin, flesh, and bones—is overwhelmed by a sensual languor and your mind becomes hazy as if you were falling asleep. That's when the essence emerges, and that's what is meant by spending. It was shown in the fifth picture in the album. You saw it, so surely you know what I mean?"

"And according to you, one can come back to life after spending? One doesn't really die?"

"A man and a woman spend every time they do it. There are some women whose essence comes very quickly and who spend dozens of times while the man spends only once. Now *that's* what I call pleasure! Of course you don't die!"

"For pleasure like that I'd be willing to die. And to think one doesn't even have to! In that case, from now on I'm going to spend every day and every night."

Vesperus laughed gaily. "Didn't I give you the right advice, though? Isn't this album a treasure?"

"Oh, it *is*! It would be so nice if we'd bought our own copy and could keep it and look at it often. I'm afraid your friend may come and take this one back."

"That was just a fib. The truth is I *did* buy it."

Jade Scent was overjoyed.

They got up and dressed and then looked at the erotic album again until they became excited and had sex once more. From that day forward they were perfectly adjusted and more deeply in love than ever. After looking at the erotic pictures, Jade Scent was converted from puritanism to libertinism. When making love at night, far from practicing the Doctrine of the Mean, she favored the novel and the exotic. She was quite amenable to Dousing the Candle and Fetching the Fire from the Other Side of the Mountain, and so insistent was she on putting her tiny feet over her husband's shoulders that next morning he had to exert herculean efforts to get them down again. Needless to say, in time she became adept at uttering passionate cries during intercourse and also at the kind of wanton behavior that enhanced his excitement.

In order to enhance hers, Vesperus paid a visit to the bookstore and bought a quantity of erotic works, such as *The Unofficial History of the Embroidered Couch, The Life of the Lord of Perfect Satisfaction*, and *The Foolish Woman's Story*,[37] a dozen or so titles in a boxed set, which he left on the table for her to peruse. The books she had been studying he put away, lest she revert to her old ways and display her puritanical nature again.

The lute and the zither are inadequate symbols for the harmony of their bedroom bliss, just as the bell and the drum are incapable of expressing their joy. Even if you were to paint three hundred and sixty erotic pictures, they would not suffice to depict the lovemaking of Vesperus and Jade Scent. In later times a poet composed a lyric on the pleasure this couple took in looking at their album. It ran,

> She's on his lap by the bedroom window,
> While he on her scented shoulder leans.
> As they open the book and linger upon its scenes,

---

37. *Xiuta yeshi, Ruyi Jun zhuan*, and *Chi pozi zhuan*, respectively. The first was written by the playwright Lü Tiancheng about 1600, the second by an anonymous author perhaps in the middle of the sixteenth century, and the third by another anonymous author in the early decades of the seventeenth.

She finds these joys aren't secrets, after all,
But age-old lore.

Her hair disordered more and more,
They tumble like a phoenix pair;
Nine times in ten the lotuses point up.
Immortal-like, she'd play the scenes forever,
With joys as rare.
(To the tune of "The Flowerseller's Cry")

With one exception Vesperus could be described as having reached the pinnacle of happiness. But although his marriage was exceptionally harmonious, his relations with his father-in-law were difficult. Why was that? Because Master Iron Door was a staunchly conservative gentleman who preferred austerity to luxury and who liked to discuss moral issues while abominating all talk of love. He had regretted his choice of son-in-law from the moment Vesperus arrived in the house with his brilliant clothes and frivolous manner.

"The fellow is all show, no substance," he sighed to himself. "He'll never amount to much, and my daughter won't have a husband worthy of the name. The trouble is that the betrothal gifts have all been received and the match arranged, and it cannot be undone. I'll have to make the best of a bad situation by letting him marry her and then trying to mold him into a gentleman with a father's firm hand."

He was unsparing in his criticism. Not only did he scold and lecture his son-in-law for every slip in speech or action, he would carry on if Vesperus showed the slightest impropriety of carriage or posture.

However, as the proverb says, "Mountains and rivers are easier to change than a man's nature." Not only did Vesperus have a young man's temperament, he had never known an adult's restraint since losing his parents many years before. How could he endure this daily torture? Several times he came close to fighting back, but because he did not want to embarrass his wife and jeopardize his marital bliss, he felt obliged to suffer in silence.

But at length the abuse became too much to bear. It was only because I admired his daughter's beauty, he said to himself, and because he refused to let her marry out of the family but insisted on a live-in son-in-law that I pocketed my pride and joined his household. I was not some half-starved, ill-clad pauper with designs on his father-in-law's property, so why does he have to use his position to tyrannize me like this? It's enough that I don't try to change him, pedant though he is. Why is he so determined to change me? What's more, a romantic young genius like myself will want to enjoy a few celebrated amours at some stage. That daughter of his is hardly going to be enough wife for me! But if he keeps me under such strict supervision, I'll never be able to put a foot wrong or say a word out of place! If I step out of line, he's sure to sentence me to death!

I must think this through carefully. I can't stop him and I can't endure him, either, so there's just one solution: I'll have to leave her in his care while I go off somewhere else on the pretext of furthering my studies. I already have the most beautiful woman in the world as my wife, but if I met up with the second most beautiful, even if I couldn't marry her, I wouldn't mind fulfilling my destiny with a brief affair.

Having made up his mind, he was about to tell Jade Scent and then ask her father's permission, when the thought occurred to him that, because of her craving for sex, she would never let him go and, once she was against it, he could hardly go and ask permission from her father. The only course was to consult his father-in-law first behind her back.

"Your son-in-law is living in a remote place and has been

poorly educated," he said. "I lack enlightened teachers and helpful friends, and I will never make any progress in my studies or succeed in the examinations. I am thinking of taking leave of you, father-in-law, and traveling about the country to broaden my mind. When I find an enlightened teacher and helpful friends, I'll set to and study. Then, at examination time, I'll travel to the provincial capital and take the examinations. Perhaps I'll succeed and justify your inviting me to be your son-in-law. Would you permit me to go?"

"In the six months you've been living here as my son-in-law," replied the Master, "this is the first sensible observation you've made. Normally it's only dissolute stuff that you come out with. I find it admirable that you are willing to leave home for the sake of your studies. Why shouldn't I permit it?"

"Father-in-law, *you* may agree, but I'm afraid that your daughter will say I'm lacking in affection for proposing to go away so soon after our marriage. May I suggest that we maintain that the idea originated with you rather than me? That way I'll be able to carry out my plan without any obstacle."

"Very well," said the Master.

In his daughter's presence he urged Vesperus to travel for the sake of his studies. When Vesperus feigned reluctance, the Master put on a stern expression and gave him a severe dressing down, after which he assented. At the unexpected news that her husband was leaving, Jade Scent, who was just then at the height of her enjoyment, felt like a baby being weaned of the breast, her anguish was so unbearable. Of course she threw farewell party after farewell party for the traveler and gave him gift after parting gift. She also insisted that he pay in advance all the debts for which he would have been liable after his departure. And Vesperus, mindful of how lonely he might be on the journey and of how at any given time he might have no woman to console himself with, made every effort to oblige, like someone who puts on a banquet for a guest and then enjoys it himself. They made love several nights in succession, and only they could know how indescribably blissful those nights were.

Before his departure Vesperus thought of leaving one of his servants behind to attend to the chores. Because the Master was a miser who begrudged providing board for his servants, his whole household consisted of only the three family members and two maidservants, who had been part of the wedding settlement. He had no manservant at all, which was the reason for Vesperus's concern. Summoning his pages, Vesperus stood them in front of the Master and invited him to choose one. To his surprise neither was acceptable.

What was the reason? Vesperus was amphibious—that is to say, given to both homosexual and heterosexual pleasures. His pages were always under twenty, handsome young fellows with slicked hair or sly young rogues who were beautifully dressed. Master Iron Door had often in his mind urged Vesperus to send them packing, and now that he was to choose one of them as a servant, he was troubled.

We do need someone to fetch and carry for us, he thought, but with my son-in-law away and my daughter on her own, how can I have these pretty boys in and out of the house? Looking after her is far more important than getting the chores done. I must on no account do something I'll come to regret.

To Vesperus he replied, "You're the only one who has any use for these good-for-nothings. I certainly don't want them, so see you take them off with you. If I need help, I'll always be able to get someone. Don't worry about the chores."

Since Master Iron Door was so adamant, Vesperus did not dare press the point. But knowing that his father-in-law might be too stingy to hire any help, he thought it best to leave a few taels behind to pay for a servant. Then he departed, accompanied by the pages he had brought with him.

This chapter has told the full story of Vesperus's first match with a beautiful girl. There are many more extraordinary encounters to come, so listen carefully as the chapters unfold.

CRITIQUE

When the author is exhorting his audience with talk of moral principle, he makes their hair stand on end, and when he sets out to move them with accounts of sexual passion, he drives them wild. Ignorant people will regard this ambivalence of his as a flaw, thus missing the point that the passages where he moves his audience so ingeniously are precisely the occasions when he is most intent on exhorting them to moral behavior. Think what a virtuous girl Jade Scent was before she saw the erotic pictures and how wanton she became after reading their comments! Chastity and wantonness, nobility and baseness, decided in just a moment of time! And all of it the man's fault, for leading her into temptation! Can husbands afford not to pay heed?

CHAPTER *F*OUR

*A traveler bemoans his solitude while spending a night
   in the wilds,
And a thief discourses on sexual passion to pass the
   time.*

Poem:
   The puritan preaches morality,
   The libertine his creed.
   But both need listeners predisposed,
   If they're going to succeed.

After taking leave of his wife and father-in-law, Vesperus set
out on his study tour. He had no particular destination in
mind, but merely let his legs carry him wherever they would.
So long as there was a beautiful girl somewhere, he thought,
that was where he would settle down. At each prefectural or

county town he came to, he stayed several months. As a brilliant young man of letters, he easily qualified for local society. He was fond of joining literary circles, had published a great deal, and was known by name to educated men for hundreds of miles around. Wherever he went, he found friends eager to take him off to join their groups.

For Vesperus, however, writing and the social life that went with it were of minor significance beside his quest for a beautiful girl. Every day at dawn he would get up and patrol the town from its main streets to its back alleys. Unfortunately all the women he saw were quite ordinary, and he never came across another outstanding beauty, which was a disappointment that preyed on his mind and tongue; for whatever he was doing, he would mutter, "Such a fine place, yet not a single girl worth looking at!" Over and over he would mutter these words wherever he went, even on trips to the privy. His complaint ultimately became such a habit with him that he would blurt it out before acquaintances and strangers alike, a fact that led his fellow students to call him sex-crazy behind his back.

One day while he was staying at an inn in the countryside, both of his pages fell ill and were confined to bed. Vesperus wanted to go for a walk but feared it would detract from his dignity if some woman saw him without an escort, and so he remained alone in his room, bored beyond endurance. Just at the height of his boredom, a guest from the next room paid him a visit.

"You're all on your own, sir," said the visitor, "and I daresay you're feeling lonely. I have a jar of wine in my room, and if you have no objection, I'd like to invite you for a drink."

"Meeting by chance," said Vesperus, "one mustn't impose. If we're going to drink together, you must let me be the host."

"And I've always heard that educated men *like* to be unconventional! Why so formal? As the proverb says, 'Within the four seas, all men are brothers.' And there's another one, too: 'Many's the time men meet by chance.' I may have a humble station in life, but there's nothing I enjoy more than making friends. However, your prospects are so grand that in the ordinary way I would never have presumed to make your acquaintance. So this is a rare encounter, our staying at the same inn! What harm would there be in your condescending to join me?"

In his state of acute boredom Vesperus was only too eager to have someone to talk to and, on finding himself so earnestly invited, he promptly accepted. His host seated him in the place of honor, while he himself sat to one side, an arrangement over which Vesperus protested, insisting he take the seat opposite. After a few casual remarks, they exchanged their names. Vesperus revealed his sobriquet and asked his host's.

"As an educated man, sir, you have a sobriquet," said the other. "But I am a vulgar fellow and have no such elegant title, just the nickname A Match for the Knave of Kunlun. However, you'll find that everyone within a hundred miles of here recognizes that name."

"It's most unusual. How did you come to choose it?"

"If I tell you, I'm afraid you'll be scared. And even if you're not scared, you'll want to leave at once and not drink with me anymore."

"I'm a man of some courage myself, you know, as well as a free spirit. I wouldn't be scared even if it was an immortal or a ghost there in front of me. And as for such things as status and education, I pay them even less attention. As everybody knows, there was a barnyard mimic as well as a sneak thief among the heroes in the Lord of Mengchang's entourage, and Jing Ke used to get drunk with a dogmeat butcher in the marketplace of Yan.[38] So long as we get on together, why wouldn't I drink with you?"

"In that case there's no harm in telling you. I'm a professional thief, a specialist in breaking and entering. A rich man's tower may be thousands of feet high and his walls hundreds of courses thick; if I choose not to try, fine, but if I go there in search of money, I'll get straight to his bedside with the greatest of ease, bundle up his valuables, and make my getaway so cleanly that he won't know he's been robbed until the next day. They say there used to be a Knave of Kunlun who got over the wall into General Guo's palace and abducted a Girl in Red, but he did it only once, whereas I've done that kind of thing hundreds of times.[39] Anyway that's why I'm called A Match for the Knave."

Vesperus was aghast. "But since you've been doing this for a long time and have earned a name for yourself that everyone knows, surely you must have fallen foul of the law?"

"If I did that," replied the Knave, "I'd be no hero. As the proverb says, 'You have to have the goods to catch the thief.' When the stolen goods can't be found, I point that out, and no one dares lay a finger on me. In fact everyone around here tries to get into my good books, because they're afraid I'll ruin them if they so much as cross me. But I'm not without honor, you know. I do have my Five Abstentions from Theft."

"And what are they?"

"I don't rob unlucky people, lucky people, people I know, people I've robbed once already, or people who take no precautions."

---

38. The Lord of Mengchang was the archetypal feudal patron. Jing Ke attempted to assassinate the First Emperor of the Qin. Biographies of both men appear in the *Shi ji*.

39. The Girl in Red appears in the Tang story "Kunlun nu."

"Those terms are rather intriguing. Won't you please explain?"

"If people have suffered some blow such as an illness, a death in the family, or some natural disaster and are in terrible anguish over it, robbing them would be like pouring oil on the flames—too much for them to bear. That's why I won't do it.

"If a family has something to celebrate, such as a wedding, the birth of a son, or a new house, and I were to go and rob them in the midst of the festivities, the loss of property would be far less important than the ill fortune I'd be bringing them, ill fortune that would dog them in the future. That's why I won't do it.

"I don't consider it wrong to steal from people I've never met, people I know but who don't know me, or people who know me but aren't willing to associate with me. But in the case of people I meet and greet every day, if I were to rob them, they'd never suspect me and I'd feel a bit ashamed when I saw them next. For instance, I invited you to join me for a drink just now. If you'd refused, you'd have shown yourself to be a snob who looked down on me and, no matter where you lived, I'd never have let you get away with it. But you were happy to come over and sit here opposite me. Someone as congenial as that—how could I bring myself to rob him?

"In the case of a rich man who has never been robbed despite all his wealth, I'll condescend to pay him a call, to hit him up for a contribution, as it were. What's wrong with that? But if I've robbed him once already and gotten my share, I'd have to be a monster of greed to go on plaguing him. So that, too, is something I won't do.

"But those timid souls who worry about thieves all day and guard against them all night, who never stop talking about thieves, they treat me without any respect, so I do the same with them. I rob them a couple of times and show them I'm smarter than they are and all too easy to underestimate, just so that they won't look down on us thieves anymore.

"But if it's a bighearted, generous man for whom money is just a matter of chance, anyway, the sort of man who will let you steal a little if you need it, either by neglecting to shut his gate or deliberately leaving his door open, if I stole from a man like that, I'd be a coward and a bully, a thieving rat or cur, as they say. It is not something that our great mentor, Robber Zhi, would ever have stooped to, so how can I do it?[40]

"Those are my Five Abstentions from Theft. All my life I've benefited from them. People far and wide know about these qualities of mine, and although they realize I'm a thief, they don't treat me as one and they take no precautions. Since they don't consider it a disgrace to associate with me, I don't consider it one either. If you have no objection, let's take an oath of brotherhood. Should you ever need my help, I'll do my level best to serve you, to the death if necessary. This is not one of those oaths of brotherhood you educated men swear, which amount to helping a brother in good times but begging off in bad. We thieves aren't like that."

As he listened to the other's speech, Vesperus had been nodding in rapid succession. Now he heaved a sigh.

I never expected to find such a hero among thieves, he mused. If I make friends with him, the one case in which I might need his help would be if I heard of some outstanding beauty—like the Girl in Red or Red Whisk—who was living in a great mansion where I mightn't be able to communicate with her, let alone meet her.[41] How marvelous if I could count

---

40. Zhi is the archetypal robber referred to in the *Analects* of Confucius as well as in the *Zhuang Zi*.

41. Red Whisk appears in the Tang story "Curlybeard" (*Qiuran ke zhuan*).

on him to play the role of Kunlun! Perhaps meeting him today means that I have an exceptional destiny in store for me and Heaven has sent a supernatural being to help me achieve it.

At this prospect he began to jump for joy. But the Knave's suggestion that they swear an oath of brotherhood gave him pause. Although he replied, "Capital," his tone was less than enthusiastic.

The Knave guessed his thoughts. "You may say you agree, but in your heart you haven't quite agreed. You're not afraid, by any chance, that I'll involve you in a lawsuit? Forget for the moment that my exceptional skills will keep me out of the courts; even if I got into trouble, I'd go to my death if need be, rather than drag an innocent person down with me. So don't give it a second thought."

Now that the Knave had answered his reservations, Vesperus readily accepted, not daring to make any excuses. They contributed to a three-animal sacrifice and then, after writing out their dates of birth, smeared their mouths with blood and took an oath to live or die together. Since the Knave was older than Vesperus, they addressed each other as *younger brother* and *elder brother*, respectively. Then they enjoyed what was left of the sacrificial meats and ate and drank until midnight, by which time the table was littered with cups and dishes.

They were about to go to their rooms, when Vesperus said, "We'll be lonely sleeping in separate rooms. Why not come and share my bed and we'll pass the night in heart-to-heart talk?"

"Good idea," said the Knave, and they undressed and got into bed.

Vesperus had been so preoccupied with drinking and talking that he had quite forgotten the complaint that was normally on his lips. But now, with the drinking and talking over, as he got into bed and was about to drop off to sleep, he reverted to form. He came out with his grievance and repeated it several times.

"There are beautiful women everywhere," protested the Knave. "What makes you say that? Are you still unmarried, by any chance, and traveling about in search of a wife?"

"No, no, I already have a wife. But how can a man be expected to depend on just one woman for company all his life? After all, he needs a few women besides his wife just for the change of scenery! To be quite candid, brother, I have an exceptionally amorous nature. Wealth and honor are within my grasp, but they don't interest me at all. This is the one thing that matters. The journey I'm on is nominally to advance my studies but actually to look for women. I've been to many cities and towns, but all the women I've seen have either been larded with makeup to hide their dark complexions or covered in jewels to hide their brown hair. I've not met a single natural beauty, one who didn't need to adorn herself. I've lost heart, and that's why I say this all the time, to vent my frustration and despair."

"You're quite wrong there, brother. Good women never let themselves be seen, or rather, the only ones who do are not good women. Even among prostitutes, not to mention girls of good family, it is only the ugliest ones that nobody wants who will stand in doorways and try to sell you their wares. Those with any reputation at all sit inside and wait for the man to call on them, and even then they play hard to get and only come out after you've asked for them several times. You surely don't imagine that an unmarried girl of good family or a wife or concubine from a great household is going to stand in her doorway and display herself, do you? If you really want to know whether there are any good women about, you ought to come and ask me."

At this suggestion Vesperus's head jerked up involuntarily. "Now, that's a surprise! Since you don't take the stage yourself where love is concerned, how would you know anything about it?"

"I may not take the stage," said the Knave, "but I have a better view of the action than anyone else. Even the principals have only a general idea of what's going on. They're in no position to know all the details."

"Why is that?"

"Tell me, are beautiful girls more plentiful in rich and eminent households or in poor and humble ones?"

"Oh, in rich and eminent households, of course. Poor men can't afford them."

"Well, then, can you get a more accurate view of the beautiful girls in the rich and eminent households when they're fully dressed and made up or when they're undressed and have washed off all their makeup?"

"Of course, it's only after they've washed off their makeup that you see their natural beauty. When they're dressed and made up, how can you tell *anything*?"

"You see my point," said the Knave. "We thieves, of course, don't choose to go near the houses of the poor and humble. The houses we frequent are full of girls hung with jewels and dressed in the finest silks, and so naturally we get to see them in great numbers. Moreover, we time our visits, not for the daytime but for the dead of night, when they may be sitting undressed in the moonlight or else sleeping beside a lamp with the bedcurtains open. For fear the girl may not be asleep, I don't dare take anything at first, but hide in some dark corner with my eyes riveted on her body to make sure she's not stirring. Only when she's asleep do I set to work. Thus for the better part of an hour I have my eyes on her, and during that time nothing escapes me, not her eyes or face or figure or complexion, not even the depth of her vagina or the growth of her pubic hair. I have a mental record of which women are good-looking and which aren't in the houses of all the rich men and officials within a hundred miles of here. If you want to go in for this, you'll need my advice."

At this point Vesperus, who had been lying inside the bedclothes, suddenly sat bolt upright, exposing his chest and back.

"That's right!" he exclaimed. "You can't see the women in a great household, no matter who you are. Or if you do see them, it's never a good view that you get. You thieves are the only ones who are able to see them properly! If you hadn't brought this up, I'd have missed a glorious opportunity. But it raises another question in my mind: when you see such beautiful women, with such well-developed vulvas, what happens if your excitement gets too much for you and you can't control yourself?"

"When I first saw such sights as a young man, I couldn't control myself and would often sit there in the darkness and shoot my handgun at the woman, making believe I was doing it with her. Later, as I saw more of them, they came to mean less and less. Gradually a vulva came to resemble some kitchen utensil and aroused about as much feeling in me. Only when I saw a woman doing it with her husband and heard the moans coming from their mouths and the pumping sound from down below did I get a little excited."

Now that the Knave was touching on such fascinating subject matter, Vesperus, who was sitting up in bed not far away, feared that even the remaining two or three feet would lessen the impact of what was being said, so he flipped over and lay beside the Knave.

"If you're not too bored with such trivialities," the Knave went on, "let me tell you one or two of the things I've seen and heard, so you'll appreciate that, although I may be a thief, I am also a spy in the camp of love and a chronicler of women's ways, not some dumb know-nothing who can't even write the word *love*."

"Splendid! If you'll do that, one night of talk with you will be worth more than ten years of study. Do go ahead."

"I've seen so many things, I hardly know where to begin. Ask me anything you like and I'll try to answer."

"Fine. Well, then, which are more common, the women who like it or the ones who don't?"

"Oh, the women who like it, of course. Still, there are those who don't. In general, out of every hundred women you'll find only one or two who don't like it. But even among those who do, there are two kinds: those who like doing it and say so, and those who try to give the impression they don't like it even though they do. Only after their husbands have forced them on stage do these latter ones show their true colors.

"Of the two kinds, it is the former that is the easier to dispatch. At first, as I watched from a dark corner while a wife brazenly urged her husband to do it, I thought she must be a real wanton whose energy would last all night, but, lo and behold, she spent after just a few thrusts and then felt drowsy and only wanted to sleep. She no longer cared if her husband did it or not, and she gave up trying to spur him into action or keep him up to the mark. By contrast, the woman who really wants it but pretends she doesn't is terribly hard to live with. I was robbing a house once and saw the husband trying to get his unwilling wife to do it. When he mounted her, she pushed him off, so he concluded she genuinely didn't want to and went to sleep and began snoring. But then she set herself to tossing and turning in bed in order to get him to wake up. When he didn't wake up, she shook him. But he was sound asleep and still didn't wake up. So she started screaming, 'Thief! Thief!' Anyone else in my position would have been frightened off at that point, but I realized she wasn't really crying thief, she just wanted her husband to wake up and have sex with her. And so it proved. He woke up with a start, and she was ready with a clever excuse: 'The cat was chasing a mouse and it jumped down and made a noise that I mistook for a burglar. Actually it wasn't anything.' She clasped him tightly and rubbed her vulva beside his penis until he got excited and mounted her. At first, when he thrust, she managed to refrain from uttering any cries of passion, but after several hundred strokes she started to moan and her fluid came in a steady stream. She let him thrust a while and then wipe up, in constant attendance on her. At midnight her husband spent, but her own passions were still at their height. She was greatly distressed at his wanting to stop, but she couldn't bring herself to ask him to continue. Her only solution was to start sighing and groaning as if she were ill in order to get him to rub her chest and stomach, thus preventing him from sleeping. It was too much for the husband, who couldn't help mounting her and beginning all over again. This went on until cockcrow, keeping me up all night. Then, just as I was about to gather up their valuables, dawn broke and I had to sneak away, and I never did manage to rob them. But that is how I know that this kind of woman is hard to live with."

"Indeed. But let me ask you this, are most women capable of passionate cries while they're having sex?"

"Most are, of course. Still, there are those who aren't, probably one or two in every ten. But women have three kinds of cries, which sound very different even when expressed in the same words. We thieves are the only ones who can tell the difference. Even the men having sex with them don't know."

"What are they?"

"When they start, the women aren't feeling any pleasure and have no desire to cry out. They're just putting on an act to get their husbands excited. You can tell that from the sound they make; in general, although they cry out, they don't move at all and their words are distinct rather than garbled. When they begin to feel pleasure, not only are their minds and mouths full of sensuality, every part of their bodies is starting to feel the same way. The cries are audible, but the words come out incoherent and disjointed. When their pleasure reaches its climax, their energies flag, their arms and legs go limp, and they couldn't utter any cries even if they wanted to. Now the sound comes from their throats rather than their mouths and is barely audible.

"But even this barely audible sound is too much for the listener. I was robbing a house once and saw a husband and wife having sex. At first as they tumbled about, the noise she made was deafening, but it had not the slightest effect on me. Then she fell silent and stopped moving, as if her husband had done her to death. I cocked an ear and drew closer. All I could hear was a wheezing and gasping from her throat that sounded like something between speech and a sigh, and I knew she had reached her climax. A wave of excitement swept over me, I began to tingle all over, and my semen came of its own accord without resort to the handgun. That is how I know women are capable of this sort of cry as well."

At this point Vesperus heard in his imagination the most wanton of women uttering her cries of passion in his ear, and his body began to tingle all over, too, and before he knew it his long-suppressed semen was spreading over the mat.

There were more questions he wanted to ask, but it was now broad daylight. The two men got up, washed, and then sat down again to continue their talk, which was full of the same kind of fascinating information. The lecturer may occasionally have shown signs of fatigue, but his listener's interest never flagged, and after several days of intimate conversation an even closer bond had formed between them.

"I've seen many women since I left home," said Vesperus at this stage, "but none who has taken my fancy, and I'd come to the conclusion that there are no beautiful girls left in the world. From what you say, though, you've seen girls like that not once but many times. Since I'm devoting my life to sex, I feel thrice blessed in getting to know you, and I'd be missing a golden opportunity if I failed to entrust you with this concern of mine. I beg you, brother, to pick out the most beautiful girl from among those you've seen and think up some way for me to get a look at her. If she really is strikingly beautiful, well, to be candid, I was born under the lucky star of love. All my life it's been the same way. Once I meet a woman, I don't need to seek her out, she comes looking for me. When the time is right, I'll ask you to pull off one of your miracles and arrange a rendezvous. Who knows, perhaps you as the reincarnation of the Knave of Kunlun may come to my aid as a latter-day Master Cui?"

The Knave shook his head. "No, I can't do that, because I've vowed never to rob any people I've robbed before. Having robbed them once, I couldn't bring myself to rob them of their property again, let alone of their womenfolk's chastity! But I'll make a point of watching out from now on. When I enter someone's house and see a beautiful girl, I won't necessarily take anything, I'll come back and consult you about a rendezvous. That's something I *can* do for you."

"I failed to give a gallant man his due," said Vesperus. "My suggestion was presumptuous, I now realize. There is one thing I must mention, though: I am grateful for your offer, but if you find a strikingly beautiful girl, whatever you do, don't steal anything. Don't let the sight of her valuables tempt you into forgetting your promise. If you can arrange something for me, I'll make a point of rewarding you."

"Now you really *have* failed to give a gallant man his due! If I were looking for a reward, I'd do better to take what you have on you right now. Why shouldn't I be tempted by the sight of *your* valuables? Even if you make a point of rewarding me, the reward will be just the promise of a contribution or two after you're in office. I can well imagine what those contributions will be worth; ten of them together wouldn't equal what I make from a single robbery. *That* kind of reward you can forget about. I'm promising you a beautiful girl. Of course, when I find one for you, the onus of seducing her will be on you. I can't guarantee everything!"

"I'm a specialist in the art of seduction," said Vesperus. "You can set your mind at rest."

"Now that you've met me," said the Knave, "there's no need to go off anywhere else. Why not rent some rooms here and get on with your studies? But don't depend solely on me. If you see someone good, you should go ahead on your own. If I find someone, I'll come and report. With both of us on the lookout, we're sure to find one or two. We can hardly draw a complete blank."

Jubilant, Vesperus told his servants to look for lodgings. Then, before letting the Knave take his leave, he insisted on bowing another four times in friendship. With sworn brothers in the past, his friendships had been cemented with eight bows; only in the Knave's case had he given as many as twelve. In later times someone wrote a poem pointing out the error of Vesperus's ways, namely, his lechery and his consorting with a criminal. The poem ran,

Since lust misleads us, dims our sight,
He took thief for hero in lust's despair.
Then swearing an oath, he forged a bond
With the lowliest creatures of earth and air.

Having bent the knee to a humble thief,
How should he answer the emperor's grace?
Your views, good sir, are enlightened indeed;
In the world today we honor the base.

CRITIQUE

The Knave's character is ten times better than Vesperus's. It was not Vesperus, but the Knave, who swore brotherhood with a thief.

Lone Peak's three abstentions and the Knave's five are the most remarkable and delightful writing of all time, something quite unparalleled in fiction. Even if you tried, you couldn't prevent them from enjoying a wide circulation!

CHAPTER *FIVE*

In selecting beauties, he rigorously compiles a list of
  names;
For personal reasons, he leniently admits an older
  woman.

Poem:
  Her girlish beauty's on display;
  How passionate? One cannot say.
  In bed she oughtn't to be shy,
  For soldiers must not run away.
  Once a mother, already old,
  Until then, a simple maid.
  Her sole desire, that beauty stay;
  But graying locks can't be delayed.

After parting from the Knave, Vesperus took up residence in
a temple that was a secondary abode for the Immortal Zhang,
god of fertility. It had few rooms, which normally were not

rented to travelers. But because Vesperus was prepared to pay a very high rent—other places charged one tael a month and he offered two—the Taoist priests, in their eagerness for a paltry profit, made an exception in his case.

Why was he willing to pay such a high rent to stay at this temple? Because the Immortal Zhang was extremely efficacious and women flocked to him from far and wide to pray for sons. It was Vesperus's idea to treat the temple as an examination hall, and that was his purpose in moving there. Sure enough, he found that every day brought several groups of ladies to the temple to burn incense, ladies who differed from the women attending other temples in that there were always one or two of them in every ten who were tolerably attractive.

Why should that be, you ask. Surely Vesperus had not posted a notice banning all ugly women and admitting only the pretty ones? You must understand that every temple has its women visitors, who encompass the old, the middle-aged, and the young. Of these the old and middle-aged make up about two-thirds and the young one-third; thus the good-looking women are outnumbered by the rest. But the women who came to this temple were all there to pray for sons. Now, old women are beyond menopause and cannot bear children, while middle-aged women are approaching it and have lost interest in child-bearing; thus the women who came there to pray for sons were all young. If any mature women did come along as companions, they were few in number. For the five or six years following the age of thirteen, all girls, good-looking or not, have a certain bloom in their cheeks that men find subtly appealing. That was why, out of every ten visitors, there were always one or two who were tolerably attractive.

Vesperus rose early each morning and, dressed as smartly as the leading man in a play, paced endlessly back and forth in front of the Immortal's throne. When he saw any women approaching, he would duck out of sight behind the throne and listen while the Taoist priests communicated the women's prayers. He would watch as the women took incense sticks and knelt down, carefully observing their looks and demeanor and then dashing out when they least expected it.

At sight of his peerless looks and ethereal manner, the women would gasp in astonishment, assuming that the sincerity of their prayers had brought the Immortal's statue to life to provide them with sons. Not until Vesperus came down the steps and swaggered about did they realize that he was a mere human being, by which time their souls had been captured by this living Immortal Zhang. So wild with desire did he drive them that they sent him loving glances and meaningful winks and could scarcely tear themselves away. Some dropped their handkerchiefs on purpose, while others left their fans behind. Vesperus could count on receiving several such tokens of admiration each day.

From this time on, his behavior grew quite irresponsible and his mind ever more depraved. He went so far as to proclaim, "I *deserve* to enjoy the most beautiful women in the world. A man as handsome as I am *deserves* to have women dancing attendance on him. There's nothing strange about that!"

On moving to the temple he had put together a small notebook, which he kept in his pocket. On the cover were inscribed the words:

GARNER THE BEAUTIES OF SPRING FROM FAR AND WIDE

Any woman who came to the temple to pray and who possessed a degree of beauty would have her particulars entered in the notebook as follows: name, age, husband's surname and personal name, address. Beside her name Vesperus drew circles in red ink to indicate her ranking: three circles for *summa cum laude*; two for *magna cum laude*; and one for *cum laude*. After each name he added comments in parallel-prose style like those written on examination scripts, to describe the woman's good points.

Storyteller, what you've just said doesn't tally with what you said before. When the women came into the temple, all Vesperus could do was stand aside and observe them. That way he wouldn't have learned the women's own names, let alone their husbands' names and addresses! Are you trying to tell us that he stopped them and asked them their particulars?

Gentle reader, you've missed the point again. When a woman goes into a temple to pray, she invariably has a priest beside her to communicate her prayer. When she comes in, he always asks her, "What is your surname, please? Your personal name? Your age? Which believer's wife are you? Where do you live?" Even if she doesn't answer the questions herself, she'll have a servant or a maid there to answer for her. As he listened, Vesperus made mental notes about each woman and then entered them in his book after she had left. What's so hard to believe about that?

Within the space of a few months Vesperus had garnered almost all the beauties in the district. There was just one problem, however. Although he was lenient about admitting people to the examination, he was extremely strict in his grading. Many names were entered in his book, but all in the second or third categories; there was not a single name to which he gave three circles.

My lifelong ambition, he thought, was to marry the most beautiful girl in the world. I used to think that the one I married was the most beautiful, but in the light of my recent experience I see that there are many others who are on a par with her. Clearly she doesn't qualify as *the* most beautiful. But it makes no sense to have a Secunda and a Tertia but no Prima.[42] Anyway, if a Prima does exist somewhere, I have yet to meet her. All those I see as I search and search are *cum laude* talent. I'll keep this by me as an alternate list, and if I never meet the one I'm looking for, I'll take it out and do the best I can with it. Meanwhile I'll wait and see what the next few days will bring.

From this point on, not only was his grading even stricter, his admissions policy was also tightened up. One day, in a state of mental exhaustion, he was taking a nap in his room when one of his pages burst in and announced, "Master, come and see the beautiful girls! Come at once, or you'll miss them."

Vesperus promptly arose, put on a new cap and an elegant gown, and then stopped to check his appearance in the mirror, all of which took a little time. When he got outside, he saw two girls, one dressed in pale rose, the other in lotus pink. Their companion was also a beauty, although somewhat older. Having burned their incense, the three women were on their way out of the temple when Vesperus caught a glimpse of them from a distance. The two girls looked to him like the Goddess of Mount Wu and the Fairy of the River Luo[43]—in a different class altogether from the women he had seen so far.

Now, the way to look at a woman is the same as the way you look at calligraphy or painting. There is no need to study a scroll brushstroke by brushstroke; all you have to do is hang it up at a distance and judge its power. If it shows adequate

---

42. The terms are those for the top candidates in the civil service examinations (*zhuangyuan*, etc.). Their Latin equivalents have been feminized here.

43. The divine beings of the "Gaotang Rhapsody" (attributed to Song Yu, third century B.C.) and the "Luo Goddess Rhapsody" of Cao Zhi, respectively.

power, it is a masterpiece; if its power is blocked and the scroll lacks vitality, it is no better than a print; however fine its brush technique, it is mere hackwork and hence worthless. Now, if a woman's beauty has to be examined close up to reveal itself, it will be limited at best. The qualities of a truly beautiful woman cannot be obscured, even though seen through a curtain of rain, mist, flowers, or bamboo. Even if she is glimpsed through a crack in the door or has hidden herself in the dark, a sense of her charm will emanate of its own accord and make the observer marvel, "How comes it she is like a heavenly one, how comes it she is like a god?"[44] If you think these qualities reside in her physical form, you are wrong; but if you think they lie outside of her physical form, you are also wrong. They are beyond explanation, hence marvelous.

At sight of the girls, Vesperus went out of his mind. Since they had not yet reached the gate, he flew after them and, kneeling down outside the threshold, began kowtowing nonstop. His pages and the priest were struck dumb, terrified the women would make a scene. But there was a method in Vesperus's madness, for he was calculating along these lines: If they are willing to go down this path with me, they will realize that I kowtowed because I saw how beautiful they were and was overcome with love; they can hardly return my greeting in public, but I doubt that they will make much of a scene. If, on the other hand, they are proper, highly principled girls and do make a scene, I'll just claim that I was visiting the temple to pray for a son and that, on noticing some women in there already, I knelt down and kowtowed outside to avoid mixed company. They can't possibly know I'm staying in the temple and refute me. Only because he had this ingenious plan

---

44. The lines come from the song "Junzi jie lao" of the *Poetry Classic*. See Arthur Waley, trans., *The Book of Songs*, p. 77.

up his sleeve and felt himself on safe ground did he dare kowtow.

Just as he had supposed, the three women knew nothing about him. Thinking he had come there to pray for a son, they withdrew to one side and waited for him to finish. As he kowtowed, the two younger women turned and gave him a look, but it was not clear to him whether it was a look of interest or indifference. The older beauty, however, faced him squarely and put on a regular performance. With her hand over her mouth, she dissolved into giggles, nudging the two girls as if to get them to turn and acknowledge Vesperus's kowtows with her. As she departed, she also sent him a couple of sidelong glances.

For a long time Vesperus remained stupefied, unable to utter a sound. Only when the women were half a mile away did he turn to the priest: "Those three just now—which household are they from? They're so *beautiful*!" But the priest, who had seen Vesperus's wildness almost result in an incident, was still furious with him and would not tell him anything.

Vesperus considered following them home, but they were now too far away to overtake, so he returned to his room and sat there brooding. "How terrible!" he said to himself. "I know the names and addresses of all those women who don't appeal to me, but not of these two who do. What a pity I've let such peerless beauties slip through my fingers! How will I ever get over it?"

He took out the notebook and placed it in front of him, intending to add the two women to his list. But then he realized, on picking up his brush, that he did not know what names to put down. So he wrote a short introductory note:

On the _____ day of the _____ month, met two outstanding beauties. As their names are unknown to me, for the time being I name them for the colors of the dresses they were wearing. Apparent ages, temperaments noted below, to aid in search:

Pale Rose Maid. Age about sixteen or seventeen. Judging from emotional attitude, seems married only short time, with sexual desires as yet undeveloped.

Comment:

Graceful as a cloud in motion, elegant as a column of jade. With ruby lips apart, looks as pretty as a flower that understands speech. Walking with delicate steps, moves as lightly as a swallow just able to fly. Brows constantly knitted, but not with grief—it's true that Xishi was given to frowning![45] Eyes reluctant to open, though not from weariness—it's a fact that Yang Guifei was fond of sleep![46]

Even more endearing is the way she offers others her heart rather than gifts; on parting she left no trinket behind. She showed me her thoughts rather than her actions; on leaving she cast no backward glance. Surely a hermit among women, a recluse of the boudoir! If I place her in the highest group, who will deny she deserves it?

Lotus Pink Beauty. Age in her twenties. From her expression, seems to have been long married but without exhaustion of original yin.

Comment:

A beauty soft and graceful, a bearing as light as if dancing. Eyebrows that need no Zhang Chang to paint them, a face that requires none of He Yan's

---

45. The classic beauty. Even her frown was imitated by other women.
46. The Tang beauty, consort of Emperor Xuanzong.

powder.[47] Flesh that is between sleek and spare, its beauty being that its spareness cannot be increased nor its sleekness reduced. Makeup that is between heavy and light, its beauty being that its heaviness looks shallow and its lightness deep.

The affecting thing about her is that the melancholy of her feelings goes unrelieved, like a lotus bud overdue to open; and that the concerns of her heart go unexpressed, like a flower that dreads its fading. She deserves to rank with the first girl ahead of all other blooms and to merit the title of supreme beauty. Only the Oral Examination will determine the top candidate.

After finishing the comments, he remembered someone he had omitted. The beauty of these two goes without saying, he thought, but even the older one has not lost her youthful charm. To take just one feature, her eyes are pure gems; the pupils can positively speak. She sent me glance after glance, but because I was so intent on the others, I never responded—embarrassing thought! Her age may be rather advanced, her looks may have declined somewhat, and she may be a little too plump, but since she was with the others, she must be a relative of some kind. If only out of consideration for them I ought to be more lenient in my grading. Moreover, she was willing to join in the fun and try to get the others to look at me. Obviously she has a lot of savoir faire. If I can only find her, the others, too, will surely fall to my bow. The trouble is I've no idea where to start looking. For the present I'll just enter

---

47. Zhang, a Han official, was famous for painting his wife's eyebrows. He Yan, a Wei official of Three Kingdoms times, had a face so pale the emperor suspected him of using powder.

her in my notebook with a *summa* rating: first, as a reward for being so responsive; second, as an extension of my love for the other two; and third, so that if I do find her, I can show her this notebook and, after winning her over, gain her help with the others.

He changed the *two* of *two outstanding beauties* in the first line to *three*. Since she was wearing a dark dress, he named her

Black Belle. Age about thirty-five, but looking only fifteen. From her bearing, it would seem that her desires have been long neglected and that her passions are incandescent.

Comment:

Of effervescent feelings and mercurial mood. Her waist may be thicker than a young woman's, but the line of her eyebrows is as arched as any bride's. Her cheeks are as rosy as ever, maintaining their flowerlike, original brightness; her skin still glows, showing its jadelike, pristine beauty.

The most captivating thing about her is the way her glance, without any movement of the eyes, flashes as vividly as lightning amid the mountain crags; and the way, in her walk, without taking so much as a step, she wafts as lightly as clouds over the mountain tops. She deserves to be classed with those who express their feelings through their thoughts rather than their actions. Placed beside the other two beauties, she would not have to concede very much.

After completing his comments, he drew three large circles beside each of the names, then folded up the notebook and tucked it into his pocket. From that day forward he no longer cared whether he went to the temple to look at girls. He was preoccupied with the three beauties, but although he spent every daylight hour walking the streets with his notebook, he could find no trace of them.

The Knave has more experience than anyone else, Vesperus said to himself, and he knows this area well. Why not go and ask him? There is one problem, though. He promised to find me a mistress, and since he hasn't been around the last few days, I expect he's gone off in search of one. If I mention this to him, he'll assume I've found a suitable girl and give up his responsibilities. Moreover, without a name to go by, where would he start looking? I'll keep the matter to myself for a few days. He may find someone and come and tell me about her. You never know. One can have too much of everything in life except beautiful girls. Even if he produces dozens of them, I'll deal with his recommendations first and still have time for these three later. Thenceforth after rising each morning he either went out hoping to run into the Knave or else waited anxiously in his rooms.

One day while crossing the street he spotted his friend and hailed him. "Brother, about that promise you made me the other day. How is it I've had no response? You haven't forgotten, by any chance?"

"It's been on my mind every hour of the day. How could I possibly forget? The trouble is that there are plenty of ordinary girls out there but very few excellent ones. I've been searching all this time, and only now have I come up with one or two. In fact I was just on my way over to report when I ran into you."

Vesperus's face broke into a broad smile. "In that case this street is hardly the place to talk. Come over to my lodgings."

Linking hands, the two men walked to his lodgings. Once there, Vesperus dismissed his boys and shut his door so that he and the Knave could discuss the happy prospect in private.

Whose wife will be so fortunate as to get the services of this eminently qualified lover? And whose husband will be so unfortunate as to arouse the attentions of this devilish adulterer? There is no need, gentle reader, to remain in doubt, for the answers will be found in the next chapter.

CRITIQUE

Fiction writers always confine themselves to narrative as distinct from discourse. Or, if they do write discourse, they develop a piece to serve as prologue to the narrative and then, after reaching the *transitio,* [48] quickly wind it up, evidently fearing a hopeless confusion. How can they conduct a philosophical discussion while poised for the fray? The author of this book is the only one who can display calm amid the panic and cool amid the heat. Into every tense passage of narrative he inserts a piece of leisurely discourse, posing and answering his questions in such an orderly fashion that the reader, far from finding it a distraction, is loath to see it end. When the author has finished his discourse and takes up the narration again, he is able to make it dovetail perfectly with what has gone before. A true master of the art! Ever since he invented this mode, he has been the only one capable of practicing it. Those who imitate his technique merely earn the reader's boredom.

---

48. Name for part of the *eight-legged* examination essay.

CHAPTER SIX

*In embellishing a shortcoming, he boasts of a long suit;
For presenting a small object, he is mocked by a great
    expert.*

Poem:
　　If you lack great talent for the bedroom art,
　　Tempt not with lesser skills the womb of woe.
　　In the darkness Pan An's looks will go unseen;
　　What use are Cao Zhi's rhymes before the foe?
　　After his dream King Xiang returned to Chu;[49]
　　Pray ask him why he ever climbed Mount Wu.
　　You expect from birth love's perfect instrument?
　　Then see that its size and design are left to you.

---

49. King Xiang had the romantic encounter described in the "Gaotang
Rhapsody."

The Knave took a seat and opened the discussion: "Well, brother, any interesting contacts?"

Fearing that the Knave merely wanted to shed his responsibilities, Vesperus said no, then went quickly on: "Brother, that one you mentioned just now—what family does she belong to? Where do they live? How old is she? How would you rate her looks? Do tell me."

"I've found you not one but three. I'll tell you all about them and let you make your own choice. But you can have only one, you mustn't get greedy and hanker after all three. That would never do."

I have these three girls on my mind, thought Vesperus, and here he is talking about three girls too. I wonder if his three could be the same ones I saw? If so, I need seduce only one of them for the other two to come around of their own accord. I wouldn't even *need* his help in that.

"Of course not," he replied. "One would be ample, thank you. I'd never dream of being so greedy."

"Just as well," said the Knave. "The only problem is that everybody has his likes and dislikes, and someone I think beautiful may not seem so to you. I've found these three girls, but I'm not sure they'll appeal to you."

"Brother, you have such a wealth of experience that you must be a good judge. It's possible that a woman who took my fancy might not seem beautiful to you, but hardly the other way around."

"Well, then, let me ask you this: do you prefer your women plump or slender?"

"A plump figure has its attractions, just as a slender one does. But a woman must not be so plump as to fill out her clothes or so slender as to look bony. So long as she is plump or slender within a suitable range, she'll appeal to me."

"In that case you'll find all three to your liking. Now let

me ask you this: in matters of sex, do you prefer them passionate or prudish?"

"Why, passionate, of course. It's no fun having a prudish woman in bed with you. It's simpler sleeping on your own. I've always been dead scared of prudes."

The Knave shook his head. "In that case, none of these will be right for you."

"Tell me, brother, how do you know they're prudish?"

"As it happens, they all belong to the same school—supremely beautiful but lacking experience in lovemaking."

"But that's no obstacle! So long as the basic quality is there, passionate behavior can always be instilled. To be quite frank with you, my own wife was a prude at first, utterly ignorant about lovemaking she was; but it took me only a few days to educate her out of it. Now, believe it or not, she's almost too passionate. So long as these women really are beautiful, I have my own ways of changing them should they be a little on the prudish side."

"Well, that takes care of that. There's just one other question I have for you: do you need to take possession as soon as you meet, or are you willing to hold off for a few months while waiting for her to come to hand?"

"Frankly, brother, my desires are always at fever pitch. If I have to go a few nights without a woman, I'll have a wet dream. In all the time I've been away from home, I've not visited a brothel once, and by now I'm simply frantic. If I fail to meet a beautiful girl, I daresay I'll be able to scrape by, but if I do find one, and we have some feeling for each other, I don't think I could contain myself any longer."

"In that case let's confine ourselves to this one and ignore the other two. They belong to a rich and distinguished family and would be difficult to obtain at short notice. This one is the wife of a poor man and should be easy to get. I don't frequent poor people's houses, but the promise I made to you has been very much on my mind, and I've made a point of looking closely at every woman I saw, by day or night.

"One day I was walking along the street when I noticed this woman sitting in her doorway behind a bamboo curtain. Although I saw her only through the curtain and did not get a clear view, I was struck by the pink and white glow of her complexion, like some priceless pearl radiating light. When I looked again, this time at how graceful her figure was, she seemed like a great beauty's portrait hanging there inside the curtain and gently swaying in the breeze. The sight held me rooted to the spot, unable to walk on. I stood there opposite her house for a while and then noticed a man coming out, a coarse-looking character in shabby clothes who was taking a roll of silk to market. I went and asked the neighbors about them and learned that the man's surname was Quan, that due to his reputation for honesty he was known as Honest Quan, and that the woman was his wife. I was worried about not getting a close enough view of her through the curtain, so I went by a few days later, and there she was again, sitting in her doorway. Before she had time to do anything, I whipped the curtain aside, burst in, and told her that I had come to buy silk from her husband.

" 'My husband is away,' she replied. 'But if it's silk you want, we have plenty of it. Let me get some out for you to look at.' But despite what she said, she made no move to get the silk. I talked her into getting some, just to see what her hands and feet were like. Her fingers were like lotus shoots, as delicate and tapering as you could possibly imagine. Her feet were less than three inches long, and she was not wearing high heels either, so there was no artifice involved. I had now seen her hands and feet, but not the rest of her, and I had no idea whether her skin was light or dark in tone, and so I came up with another ploy. Spying another roll of silk on the top of the case, I said, 'None of this is good enough. Could you get me down that roll from on top? I'd like to take a look at it.'

"She nodded, and raised her arms over her head to get it down. It was a hot day, you understand, and she was wearing nothing but an unlined silk dress. As she raised her arms, her loose sleeves fell all the way back to her shoulders, so that not only were her arms exposed, her breasts were faintly visible too. They were truly as white as snow, as smooth as a mirror, as fine as powder. No doubt about it, she belongs in the top group of all the women I have ever seen. I was embarrassed to be giving her so much trouble and felt obliged to buy a roll of silk. But before I go any further, let me ask you this, brother: do you like this woman and would you want her?"

"She sounds like perfection itself. Of course I do! But how can I see her and then, once I've seen her, how can I get her?"

"There's no problem there. It'll cost a little money, that's all. I'll go and get a few ingots now, and then we'll set off for her place and wait until her husband leaves home. We'll proceed as I did before, bursting in and asking for silk. You'll be able to tell at a glance whether she appeals to you. The only question is whether you like her, for I've no doubt that she'll like you. After facing that coarse-looking husband of hers day after day—honest he may be, but he has absolutely no appeal—she's bound to be aroused by the very sight of you. Give her the impression you're making advances and, if she doesn't take immediate offense, we'll come back and think how to proceed. I guarantee that within three days she'll be yours. Afterward, if you want to arrange a marriage, I'll see to that too."

"I'd be grateful to all eternity. But there is one thing that puzzles me. Since you possess such marvelous ingenuity and supernatural power, I should have thought there'd be nothing in the world you couldn't do. How is it that you can get me this one and not the other two? Is it really because a poor man is easy to take advantage of but you don't dare provoke the rich and mighty?"

"In every other matter that's the case; the poor man *is* easier to take advantage of and the rich man more dangerous to provoke. But with adultery the opposite holds true."

"Why is that?" asked Vesperus.

"A rich man is sure to have several wives and concubines, and while he is sleeping with one of them, the others will be left on their own. As the old saying goes, 'Once you're well fed and clothed, your thoughts turn to sex.' Those women, being well fed and well dressed, have nothing else to think about but sex. When a woman like that is feeling frustrated and a man slips into her bed—a man, the very thing she has been longing for!—she is hardly going to push him out again. Even if her husband catches them in the act, although he may feel like seizing them and dragging them off to court, still, as a rich and distinguished man he will fear the resultant loss of face. Alternatively, although he may feel like killing them both on the spot, he won't want to give up such a beautiful girl, and if he can't bear to sacrifice her, how can he justify killing her lover? So he will usually suppress his anger and say nothing, playing deaf and dumb so as to give the lover a chance to escape.

"The poor man, on the other hand, has only one wife who sleeps in his arms every night. Forget that she is so preoccupied with worrying about hunger and cold that she would never have any lustful thoughts anyway. Even if she did, and tried to arrange a meeting with her lover, there'd be no place for them to have sex. If by some chance they did manage a furtive embrace and were caught in the act, her husband, as a poor man, wouldn't care about loss of face and would show them no mercy whatever. He'd either seize them and drag them off to court or else kill them both on the spot. That's why it's dangerous to provoke a poor man but easy to take advantage of a rich one."

"That's all very plausible, but how do you explain the fact that these arguments contradict what you said before?"

"It's not that I'm being inconsistent, just that those families are in precisely the opposite situations from the ones I've been talking about, which is why this one is easy to get and the other two are beyond your reach for the moment."

"I've set my heart on this one, but it wouldn't do any harm to tell me about the other two, if only to show how much trouble you've gone to in my behalf."

"One of them is in her twenties," said the Knave, "and the other no more than fifteen or sixteen. They are two sisters who are also sisters-in-law, being married to two brothers. Their husbands' family has produced officials over many generations, but no one in this generation has succeeded in the higher examinations. These two are nominal licentiates who, for all their studies, are quite ill educated. The elder brother's name is Scholar Cloud-Reposer, and he's been married to the woman in her twenties for four or five years now. The younger one's name is Scholar Cloud-Recliner, and he's been married to the fifteen- or sixteen-year-old for less than three months. Both wives are as beautiful as the woman I've just described, but they're also prudish. They don't move or say anything during sex and they give the distinct impression of not liking it. But although *they* may not like it, their husbands have no other wives or concubines to turn to, so they share their wives' bedrooms every night, which is why it would not be easy to get either woman. If you want to try, you'll need to use every trick in the book to arouse her sexual desire and then wait until her husband is away before making your move. It is not something that can be done in a month or two. The woman in the silk shop whom I mentioned has two advantages: she is easy to meet and her husband is often away. That is why it would be simpler to get her."

Noting that the description of the two women roughly fitted the two girls he had seen a few days before, Vesperus was reluctant to let the matter drop. "Brother," he said, "you are perfectly right, but there's one point you've overlooked. You said the two women are prudish and lack sexual desire and therefore it would not be easy to make a move. I suspect they may be like that only because their husbands' endowment is so tiny and their stamina so inadequate that the wives get no pleasure from sex. If they met up with me, I submit that they would soon be relieved of their prudery."

"From what I've seen," said the Knave, "their husbands' endowment can't be described as tiny or their stamina as inadequate, although it is true that they don't compare with men of the greatest proportions and capacities. That's one thing I was going to ask *you* about, worthy brother. Your sexual desires are so keen that I'm sure you have what it takes. But tell me, just what *is* the size of your endowment? And what is your stamina like? I need to know if I am to act for you with an easy mind."

Vesperus beamed. "That's one thing you needn't worry about, my good fellow. I'm not boasting when I say that my stamina and endowment are both more than adequate. They will lay a feast from which even a woman with the heartiest appetite will stagger away gorged and drunk. It will be no pauper's dinner party, I assure you, from which the guest rises sober and ravenous, complaining bitterly of her host's lack of savoir-faire."

"That's very reassuring. Still, it wouldn't do any harm to take the matter a little further. When you're making love, approximately how many thrusts can you give before letting go?"

"I've never even counted. Anyone who can keep track of

the number is bound to be of very limited sexual powers. I don't abide by any general rule when I'm making love to a woman, but I can assure you that she receives innumerable thrusts before I stop."

"Even if you can't remember the number, you must at least remember how long. Approximately how many hours can you last?"

Vesperus's actual limit was only one hour, but since he wanted the Knave to act for him, he was afraid to admit to so little, lest he give his friend an excuse for backing out, and he felt compelled to add another hour to his performance.

"I can last a good two hours," he replied. "If I tried to hold out, I daresay I might be able to last for half an hour or more beyond that."

"That's nothing out of the ordinary," said the Knave. "It doesn't qualify as a very strong performance. Such mediocre ability is ample for everyday sex with your wife, but I'm afraid it would be quite inadequate for a raid on someone else's camp."

"You're worrying unnecessarily, my good fellow," said Vesperus. "The other day I bought myself an excellent sex tonic. I have no woman at present, so I'm a warrior without a battlefield. But if an assignation can be arranged, I'll take a chance and apply some of it ahead of time. I've no doubt I shall prove to have plenty of endurance."

"Sex tonics can give you endurance only," said the Knave. "They cannot increase your size or firmness. If a man with a large endowment uses one, he'll be like a gifted graduate taking a ginseng tonic at examination time; in the examination hall his mental powers will naturally be enhanced, and he will be able to express himself well. But if a student with a very small endowment uses one, he'll be no better off than some empty-headed candidate who couldn't produce a line even if he swallowed pounds of the tonic. What's the point of his sitting in an examination cell for three days and nights if all he's doing is holding out regardless of results? Moreover, most such tonics are a swindle. Who knows whether yours will work or not? But I'm not asking whether you've tested it. What I want to know is the size and length of your endowment."

"There is no need to go into that," said Vesperus. "What I will say, though, is that it is not small."

Seeing that Vesperus was not about to respond, the Knave shot out his hand and tugged at the crotch of his friend's trousers in an effort to free the object in question. Vesperus kept evading his reach, refusing to let him do so. "If that's the way things are," said the Knave, "I won't bother you anymore. Your stamina certainly can't be described as strong. If your endowment should be puny, too, and if by some chance you fail to stimulate the woman and she cries rape, think how terrible that would be! If you got into any trouble, I would be the one who had misled you, and that is something I cannot accept."

Confronted with such vehemence from his friend, Vesperus could only smile gamely. "My endowment will certainly pass muster," he said, "but I do find it a little indelicate to have to produce it in front of a friend, and in broad daylight too. However, since you're so worried over nothing, I suppose I have no choice but to make a spectacle of myself."

With that, he undid his belt and brought out a penis that was dainty in both size and texture. Weighing it in his hand, he continued, "Here is my modest endowment. Take a look at it by all means."

The Knave approached and scrutinized it. This is what he saw:

Body a pearly white,
Head a crimson glow.

Around the base thin grasses in dense profusion rise,
Under the skin fine threads are faintly to be seen.
Bounced in the hand, it makes no sound, being lighter
    than the hand itself;
Touched with the fingers, it retains no trace, its
    muscles being so few.
In length all of two inches;
In weight a good quarter-ounce.
Solid outside, hollow inside, easy to mistake for a
    schoolboy's brush handle.
Sharp of head, tiny of eye, easy to confuse with a
    Tartar girl's pipe stem.
A twelve-year-old virgin could accommodate it,
A thirteen-year-old catamite would delight in it.
Hard as iron before the event, resembling a very long
    dried razor clam;
Bent like a bow when all is done, suggesting a very
    plump dried shrimp.

The Knave examined it, looked Vesperus in the eye, contemplated for a long time, but said nothing. Vesperus assumed he was astonished at its size.

"It is only like this when limp," he said. "When full of vigor it is even more spectacular."

"If this is what it's like when limp," said the Knave, "I can well imagine what it's like when full of vigor. I've seen all I need to, thank you. Please put it away." Then, unable to contain himself any longer, he put his hand over his mouth and burst out laughing.

"How can you be so ignorant of your own limitations, worthy brother? Your endowment is less than a third the size of other people's, and yet you propose to go off and seduce their wives! Do you imagine the women's shoes are too big for the lasts they have at home and that they need your little

peg wedged in alongside? When I saw you looking about
everywhere for women, I assumed you had a mighty instrument on you, something to strike fear into the hearts of all
who saw it. That's why I hesitated to ask you to show it to
me. I never dreamed that it would turn out to be a flesh-and-
blood hair clasp, good for titillating a woman inside her pubic
hair, perhaps, but useless in the really important place!"

"It will serve at a pinch," protested Vesperus. "Perhaps
yours is so massive that you tend to look down on everybody
else's. I'll have you know that this unworthy instrument of
mine has been much admired."

"Admired?" said the Knave. "A virgin with her maidenhead intact or else some boy who has yet to make his debut—
people like that would admire it. But apart from them, I'm
afraid everyone else would find it as hard as I do to flatter your
honorable instrument."

"You mean to tell me that *everybody's* penis is bigger than
mine?"

"I see them all the time—I must have inspected a thousand
or two, at least—and I don't think I've ever seen one quite as
delicate as yours."

"Let's leave other people's out of it. The husbands of those
women—how do their members compare with mine?"

"Not much bigger—only two or three times the size and
length."

Vesperus gave a laugh. "Now I know you're not telling
me the truth!" he said. "This shows that you don't want the
responsibility of helping me and are just looking for a way out.
Let me ask you this: Perhaps you really did see the two men
in that household as you robbed their houses at night, but as
for the woman in the silk shop, you told me yourself that you
visited her only once, in the daytime, and that you spoke only
to her and never met the husband. How can you possibly be
sure that his thing is two or three times as big as mine?"

"I saw the other two with my own eyes," said the Knave. "This one I only heard about. The first day I met her, I went and asked the neighbors about her husband, and they told me his name. Then I asked them: 'Such a beautiful woman—I wonder how she manages to get along with her stupid clod of a husband?' 'Although the husband may look coarse,' they told me, 'he is fortunate enough to have an impressive endowment and that is why the two of them rub along without any actual quarrels.' I then asked, 'How large is his endowment?' Their reply was, 'We've never measured it, but in summer, when he strips down, we've noticed it swinging about in his pants the size of a laundry beater, so we know it's impressive.' I made a mental note of that at the time, which is what led me to ask to see yours today. Why else, for no reason whatever, would I want to inspect someone's penis?"

At last it dawned on Vesperus that the Knave was telling him the truth, and he began to feel depressed. After pondering a while, he went on, "When a woman goes to bed with someone, it's not only from sexual desire, you know. It may also be because she admires his mind or is attracted by his looks. If neither his mind nor his looks amount to much, a man is forced to rely on his sexual prowess. Now I happen to be quite well endowed with looks and brains, and perhaps a woman will take that into account and be a little less demanding in the other department. I implore you to see this matter through for me. You mustn't ignore my many strong points because of a single shortcoming and abandon your idea of helping a friend."

"Talent and looks," said the Knave, "are sweeteners for the medicine of seduction. Like ginger and dates, their flavor helps get the medicine inside, but once it's in there, the medicine alone has to cure the disease; the ginger and dates are of no further use. If a man goes in for seduction and has neither looks nor talent, he'll not be able to get a foot in the door, but once he is inside, his true powers are in demand. What are you planning to do with her under the quilt, anyway, write *poems* on her pelvis? If someone with a very limited endowment and stamina manages to get in by virtue of his looks and talent and then gives a disappointing display the first few times, he will very quickly get the cold shoulder. A fellow takes his life in his hands when he goes in for adultery, and he therefore hopes for a love affair that will last a long time. Why go to such trouble if all you have in mind is two or three nights' fun? We thieves think we have to steal five hundred or a thousand taels' worth of valuables in a break-in, just to make up for the stigma we incur. For a couple of items we might as well stay home, rather than incur the stigma and have nothing to show for it. But let's ignore for the moment the man's desire for long-time pleasure. A woman who deceives her husband and has an affair must take endless precautions and suffer innumerable alarms, poor thing, in order to get some real pleasure. All well and good if she enjoys it a few hundred or even a few dozen times. But if she gets no pleasure out of the affair at all, she's no better off than a hen mounted by a rooster. The hen scarcely knows what's going on inside her before it's over. The woman's life has been wasted and her reputation lost, all for nothing! Not an easy thought to live with! Forgive me for what I'm going to say, worthy brother, but while endowment and stamina like yours are all right for keeping your wife on the straight and narrow, they are not enough to sustain any wild ideas about debauching other men's wives and daughters. Luckily I was shrewd enough to measure the customer before cutting the cloth. If I'd simply set to work without asking your measurements, the garments would have been far too big for you. What a waste of material! And apart altogether from the woman's resentment, I'm afraid you, too, would have blamed me in your heart for not acting in good faith but deliberately choosing someone too large for you so as to get myself off the hook. I'm a straightforward sort of fellow, and I put things crudely, but I hope you won't hold it against me. From now on if you need any money or clothing, I'm only too ready to provide it. But as to this other matter, I simply cannot do your bidding."

From the forcefulness with which the Knave spoke, Vesperus realized that the affair was a lost cause. He knew, too, that the money and clothing would be stolen goods, and he was afraid of the trouble they could land him in.

"I am in rather a difficult spot," he said, "but I haven't spent all my travel money yet, and I still have a few plain garments left. I would not want to put you to any expense."

After saying a few things to comfort his friend, the Knave made as if to leave. Vesperus, his hopes dashed, could not find it in his heart to ask him to stay, and showed him to the gate.

After this frustration did Vesperus curb his desires? Did he reform? The reader is not the only one who is perplexed over these issues; the author himself is not sure, either, and will have to continue into the next chapter before he resolves them. Thus far, although Vesperus's mind has been corrupted, his conduct is without blemish. He is still, believe it or not, a man who *could* lead a virtuous life.

CRITIQUE

Each passage of discourse is bound to contain several superb images that invariably delight the reader and cause him to burst out laughing. They are too numerous to list in full, but two examples may be cited: the likening of sex tonics to examination tonics and the comparison of talent and looks with medicinal sweeteners. Humorous though these remarks are, they also contain a profound truth. I don't know how many thousand apertures the author's mind possesses, to radiate such brilliance!

CHAPTER *SEVEN*

Complaining of his physical endowment, he laments
*   with hand on groin;*
Hoping to rectify his failing, he prays on bended knee.

Lyric:
> Men's desires, how hard to satisfy!
> They weep, who've never known adversity.
> And other unfortunates there are,
> Who in the midst of joy will heave a sigh:
> "I have no luck!" they'll cry,
> All because their desires are set too high.
> (To the tune "Dreamlike Song")

Let us tell how Vesperus's joyous mood was swept clean away
by what the Knave had said. After the latter's departure, he was
like a dead man, unable to bring himself either to speak or to
eat. He sat alone in his room, turning the following thoughts

over and over in his mind: In the course of my twenty-odd years I've seen a great many things in this world, but I've rarely seen another man's penis. Ordinary people keep theirs tucked away under their clothes, where naturally they can't be seen. The only time anyone showed me his was when those nancy-boys took down their trousers and did it with me, but they were younger than I was and naturally their things were smaller than mine. Since the only ones I ever saw were smaller, mine appeared larger. When I was young and played the nancy-boy myself with my schoolmates, we did see each other's things, but we were all of an age and naturally we were about the same size. I came to regard that size as normal and assumed from my own experience that everybody's was much the same. But he claims he has never seen one as small as mine. If so, it's utterly useless! What good is it?

There's one thing that puzzles me, though, Vesperus reflected. When I had sex with my wife, she enjoyed it every bit as much as I did. And in the days when I used to visit courtesans and seduce maids, they would cry out with passion and spend, too, which they never would have done if this thing hadn't brought them pleasure! If it's so useless now, why wasn't it useless then? Why has it become useless all of a sudden? Obviously he must have been deceiving me in order to get out of his commitments.

Thus a moment of suspicion was followed by a moment of wild hope, after which Vesperus suddenly awoke to the truth: No, that's not it, he said to himself. My wife's vagina was quite unformed before I developed it. Now its dimensions match my own exactly—a perfect fit, with no room to spare, between my shortness and thinness and her smallness and shallowness, which is why she enjoys it. It's like cleaning your ears. If a tiny cleaner is inserted in a tiny ear and twiddled about, it gives a pleasant sensation, whereas in a large ear it may have little or no effect.

The Knave told me the other day that women have ways of faking their cries. Who knows whether the maids and courtesans I slept with may not have felt *obliged* to flatter me after accepting my money and presents? In fact perhaps they didn't even *want* to give any cries at all, but just faked them to deceive me. And if their cries can be faked, why not their spending too? The things he told me may not be entirely reliable, but they can't simply be dismissed either. From now on, whenever I meet someone, I'll make a point of looking at his penis to see if it bears out what the Knave says.

Henceforth, whenever he attended a literary gathering and one of his friends went out to relieve himself, Vesperus would follow along and do likewise, glancing first at his friend's penis and then back at his own. It was true; everybody's was more impressive than his. Even when he was going along the road and noticed someone relieving himself outdoors, he would be sure to scrutinize the man's organ out of the corner of his eye.

Nothing in the world is proof against self-doubt. Before, when he thought he had a large penis, even if he had met up with a Xue Aocao, he would have concluded his was better because Xue's was mainly for show and might be of no practical use.[50] But now that he was consumed with fears about his own size, even if he had seen a boy's, he'd have felt, *The boy's is better than mine, for even if mine is the same size, it may not be as firm as his.*

For these thoughts, gentle reader, you must not laugh at him. This was a golden opportunity to purge himself of evil and lay a foundation for cultivating his virtue and reforming his conduct. Who knows, perhaps Lu Nanzi, who shut his door against an importunate widow, and Liuxia Hui, who kept his

---

50. Xue, the fabled lover of the Empress Wu, was noted for the enormous size of his penis. See the *Ruyi Jun zhuan*.

self-control with a girl on his knee, may have shared these very thoughts of his, thoughts that have made them the leading paragons of all time.

After Vesperus had completed his comparative studies, his desires began to slacken and he became less and less inclined to run risks for the sake of sex. Although the Knave's advice was harsh medicine, he thought, I shall just have to swallow it. At least he is a man! I felt like hiding my face in shame when he laughed at me, but think how I'd have felt if I'd been having sex with a woman and right in the middle she had come out with some scathing remark! What should I have done then, stopped and withdrawn, or stayed on until I was ejected? From now on, I'm going to give up all thought of seduction and devote myself wholeheartedly to my proper task. If I can succeed in the examinations, I'll put up some money and buy a couple of virgins as concubines. Theirs will be smaller than mine, and naturally I'll earn their appreciation rather than their contempt. Why waste my energy on all these religious exercises?

After this decision, he gave up his frivolous pursuits and concentrated on his studies. If he noticed any women coming to burn incense, he no longer rushed off to look at them. In fact, if he met any outside the temple, he would duck inside to avoid them, lest they discern his contours through his unlined summer gown and have a private snicker at his expense. Needless to say, if he met a woman in the street, he would hang his head and pass quickly by.

However, because he was a young man in his prime, a certain tumescence made itself felt after a week or two of this harsh regime. His answer was to add a cummerbund to hide this one shortcoming of his from women's prying eyes. As for his other, outstanding features, he was still more than willing to flaunt them.

One day while walking along one of the streets, he observed a young woman open her door curtain and start chatting with a neighbor across the street, revealing her profile as she did so. Seeing this from a distance, he at once shortened his pace and advanced very slowly to listen to her voice and look at her face. Her enunciation was as clear, sweet, and perfectly cadenced as the sound of a panpipe or a flute; every word she uttered left an echo lingering in the ear. On reaching her doorway, Vesperus looked closely at her face and figure. She bore a strong resemblance to the woman the Knave had described: her face was like a priceless pearl radiating light while her figure was like a great beauty's portrait swaying in the breeze behind the curtain. "Perhaps she is the one he mentioned," he surmised.

After a moment's observation, he walked past a few more houses and then asked a bystander, "Is there a silk merchant here by the name of Honest Quan? You wouldn't happen to know where he lives, I suppose?"

"You've just passed his house," said the bystander. "Inside that curtain there, where the woman is talking—that's his place."

His hunch confirmed, Vesperus turned around and took another good look at her before going back to his lodgings. When the Knave described her beauty to me, he thought, I didn't believe him. I felt that, although he claimed to be a connoisseur, he might not be the best judge of quality. I never dreamed he'd have such a marvelous eye! Since he judged this one so perfectly, it goes without saying that his judgment of the other two will be equally reliable. To think that such classic beauties are available and such an extraordinary gallant stands ready to help, and yet I'm missing out on three heaven-sent chances just because this thing of mine has let me down! Oh, the frustration of it all!

After a moment's fury he shut his door, undid his belt, and, taking out his penis, examined it from every angle. Then rage seized him again and he longed to fetch a sharp knife and cut it off, ridding himself forever of this sorry excuse for a penis that was attached to his body for all to see. After a moment he launched into a bitter tirade: "This is all the Lord of Heaven's fault! If you wanted to indulge me, you should have indulged me all the way; why did you have to leave me with this handicap? My looks and talent are only for show, they're of no practical use. You endowed me liberally enough with them, but in the case of this all-important item you wouldn't even lift a finger to help! Do you mean to tell me that adding a few inches to its length and circumference would have cost you any endowment? Why not use someone else's surplus to make up my shortage? Even if bodily material can't be exchanged once people have been endowed, why not take some flesh from my own legs, some sinew from under my skin, some of my body's strength, and redistribute it here? That would have been ample. Instead, why did you take the material needed here and distribute it elsewhere, so that what I really need becomes useless and the things I don't need I have too much of? No doubt about it, this is all the Lord of Heaven's fault! I've seen this beautiful girl, but I don't dare make a move. I'm like a starving man who sees a dish of food with the most wonderful aroma but can't swallow it because his mouth is full of sores. It's enough to make one weep!" And he began to sob bitterly.

Later he went over to the temple, where he strolled about trying to shake off his depression. There he happened to notice a new poster stuck on the screen wall outside the temple gate. Its message, cast in the form of a four-line verse, differed from all the other messages; it was as if the Lord of Heaven had heard his piteous weeping and sent an immortal down to Earth to relieve his misery. It read,

A TRUE MAN FROM A DISTANT LAND
HAS COME TO TEACH THE BEDROOM ART.
HE CAN TAKE A PUNY GROIN
AND TURN IT INTO A MIGHTY PART.

The space beneath the poem, which was in large script, was filled with a line or two of tiny characters:

Passing through this area, I have taken lodging in room _____ in the _____ Temple. Those interested in receiving instruction should make haste to honor me with a visit. If they delay, they will be too late for a consultation.

Vesperus read both poem and postscript several times. So great was his astonishment that he burst into wild laughter. "What an amazing thing! Just when I'm at my wit's end about the size of my penis, along comes this immortal peddling his art and puts up a poster where I happen to see it! It *has* to be Heaven's will!"

He flew into the temple, sealed up some introductory gifts, and put them into a small box, which he had one of his pages carry while he found his way to the address given in the poster.

The adept in question proved to be an old man of awe-inspiring appearance, with a boyish face and white hair. At the sight of Vesperus he folded his hands in front of him and asked, "Well, my good sir, have you come to study the bedroom art?"

"Yes," said Vesperus.

"Which program are you interested in, the one in altruism or the one in egotism?"

"Let me ask, venerable sir," said Vesperus, "what you mean by altruism and egotism?"

"If your sole desire is to serve the woman and bring her

pleasure without attempting to gain any yourself, that is an easy art to learn. You just take a little sperm-suppressant to make your semen come more slowly, rub some analgesic ointment on your penis to numb it until it has no more feeling than a lump of iron, and you'll no longer care whether you spend or not. That's what I mean by altruism.

"If, on the other hand, you wish to attain pleasure *with* the woman, so that every sensation her vagina feels your penis feels too, and so that with every withdrawal you both come back to life and with every thrust you both begin to die, now *that* is mutual pleasure, true enjoyment. The trouble is that at the height of pleasure you will both inevitably want to spend, and the woman will be afraid of spending too late and the man of spending too soon. The most difficult art of all is to get the man to spend less the more he enjoys himself and the woman to enjoy herself more the more she spends. That kind of pleasure is much harder to attain; self-cultivation is the main requirement, supplemented by medication. If you wish to study it, you will have to accompany me on my travels for several years and gradually reach enlightenment before you attain the reality. It is not something that can be mastered in a day or a night."

"In that case I can't study it," said Vesperus. "It will have to be the course in altruism. I already have some of that vital medicine in my lodgings and I won't presume to ask you for more. But it's a commonplace technique at best, one that enables you to hold out but not to increase your size. Your poster claims that you can 'take a puny groin and turn it into a mighty part,' and that was what brought me here to seek instruction. What method is it, I wonder, that can actually effect a change?"

"There are various methods, from which one must choose according to the client's capacity. First, one must see the original size. Second, one must ask how much of an increase the client wants. And third, one must ask if he can bear it and if he is prepared to make the sacrifice. Only when those three questions have been answered can one decide which procedure to use. It is not a casual decision, by any means."

"What if it is large to begin with?" asked Vesperus. "Or small to begin with? What happens if you enlarge it a lot? Or a little? What if one *can* bear it and *is* prepared to make the sacrifice? And what if one can't? Please advise me on all these points so that I can make my choice."

"If the original size is not particularly small and only a modest increase is sought, the treatment is quite simple. You needn't even ask the client any questions. All you have to do is rub some analgesic on his member to make it insensitive and then fumigate and cleanse it with medication. With every fumigation and cleansing it must be kneaded and pulled. The fumigation is to make it firmer and the cleansing to make it stronger; the kneading is to make it thicker and the pulling to make it longer. If you do this for three days and nights, you can increase the original size by up to a third. This is a procedure that people are happy to consent to and that they need have no qualms about, so you apply it right off without asking any questions.

"If the original is small and the client wants to increase it by a large amount, the procedure involves an operation, hence the client must be asked if he can bear it and is prepared to make the sacrifice. If he is a timid soul unwilling to take the risk, you should stop right there. But if he puts lovemaking above life itself, you proceed without hesitation to a restructuring. For that you need a dog and a bitch, which you shut up in an empty room, where they will naturally start copulating. You wait until they are right in the middle of the act, then pull them apart. A dog's penis is an extremely hot organ that expands, on entering the vulva, to several times its former size; even after ejaculation it cannot be withdrawn for a long time, let alone before. You seize this moment to amputate it with a sharp knife, after which you cut open the bitch's vagina and extract the dog's penis, slice it into four strips, and then, after quickly numbing the client's penis with an analgesic to render it insensitive to pain, make four deep incisions on the sides, top, and bottom. You force one of the strips from the dog's penis, still hot, into each incision and promptly apply a miracle dressing to close the wound. In all this your one fear is that the incision be done incorrectly, for that would harm the client's penile vessels and render him impotent. But so long as the vessels are unharmed, there is no cause for concern. After a month of recuperation, the parts inside the dressing will have grown together so completely that they are no longer recognizable as human or canine. When, after a further period of recuperation, the patient engages in sex, the heat generated will be as intense as a dog's. Before the penis enters the vagina, it will look several times its original size, but once it enters, it will grow several times as big again. In effect one penis has been turned into dozens of penises. You don't think the vagina feels any pleasure, eh? You don't think the woman enjoys it?"

On hearing these words, Vesperus felt as if resurrected from the dead. Before he could so much as reply, he found himself on his knees, pleading, "If you can do this for me, you will be restoring me to life!"

The adept quickly helped Vesperus to his feet. "You need only recognize me as your teacher. Why this elaborate ceremony?"

"Your student has a highly lecherous nature and regards sex as life itself. Unfortunately I am handicapped by a natural endowment that prevents me from fulfilling my aspirations. This meeting with an immortal is the luckiest encounter ever! I wouldn't dare give you anything less than a royal obeisance before imploring you to help me." He then called to the page to bring forward the gifts, which he proffered with his own hands. "Just a few unworthy presents to mark your acceptance of me as a student. After the restructuring, I shall make every effort to reward you. I will never go back on my obligations."

"But what I told you is only the way it works in theory; there is a ninety-percent chance that it won't be possible. I'm afraid I cannot accept your magnificent gifts without further assurances."

"But it *has* to be possible!" exclaimed Vesperus. "It's my nature to disregard life itself for the sake of lovemaking. If, by the grace of Heaven, the restructuring turns out well and a puny groin is transformed into a mighty part, I shall of course be immensely grateful to you and sing your praises everywhere. But even if there's a mistake in the course of the operation and a slip of the scalpel costs me my life, that will be the fault of my destiny and I'll bear you no ill-will from the Nine Springs.[51] Please, venerable sir, there's no need to hesitate a moment longer."

"If I weren't familiar with this procedure and confident of the outcome, I wouldn't dream of gambling with a man's life! What concerns me is not the danger but the three drawbacks that result from restructuring, all of which will give you trouble. That is why I don't take this decision lightly. Let me explain those drawbacks, for only if you consent to all three of them will I accede to your request. If there is a single one you don't consent to, I shall be unable to proceed."

"What are they? Please tell me."

"The first is that you must wait a hundred and twenty days after the operation before having sex. If you have sex just once within that period, it will damage you internally and cause the human and canine parts to rupture. And not only will the implants fail to take, your own penis will fester and drop off.

---

51. The world of the dead.

That was why I raised the question of whether you could bear it. What I meant was not whether you could bear the pain but whether you could bear to abstain from sex.

"The second drawback is that only a woman in her twenties or thirties will be able to accommodate you. A girl under twenty, even if she has lost her maidenhead, will suffer terribly during her first encounter with you, unless she has already given birth. The same caveat applies with even greater force to virgins, needless to say. You will be killing every one of them that you sleep with. There will be no chance survivors. Unless you undertake not to marry a virgin and not to sleep with any young women, I shan't proceed with the operation. Otherwise, not only will *your* moral credit be damaged, I, too, as your accessory, will be guilty of a grievous sin.

"The third drawback is that, although your acquired strength will be more than ample, some of your innate supply of vital energy will inevitably escape during the operation. There will certainly not be enough left, and hence no guarantee that you will ever be able to have children. Any children you do have will tend to die young. That is what I meant when I spoke of making a sacrifice. I was not asking whether you were prepared to sacrifice your life, or even whether you were afraid of death, but whether you would sacrifice your chances of marrying a virgin and having children.

"I've observed that you are a young man of great ambition. In the first place your sexual desires are too urgent to allow you to go three months without sex. Secondly your sexual appetites are too great for you to guarantee not to sleep with a virgin at some point. And thirdly you're still very young. I daresay you don't have any sons yet, or at least not more than one or two. That is how I know that these three things will give you trouble. When you first heard of the operation, you thought only of its benefits, not of its dangers, and you got excited and wanted to start at once. Now that you know the dangers as well as the benefits, you'll not be so quick to experiment."

"None of those drawbacks troubles me in the slightest," said Vesperus. "Set your mind at rest, my good sir, and get on with the restructuring."

"How can they not trouble you?"

"I'm living in rented rooms," said Vesperus, "which is very different from living at home. If I don't have the operation, I'll still be sleeping on my own every night, so if I do have it, what will I be giving up? Your first drawback doesn't bother me and is no reason for not going ahead. As for women, it is only one's first wife who has to be a virgin; with maids and concubines it doesn't matter. Since I already have a wife, there's no need for me to worry. Moreover, virgins make the least satisfactory sexual partners. They know nothing whatever of sex or passion, and the men who sleep with them are just trying to make a name for themselves; they certainly derive no pleasure from it. For real enjoyment you need a woman in her twenties who will know something about opening, development, reversal, and closure. Because sex is really like an essay, in which each section has its mode of organization and each stage its type of parallelism. This is well beyond the capacity of a child just learning how to write.

"Thus your second drawback doesn't bother me either; in fact it suits me. It is certainly no reason for not going ahead. As for sons, other men may set great store by them, but I don't. Worthy, filial sons are far fewer than the unworthy, incorrigible kind. How many sons are there like King Wu, who excelled at continuing the family line? How many sons are there like Master Zeng, who scrupulously honored his parents' wishes? If I were lucky enough to have a good son, I'd give him a free start in life and he'd support me in my old age, but that would be merely a fair exchange—nothing out of the ordinary. If I had an unworthy, unfilial son, he'd lose the property and make me die of apoplexy, and when that happened, I'd bitterly regret having had sex once too often, emitting my sperm and blood to such a sorry end.

"That is what happens to people with sons. However, at least one or two men in every ten will have no sons at all, because that is their fate. You're surely not going to tell me it's because all their vital energy escaped during penile reconstruction? The mere fact that I have this wish is a sign that I'm not due to have any sons. I am quite prepared to have none, I definitely want to have the operation, and I assure you that I'll have no second thoughts. Obviously Heaven and Earth, as well as my ancestors, are aware that it's my fate to have no sons, so they're not trying to stop me. It's yet another sign that I'm not due to have any.

"And if I'm not fated to have sons, it doesn't make any difference whether I have the operation or not. If by some chance I should be fated to have a son, my vital energy may congeal during the operation and not escape completely, and I may still father a child who will survive to maturity. These are things that cannot be anticipated, and I won't set my heart on them, just resign myself to being childless.

"So as to your two requirements, sir, I *can* bear to wait and I *am* willing to make the sacrifice. In my eyes your drawbacks are actually advantages. There is no need for any further doubts about me. Please go ahead with the restructuring."

"Since you are so set on it," said the adept, "I shall certainly go ahead. I have no desire to create difficulties. Well, now, we shall have to set a date for surgery and decide whether it should be done at your honorable establishment or in my humble abode. It must be done in secrecy, without a soul knowing, because if someone heard about it and came along to spy on us, we would find it impossible to carry on."

"My humble quarters are very cramped," said Vesperus,

"and there are people coming by all the time. It would be embarrassing if they saw us, and we could hardly continue. It would be better to use your honorable abode."

Once the arrangements had been agreed on, the adept accepted the gifts. Then, asking Vesperus his age and date of birth, he took out an almanac and chose three or four dates, all of which were *fire* days. (The penis belongs to the fire element, because "in the time of fire, the yang is strongest.") From among the dates he chose one for the surgery that did not clash with his patient's destiny. Vesperus then took his leave and returned to his lodgings in a euphoric mood.

This incident was the root cause of all the evil he was to do during the rest of his life. Clearly it is wrong to study the bedroom art, for once learned, it tends to corrupt our thinking. If officials wish to apprehend adulterers, all they need do is lie in wait for them at the sex-aids shop. For the man has not been born who buys sex tonics and studies the bedroom art for the sole purpose of pleasing his wife.

CRITIQUE

If anyone else were writing this book, he would certainly have told us how, after the Knave dashed his hopes, Vesperus realized that his penis was inadequate and sought desperately for someone to rectify it. After the rectification, this writer would have enjoyed telling how Vesperus lusted after women, in order to excite his readers and silence any criticism that his narrative had too many branches and too little trunk. Such a writer would never have been willing to insert the passage in which Vesperus stops looking at women, the passage in which a young libertine is suddenly transformed into a puritan. Only our author, with the eye of a dispassionate observer, would devote his attention to such an episode, looking back and lingering over it, reluctant simply to tell it and be done with it. No doubt there is a profound meaning here. The author is not merely concocting an interesting turn of events to liven up his narrative, he is providing adulterers with a way to turn back. Had Vesperus really changed his ways, he would not be about to lose his reputation or moral credit, nor would his wife and concubine be about to pay for his sins of the flesh. It is clear that even the worst sinner becomes a good man once he wishes to repent his sins, but that he must not have a further change of heart after repenting.

Readers should pay particular attention to this kind of passage, chewing the olive inside the date until they can taste its flavor. The author's profundity is apparent well before the end of his book.

CHAPTER *E*IGHT

After Vesperus cultivates himself for three months, a
friend eyes him anew;
When he flaunts his looks just once, a beauty loses her
heart.

Lyric:

Song Yu's brilliance, Pan An's beauty,
The grace of the willow tree,
Youth like the flowery season's start,
A temper mild, a patient heart—
With these five things a seducer you can be.

Two other things there are, both hard to counterfeit:
Be born with a lover's grace
And by love's lucky star be blessed.
With these seven things, if you start your quest,
Expense of spirit is all you'll have to face.
(To the tune "Butterflies Adoring the Flowers")

Taking leave of the adept, Vesperus returned to his lodgings, where he lay in bed contemplating the sexual adventures he would enjoy after reconstruction. He felt the excitement building up in him.

I've been living the single life for ages, he reflected, and my heart is choked with long-repressed desire. I'll never be able to bear the period of enforced impotence after tomorrow's operation. Before I go under the knife, I ought to take this chance to find a woman and have a bout or two with her. It would act like a dose of rhubarb and purge all the emotional congestion from my system.

Preoccupied by these concerns, Vesperus had trouble sleeping. He was about to get up and go in search of a prostitute when it occurred to him that by this hour prostitutes would be busy with their clients and reluctant to open their doors to him. For a while he endured the frustration, then realized, I have emergency relief right here at hand! Why not get it out and put it to use? I've been ignoring the unbolted south gate while trying the blocked-off north road.[52] He then called one of his pages into bed, to serve as a woman and allow him to work off his desire.

He possessed two pages, one named Satchel, the other Sheath. Because Satchel, who was only fifteen, could read a little, Vesperus had entrusted his books to the boy's care as if he were a satchel, hence the name. To Sheath, who was a few years older, Vesperus had entrusted his antique sword, an heirloom, as if he were a sheath, hence *his* name. Both boys were attractive; indeed, apart from their big feet, they were on a par with the most beautiful women. But Sheath was somewhat artless and lacking in coquetry, and although Vesperus had frequently dallied with him, he had never been completely

---

52. The words for *south* and *male* are both pronounced *nan*.

satisfied. Satchel, on the other hand, although younger, was extremely artful and an expert sexual partner. While joining Vesperus in his pleasures, he was able, like a woman, both to raise his buttocks to meet Vesperus's thrusts and also to utter cries of passion. Vesperus favored him, and so on this occasion it was Satchel, not Sheath, whom he called into bed to help him vent his now violent desires.

Satchel waited until he had finished, then asked in a coquettish tone, "Master, you've been so preoccupied with women that you've completely neglected the two of us. Why this sudden interest in reopening the old accounts?"

"This is not sex we're having tonight," said Vesperus. "This is a farewell."

"A farewell? Surely you couldn't bear to part with us?"

"Who said anything about selling you? Perhaps the word *farewell* needs some clarification: I'm not the one saying farewell, it's my penis that's saying farewell to your buttocks."

"But why?"

"Well, as you know, I'm due to have my penis restructured in a day or two. After the operation it will be dozens of times bigger than it is now. Even a woman whose vagina is a little on the tight side will no longer be able to receive me. So after tonight you and I won't be able to have sex again. If that's not a farewell, I don't know what is!"

"Perhaps yours *is* rather small, but why would you want to restructure it?"

Vesperus explained that women differed from boys in preferring the large to the small.

"So after surgery you intend to seduce girls? You'll have no use for us?"

"That's right."

"When you go off on your seductions, you'll need to have an escort. Take me along, and if there are any girls left over whom you don't have time for, give one to me so that I can see what sex with a woman is like. That way I'll not have wasted my time in the service of a great lover."

"That's easily arranged. A well-fed general doesn't starve his troops, you know. While their mistresses are sleeping with me, you shall have any maid you want. And not just one, but dozens, hundreds . . ."

Satchel was so delighted that he climbed on top of Vesperus and doused the flesh-colored candle.

Vesperus slept the rest of that night. The next morning he assembled the things he would need. He bought an extremely plump, sturdy dog; he found a bitch to match with it; and he kept them in separate quarters in his lodgings until the next day, when he told Satchel to fetch the dogs and accompany him. Sheath was to prepare the wine and bring it along later.

Since he dealt in such secret techniques, the adept had found himself a large, very private place surrounded by open land where there were no casual visitors. Once the gate was shut, it offered the ideal setting for the operation. To prepare for the surgery, he applied analgesic to Vesperus's penis. At the first application of the ointment, Vesperus felt as if his organ had been plunged into cold water and then as if he had no organ at all, for he felt no sensation when it was pinched and scratched. Some of his tension left him at that point, as it dawned on him that he would feel no pain during surgery.

Before long the wine arrived, and Vesperus and the adept drank as they waited for the dog and bitch to couple.

These two hot-blooded creatures were apparently under the impression that their new master wanted to do them a special favor and had purposely brought them to some out-of-the-way place where they could couple freely, without interruption from other males dashing up to pick fights or other females acting jealous. And so, not daring to betray their master's generosity, they spliced themselves together as soon as they were in each other's company. Little did they realize, however, that theirs was an impecunious master who meant to appropriate their very endowment.

The dogs had been brought to the operating room with ropes around their necks, and the ropes had not been removed. Now that the dogs were enthusiastically coupling, all that Satchel and Sheath had to do was give a strong tug on the ropes for them to be pulled half apart like a severed lotus root with its fibers still entwined. The male could not bear to be parted and began to bark furiously, while his hind legs tried to grip the female's vulva and prevent it from slipping away. To his surprise, he could not hold on, and both vulva and penis were removed together. The female could not bear the thought of separation any more than the male, and she barked furiously, too, her hind legs holding his penis to prevent it from slipping out. To her surprise, the penis could not be held either, but was removed along with her vulva.

After cutting out the dog's penis, the adept quickly made the incisions in Vesperus's penis and, having sliced the dog's into strips, packed one strip, still hot, into each incision. He then applied a miracle drug and bandaged it up. Once the operation was over, he and Vesperus resumed their drinking.

Vesperus asked the adept if he might stay the night. The two men shared the same bed, and in the course of the night the adept passed along much tactical information. Next day Vesperus returned home to begin his convalescence.

During the next three months, thanks to his self-control, he never once looked at a woman or entertained a lascivious thought. He neither peeked at his restructured penis nor felt it with his hand, but acted as if it was still the same. Only when the critical period was over did he take off the bandages, clean it out, and examine it closely, at which point he let out a whoop of laughter. "It's simply *magnificent*! It really *is* different! With an amazing thing like this, I'll be able to run *wild*!"

After another day or two, just as he was thinking of going

to look for the Knave and urging him to make good on his promise, the latter happened to come by.

"Worthy brother," said the Knave, "you haven't been out in ages, just stayed quietly at home. You must have made a lot of progress in your examination studies."

"None at all, although I have made a little progress in my study of bedroom techniques."

The Knave smiled. "If you're not born with the right capacity, the progress will always be limited, I'm afraid. I would urge you not to spend your time on that subject."

"Just what are you suggesting, brother? When you meet a gentleman again after three days, you should look at him with a fresh eye, you know. An even fresher eye in my case, for you've not seen me in three months! Do I still have to put up with your insults, even if I've made some progress?"

"If you've made any progress, it will be merely cosmetic and won't affect the real issue. You're like a man in combat training; if he has an exceptional physique and strength, he'll naturally be in great demand. But if he's less than three feet tall and can't lift ten pounds, even if he practices constantly and masters all eighteen techniques, he'll have to confine his fighting to the puppet theatre. He can hardly take part in real combat!"

"Brother, you're going farther and farther astray! Have you never seen a boy three feet tall develop into a husky man? Have you never heard that before an army races with the speed of a hare, it's as demure as a maiden?[53] Only dead men's penises can shrink but not grow. What living man's thing never grows, but stays predictably the same?"

"I simply don't believe it. The pecker on a twelve- or

---

53. The image comes originally from the famous military treatise *Sun Zi*.

thirteen-year-old boy who has never produced a drop may grow by the day, but in the case of a man in his twenties, if his penis is going to develop at all, it will do so very little, by millimeters rather than centimeters."

"If it were just a matter of centimeters, you wouldn't notice the difference. It would only be noteworthy if it grew several times bigger."

"Impossible! We may have get-rich-quick millionaires, but there are no get-big-quick penises! Anyway take it out and let me see it."

"The last time I did that I had to put up with a stream of ridicule from you. That same day I made a solemn vow never to show my penis to anyone ever again. Then I stuck the vow on my wall. I'm not going to make a spectacle of myself a second time."

"Stop making fun of me, brother, and hurry up and show me. I hope it *has* grown a bit. If so, I shall offer it my humblest apologies."

"A verbal apology won't suffice. Only if you find it a real opportunity for action, to try it out and give it encouragement, will you be showing a desire to foster talent."

"You're right. If it really has developed, I'll foster it with that affair we spoke of."

"Very well, then, I suppose I shall have to make a spectacle of myself all over again."

It was the beginning of winter, and Vesperus was wearing a padded jacket and lined trousers. Thinking his clothes would be too bulky to allow a close inspection, he tied his sash around his waist, tucked up his shirt, and let down his trousers. Then he presented his penis with both hands, like the Persian offering up his jewel.

"Well, has it made any progress? Take a look."

The Knave, who was standing some way off, thought he must have obtained a donkey's member from somewhere and attached it to his waist. Not until he came close and scrutinized it did he realize that it was the genuine article. He gaped in astonishment.

"What method did you use to turn that puny object into something so impressive?"

"I don't know exactly, but after you provoked it, it suddenly pulled itself together in an effort to do me credit. There was no holding it back."

"Don't you try to fool me! I can see the surgical scars, as well as four strips of a different color. Come on now, tell me the truth, what ingenious technique is behind all this?"

Vesperus could hold out no longer against his friend's questions. He proceeded to relate how he had met the adept and undergone transplant surgery with the aid of a dog's penis.

"The lengths you go to for the sake of sex! You'll obviously succeed, because you'll let nothing stand in your way. I can see I have no choice but to help you out in this affair. Luckily I still have a few pieces of gold on me. Let's go over to her place now and see if there's any opening."

Overjoyed, Vesperus hastily changed his clothes, put on a new cap, and went out with the Knave. When they came near her shop, the Knave asked him to wait while he went ahead and spied out the land.

Before long he was back, a broad grin on his face. "Congratulations! You're in luck! Provided you have the right destiny, you can pull it off tonight."

"But we've never even met," said Vesperus. "How can you be so sure about tonight?"

"I've just heard from the neighbors that her husband is off on a buying trip and won't be back for over ten days. You'll burst in with me and start making advances to her. If she shows any liking for you, I'll find a way to get you in there tonight. You'll be able to count on ten days of pleasure with her."

"I shall owe everything to you."

When they reached the shop, the woman was sitting inside, spinning silk. The Knave pushed the bamboo curtain aside and he and Vesperus burst in.

"Is Master Quan at home?"

"No, he's away buying silk," she replied.

"I was thinking of buying a few pounds. Since he isn't here, what shall I do?"

"You could always go somewhere else for it."

Vesperus intervened. "We could get it anywhere, of course, but we've been customers of yours for a long time and would prefer not to patronize someone else. Moreover, other people's silk may not be of the highest quality. We feel more confident buying from you."

"If you're customers of ours, how is it I don't know you?"

"Where's your memory, ma'am?" put in the Knave. "I was in here last summer buying silk. Your husband was away then, too, and you served me yourself. You got a roll down from on top and sold it to me. Surely you haven't forgotten?"

"No, I do remember that."

"Since you remember," said Vesperus, "you must know we haven't come here to haggle. If you have some silk, bring it out and sell it to us. Why drive business away to your competitors?"

"I do have a few pounds," she said, "but I don't know if they'll meet your requirements."

"How could *your* silk not meet our requirements? It is more likely *too* good. I'm afraid a poor student like me may not be able to afford it."

"You're too kind. Well, won't you take a seat while I get it out?"

The Knave made Vesperus take the upper seat, which was closer, so that he could flirt with her more easily.

The woman brought out a roll of silk and handed it to Vesperus. As she did so, she remained impassive and did not look closely at him.

Before he even took the silk, Vesperus said, "This is too yellow. I'm afraid it won't do." Then, after taking it and inspecting it, he said to the Knave, "That's funny! In madam's hands it looked a yellowy brown, but in mine it's white again. How do you account for that?" He pretended to ponder the answer, then went on: "I know! Madam's hands are too white, and so they make the silk look yellow by comparison. My hands are dark, and so they make it look white."

When she heard this remark, her eyes fastened on Vesperus's hands and examined them. "Your honorable hands can hardly be called dark," she said at last. Despite this, she retained her serious expression, with no trace of a smile.

"His hands may not be dark as compared with mine," said the Knave, "but compared with madam's they're certainly not white."

"If you think the silk is white, why don't you buy it?" she asked.

"But it's white only in comparison with my unworthy hands," said Vesperus. "Obviously it's not really white. Only silk the color of madam's honorable hands will do. Please bring some out and show it to us."

"Where in the world are you going to find silk as white as that?" asked the Knave. "If we could only get some the color of your complexion, it would be all right."

At this remark the woman's eyes fastened on Vesperus's face and examined it. This time her face lit up with pleasure. "I'm afraid there's no silk in the world as white as that," she said with a smile.

Gentle reader, why do you suppose she smiled now but not before? Why do you think she looked closely at him now but not before? The truth is she was nearsighted and could see nobody more than a few feet away. When Vesperus entered the shop, she thought he was just another customer. Then, when she heard him describe himself as a poor student, she realized he was a licentiate, but still thought him ordinary and did not scrutinize him. Because she had to strain her eyes in order to see people, she never looked closely at a man on meeting him.

In general, among nearsighted women the pretty ones outnumber the ugly and the intelligent the stupid. But there is one thing to remember about them all: Their desire for sex is fully equal to that of those men with lustful eyes. Both types throw themselves wholeheartedly into sex without any respite. There is an old saying that goes:

A nearsighted wife
Won't be idle in bed.

Suppose an oversexed woman were able to see people at a distance. If she saw a handsome man, her desires might well be aroused and her lifelong chastity lost. That is why the Creator, in endowing her with human form, had the brilliant idea of giving her these eyes, to prevent her from seeing anyone—not even a Pan An or a Song Yu—except her husband, thus avoiding a great deal of retribution. Historically the vast majority of nearsighted women have preserved their chastity while only a small minority have gone astray.

Because her eyes kept her out of trouble, she'd never have known if a man was standing before her all day making eyes at her. He might just as well have been wrapped in a blanket of fog. But now that she had seen Vesperus's hands and face, she was dazzled, captivated.

She turned to him. "Well, sir, do you really want to buy some? If you do, I have a roll of excellent quality that I'll be glad to bring out and show you."

"That's what we came for," said Vesperus. "Of course we want to buy some. Please show me what you've got."

She went into the shop and returned with a roll of silk, at the same time telling her maid, a scabby-headed young girl, to serve tea to the Knave and Vesperus.

Vesperus did not finish his tea, but left half a cup in tribute to his hostess, a gesture that she acknowledged with a smile before handing him the silk. As he received it, he took the chance to squeeze her hand, and she, although affecting not to notice, responded by scratching his hand with a fingernail.

"This *is* an excellent roll," said the Knave. "Let's take it and be on our way."

He gave the purse to Vesperus, who weighed out the amount she asked for and handed it over.

"Please note that it's in full ingots," he said.

"If it's in full ingots," she replied, "I'm afraid it may look good on the outside but be worthless inside."

"If you're worried about it, ma'am, why not keep both the silk and the silver here and this evening I'll come back and break open one of the ingots and try it out for you? I'm not exaggerating when I say that our silver is as good as we are, the same on the inside as on the outside."

"That won't be necessary," she said. "If it's all right, we can do business again. Otherwise you'll be a one-time customer."

Picking up the silk, the Knave urged Vesperus out of the shop. As he left, Vesperus cast several lingering glances behind. Although she couldn't see, she understood and narrowed her eyes to two slits in an expression that was neither happy nor sad.

Back at his lodgings, Vesperus conferred with the Knave. "I feel I have an excellent chance there. But what means of entry shall we use? We can't afford to take any risks."

"I've made careful inquiries," said the Knave, "and there's

no one else in the house except that maid we saw just now. She's only ten or eleven. She'll be asleep as soon as she falls into bed and won't hear a sound the rest of the night. The house is obvious enough—no upstairs, no cellar. It won't hold me up in the least. If we go through the wall, someone will spot us and you won't be able to pay her a second visit. I'll just have to carry you up to the roof on my back, remove a few tiles, pull out a rafter, and let you descend from on high."

"What if the neighbors hear and cry thief?"

"With me beside you, that's not likely to happen, so don't worry. The one thing that concerns me is her remark—did you hear?—that she was afraid you might look good on the outside but be worthless inside, and that if you didn't please her you'd be a one-time customer. Doesn't it bear out what I told you? You'll have to do your damnedest not to let her flunk you. Otherwise you'll be admitted to a first examination but not to a second or a third."

"It will never come to that," said Vesperus. "If you doubt me, why not keep watch from some vantage point?"

They joked together while waiting impatiently for "the golden crow to descend in the west and the jade hare to rise in the east," when the time would come for Vesperus's examination. But we do not yet know what method the examiner will adopt and will have to wait until the questions are handed out.

CRITIQUE

Fiction is parable and, as such, its content is obviously not factual. I hope that readers will not distort the author's intention by focusing on his literal meaning. The surgical implant of a dog's member into a human being, as related in this chapter, is a palpable absurdity, which implies that Vesperus's actions are going to be bestial in nature. Similarly, in Chapter

Three, when he swore friendship with the Knave and even acknowledged him as an elder brother, the implication was that his character and aspirations were lower than those of a burglar. Both incidents are scathing expressions of deep loathing, tantamount to reviling him as a cur or a crook. People must not mistake condemnation for praise and fantasy for reality and think it right to mutilate dogs and fraternize with burglars. But if the bearer of the warning is slandered as the promoter of the very vice he is warning against, he will merely be sharing the same fate that writers have always suffered.

In Chapter Six, the Knave described this woman as prudish, as unversed in passion, whereas in the silk-shop incident in this chapter she matches Vesperus blow for blow in repartee. Not only is she not prudish, she is extremely seductive, a fact that flatly contradicts what the Knave has said. No doubt ignorant readers had concluded that the novel's stitching was not fine enough and had criticized the author for it, never dreaming that he would have nearsightedness in mind as a pivot, and that *that* was the reason for the apparent inconsistency. The author deliberately set an ingenious ambush so as to lure people into attacking him—a clear case of literary deception. The reason the woman was described as prudish is that she was nearsighted; she didn't see the handsome young man in front of her and had no occasion to behave seductively. Similarly the reason she is now shown as seductive is also that she is nearsighted; suddenly she sees a handsome young man in front of her and cannot maintain her prudishness any longer. Obviously nearsighted women should never be allowed to set eyes on handsome young men. Readers should understand that the author is using her as an example in his moral instruction of women, not just as a means of livening up his plot.

CHAPTER *N*INE

One woman, although adept at the rarest sensuality,
  upholds basic principle,
While another, although ready for leftover pleasures,
  takes first prize.

Poem:

> Wanton bawds talk much of chastity
> And gain thereby a false celebrity.
> Others there are, of snow-white purity,
> Who're only roused by rare depravity.

Let us tell now of Honest Quan's wife, whose childhood name
was Fragrance. Her father was a village schoolmaster who gave
her lessons in reading and writing from early childhood. She
proved an extremely apt pupil, and because she was also very
pretty, her parents were unwilling to rush her into an early
marriage. When she was fifteen, a young student who had
topped the list in the Boys' Examination sent a go-between

along with a proposal, and Fragrance's father, who felt the youth showed some promise, betrothed her to him. Unfortunately after just one year of marriage he died of general debility.

Fragrance remained in mourning for a full year before marrying Honest Quan. Although hers was a highly sensual nature, she had a good grasp of basic principle, and whenever she heard talk of some woman's going astray, she would laugh at her behind her back, on one occasion declaring to her companions, "Because we failed to cultivate our virtue in our last existence, we've been born female in this one and are forced to spend our lives in the women's quarters. There's no sightseeing or visiting for us, as there is for men. Sex is the one diversion we have in our lives, and surely no one can tell us not to enjoy that! But we were created man and wife by Heaven and Earth and matched in marriage by our parents, and so naturally it is right and proper to enjoy ourselves with our husbands, while sex with any other man is a moral transgression. If our husbands hear of it, it will bring us curses and a beating, and if the news becomes public, it will create a scandal. Beatings and scandal aside, if a woman does not have sex, well and good. But if she *is* going to have it, she should at least see that she enjoys it. After all, when you're with your husband after the day's work is done, you undress, get into bed together, and take things from the beginning in an ordered, leisurely way until eventually you reach a degree of ecstasy. What enjoyment is there in some furtive, fumbling encounter in which your only concern in the midst of your panic is to finish up as hastily as possible, whether you've hit the mark or not? What's more, there's nothing to eat when you're famished and more than enough when you're well fed and, just as with food and drink, you get sick from the continual feast and famine. How ridiculous those women are who go astray! Why didn't they use those same eyes to pick out a good husband in the first place as they used for picking out a lover later on? If they're impressed by a mere name, let them choose someone cultivated. If it's appearance they want, let them choose someone good-looking. And if it's neither a name nor good looks that attracts them, but the reality of sexual performance, they ought to find someone robust and vigorous. That way they'll not go wrong and they'll be able to enjoy the real thing. There's simply no need to abandon your husband and take a lover!"

Her companions listened and said, "She speaks from experience, so naturally her advice is somewhat different. It comes from the heart, but it's also rather entertaining."

In what sense was she a woman of experience? As a girl she had valued three things in a man—a name, good looks, and sexual ability—and in her heart she wanted a husband who possessed all three. When she married the student, she knew he had talent and was quite handsome, and she assumed he had the third quality as well. But to her great disappointment, his endowment was impossibly small and he had no stamina whatsoever. When he mounted her, she had scarcely begun to warm up before he had to dismount. But she was a hard-driving woman who refused to let him shirk his duties, and once her passions were aroused, she would urge him on again. No man with a weak constitution could survive such grueling demands, and in less than a year he was dead of general debility.

After this ordeal she realized that talent and looks, however attractive, serve no practical end. If all three qualities cannot be found together in a man, one should discard the illusory ones in favor of the real, which was why, when she came to choose another husband, she did not insist on an educated man, or even on a handsome one, but chose a robust and vigorous man for strictly practical ends.

Observing that Honest Quan, although coarse-grained and

dull-witted, had the strength of a tiger, she knew he would also have the necessary practical qualifications, so she married him without even asking about the state of his finances. She had chosen him for his strength and had no idea of the size of his weapon. She merely assumed that a man of great physical strength would not need the longest spear or the biggest battle-axe to gain the victory, that even with a short sword or a thin blade he would still be able to defeat the foe. She never dreamed that his weapon would prove to be an eighteen-foot lance that a weak person could scarcely lift or someone with small hands even grasp. She was delighted and clung to him with utter devotion from the day of her marriage, not once entertaining a wayward thought.

His was a small business that brought in only a meager income, so she rose early to spin silk for him, contributing some cash each day. Far from her living off his earnings, he had to live off hers.

That day, as fate would have it, she had opened the curtain and was chatting with the woman across the lane when Vesperus passed by and got two close-up views of her. But because of her own nearsightedness, all she saw was the vague outline of a man dawdling in front of her shop; she had no idea what he looked like. Not so the woman across the lane, however, who enjoyed an excellent view.

This woman was in her thirties, and her husband, like Fragrance's, was a silk merchant. He and Honest Quan would go off on business trips together, and although they did not pool their resources, they were partners in every other respect. The wife was exceedingly ugly and also oversexed, but partly because her signboard was not attractive enough and partly because her husband was a violent man who beat and abused her for the slightest misdemeanor, she was afraid to do anything rash.

That day she got a good view of Vesperus from head to toe and, as soon as he had left, she crossed the lane to her neighbor's.

"That was a terribly handsome man walking up and down just now, looking at you. Did you notice?"

"You know how well *I* see, with my eyes! I sit here, and not a day goes by that a few men don't look at me through the screen. Well, let them look. What's the good of noticing anyway?"

"With the ordinary run of men, someone like you wouldn't find it worthwhile to let them look; but with a man like this, you'd let him stand in front of your door and look at you for days on end."

"You mean he's better than perfect?"

"Not just better—ten times better, in my opinion. I stand in my doorway all the time and on any given day I see hundreds and thousands of men, but I've never seen one as handsome as this fellow. There's nothing to compare with the pure whiteness of his complexion. His eyes and eyebrows, nose, ears—everything about him is simply *adorable*! He's as gorgeous as a figure on a silk fan. Even if an artist were to paint a portrait as handsome as he is, it could never capture that romantic look. He makes you just *die* of longing!"

"You describe him so vividly, it's comical. Frankly I don't believe such a paragon exists. And if he did exist, he would stick to his business and I to mine, and I'd never even learn his name. So what's the point of longing for him?"

"You may not long for him, but I saw how he longs for you. Half out of his mind, he was. He was going to leave, but couldn't bear to. Then he was going to stay, but he was afraid of what people might think, so he had to leave. But after a while, there he was back again. Even when he left, he couldn't bear to part from you. Isn't that pathetic? You didn't see him, so naturally you're not in love with him. But I saw him and I'm lovesick on your account. How's that for a strange thing?"

"I imagine he was reacting to seeing you, not me. You're too embarrassed to admit he's in love with you, so you put it all on me."

"He fall for me—with *my* looks! It *was* you, I assure you. If you don't believe me, he's bound to come by again, and when I see him in the distance, I'll let you know. Then you can come out and see him and also give him a chance to see you."

"Let's wait until he comes back and then decide."

After many other intriguing remarks, the neighbor retreated to her house. For the next few days Fragrance was on the lookout, but a great deal of time elapsed without her seeing him again, and by the time he came in to buy silk, she had dismissed him from her mind. Then, on seeing how handsome he was, she naturally recalled the earlier conversation.

He must be the one we spoke of, she thought, after he had left. In appearance he is in a class of his own, but I know nothing yet about his inner talents. If I'm going to lose my good name, I ought at least to get some real enjoyment in exchange. If appearance is all I want, I can get him to come back for silk every day and gaze at him to my heart's content; there's no need to do anything more. Just now he joked about breaking it open and trying it out. He was talking about the silver, of course, but he meant it as a double entendre. If he does come tonight, ought I to reject him or let him stay? Is my reputation going to be decided, once and for all, for better or for worse, in this one moment? I must give this some serious thought.

While she was in the midst of her dilemma, her neighbor came over.

"Mrs. Quan, did you recognize that man buying silk from you?"

"No."

"But he's the one I told you about! Didn't you realize? Is there another man in the world as handsome as he is?"

"Handsome, yes, I grant you that, but altogether too light and frivolous, not at all like a proper gentleman."

"Now you're getting all moralistic again! When would a proper gentleman ever come around looking at women? Let's just admire his looks and not put him on the scales. Who cares if he's light or not?"

"That's all very well, but in front of other people he ought to be a bit more serious. He made all kinds of advances just now. It's fortunate my husband wasn't at home. He would never have let him get away with it!"

"What advances? Do tell."

"It was all so juvenile, there's no point in describing it."

The neighbor had an extremely prurient mind and, on hearing talk of advances, she imagined that Vesperus must somehow have dragged Fragrance off to bed. Fairly trembling with excitement, she pinched and patted her to make her tell, and Fragrance finally gave in. "He wasn't alone. He had a companion with him. His flirting was just a matter of making eyes at me, very suggestively, while he was talking. What else did you imagine?"

"And did you give him any encouragement in return?"

"He was lucky I didn't tell him off. What encouragement would I give him?"

"That shows a real lack of feeling on your part. Now don't take me wrong, but there's not another woman in the world as beautiful as you are, and not another man as handsome as he is, either. You two were meant for each other. It's a match made in Heaven. You ought to have been husband and wife, but since that cannot be, you should at least fulfill your deepest desires by becoming lovers. Don't take me wrong if I say that Master Quan is not a proper match for you. A fresh flower stuck in a dungheap, that's what you are, and a crying shame it is. If this man doesn't come back, never mind; but if he does, and you have no one else to take the part, I'll gladly come over and play the matchmaker for you. Why, if you made love with him a couple of times, it would justify your whole existence. Now don't get all moralistic. It's only widows who don't remarry that get the memorial arches built in their honor, you know. Whoever heard of a married woman getting a commendation from the government for not taking a lover? Am I right?"

The whole time the neighbor held forth, Fragrance was busy calculating to herself: It looks as if she's madly in love with him. If I go in for this affair, since she lives just over the way, I'll have to give her a piece of the action or she'll wreck everything. But I still don't know about that fellow's capacity. Why not let her have first turn, as if she were sitting an exam in my place? Then, if he proves to have the capacity, I'll sit the next one myself. I need hardly fear that an ugly woman like that will steal his affections. If he's not up to it, all I have to do is make a scene and drive him out, and my good name will be as good as ever. Brilliant!

Her mind was made up.

"That sort of thing is not really my line," she said. "If he comes back again, rather than your being my matchmaker, why not let me be yours, so that the two of you can enjoy yourselves a few times?"

"Don't be ridiculous! You don't mean what you're saying, but even if you did, he'd never want an ugly woman like me. If you wish to do me a favor, let me burst in on you after you've been to bed with him a couple of times. You can pretend to be embarrassed and insist that I join in, as if we were taking turns at being the banker in a gaming house. That just might work."

"I *did* mean what I said, and I know how it can be done,

too. I noticed how awfully persistent the man can be. I tried
to snub him, but I can't have been stern enough, because just
before leaving he joked about trying to sneak in here tonight. Our husbands are away, and there's hardly anyone at
home. Lock your place up tonight and come over here to
sleep. We'll blow out the lamp, and I'll hide. Then, if he
does come, you pretend to be me and sleep with him. Afterward he'll have to sneak away in the dark and will never
suspect it was you in my place. Consider you're doing me a
favor, as well as preserving my good name. Now isn't that a
wonderful idea?"

"From what you say, I gather you've already told him he
can come. I'm tickled to death at the idea, of course, and I
couldn't turn it down even if I wanted to. But there's one
thing I don't understand. Why would you let him come here
and not go to bed with him yourself? No virtuous woman has
ever behaved like that."

"I'm not acting hypocritical or covering my ears as I steal
the bell. The fact is, I've already savored every bedroom
pleasure there is. No one is a match for my husband where
virility's concerned, and someone who has enjoyed a banquet
will turn up her nose at a scratch meal. If the food's mediocre,
better not try it. That's why I won't compromise."

"I know what you have in mind. Master Quan's endowment is well known around here. You've been shaped on a big
last and you're afraid that a child's one won't do. So you want
me to spy out the land for you. Well, I'm more than prepared
to sacrifice myself, because it's no great hardship to play the
spy in this case. There's just one thing, though: you must wait
until I've thoroughly enjoyed myself, not come charging on
to the battlefield at the critical moment, leaving me in a bind
as to whether to advance or retreat. There's an old saying you
ought to keep in mind: 'When feeding a priest, you might just
as well bury him alive as not let him eat his fill.' "

"I'm not expecting any such luck. You can set your mind at rest."

Having agreed on their plans, the two women waited until it was time to put them into effect.

This was a momentary stroke of luck for the ugly neighbor. She has received this splendid assignment, and it is her shoe that the brand-new, freshly restructured last will be the first to shape. If you wish to learn the last's proportions, you must wait a little while until the event takes place.

CRITIQUE

Fragrance's plan for taking a lover is absolutely masterly, a variation on the principle that it's a wise subject who knows how to choose the right lord and master. How different she is from some passive observer with no purpose in mind! What a pity she met the adulterer at this stage, for the meeting will lead her to a career of good works! If Vesperus had acted three months earlier than he did, the neighbor's loss of her chastity would have coincided with Fragrance's preservation of hers. If there are any enlightened officials about who are interested in erecting a commemorative arch or shrine, I have an honorand to propose whose name is as fragrant and glorious as that of the chaste maid of "I Want to Get Married."[54] She opened up a convenient new route within Confucian morality, and for a thousand years to come all those women who, despite their disloyal thoughts, manage to avoid taking another husband will be able to look up to her as a pioneer.

---

54. A story that is told in Chapter Seventeen.

CHAPTER *TEN*

By listening to her precursor, she finds a strong
opponent;
By allowing a little grace, she fosters a true talent.

Poem:
   Beauty, while enjoying herself,
   Should allow her lover some rest.
   To spare a thought for the morrow's sport—
   Mightn't that be lust at its best?

Let us tell how the neighbor went home rejoicing in her
enviable assignment. She got some cloths ready for wiping up
her secretions, lest they soak her friend's bedding, then waited
impatiently until evening, when she locked her door and
crossed the lane.

Fragrance decided to play a trick on her. "I'm afraid I've
brought you here on false pretenses," she said. "I've just re-

ceived a note: someone has taken him drinking and he can't get away, but he would like to set another date. You might as well go home again."

The neighbor was so upset her nostrils flared and her eyes flashed. She blamed Fragrance for not sending a message right back insisting that he come, but at the same time she strongly suspected that Fragrance now regretted the whole arrangement and wanted to get rid of her and have him all to herself. Fragrance let the protests continue for some time before explaining, with a laugh, "I was only having you on. He should be here any moment now. You'd better get ready to go to bed with him."

She heated a bowl of water so that she and the neighbor could wash their private parts, then placed an easy chair across from the bed, her intention being to lie back and listen while the other two had sex. She told the neighbor to bolt the door and stand quietly behind it, for when her visitor came, he would knock very lightly. She was to let him in at the first knock, not force him to knock again and again, which might alert the people next door. After letting him in, she was to replace the bolt before taking him to bed, where she should keep her voice down, lest he recognize her.

The woman nodded and sent Fragrance off to lie down, while she stood guard by the door. She had waited a solid two hours without anyone coming, and was just going in to ask Fragrance's advice, when in the darkness someone suddenly clasped her in his arms and kissed her. She leaped to the conclusion that it was Fragrance playing another of her tricks, this time by pretending to be a man, so she felt for the person's crotch. On reaching downward, however, she found a very large object butting at her hand and realized this was the visitor they were expecting.

Affecting a sweet, girlish voice, she asked, "How ever did you get in, dear heart?"

"Through the roof," said Vesperus.

"What a clever sweetheart! Well, now you're here, let's go to bed."

They unclasped—and undressed. Well before Vesperus, the woman had undressed completely and was lying on her back. When Vesperus mounted her and felt for her feet to put them over his shoulders, he couldn't find them; from the moment she had gotten into bed, her feet had been up and her vagina open, waiting for his penis.

I never suspected she was such a wanton, thought Vesperus. But since she is, I won't need my gentler techniques. I shall have to start off with a show of strength.

Raising himself a foot or more above her vagina, he thrust out his penis and attacked.

She began squealing like a slaughtered pig. "Oh, no! Be gentle, please!"

Vesperus parted the labia with his hands and began to work his way slowly inside. But time went by and no more than an inch of the glans had penetrated.

"The gentler I am," he said, "the harder it is to enter. I'll need to be a bit more vigorous, I'm afraid. You'll just have to put up with a little pain before you start enjoying yourself."

He attacked once more, which only set her squealing again. "Don't! Don't! Use some spit at least!"

"Spit is for virgins only; that's an inviolable rule. We'll just have to do it dry." He attacked again.

"Don't! This isn't working! If you won't break your rule, please withdraw and let *me* put some on."

"That would be better."

After he withdrew, she spat copiously into her palm. She then opened her labia and put half the spittle inside. The rest she rubbed on his penis.

"Now there shouldn't be any problem, but take it easy as you enter."

Vesperus, however, was eager to display his prowess and refused to take things easy. He raised her legs and, with a sudden swish, that long, thick object of his buried itself to the hilt inside her.

She began squealing again. "How is it you intellectuals are so *rough*? Don't you care whether we live or die? All the way in the first time! I don't have room! Take it out a little."

"You don't have room? You don't think it's still outside surely? I'll have to move it a bit. Don't be left out in the cold!"

Laughing, he began to move again. She could not bear the first few thrusts and let out an *aiya*! with each one. But then, after fifty or more thrusts, nothing more was heard from her—until, after a hundred, she began crying *aiya*! once more, but in delight now, rather than pain. (*Aiya* has a range of meanings.)

After several hundred strokes she began making numerous wanton moves and uttering countless cries of passion, enough to make it impossible for a man to restrain himself. Vesperus had to speed up his onslaught and force her to spend so that he could spend along with her. But she was not without guile, for although she had spent several times already, she replied, "No, not yet," when he asked her.

Why didn't she tell the truth? Because, as a stand-in, she feared she would lose her place the moment Fragrance heard her say she was satisfied. As the saying goes, "If you're going to be robbed by a powerful official, the longer you can put it off the better."

Vesperus took her at her word and did not dare spend. But as he thrust away, he gradually lost control of himself and had to do so, contriving only to hide the fact from his partner. After that he did not dare stop, but kept going like a drunken man on a donkey, nodding his head every step of the way, with none of his former élan.

Noticing that his penis hung back from the fray, she asked,

"Sweetheart, have you spent?" Vesperus was afraid she would laugh at him for his lack of stamina and felt compelled to say no. Before her question he had been getting weaker with every thrust, but now he was like a dozing schoolboy struck by the teacher who suddenly works twice as hard as before. He pulled himself together and gave several hundred thrusts in succession without even pausing to catch his breath.

She began to cry out. "Dear heart, I'm spending! I'm dying! I can't bear another thrust. Hold me in your arms and let's sleep together. Mind you don't move."

At this point Vesperus stopped and, with his penis still inside her, they fell into a sound sleep.

Although she had an ugly face, she was blessed with small feet. And although her skin was as dark as could be, it was not really coarse. That was why, during all the time they had sex together, it never occurred to him that she might be a substitute.

Let us tell now of Fragrance, who was lying hidden beside the bed listening intently to everything that went on. At first, on hearing the woman cry out in pain, Fragrance knew that Vesperus's instrument, far from being insignificant, must at least be serviceable, and she relaxed somewhat. Then, when she noted that his technique was that of a master and that he varied his pace like a man of experience, she relaxed completely. In the middle, when he slackened off, she felt a certain contempt for him, but later, when his morale picked up again and he strove harder than ever, she said to herself with deep satisfaction, "Obviously he is a hero of the boudoir, a champion of sex. What else is there to say? I need have no regrets about losing my virtue to him. I'd slip in beside him while he's asleep and explain everything, except that he hasn't seen *her* yet and may think she's better than I am. I'll have to find some other approach. Moreover, I wouldn't look my best without an ugly woman to point up the contrast. When a man has fought long and hard, he may not be able to rise and fight again unless you have something to tempt him with."

Tiptoeing into the kitchen, she lit the fire and ladled some water into a pot, then picked up a taper and waited until it caught before marching into the bedroom, candle in hand. There she ripped aside the bedcurtain and tore off the covers, declaring, "What scoundrel is this who has forced his way into someone's house in the dead of night and seized a woman for his lustful purposes? What's the meaning of it? Kindly get up and tell me just what's going on in here?"

Startled from his dream, Vesperus leaped to the conclusion that Fragrance's husband had been hiding in the house waiting for him to go to bed with her so that he could catch him *in flagrante* and extort blackmail. His teeth chattering with fear, he broke out into a cold sweat. But when he looked up, there in front of him stood the same woman he had spoken to that day and slept with that night. "Can there be *another* one like her in the house?" he wondered aloud.

Then he bent his head to take a closer look at the woman in his arms and found that she was an insufferably ugly creature, with a face full of dark pockmarks, hair that was short and yellowy brown, and skin the color of an unscoured Jinhua ham.

"Who are *you*?" he exclaimed in astonishment.

"Don't be alarmed," she said. "I've just been spying out the land for her. I'm her neighbor from across the lane, the one she was talking to the other day when you came by. She thought your looks were fine, but that you mightn't be of any practical use. She felt she'd be risking the stigma of adultery to no purpose, so she invited me over to try you out. I imagine you've passed the test and can sleep with her. By rights I ought to stay and get another reward before I leave, but it would spoil your enjoyment to have an interloper around. I'd better go off home and content myself with being the best helpmate in the world."

She got up, pulled on her jacket and trousers, and draped her underclothes and the sopping wet cloths over her arm. On leaving she addressed Vesperus again: "I may have an ugly face, but I've served you well, because this lovemaking was all my idea. The fact that we slept together was due in the first place to her kindness, but also to our being destined for each other. If you do come back, and if you have some time on your hands, I hope you will sleep with me again. Don't be heartless, now." Then she turned to Fragrance, bowed several times in gratitude to her hostess, and left.

Vesperus, who felt as if he were sobering up from a binge or awakening from a dream, thanked the Knave fervently in his heart. Without his salutary advice to needle me into surgery, I'd have been like Su Qin when he tried to make the grade in the state of Qin—I'd have failed and been driven out with nothing to show for my efforts!

After escorting the neighbor out, Fragrance replaced the latch and came back.

"I knew you wouldn't be able to leave me alone tonight," she said, "and that's why I found a substitute to wait up for you. Now that you've slept with her, I consider the account closed. What are you doing here? Why are you in my bed?"

"Not only is your account still open, I intend to add to your sins. It's past midnight and will soon be daybreak. Hurry up and come to bed. We haven't time for gossip."

"You really want to sleep with me?"

"I really do."

"In that case you'll have to get up, put on a gown, and see to a certain very important thing."

"What else is important, apart from this?"

"Don't ask. Just get up."

As she spoke, she went into the kitchen and ladled the water she had heated into a bidet, which she brought in and set beside the bed.

"Up you get and wash. You're not going to spread other people's muck all over me!"

"You have a point. That *is* important. But I not only slept with her, I also kissed her several times. By the same token I ought to rinse my mouth, too."

"You don't need to rinse your mouth. I don't go in for *that* kind of thing."

"There you go again! You mean to say you'll write a *zhong* below but not a *lü* above?"[55]

Just as he was going off to look for something to scoop the water up in, he noticed a bowl of hot water already in the bidet with a toothbrush on top of it. What a thoughtful girl! he said to himself. If she hadn't done this, she'd have shown herself a slattern, none too particular about the pure and the impure.

Fragrance let him rinse out his mouth and wash, then sat on the bidet and washed the lower part of her own body.

She had already washed herself when the neighbor did, so why did she wash again, you ask. You must understand that while lying beside the bed listening to Vesperus having sex, she had been drenched in her own secretions. She was afraid Vesperus might feel the dampness and make fun of her, so she washed herself a second time. Afterward she took a damp cloth and wiped the bed mat with it. She also fetched a fresh cloth from the trunk and placed it beside the pillow, then blew out the lamp and sat on the bed and undressed, taking off every-

---

55. The character *zhong* consists of a circle bisected by a straight line. The character *lü* consists of two mouths linked together.

thing but her breastband and drawers, which she left to Vesperus.

Vesperus put his arms around her and kissed her as he undid the band. When cupped, her breasts did not even fill up his hands, but when stroked flat they covered her entire chest. They were dainty and soft to the touch, because there was no hardness in her breast. When he took off her drawers and felt her vagina, he found that in softness and daintiness it equaled her breasts and that in smoothness it surpassed them.

He let her lie back, then placed her tiny feet over his shoulders and raised himself above her just as he had done with the ugly neighbor. He then drove in a long way, to make her suffer a little at first in order to taste a keener pleasure afterward. But, despite all his pounding, Fragrance seemed totally oblivious to both pain and pleasure.

Everything the Knave warned me about has come true! thought Vesperus. Without that gross thing of Honest Quan's, how could she have become as large as this? If I'd not had the restructuring, I'd have been like a grain of rice lost in a granary, a fish scale adrift in the ocean! How could I ever have anticipated anything like this? Since my show of force has failed to impress her, I'll have to use some strategy.

He took the pillow out from under her head, inserted it under her hips, and then, having set his new strategy, engaged her again. Fragrance, who had not yet begun to enjoy herself, saw him remove the pillow but not replace it, and she realized he was an expert.

Now, taking out a pillow and using it to bolster a woman's hips is a routine technique; why should it make him an expert? You must understand that the principles of sexual intercourse are exactly like those of warfare; only a man who can estimate the enemy forces will make a skillful general. If he knows a woman's depth, he will know how far to advance and retreat;

if she knows his length, she will know how to meet and return his thrusts. This is what is meant by the saying, "The key to victory lies in knowing your own and the enemy's strength." Penises differ in length, just as vaginas differ in depth. If a vagina is shallow, a very long penis will be useless, for during intercourse there will be a constant sense of idle capacity. If the penis penetrates all the way, the woman will not only feel no pleasure, she will be in actual pain, and how can the man enjoy himself on his own? If the vagina is deep, an extremely long instrument is necessary; if it is even a little short, it will bring no pleasure.

But the size of a penis is fixed, so how can it be lengthened? In such a case one must find some way of supplementing it. The region between the stomach and the thighs needs bolstering so that the vulva is raised to meet the penis, making it easier for the man's thrusts to reach all the way. Thus the technique of bolstering the hips is to be used only in the case of a short penis and a deep vagina; one should not conclude that a pillow is essential for all intercourse. These facts explain why a short penis can be treated but not a thin one; why it is better to be short and thick than long and thin; and why the adept, in restructuring Vesperus's penis, had tried to make it thicker but not longer.

Now, Fragrance was deep and Vesperus short, so in moving quickly to bolster her with a pillow was he not proving himself an expert? The general principle is known to all, but as for placing a pillow under the woman's hips and leaving nothing under her head, that particular formula has never been understood before.

If a woman has one pillow under her hips already and another is then placed under her head, the upper part of her body, a little over two feet in length, will be forced into a concave shape. It amounts to breaking her in the middle and then piling a man's weight on top of her. Can't you imagine how uncomfortable and even painful it is? What's more, if her head is resting on a pillow, her face will be forced down so that her mouth is no longer opposite the man's, which makes kissing awkward. He has to bend down to meet her lips, while she has to force her head up to meet his. Such a waste of effort, and all because of a single pillow! Therefore nothing should be allowed to remain under the woman's head during intercourse, whether or not her hips are bolstered. A capable lover will push the pillow aside before he starts, letting the woman's hair lie on the bed mat and her lips, face, organs, and limbs all coincide with his. The upper and lower orifices differ from the other parts; they not only coincide, they fit, and they not only fit, they interpenetrate. His jade whisk enters her vagina, while her crimson tongue enters his mouth, allowing her to play the aggressor, too, and achieve a balance of sexual pleasure as well as a perfect fit.

While with one hand Vesperus removed the pillow, with the other he supported her head and laid it on the bed mat, where she faced directly upward, in the right position for kissing. That was why Fragrance was secretly pleased; she realized that he was an expert.

After placing the pillow under her hips, Vesperus raised her tiny feet over his shoulders and, supporting himself with his arms, employed all his skills and thrust as hard as he could. With each retreat he withdrew halfway, but with each thrust he plunged in to the base. There is a point worth noting here: He withdrew quickly, but he thrust slowly. Why was that? He was afraid there might be trouble if he thrust rapidly and made such a noise inside her as to alert the neighbors, so he dared not let himself go.

After a while her vagina began to feel tighter—it was no longer the vast, shapeless thing it had been—and Vesperus knew the dog's parts had flared up and his penis begun to grow. His vigor now increased a hundredfold and his thrusts came faster and faster. Hitherto Fragrance had shown no reaction, but now she wriggled from side to side and exclaimed, "Dearest, it's starting to feel nice."

"I've only just begun, my sweet," said Vesperus. "It can't be feeling nice yet. Wait until I've done some more and see how you like it then. There's just one thing that bothers me, though; I never like doing it silently, and if I'm going to get excited, I need to hear the sounds from inside. The trouble is that this house of yours is so cramped I'm afraid the neighbors will hear if I let myself go. What shall I do?"

"That's no problem. On one side of us there's a vacant lot and on the other a kitchen, where no one sleeps. So go right ahead, there's no need to worry."

"Perfect!" Vesperus exclaimed.

His technique was now exactly the opposite. He withdrew slowly but thrust rapidly, and when he thrust, he did so as noisily as any beggar beating on his ribs with a brick to gain public sympathy. After a spell of earth-shaking activity, Fragrance's passions were in full flow, and she kept crying "darling boy" over and over again, as her fluid spread everywhere.

Noticing the flood, Vesperus was about to pause and wipe it up, but when he groped for the cloth, she snatched it away.

Why did she do that? Because she had an instinctive dislike of silent sex, much like Vesperus, and, of the things she most enjoyed, her deepest pleasure came from the sound of sexual activity. In general the more the fluid the greater the sound, and that was why, even if she was streaming with fluid until her body was drenched, she would never let her husband wipe it up. Only when they had finished would she sit up and clean herself. It was an obsession with her—a singular feature that can be spoken of to the enlightened, if not to the vulgar. Seeing her reluctance, Vesperus guessed the reason and resumed his activity even more resoundingly than before. After more earthshaking thrusts she clasped him tightly.

"Dearest, I'm going to spend. Spend with me, please."

But Vesperus wanted to display his prowess and was not ready to spend.

"You've convinced me of your powers," said Fragrance. "You're not a phony, by any means. You haven't stopped all night, you've taken on two women, and the effort must have drained your energies. Do save a little for tomorrow night. Don't ruin yourself and deprive me of my pleasure."

At these endearing words Vesperus clasped her in a tight embrace and wished he could have forced his whole body inside her. After more furious thrusting they finished together.

They scarcely had time to say anything more before it was daybreak. Fragrance was afraid Vesperus would be seen if he stayed any longer, so she urged him to get up. Then she dressed, too, and saw him to the door.

From this point on he continued in the same fashion—arriving at night, departing at dawn—except that he no longer played the gentleman of the rooftops, but came in through the door. On one or two occasions he could not bear to leave and hid in her house all day. Fragrance told people that she was sick and could not go out or receive visitors, and the two of them went about in broad daylight without a stitch of clothing on, the mere sight of each other's snow-white flesh serving to stir their passions.

Every second or third night the ugly neighbor would drop by. Vesperus could not very well reject her totally and would occasionally pay her some superficial attention. Although he was unable to satisfy her fully, he could not afford to let her become resentful.

Several other neighbors had an inkling of what was going on, but they all thought it was the Knave who was the adulterer; they never imagined he would consent to act for anyone else. For fear he would get angry and retaliate, they shut their doors before dark and ignored everything that went on outside. Thus the two lovers slept together for over ten nights without the least apprehension until Honest Quan's return, at which point Vesperus's visits came to an abrupt end.

The Knave was afraid Vesperus's youthful passions would get him into trouble, so he forbade him to go near her door even in the daytime to spy out the situation. Instead he himself would play the part of Hongniang.[56] On the pretext of buying silk, he was constantly carrying messages back and forth between the lovers. On several of these occasions Honest Quan was at home, but he took the Knave for a businessman accustomed to dealing with his wife and stood aside to let them talk. Quan was a completely honest and straightforward man who never played anyone false, which is why he was known as Honest—a fact that inspires a certain faith in nicknames. After all, even Xu Shao[57] used to pin an apt label on his neighbors at the beginning of each month. Nicknames differ from sobriquets, which we select ourselves and for which we pick the most flattering combinations. When we choose our friends, we don't need to look at their character or conduct to know if they will be suitable; we need only ask what their nicknames are.

CRITIQUE

What a pity that a secret lost since antiquity, a formula that could not be purchased for a thousand taels, has been revealed to the public!

---

56. The maid in *The West Chamber*, who carries messages between the lovers.

57. An Eastern Han figure famous for regular, pithy criticism of his neighbors.

CHAPTER ELEVEN

A housebreaking hero throws his money about,
And clandestine lovers become husband and wife.

Poem:
> Many are the robbers living in the greenwood
> Who'll meet a friend and treat him lavishly.
> Many, too, the robbers among the official classes;
> Why don't they show an equal sympathy?

When Fragrance had been sleeping with Vesperus for ten nights or more and their passion was at its height, the affair was abruptly terminated by her husband's return. Her frustration was indescribable.

I used to think, she said to herself, that talent and looks in a man never went together with performance. That was why I passed them both up and regarded that coarse, stupid creature of mine as such a treasure, letting myself in for a life of constant hardship to help him earn a living. I never dreamed there might be anyone who combined all three qualities. If I'd not met this genius, my beauty would have been wasted, and I'd have been no better off than the ugly woman across the way! It's no good regretting what's past, but I'm not going to waste any more of my life! As the maxim says, "An upright person doesn't do underhand things." If a woman does not lose her honor, fine. But if she does, she might as well be bold and resolute enough to leave her husband for her lover and so avoid having to divide herself between them. I've often said that you can only afford to take a lover if you have Red Whisk's eye for a hero and Zhuo Wenjun's boldness. And provided you take just one lover during your whole life and stick with him, even the words *take a lover* will be rectified in due course. Eventually you'll receive honors and a title and qualify as a true heroine.

Those weak, useless creatures who scarcely manage to consummate their love and then waste the rest of their lives on their lovers, in some cases never seeing them again and even pining to death—aren't they ridiculous? The formula for taking a lover is composed of two terms, *adultery* and *elopement,* which are inseparable. If you're going to commit adultery, you have to elope. If you think you'll never be able to elope, you'd do far better to remain faithful to your husband and so escape retribution for your sins! Why barter away your honor and even your life for a moment of joy?

Having made her decision, she wrote a letter to Vesperus proposing that they elope. As a girl in her mother's household, she had loved reading and writing, but on becoming a merchant's wife she had neglected her skills and now wrote as she spoke, without any literary flavor at all. But although she was ill versed in the art of composition, she wrote straight from the heart, unlike those talented young ladies whose letters

submerge all trace of feeling under a welter of subtle implication, forcing people to read them as literary texts rather than
as letters.

Her letter ran,

To my lover, Scholar Vesperus:
Ever since you stopped coming to see me, I have spent
all day in front of my food unable to swallow it. If
I force myself to eat some, it is only a third at best.
Obviously my heart and other organs must have
shrunk to a fraction of their former size; it is not just
my face and body that have withered until they
scarcely look human. Not having seen me, how would
you know the state I'm in? I have now made up my
mind to spend the rest of my life with you, and you
must arrange it at once. Either trouble the Knave to
come and abduct me or I'll do a Red Whisk and run
away to join you. Just settle the date and the place
where you'll be waiting, lest we miss each other and
I be lost to the fisherman who gets the profit.[58] This
is very important, so take note! If you are worried
about the consequences and hesitate to run the risk,
then you are a faithless wretch. You may write and tell
me, but from that moment on I'll break with you and
never see you again. If I should see you, I have sharp
teeth and they'll take a bite out of my false-hearted
lover and eat it as I would pigmeat or dogmeat!
    As for all those lovers' oaths sworn on pain of
death, they are just cynical ploys used by heartless

---

58. According to the parable, a crane and a clam were preoccupied
with fighting each other, when a fisherman came by and caught them both.

women to deceive men, and I cannot bear to utter them.

Respectfully, Fragrance, the concubine you favored with your love.

After finishing the letter, she stood by the door until she saw the Knave walking by. But upon giving it to him, she began to worry that Vesperus would be too timid for such a dangerous venture, and she conceived the idea of picking quarrels with Honest Quan until he couldn't stand her and would be willing to follow the precedent of Zhu Maichen and let her go.[59]

Feigning constant illness, she gave up her spinning. Her husband even had to make the tea and do the cooking. If the tea was a little cold, she would accuse him of not boiling the water, and if the food was a little tough, she would complain that he had not cooked it properly. She got up every morning at dawn and nagged steadily until evening, stopping only when she went to bed. He had to be ten times as diligent as before if he was to get safely through the night; otherwise she would order him out at midnight to make tea or prepare medicine, and that would be the end of his uninterrupted sleep.

When they had sex, she used the same means by which she had disposed of her first husband, hoping to send Quan on his way and leave herself free to marry someone perfect in all three respects. Faced with her scorn and loathing in the daytime, Quan did his utmost to serve her at night, to atone for his misdeeds. To his dismay, however, his nocturnal efforts did nothing to make up for his daytime delinquencies. She had scarcely gotten out of bed than her whole attitude changed,

---

59. Zhu was a woodcutter whose wife grew impatient with poverty and left him—just before he succeeded in life.

striking fear into his heart before she opened her mouth. In less than two months she had so worn down her tiger of a husband that his bones stood out like matchsticks and he barely clung to life.

When the neighbors saw what was happening, they felt indignant, but because of their fear of the Knave they were reluctant to tell Quan. He, however, noticing this sudden change in a wife who had previously been so contented and affectionate, realized that there must be a reason behind it and continued to question them.

"Was there any outsider at the house while I was away? Did you notice anything going on?"

At first they made out they knew nothing, but at length, under the pressure of his questioning, they took pity on him as an honest man about to die at the hands of an adulterous wife and felt obliged to respond. "Well," they replied, "yes, there *was* someone who made a few visits to your house, but he is not the kind of customer you would want to provoke. If you do, it will be just as the proverb says: 'An open thrust is easy to dodge, but a sneak attack is hard to avoid.' Not only will you fail to stop him, you could suffer a very nasty accident."

"Who is this man, that he's so dangerous?"

"None other than the dreaded, world-famous miracle thief, A Match for the Knave of Kunlun. He was passing by your house a while ago when he saw what a good-looking woman your wife is and came over and asked whose wife she was. We told him she was yours, and he said, 'What a mismatch for this woman to be married to a husband like that! Do they get along all right?' We assured him you got on very well indeed. Then later he noticed you were away on business and came and asked us, 'How long will Honest Quan be away?' We assumed that he wanted to buy some silk and told him, 'The whole trip will take ten days or more.'

"But from then on, we heard noises coming from your house every night, as if there were people talking in there. If it had been anyone other than the Knave, we'd have gone and investigated. But you know how it is, you'd sooner provoke the God of the Years than this fellow.[60] Even if you leave him alone, he may still come and get you, but if you offend him, you're in real trouble. Moreover, there's no provision in the law for neighbors to seize people in adultery. And so we let him come and go as he pleased. He slept there ten or more nights, until you came back and the road closed again. We're telling *you* this, but you've got to keep it to yourself and be on your guard at all times against revealing it to anyone else, or it will bring disaster down on all of us. Even in front of your wife you'll have to control your feelings and not give yourself away. Otherwise she'll let him know, and none of us will be left in peace. If we're lucky, we'll lose only our property; if we're unlucky, we'll lose our lives as well."

"I saw him coming in to buy silk all the time and I was surprised he was such a big customer. So this is why! Well, gentlemen, if you hadn't told me, I would never have known, so I shall respect your wishes and not tell anyone. But the day will come when he'll fall into my hands, and when I've caught him and cut off his head, I shall ask you to back me up."

"That's foolish talk," said the neighbors. "As the saying goes, 'You have to have the goods to arrest the thief, and you have to catch them in the act to prove adultery.' He's been a thief all his life, and he's never once been found with the goods on him. Do you really suppose that after a few nights of adultery he's going to let you catch him in the act? Now, don't take offense, but that wife of yours isn't yours anymore. If he

---

60. Taisui, who presides over the planet Jupiter. A baleful god, he punishes those who offend his taboos even slightly.

carries her off with him one day, just be happy if you don't have to provide the dowry."

"How could he do that?"

"An old technique of his, haven't you heard?" asked the neighbors. "A wall may be dozens of feet high, but he'll clear it at a single bound! Or it may be hundreds of courses thick, and he'll get through it the first time! That cottage of yours will give him no trouble at all. He's sure to get in, by one means or another, and not only will your wife be taken off, all your property may well go with her as dowry. You'll have to be on your guard against a double loss."

Honest Quan grew even more alarmed and, kneeling down in front of the neighbors, begged them to think of some plan for avoiding such a disaster. The neighbors sympathized with his plight and tried to think of a solution. Some urged him to divorce his wife and cut off the danger at the root. Others told him to take his wife and flee with her to some distant place. Quan was in a dilemma until another neighbor, a man of some experience, offered his opinion.

"Neither solution will work," he said. "Even if Quan's wife could be evicted under the law, he hasn't gathered any evidence. On what grounds is he going to divorce her? And the Knave knows every road in the land. He'll track you down no matter where you move to, and when he does, you'll have delivered your life into his hands, I'm afraid. In my humble opinion, the only thing to do is make the best of a bad deal. Since your wife has no desire to stay with you, there's no point in trying to keep her. You'd be far better off getting a little money from selling her, so that you won't suffer a loss. If you sell her to anyone other than the Knave, she'll refuse to go, and when he hears about it, he'll resent your trying to break up his affair and will retaliate. The best thing would be to sell her to him. A thief can easily get his hands on some money, and since he's in love with your wife, he may be willing to put up a hundred or two. With that you should have no difficulty getting a second wife. Find a homely one who'll give you no trouble, and you'll be ahead in two respects: you'll have a wife and you'll be able to keep your property."

"Excellent idea!" said Quan. "Although it's not what a husband ought to be doing, it's the only option I have. But there's just one problem. I can hardly ask him myself, so I shall need a middleman. Would one of you gentlemen be willing to act for me?"

"If that's what you want," said the neighbors, "we wouldn't mind helping out. But once you've sold her, you're not to go stirring up trouble by saying we conspired with a scoundrel to seize your wife."

"If this works out, I will owe my life and property to you gentlemen. I would never do anything so two-faced."

"Quan is an honest man," said the experienced neighbor. "He'd never do such a thing, you can set your minds at rest."

They consulted and chose someone known for his diplomatic skills to go and negotiate with the Knave the next day.

Meanwhile, ever since parting from Fragrance, Vesperus had been suffering from lovesickness. In his desperate state he was counting on the Knave's magical powers to reunite him with Fragrance.

"If you want her abducted," said the Knave, "that's no trouble. The only problem is that you won't be able to go on living here afterward. If you wish to be husband and wife, you'll have to take her to the ends of the earth, somewhere you can't be traced, and settle down there. Are you prepared to do that? It's a question you'll have to decide before I can take any action."

Because of the two other *summa* beauties whom he had yet

to seduce, Vesperus was reluctant to leave the area. At first he could not make up his mind, but then, seeing how outspoken Fragrance was in her letter, he felt in honor bound to agree.

"I'll never be able to drop out of sight unless I move a long way off. Of course I'm ready to leave."

"In that case it will be simple," said the Knave, "except for one thing. Abducting a man's wife is a far more serious crime than stealing his money. Money is all a matter of chance anyway; if you lose it today, you can always earn some more tomorrow. But if a man's primary wife is abducted, the loss will be too much for him. Moreover, Honest Quan is poor. If he loses this wife, how will he ever be able to afford another one? A man's life is at risk if you push him too far. We need to think of some form of consolation for the victim. We should bring a hundred or more taels with us when we abduct his wife and leave them in his house, as if to suggest that he take them and buy himself another wife. If we deprive him of one wife but enable him to get another, it may not help our moral credit at all, but at least I'll have been true to myself as a hero."

"That would be the perfect plan, except that I'm embarrassingly short of money and there's nowhere I can get any. I'd have to trouble you for it, as a friend, and that is something I'd feel very uncomfortable about."

"Where *my* money's concerned, it's easy come, easy go," said the Knave. "If I begrudged you the money, do you think I'd have dared to speak up so boldly? Just leave the expenses to me. Write to her and say that I'll go and get her whenever she wishes, so long as Quan isn't at home; tell her there's nothing for her to worry about."

Vesperus was in high spirits as he hastily ground up the ink. Because her letter had been simply written, he replied in the same simple language, to save her trouble in interpreting it. The letter ran,

To Mistress Fragrance:

The two months since we parted seem like decades. Your heart and other organs have wasted half away, while mine have swollen to the same extent. Otherwise why would they block my throat so that I cannot swallow a morsel of food? I have been pleading all this while with the Knave to help us, but he was afraid that you were not fully committed and did not dare embark on it lightly. However, when he saw your letter to me, he realized that your love was as firm as iron or stone and he now undertakes to try his best. To do as Red Whisk did would be far too dangerous; with him helping us, it would be better just to emulate the Girl in Red. It is hard to predict when our tryst will occur, but the day your warden leaves home will be the same day Chang'e flees to the moon.[61] Send us the glad tidings as soon as you know, so that we can take action. If I prove faithless, whether I am pigmeat or dogmeat, your honorable mouth will not need to bite me, for there will be crows and curs aplenty to drag me off and devour me. I shall say no more.

Respectfully,

As a precaution I shall not sign my name.

After delivering the letter to Fragrance, the Knave took out a hundred and twenty taels and packed them up in readiness. But while he and Vesperus waited anxiously for news, Quan never left the house. Then one day, to the Knave's

---

61. The woman in Chinese mythology who stole her husband's elixir of immortality and fled to the moon.

surprise, one of Quan's neighbors appeared and, after exchanging a few casual remarks, came to the point.

"Honest Quan's business has been losing money and he can't make ends meet. As a result he is unable to keep his wife and proposes to sell her. It occurred to me that other people either had no money at all or else hadn't enough to keep her, whereas you, with your great generosity in helping others, might come to the rescue. So I'm here to beg you to do a good deed that would not only save this woman from starvation but that would also provide Honest Quan with some bride money as capital. You would be doing a great service to two people."

The Knave was perplexed. What an extraordinary thing! Here was I, just about to go off and see to him, when he sends someone over with an offer to sell her, as if he knew what I had in mind. He may have heard that I was acting for someone and, thinking he could not escape my trap, he may have decided to take this way out. Since he has done so, I'd better buy her openly rather than covertly. Why take the money along and then abduct her?

"Why on earth would he want to sell his wife?" he asked the neighbor.

"He's been driven to it by poverty, nothing else."

"In that case is the wife willing to leave him for someone else?"

"She can't stand the misery at home and is eager to get away. There's no question of her willingness."

"What would the price be?"

"He intended to ask for two hundred, but you don't need to stick to that. As long as he gets a bit over half, I daresay he'd be satisfied."

"In that case let's make it a hundred and twenty."

Having obtained the Knave's consent, the neighbor asked him to weigh out the money while he sent for Quan to come and close the deal.

The Knave's first idea had been to name Vesperus as principal and the neighbor and himself as intermediaries, but he thought better of it. It's a risky business taking another man's wife, he reflected. My reputation is sufficient to deter anyone from hauling me into court, but if I let him give his name, he'll be in trouble at once. So he said nothing about Vesperus, and he made out he was taking Fragrance as his own concubine.

Quan arrived and a marriage certificate was drawn up, to which he affixed his thumbprint. The neighbor also made his mark and passed the paper to the Knave, who handed over a packet of silver in the amount promised plus another ten taels as broker's fee for the neighbor.

That same day, still without letting Vesperus know, the Knave hired a sedan chair and fetched Fragrance. Only after he had found a house, furnished it, and engaged a maid for her, did he arrange the wedding and see the couple to their bridal chamber—behavior unsurpassed even by Bao Shuya with his loyal friendship or Curlybeard with his gallantry.[62] The only pity is that the Knave answered the wrong question in the examination and cannot qualify as a true hero. If he had applied his loyalty to the case of a worthy friend and his gallantry in a real emergency, he would have been entitled not only to rank as a hero among robbers but also to feel superior to the official classes.

------

62. Bao, who lived in the early part of the Zhou dynasty, was famous for his self-sacrificing friendship with Guan Zhong. Curlybeard is the hero of the Tang story of that name.

CHAPTER *T*WELVE

By means of kowtowing, he succeeds in seduction;
In spite of her jealousy, she arranges a pact.

Lyric:
    My love I dearly love,
    My love I idolize.
    But jealousy springs from love too dear;
    I glare—but with the fondest eyes.

    This beauty I hold dear,
    That beauty I adore.
    If I can get these beauties not to fight,
    Romantically, my fame will soar.
    (To the tune "Love Eternal")

Once Vesperus and Fragrance had become husband and wife,
they enjoyed themselves to the full, day and night, hot weather

and cold. After joining his household, she had just one period and then became pregnant. Vesperus was delighted at the news, believing that the adept had been proven wrong and that he could still father a child. His instrument of pleasure had been successfully restructured.

After four or five months her body began to swell up, making sex a little awkward. Normally Vesperus would stop thrusting only when there were no more cries to be heard from her, and now, on hearing a cry of alarm, he was not startled enough to detach himself, draw in his stomach, and proceed less passionately. As a result she told him that rather than exhaust himself, he should put off sex for the time being and husband his strength for a grand celebration after the baby's birth. From that time on they slept in separate rooms.

Vesperus spent his nights in the study where, amid peace and quiet, he inevitably longed for action, hoping for another affair. Before his marriage to Fragrance, he had felt that if only he could have her, he would be able to get through life without ever taking another mistress. But once he had married her, he began to think how much nicer it would be if he had another one like her, to form a pair. Although the idea occurred to him soon after the wedding, he was still able to enjoy himself, so he shelved it. In his present state of frustration, however, he began to treat this shelved idea as a matter of the highest priority.

"Of all the women I've seen," he thought, "only those two whose names I don't know are truly outstanding, fit to put beside the one I've just married. Unfortunately I don't know where they live or even where to start looking for them. I'll have to content myself with the second best and turn to someone from the *magna* class in my notebook for relief in this present crisis. There'll be time enough later on, when I'm free, to go looking for the others."

Without letting Fragrance know what he was doing, he shut the study door, took out his notebook, and leafed methodically through it until he came to the name Cloud of Scent. Although his comments on her amounted to no more than a few sentences, they were a little more positive than the rest; they were straightforward praise without irony, whereas the other comments were either praise with a dash of criticism or criticism with a dash of praise. She clearly stood at the head of the *magna* class and only a notch below Pale Rose Maid and Lotus Pink Beauty.

Comment:
There are many special features to her beauty. She has grace to spare. She trips so lightly as to leave no sign, and could be lifted on the palm of the hand. Her charm is unaffected, and her looks are as in a painting. The breeze wafts a rare fragrance from her, as if she were steeped in the scent of flowers. At her side one hears exquisite tones, like the warbling of innumerable orioles. She is without doubt an outstanding beauty, the most charming of women. I place her in the *magna* class, above the other beauties.

Rereading his comments, Vesperus recalled her face and remembered her as being in her twenties, a young woman who gave an impression of great charm. As she passed by, he had sensed a fragrance imbued with freshness and sweetness that was quite unlike the perfumes women use on their clothes or skin. After she departed, he had found a fan with a poem on it lying beside the incense altar and realized that she had left it for him. She was on his mind for days, and he fully intended to seek her out. But after meeting with the two *summa* women, he had begun to treat her as "a fish thrown back into the river." When he came upon this comment in his notebook, however, he felt the cold ashes of his desire rekindling and examined the tiny handwriting that followed the comment to see her address. It turned out that she was living in the same lane as he was!

He was overjoyed. There cannot be more than a few dozen families in this lane, he said to himself, so she must live quite close by. It shouldn't be too difficult to get hold of her. He went out at once to ask where her house was.

Little did he realize that he had been aided in his evil plans by the neatest of coincidences. It was as if the gods of Heaven and Earth were aiding the evildoer—for she proved to be his next-door neighbor, with only a wall in between! His study even backed onto her bedroom! Her husband, whose sobriquet was Master Felix, was a licentiate in his fifties, a man as long on talent as he was short on virtue, with a reputation as high as his character was low. Cloud was his second wife, his first wife having died. He ran a school and lived away from home, returning each month for only one or two nights.

This must mean we are destined for each other, thought Vesperus. Supernatural powers have brought me here so that I can enjoy myself with her. Such a convenient arrangement— how can I fail to take advantage of it?

Back and forth he paced, trying to think of a plan of action while surveying the terrain. The wall outside the study was not high, but it was part of the house and he could not get over it. The wall inside was not very substantial, but he could not drive a hole through it, because it was built of whitewashed brick and any attempt would have left obvious traces on both sides.

So he abandoned the classic methods found in literature and went neither through the wall nor over it, but decided instead to rehearse his own text and drop down through the roof. However, on looking up, he noticed a section three feet high and five feet wide along the top of the wall where the bricks had not reached and the wall had been finished off in wood.

Now that I've found this gap, he said to himself, I won't need to get up on the roof. Why not adapt the expression "drive a hole, climb a wall"? All I need do is pry a few boards off the wooden section and I shouldn't have any trouble getting over the wall. He fetched a ladder and leaned it against the wall, then brought from the study a set of tools that he had purchased but never used, a carton containing a knife, ax, saw, and chisel. Because he had never had occasion to use it, Vesperus had thought it useless and kept it in his study only as a curiosity. Little did he realize that there is nothing in the world without its function; for the tool kit, he had found a function in adultery.

Carrying his set of tools, he climbed up the ladder and took a close look at the wooden section. Fortunately, strong as it was, there were cracks in it. When it was being built, the boards had been tapped into place one by one, not mortised together, which would have made them impossible to budge. He set to work with a small file to grind away a fraction of an inch from the top of one of the boards so that there would be no resistance when he pried it off. Next he inserted a small chisel into the crack and jimmied the board toward himself. Before he realized it, one board was off, and when he went to jimmy the second board, he found he needed no tools at all; one pull and, with nothing to hold it in place, the board came away with ease.

After taking off two or three boards, he craned his neck through to survey the scene. What met his eyes was a woman relieving herself on a commode. Before tying her trousers up again, she went to replace the cover, but it slipped from her hand and, in stretching down to pick it up, she bent her slim waist and raised a fine pair of slender buttocks in the air. The back part of her vulva was directly in front of him. Observing her from behind, he was still not certain that she was the woman he was seeking. But when she pulled up her trousers and turned around, he saw her face and knew that she was indeed the one he had admired, now more fetching than ever.

He was about to call her, but feared someone else might hear. It also occurred to him that she wouldn't know him, hidden as he was, and would scarcely be inclined to give him a welcome. It would be awkward if she made a scene. He would have to think of some way of enticing her up to see him. One look at my face, he thought, and I won't have to plead with her. She'll come to hand of her own accord.

Puzzling over what to do, he suddenly remembered the fan with the three Tang poems on it in her handwriting. "I expect she still remembers. I'll leave the wall open and go and find the poems. When she hears me reciting, she'll understand and come up to see me, at which point I'll work on her with a few clever remarks. She's bound to fall for my line."

He scampered down the ladder and opened the trunk in search of the fan. While staying in the temple, each time he had picked up one of the many tokens of admiration left for him, he had put it away for safekeeping against the day when he found the woman and needed it in convincing her. Confident the women would be willing if only he had something to offer them, he treated the tokens as treasures and saw to it that they were not mislaid. Lest they get mixed up with his other possessions and be impossible to find in a hurry, he had had another trunk made for them, on the lid of which was inscribed, in two columns of four large characters for easy recognition, a line from one of the "Songs of the States" in the *Poetry Classic*:[63]

| BEAUTIFUL | GIFTS |
| WOMEN | FROM |

As he opened the trunk, tipped out its romantic contents, and picked them over, the first fan he turned up was hers. Its calligraphy, he noted on opening it, was not of the highest artistry but did possess a certain charm. Its three four-line poems were by the Tang genius Academician Li, to the tune "Peaceful Melody." They were written when Emperor Xuan-zong was admiring the tree peonies with Lady Guifei and called Li into the palace to celebrate the occasion.

Vesperus would not have dreamed of reciting the poems without the correct preparation. He changed into his best clothes and cap, then lit an incense burner filled with the finest incense. Finally he cleared his throat and, like a singer of Kun opera rendering a long, slow tune, enunciated the poems syllable by syllable so that she could hear them clearly.

Poem One
Like clouds her garments are, like a flower her face,
As zephyrs brush the rail-top's shimmering dew.
Should you fail to find her on the Mount of Jades,
You may meet her on Jasper Terrace beneath the
    moon.

Poem Two
A sprig of crimson radiance, scent-bedewed,
Spells clouds and rain and an emperor's broken heart.

---

63. From the song "Jing nü" in the *Poetry Classic*. See *The Book of Songs*, p. 33: "But you were given by a beautiful girl."

In the palaces of Han who is there to compare?
One pities even The Swallow, fresh adorned.

Poem Three
They rejoice, the noble flower and peerless beauty,
Watched by the king of kings with indulgent smile.
Gone is the pain that the vernal zephyrs bring,
As in Aloeswood she leans upon the rail.[64]

He recited the poems again. When there was still no response after ten recitations, he read out the date and the calligrapher's name as well, like the dialogue in the middle of an aria. He thought he might just as well let her hear properly, so he repeated those items several times, too, whereupon from the top of the wall there suddenly came a barely audible sound that was something between a cough and a sigh. Vesperus knew that she had climbed up there, so he rounded on the fan and denounced it: "Because of this fan, someone was almost driven to his death. The fan is here, but where is she? If she can be found, I should give it back to her. What's the point of keeping it?"

A reply came from the top of the wall: "The fan's owner is over here. Please throw it up to me. There's no need to be so bitter about it."

Looking up, Vesperus pretended to be astonished: "So the

___
64. The Mount of Jades and Jasper Terrace are abodes of the immortals. The clouds and the rain refer to King Xiang's erotic encounter on Mount Wu. Swallow is Zhao Feiyan, a palace beauty of the Han dynasty. The spring winds strip the flowers from the trees, as beauty is ravaged by time; spring is thus the season for the pangs of unfulfilled love. Aloeswood is the name of the pavilion in which the Emperor and Guifei were sitting when Li Bai was allegedly called in to compose the poems.

peerless beauty is close at hand after all! There was no need for me to be lovesick all this time! Now I shan't die!" So saying, he bounded up the ladder, took her in his arms, and kissed her so that their tongues copulated together.

"Where have you been all this time, that I never saw you again?" asked Cloud. "And why are you in this place all of a sudden and reciting the poems on my fan?"

"I live here. I'm your next-door neighbor. Didn't you know?"

"There are other people living there. I've never noticed you before."

"I've only just moved in."

"Where were you living before? And why did you move here?"

Hoping to win her favor, Vesperus took the opportunity for a little deception. "I moved here on your account. Surely you realize that? When I saw you in Zhang the Immortal's Temple, I fell in love, and when you gave me a parting look and left your fan for me, I couldn't get you out of my mind. I tried everything I could think of to move here so that we could be together."

"What a romantic you are!" said Cloud, breaking into a broad smile and tapping him playfully on the shoulder. "To think, I almost did you an injustice! But whom do you have living with you?"

"Just a concubine a friend gave me. She's not been with me long. The rest of my family I left at home."

"But why didn't you come by before you moved here? You've made me positively sick, longing for you all this time!"

"At first I couldn't find out where you lived, so there was no way I could see you. As soon as I heard, I moved here to be with you."

"When did you move here, then?"

"Less than six months ago. Four or five months at most."

Cloud's smile froze on her face. "Since you've been here all this time," she asked after a pause, "why didn't you pay any attention to me before? Why did those cold ashes of yours take so long to give off a spark?"

Vesperus knew from her tone that he had made a mistake and, flushing with embarrassment, he tried to talk his way out of trouble. "All this time I assumed your husband was at home and, since the last thing I wanted was to get you into trouble by doing something rash, I put you out of my mind and simply endured these past few months. Only just now, when I heard your husband was away teaching and there was no one else at home, did I dare make my presence known. It was caution on my part, nothing more. You surely don't think that I could forget you or that I would deliberately ignore you?"

Cloud said nothing, but retained her sardonic smile. "Well, do you still have my fan?" she asked after some thought.

"I keep it close beside me at all times. It's never away from me for an instant. I wouldn't dare lose it."

"May I see it in that case?"

Vesperus assumed that once she saw the fan her suspicions would be dispelled, her mood would change, and she would be ready to consider sex. He climbed down the ladder, wrapped the fan in a cloth, and handed it to her. To his astonishment she tore the fan into shreds and threw them into her room. Then she flung the cloth back at him.

"What a false-hearted wretch you are! I'm only glad I never got involved with you! From now on it's over between us!"

Fuming, she started down the ladder, pulling herself away from Vesperus's clutches and ignoring his entreaties. Reaching the bottom of the ladder, she burst inexplicably into tears.

Vesperus wanted to climb down and ask what the matter

was, but he was afraid of being seen, so he watched her from the top of the wall as she wept. In the midst of his predicament he heard a sudden sound from among the banana palms outside the study door, as if someone was there. Afraid it might be Fragrance, he quickly replaced the boards and climbed down.

He was puzzled. What *could* be the matter with her? he asked himself. I haven't said or done anything to upset her, so why on earth should she lose her temper like this? Judging from her reaction, she was blaming me for taking so long to contact her, which delayed our lovemaking by six months. But as the saying goes, "In the Qingming festival, it's never too late for the cold food."[65] All that matters, surely, is that I love her. Let me make up with interest all we've missed in the last six months. Why get so upset? I suspect that her reaction wasn't solely due to this, but that there's some other reason for it. What she said just now, harsh as it was, may not have represented her true feelings. It may have been just a trick to make me beg for forgiveness. I can't very well go there in the daytime, but this evening I shall have to get through the wall and find out. Whatever the rights and wrongs, I'll apologize and settle matters between us.

That day passed as slowly as a year. Vesperus waited impatiently until evening, then sent Fragrance off to bed and returned to his study. First he fastened the door and windows securely and took off his scholar's cap and outer garments. Then, putting out the lamp, he climbed up the ladder and removed the boards that he had loosened before, for all the world as if he were opening up a gateway.

He was still worried. So far so good, he thought. But if there's nothing to climb down on, I can hardly jump off a

---

65. Qingming was the spring festival, a time for tending the graves of one's ancestors. Traditionally only cold food was eaten.

twenty-foot wall! She sounded so harsh before, I'm sure she'll never come and help me if I call out. I won't be able to say a word.

As it happened, Cloud's heart proved softer than her words. Before going to bed she had left him a loophole, not taken the ultimate step in rejection. When he climbed up and stretched out his hand, Vesperus found that the ladder she had used during the day was still there waiting for him.

Overjoyed, he stepped on to it and climbed silently down, as if crossing a wooden bridge. He had gone up with an even tread and he came down with an equally even tread, untroubled by the least difficulty or danger.

Silently he felt his way to the bed, where she lay motionless. He assumed she was asleep and intended to ease his way into her bedclothes. He would take the opportunity to insert his penis into her vagina and gently awaken her, after which they would talk. That would allow him to dispense with the usual overtures. His mind made up, he stretched out a hand to lift aside the bedclothes.

Little did he realize that Cloud was not asleep, but that she had heard him very clearly as he approached. In the hope of saving herself from his overtures, she had faced the wall, pretending to be unaware of his presence. But when she felt him trying to open the bedclothes, she decided that she could hardly let him "burst unannounced into the general's tent." Unable to escape, she had to turn over and pretend to have been startled from a dream. "Who's there?" she cried out. "Creeping into people's beds in the dark!"

Vesperus whispered in her ear, "I'm the one you spoke to today. I know it was wrong of me to neglect you all this time, and I've come especially to beg your forgiveness." As he spoke, he tried to wriggle inside the bedclothes, but Cloud, furious, hugged them tightly around her and refused to let him in.

"What a heartless wretch you are! Who asked you to

come here begging forgiveness? Out, and be quick about it!"

"I've worn myself to a frazzle trying to think how to get over here and be with you! You can't call that heartless!"

"Who do you think your fine words are going to deceive? Oh, such *good* judges of quality your eyes are! You don't have some dazzling beauty to enjoy yourself with, so you turn to an ugly creature like me. You'd betray your own sweetheart to be here with me."

"The girl I have at home was given to me by a friend and I had no choice but to accept her. How can you be jealous of her?"

"It is perfectly proper to enjoy yourself with your own wife. How could I be jealous of her? But you oughtn't to involve yourself with someone like me and then banish me to the ends of the earth. If you lived a long way off and we had no chance to meet, that would be one thing. But there you were on the other side of the wall, and not a word did you utter, as if we were total strangers! A person as heartless as that I'd just as soon leave to others."

"Mistress, where do you get all of this? Apart from my wife and concubine, I've never been intimate with any other woman. This is my very first attempt at an affair. Why are you slandering me for no reason?"

"Answer me this," said Cloud. "On such-and-such a date, three women went into Zhang the Immortal's Temple to pray. Were you, or were you not, the one who admired their beauty so much that he knelt down outside the gate and kowtowed like a madman?"

"It's true. There were three women in the temple that day burning incense. I was there, too, to pray for a son, and when I saw some women already there, I thought it best not to go in, to avoid mixed company, so I knelt down and kowtowed outside the gate. But it was Zhang the Immortal I was worshipping, not the women!"

Cloud burst into laughter. "What! You've just given yourself away. If you'd denied everything, you might have gotten away with it. But since it was you, you've no case left. Do you mean to tell me that a voyeur who used to hide behind the Immortal's image would be too afraid of scandal to rush in and flirt with any woman he fancied, but would kneel down and kowtow outside the gate? That lie wouldn't deceive a two-year-old, and yet you have the nerve to try it on me!"

Vesperus realized she knew everything and that it was no use trying to cover up. He had no choice but to tell the truth, both to confess his misdeeds and also to coax the other women's whereabouts out of her.

"To tell you the truth, Mistress," he said with a smile, "I was kowtowing partly to the Immortal and partly to those women, to get them to take pity on me. But I wonder how you came to know what was going on at the temple while you were sitting at home? Who told you about it?"

"Oh, I have supernatural powers, I don't need anyone to tell me."

"Mistress, since you know what happened, you must also know where the women live and what their names and their husbands' names are. I beg you to tell me."

"You've been with them six months and you *still* have to ask me that?"

"Once more, *I don't know what you're talking about*! I've never seen them again since that first time. How can you say I've been with them six months? Oh, how can I protest this injustice?"

"You're still trying to bluff your way out of it! If you weren't with them, why didn't you come and see me these last six months? Obviously it was all their idea, to prevent you from having anything to do with me. You think I don't know that?"

"What a monstrous injustice! Not a shred of evidence, and yet you're full of suspicion!"

"If it's really not true, swear a solemn oath."

Vesperus faced the heavens and swore, "If I have ever had anything to do with those three women, may I be . . . If, far from having had anything to do with them, I so much as know their names or where they live, or have ever gone to look for them, then may I be . . ."

When Cloud heard him swear such a violent oath, her suspicions were partly assuaged. "You *really* haven't been with them?" she asked.

"I really haven't!"

"In that case you may be forgiven."

"Now that everything is cleared up," said Vesperus, "and I've done nothing wrong, won't you let me inside the bed-clothes?"

"My looks can't compare with those of the three women, so why not go and sleep with someone better-looking instead of bothering me?"

"You're being far too modest again. Whatever gives you the idea you're not as good-looking as they are?"

"There's nothing wrong with your eyes evidently. After all, it was only because you saw how gorgeous they were that you knelt down and kowtowed to them. If they'd been merely attractive, a close look, like the one I got, would have been ample. They'd never have had any kowtows!"

"That was a purely spontaneous reaction, with no conscious intent behind it. Anyway you seem to be blaming me for kowtowing to them and not to you. You think I'm making distinctions, and that's why you're complaining. If so, there's an easy solution. Let me do some more kowtowing and pay off my debt with interest."

He knelt down on the floor beside Cloud's pillow and rattled off several dozen resounding kowtows that shook the bed before Cloud stretched out a hand and helped him inside.

Vesperus wriggled inside the bedclothes so that his lower instrument met hers like a carriage on a familiar road. Understandably, since it was their first encounter and their passion for each other had been delayed by their overtures, they could stand no more ceremony in bed, and it was a case of *I want to join her* and *she wants to join me* as the two objects met like old friends in no need of an introduction.

Vesperus at once thrust in all the way. Cloud's vagina was of only average size, but her passions were aflame and she could wait no longer. She wanted to suffer a little pain so as to quell the itching sensation inside her, to put up with hardship in order to reach the frontier. Since she was able to accommodate him, Vesperus knew she was a worthy opponent, one to whom he could not offer a handicap, and he exerted all of his skill. He thrust and counterthrust in pitched battle, then insisted on withdrawing from the palace and driving into the lair itself. For the first dozen or two strokes the inside was slippery, but after fifty strokes it turned sticky. Cloud could bear the discomfort no longer and asked, "When I sleep with my husband, I find that things get easier as we go along. Why is it harder now than at the beginning?"

"The one asset I have," said Vesperus, "is this poor thing of mine, which differs from other men's in two respects: it starts small and gets large, swelling up gradually after entering the vagina like dried food soaked in water; and it starts cold and gets hot, like a flint that heats up when struck, as if about to burst into sparks. Having these two qualities, I didn't want to conceal them but to make love to you and offer them for your appreciation."

"I never believed you had such a treasure. I thought it was all a hoax. But since it's true, if you go on making me so uncomfortable, I'm afraid I'll cease to enjoy it altogether."

"You're too dry inside at present, and that's why you're feeling discomfort. But soon there'll be some fluid along to moisten things, and you'll feel quite different."

"In that case I'll put up with the pain. I may as well let you do your worst, to get some moisture flowing and put an end to this dryness."

"You're absolutely right." Placing her feet over his shoulders, he thrust hard and fast only a few dozen times before her vagina became slippery and his penis hot. Because of the former effect she ceased to feel any pain, and because of the latter she enjoyed herself more and more.

"Dearest," she said. "What you said just now was no hoax either. It really is a treasure, and I'm beginning to enjoy it."

Vesperus seized this chance to gain her favor by thrusting even more fiercely, at the same time asking in a wheedling tone, "Dear heart, if that was no hoax, it must be obvious that the other things I told you weren't a hoax either. You can trust me implicitly, so why not tell me about the three women?"

"So long as you truly love me, of course I'll tell you; but what's the hurry?"

"You're right," said Vesperus. Henceforth he said nothing and merely continued thrusting in silence.

He had been working a good two or three hours when Cloud's hands and feet suddenly turned ice-cold. She broke out into a sweat and spent three times in succession.

"Dear heart," she said to Vesperus. "I am not very strong and I can't stand any more of this battering. Hold me in your arms and let's try to get some sleep."

Vesperus did as she asked; he dismounted, lay beside her, and took her in his arms. As he lay there, he was conscious of a strange scent emanating from the bed, the same scent he had noticed on first meeting her.

"Dearest," he asked, "what is this exotic scent you perfume your clothes with? It's so delightful."

"I don't use any scent. When did you notice it?"

"That day we met, when you walked past me. And I noticed it again just now, while lying beside you. If you don't perfume your clothes, where does it come from?"

"It's nothing exotic, just a scent that comes from inside. You're quite wrong about it."

"I don't believe that any scent from inside you could have such a nice bouquet to it. If so, your body must be a treasure too."

"It's the one real asset I have, something that no other woman possesses. I'm told that at my birth, just before I appeared, a rosy cloud wafted into the room and everyone noticed an exotic scent. Then, when I came along, the cloud dispersed but not the scent, which was often found issuing from me. It was on the strength of this that I was given the name Cloud of Scent. If I sit quietly, the scent is barely perceptible, but if I exert myself and start sweating, it comes from my pores. When that happens, not only are others aware of it, I can sense it myself. Since I have this asset, I don't like to conceal it either. That day in the temple when we met, you looked so terribly handsome that I lingered a while and made eyes at you and left you my fan as a token. I was hoping you would come and seek me out so that I could offer you this scent for *your* appreciation, but to my great disappointment you never came. Only now do I get my wish."

Vesperus sniffed her body carefully all over and found that each pore gave off a wisp of scent, which convinced him that the most beautiful women are not to be chosen solely on the basis of their visual appeal, just as heroes are not to be judged solely by their physique. Clasping her in a tight embrace, he called her *dearest* several dozen times, until Cloud broke in: "Have you smelt me all over?"

"Yes."

"I'm afraid there's one place you've missed."

"No, I didn't miss anywhere."

"Yes, you did. You missed one place, where the scent differs from everywhere else. I might as well offer that for your appreciation too."

"Where is it?"

Cloud took one of his fingers in her hand and touched her vulva with it. "The smell in here is different again," she said. "If it's not asking too much, why not sniff it and see?"

Vesperus crouched down and gave several deep sniffs before scrambling up again.

"What a treasure! There's nothing more to be said, I shall love you forever!" With that, he crouched down again, parted that supreme treasure, and began licking it.

"Don't do that! It's too much! It'll be the death of me!" As she spoke, she tried to pull him up, but the harder she pulled the more furiously he licked. Using his three-inch tongue like a penis, he went back and forth, thrusting and withdrawing as in real copulation. When he sensed her fluid coming, he drew it into his mouth, gulping it down without losing a drop, after which he kept on until she spent, when he even swallowed her essence. Only then did he get up and lie on top of her again.

Cloud hugged him tightly. "Dear one, why do you love me so? There's nothing more for me to say either. I shall love you forever, too. If you truly love me, let's take a vow tonight."

"Just what I was going to suggest." They got out of bed, dressed, and took a vow before the moon and stars, praying that, among other things, "Not only may we never part in this existence, but in the next one, too, let us be husband and wife."

Then they took their clothes off again and climbed back into bed, where they began confiding their innermost secrets.

"In my opinion," said Vesperus, "there's not another woman in the world to equal you. I don't know how many virtuous lives your husband needed to be blessed with such a supreme treasure. But since he has this treasure at home, why doesn't he stay and enjoy it instead of spending all his time elsewhere, leaving you to sleep on your own? What possible reason could he have?"

"In spirit," said Cloud, "he would like to enjoy it, but he hasn't the strength, so he uses his teaching as a pretext for staying away and avoiding his duties."

"He's still only middle-aged, as I understand. Why is he so weak?"

"In his youth he was a rake who had one affair after another. Day and night he'd be off wenching. He wasted his powers so badly that now, in middle age, he's quite useless."

"How would you compare his capacity in his youth with mine tonight?"

"Much the same in point of technique, but he never had those two special features of yours."

"Mine is unique, and so is yours. Now that our two treasures have fit together, we must see that they never part. From now on I shall be over to sleep with you all the time."

"But you have a wife! How can you be over all the time? I'll be quite satisfied so long as you're not as heartless as you were before."

"I don't know what scandalmonger has been filling your ears with gossip and leaving me without a chance to defend myself. You're *still* saying I'm heartless. If I knew who it was that told you, I'd go and have it out with him!"

"To tell you the truth," said Cloud, "it was those three women."

"This is getting stranger and stranger! They should have been offended to hear such a nasty remark! How can they be so shameless as to repeat it?"

"To be frank with you, it all began with my telling them. We belong to the same family, and I call the two younger ones sister and the older one aunt. We are all on good terms, and the two sisters and I are particularly close, as close as real sisters, and keep no secrets from each other. Well, that day after I got back from the temple I told them how handsome you were, how you kept stealing glances at me, and how I fell in love with you and left you my fan. They said, 'Since he's so much in love with you and knows you fancy him, he's bound to come looking for you. How are you going to send him away?' I, too, fully expected you to come looking for me, and I waited at the gate for ten days without a sign of you.

"Then, on their return from the temple, they came to visit me and asked, 'What did he look like, that man you saw the other day? What was he wearing?' I gave them a detailed description. 'In that case,' they said, 'we've just met the man you love.' Then they asked, 'When he fell for you, did he kowtow, by any chance?' I replied, 'He had to keep his feelings hidden, of course. How could he possibly kowtow in front of all those people?' They said nothing, just looked at each other and smiled in a smug, secretive sort of way. That aroused my suspicions, and I questioned them closely until they told me in great detail, smiling all the while, how you had kowtowed to them.

"There was something awfully superior about their attitude that upset me for days. This is how my thoughts went: 'He was meeting them for the first time too. Why was he so afraid of scandal when he saw me that he didn't even bow once, whereas with them he went wild and kowtowed quite brazenly? Obviously my looks don't compare with theirs and, equally obviously, my luck doesn't equal theirs either.' If you were going to seek anyone out, you'd seek out the ones you'd kowtowed to. You wouldn't come looking for me!

"So I cut my love for you out of my heart and never went back to the gate. But I was constantly on the lookout to see if you came searching for them. Normally we are the closest of sisters, but because of this incident I began to resent them, and that was why, when we met today and you said you had waited six months before paying any attention to me, I couldn't help suspecting them. Only when you swore all those terrible oaths did I realize that nothing of the kind had occurred. This whole comedy was kowtowed into existence by you. Tell me: do you think you were right to do it?"

"With this injustice on your mind," said Vesperus, "no wonder you flared up. But since they're your sisters, they must be my sisters-in-law, and you ought to let me see them. All I have in mind is to address them as sisters-in-law and let them know that you and I are lovers. They put you down with their story about my kowtowing, so let me return the favor by putting them down, not just with these kowtows but with our lovemaking as well. How does that appeal to you?"

"There's no need for that. We're not only sisters, we've also sworn to share each other's fortunes, for better or for worse. If they had deceived me about this, they would be at fault. But since they didn't break their vow, if I now break mine and keep you for my own enjoyment, I will be the one at fault, and I couldn't bear that. When I see them, I shall have to explain things and impress on them that they mustn't forget the fish trap once they've caught the fish and try to one-up me or make me jealous. After that I'll bring you out and introduce you, to let them know that this marvelous creature is here for everyone's appreciation. That's what is meant by the saying, 'The treasures of the world ought to be shared with the people of the world.'

"There is just one thing. I want to impress on you that once you have those women, you're not to go changing your feelings for me. You must go on being just as loving to me as you were tonight. You must swear me another oath that you'll never switch."

Jubilant, Vesperus somersaulted off the bed and addressed an even more terrible oath to Heaven and Earth, then climbed

back in and began making love all over again. It was as if the
two wedding receptions had been rolled into one and both the
matchmaker and the in-laws invited. Don't you suppose the
matchmaker got drunk and the ladies ate their fill? After the
lovers had finished, they slept entwined in each other's arms
until dawn, when Cloud sent Vesperus home over his wooden
bridge. From then on they met every day and slept together
every night, and their love was deeper than that of husband
and wife.

We do not yet know when the two sisters will fall into
his hands. But enough has been said of Vesperus's infatuation
with sex, all the way from Chapter Two onward. Let us now
pause for the space of a chapter or so and take up a different
subject altogether. Of course after another scene or two of this
comedy have been played out, the male lead will reappear on
stage.

CRITIQUE

There is nothing in fiction more remarkable than *The Carnal
Prayer Mat* and nothing in *The Carnal Prayer Mat* more remarkable than this chapter. When you first read of Cloud's
outburst, you are upset; you have no idea of its cause and you
suspect the author of deliberately piling up difficulties and
dangers in order to make the reader nervous. Only when you
reach the final part do you realize that the previous section was
perfectly reasonable and logical and not in the least contrived.

Before Cloud became Vesperus's lover, she was consumed
by a baseless envy and so, after sharing her bed with him,
should she not have felt a justifiable jealousy? This is a common characteristic of women and a familiar gambit in fiction.
But not only is she not jealous, she even takes pride in playing
the celestial matchmaker and bringing three remarkable desti-
nies together.

By this time the reader is so far along the Shanyin road that he would not have time even to accept a summons from the Palace![66] Just see what triumphs Vesperus is enjoying!

---

66. This idiom is based on an anecdote in the *Shishuo xinyu*. On the road to Shanyin there was so much beautiful scenery that the traveler was completely engrossed.

CHAPTER *T*HIRTEEN

To purge his hatred, he smashes his pots and pans and
burns his boat;[67]
To avenge adultery, he sleeps on woodpiles and sups
on gall.

Poem:

As the *Spring and Autumn Annals* stressed revenge,[68]
I dare to write a novel in similar vein.
The historian Dong Hu never touched on sex,[69]
While the Zheng-Wei songs have left no moral stain.[70]
A poem on lust will chill the lustful heart,
And a tale of lechery hold the lecher back.

---

67. Two classic references; cf. *burning one's bridges*.

68. A Confucian classic, allegedly compiled by Confucius himself,
which is said to make its moral judgments implicitly.

69. A fearless historian of the sixth or seventh century B.C., whose
writings do not survive.

70. The Zheng and Wei sections contain the most risqué love songs
in the *Poetry Classic*.

Two former enemies will meet once more,
But somewhere else than on the narrow track.

Let us tell how Honest Quan gave up work after the sale of his wife, partly because he was seething with rage and partly because he could no longer face the public. Instead he spent his days sitting morosely at home, grilling the eleven-year-old maid as to when his wife had begun sleeping with the big fellow and whether anyone else had assisted him.

At first the maid was too afraid of her mistress's spite to tattle, but now that her mistress had been sold and would presumably not be returning, she revealed everything, from the dates when Fragrance and her lover had begun and ended their affair to the fact that the ugly neighbor had come over and slept with the lover too. She also revealed that it was not the *big fellow* who was the lover, but a handsome young man instead. In fact the big fellow had been assisting the young man, rather than the other way around.

At this news Quan's heart raced, and he promptly went out and asked the neighbors.

"Yes," they replied, "there *was* a handsome young man, but he came only once, unlike the Knave, who was back and forth all the time. Besides, the Knave is a proud man who would let others serve him but would not agree to serve them. He would never act for anyone else."

They were all in the dark until Fragrance married Vesperus, when the story got out and they learned of the deception. Once Quan knew the truth, he made inquiries about Vesperus's background and discovered that he was a stranger with a wife back home who had taken Fragrance as his concubine.

If the Knave had been acting in his own behalf, he thought, I would never think of appealing this wrong or of taking revenge. I'd have no choice but to put up with it in this life and settle accounts with him in the courts of Hell. But since someone else is responsible, how can I bear the rage I feel? I have to think of some way of getting even. He's not going to get away with it! If I take him to court, he'll have the Knave's help, for one thing, which means he'll have plenty of money to spend. Officials these days are always ready to do favors, and the Knave has only to ask them for one and I've lost. And secondly, the verdict in a marriage suit depends on the evidence of the middlemen, and the neighbors are so afraid of the Knave that they'll never speak up for me. So that's a blind alley.

The other ideas that occur to me are either unworkable or else unlikely to bring me satisfaction. The only solution is to go to the place he comes from, visit his home, work my way by hook or by crook into the household, and debauch his wife a few times. Now *that* would do my heart good! He debauched my wife, so I'll debauch his, paying back wrong for wrong, as they say. Even killing him wouldn't give me as much pleasure as that. "Where there's a will there's a way," as the saying goes. So long as you persevere, there's nothing you can't do. Everyone for miles around knows he seduced my wife before marrying her, and I imagine that the talk behind my back is none too pleasant. If I don't take revenge, I'll never be able to go on living here anyway, even without this injustice on my mind. Now that he has that slut of mine, I don't suppose he'll be returning home, so I'll seize the chance to go there myself. Perhaps Heaven isn't blind but will manifest its retribution and help me."

After deciding on a course of action, he sold the maid and all his furniture and effects for cash, which he combined with the hundred and twenty taels of the bride price and his trading capital. Then he took leave of his neighbors and set off, smashing his pots and pans and burning his boat.

After days of travel he arrived at his destination and put up at an inn while he found out where the house was situated and collected as much information about the family's activities as he could. Before he arrived, vengeance had seemed as simple a thing as fishing something out of his pocket, and he had scarcely given it a thought. But after finding where the house was situated and learning something of the family, he realized how difficult his task was going to be and began to worry.

He had assumed that the women's quarters in other men's houses would all be like his own; while the men were at home, the wives were naturally under strict control, but when they were away, it was as if the doors had no latches and the houses no inhabitants; anyone could go in and out at will. Little did he realize that intellectuals' families are quite different from merchants' families; only close relatives and intimate friends are allowed to cross *their* thresholds. And this family was different again from other intellectuals' families; not even close relatives and intimate friends were allowed to enter their house. Quan was in a quandary: It looks as if what I have in mind may not be possible, after all, he thought, but since I've embarked on this plan, I'm going to do my level best to carry it out. If I fail, it will be a sign of Heaven's will. After this long and difficult journey, even if I can't see how to bring it off, I'm not going to be scared away by the name Iron Door.

He was hoping to rent a room nearby where he could stay while awaiting his chance, but Iron Door's house was isolated, with open land all around it. If a married man could not have moved in next door, what chance did a bachelor from another part of the country have to settle there and carry on a seduction? Realizing there was nothing for him to rent, he set off back to his inn. But before he had gone fifty yards, he saw a wooden noticeboard nailed to a big tree beside Iron Door's house. It appeared to contain a message. Quan went over and found that there was indeed a message on it, in bold characters:

UNTILLED LAND FOR CULTIVATION
FIRST CROP RENT–FREE

Quan looked all around him; there was nothing but heath as far as the eye could see. It must be this land here, he thought. Whoever owns it, there has to be a tenant's cottage to go with it. That would be the ideal place to rent. I'd be living close by and, on the pretext of working the land, I could keep an eye on what is happening over there.

At a nearby house he asked, "Who is the owner of the untilled land? Would there be a cottage for the tenant to rent?"

"The owner's name is Master Iron Door," came the reply, "and he lives in that isolated house over there. But there's no cottage that goes with the land. He expects the tenant to find his own lodgings."

"I'm thinking of breaking the land in for him," said Quan, "and I'm wondering what kind of landlord he is."

The other shook his head. "The most impossible man in the world! If he were easier to deal with, that land would have been rented long ago."

"Impossible in what way?" asked Quan.

"According to custom you're supposed to get three years rent-free for breaking in land, but he allows only one year and demands rent from the beginning of the second. And that's just one instance. He's so stingy he begrudges providing board for servants, so he doesn't even have anyone to run his household. Being a tenant of his means doubling as a hired hand; when there's work to be done around the house, you'll be called in to do it for nothing. Three years ago someone did break the land in, but he couldn't stand being ordered about and left before the spring sowing. That's why it's unworked now."

Quan was overjoyed at the news. What concerned me was how to get inside the house, he thought. Once in, I shall have a reasonable chance. Other men can't stand being ordered about, but I'm eager to take orders. Others expect to be paid, but I'm only too ready to work for nothing. I shall need to be employed by him if I'm going to succeed, but it is not something I can arrange in a day. If his son-in-law comes back and sees through my plan, I'll be in real trouble. Luckily we've never met, enemies though we are, so that even if he does come back, he won't recognize me. All I need do is change my name and he'll never guess who I am.

He changed his name to Lai Suixin, because he had come *(lai)* to get revenge, and by getting it he would fulfill his desire *(sui xin)*. However, to save the reader from confusion, the author will continue to call him Honest Quan.

After changing his name, Quan drew up a lease and went over to the house to wait upon the owner. He knew it was no use knocking on Master Iron Door's gate and resigned himself to sitting down outside and waiting. That day no one came out, and he went back to the inn. Returning the next day, he was lucky enough to find Master Iron Door waiting outside the gate with scales and a basket to buy beancurd. He felt certain from the man's stern appearance and austere dress that it must be Iron Door, and he approached and gave a deep bow.

"Master Iron Door! Might that be your honored name, sir?"

"Yes. Why do you ask?"

"I understand you have some land that you are looking for someone to work. Since I don't have the capital for a business of my own, I'd like to rent your land and work it. Would you be willing to rent to me?"

"Breaking in land is not something for a weak or lazy fellow, you know. What about the physical labor involved? Are you a hard worker? You mustn't loaf on the job and neglect my property."

"I'm used to hard conditions, and my strength will serve

well enough. If you doubt me, why not try me out for a while? If I can't do the job, you can always let me go and take someone else on."

"I don't have a cottage for you. Where will you live?"

"That's no problem. I have no wife, only myself to worry about. Let me build myself a thatched hut at my own expense. Why pay rent for a place somewhere else while I'm farming your land?"

"Quite right. In that case you may go and draw up a lease."

"I have one right here," said Quan, handing over the lease he had prepared.

Noting Quan's coarse appearance, the Master considered he would make a good, sturdy servant, one who would not only break in the plot but also serve him as a hired hand. He accepted the lease and gave Quan permission to build a hut at his own expense.

Quan, who had plenty of money, bought lumber and thatch and engaged a couple of carpenters and thatchers, and in a few hours they had finished the job. Although just a hut, it looked bright and new. At least he had a place to call his own.

He bought a set of farm tools and early each morning would get up and, without stopping even to comb or wash, go off to the fields to cut rushes and dig the soil, in the hope that the Master would be impressed with his diligence and show him favor.

Just opposite the plot of land, Iron Door had a studio in which he spent most of his time. It was his custom to rise very early, so when he found Quan already up, he was surprised. In fact Quan had cleared a good deal of land before the Master was even out of bed. The latter was full of praise, and if any heavy work needed doing about the house, something the maids couldn't handle, Quan would be asked to do it. He did his utmost to oblige, putting twice as much effort into serving Iron Door as he did into his farming. Not only did he ask for no pay, he refused even to eat his fill. On one occasion, as he was about to leave, the Master, impressed by his hard work, offered to buy a jug of strong liquor to cheer him up. But Quan replied that hard liquor didn't agree with him, that he never touched a drop, and that in any case he would rather go home and drink something he had bought himself than involve his master in extra expense that might prevent him from being invited to help in the future.

Before setting foot in the house, he had been greatly worried. How ugly his daughter must be, he said to himself, to force her husband to leave home in search of other women! Myself, I've had a fine woman to sleep with. Supposing I manage to entice this one on stage, then take a look at that appalling face and my penis refuses to stand up? What if I'm all set to take revenge and it won't cooperate?

He cheered up considerably when he entered the house and saw a strikingly beautiful girl there, but he was still not sure of her identity. Later, on hearing the maids address her as *miss*, he realized that she was indeed the Master's daughter. A woman like that, he mused, is well worth sleeping with. Why did he leave her on her own and go off after other men's wives?

Although he forced himself to be even more patient and methodical in his plan of revenge, his penis was unwilling to be patient. It insisted on "destroying the enemy before breakfast" and raised the standard of revolt whenever he saw her. But Quan was a very cautious man, and seeing how strictly the women were segregated in this household, he never betrayed the fact that he was covertly watching her, but always passed by with his head bowed, not saying a word, like a complete prude.

Within a few months the Master, noting how hardworking, honest, and abstemious he was, had became very fond of

him. When my son-in-law left, he thought, he gave me a few
taels for hiring a servant. But most of the stewards I've seen
in other households are lazy and interested only in their victuals. Reliable men are in a distinct minority, which is why I've
hesitated to take anyone on. But a fellow like this would be
worth a lifetime's victuals. I daresay, since he's poor and has
no one to turn to, he might be willing to sell himself as a
bondservant, but there is just one problem. Bringing a single
man into the household has two drawbacks: first, since there'd
be nothing here to hold him, he might try to make off with
my valuables; second, how could the sexes be kept apart? It's
not only the maids that need watching; there are all the problems that arise from having a daughter in the house. But I do
have plenty of maids. If he were willing to sell himself, I'd be
prepared to give him one of them in marriage. With a wife
to tie him down he wouldn't be so inclined to make off. And
a wife would also keep an eye on him inside the house and
relieve me of my anxiety.

Although the Master intended to make the offer, he was
afraid that Quan might refuse, so he hesitated to come straight
out with it. One day he walked over to watch his tenant
hoeing and inadvertently sounded him out with a jesting
remark or two.

"You work so hard, and you don't waste your money. By
rights you ought to be establishing a family. Why don't you
take a wife? A man your age, and still on your own!"

"There's an old saying," said Quan. " 'By brains you can
support a thousand, but by brawn only one.' People who work
with their hands are doing well just to get by. How can I even
think of getting married?"

"But a man *needs* a wife and children in his life. Since you
can't afford to marry, why not join the staff of some household
that would provide you with a wife? If you have a child,
there'd be someone left behind to burn paper money for you

after you're gone. Why slave away all your life and have nothing to show for it at the end?"

Quan realized from these remarks that the Master was thinking of taking him into his household, and he responded with a ploy of his own. " 'A big tree gives good shelter,' " he replied. "I'm familiar with that proverb of course. But being dependent is no simple matter either. For one thing, you may have a hard-hearted master who beats and curses you instead of thanking you, even if you've been toiling for him all day like an ox. Secondly, the other people on his staff may not accept you. They were there before you came along, and they expect you to truckle to them. And if they're not prepared to exert themselves for their master, they'll be afraid that your loyalty will show them up, so they'll set the master against you and make it impossible for you to stay. I've often seen that sort of injustice in gentry households, which is why I'd have to think long and hard before joining one."

"Those gentry households are very grand and have numbers of servants, among whom you always get discord and indifference, which is why such injustices occur. But in a household of moderate size, the master would be able to tell how good his staff were. Moreover, you would have very few colleagues and no problem fitting in. Take the case of a household the size of mine, for example, with a master as enlightened as I am. Would you be interested in that, supposing there was a wife there waiting for you?"

"Oh, that would be ideal! Of *course* I'd be interested."

"Well, to be quite frank with you, I do need a servant. The only reason I don't have one now is that I haven't found anybody suitable. Seeing what an honest, hardworking fellow you are, I've considered taking you on, and that is why I've been asking you these questions. If you really are willing, go ahead and draw up a contract stating how many taels you will need as a bond, and I'll see to it. Then the day you join my household, I'll pick out a maid for you as a wife. What do you say?"

"That way I'd have someone to turn to the rest of my life! I'll bring the contract over tomorrow. But there's one point I'd like to make. My sexual desires are very modest, and it's not important to me whether I have a wife or not. Why not go slow for the time being? There'll be plenty of time to give me a wife after I've put in a few years' service and my strength has begun to fail. At present all I want to do is serve you with all my heart, not have some woman sapping all the energy I shall need for the household chores and the farmwork. As for this so-called bond price, there's even less need to talk about it. Since I'm selling myself and don't have any parents or brothers left, there's no one for me to give the money to. Once I'm part of your household, so long as I have my food and clothing, I shall be perfectly all right. What would I need money for? But if the contract doesn't mention a sum, I suppose I can't be said to have sold myself. You can put down whatever you wish, but in fact you won't need to spend any money on me at all."

The Master's face broke into a broad smile. "Ah, it does my heart good to hear you say that! Anyone can see that you're a faithful servant. But you can decline only one of my offers, not both. If you don't collect your price, perhaps the money can remain in my keeping until such time as you need to have clothes made. But it simply won't do not to take a wife. People who sell themselves as bondservants have always done so to obtain wives and enjoy a little married pleasure. So why don't *you* want to? If you won't take either your bond price or a wife, you'd seem completely independent, and even though you addressed me as master, I'd feel very awkward calling you my servant and very uneasy about giving you orders. If you're going to insist on that, I'm afraid I cannot take you on."

"I know what's at the back of your mind, sir," said Quan. "You're afraid I'm not dependable, and you think that one day I'll want to leave. You wish to give me a wife to prevent me from being disloyal. Well, I'm not such a scoundrel, I assure you, but since you're so concerned, I shall accept your offer."

After this clarification Quan did not wait until the next day, but drew up a contract and submitted it to the Master that evening. The Master didn't wait either, but gave him a maid in marriage the same evening. He tore down the hut and told Quan to move into his house. Previously he had called him Lai Suixin, but now he called him simply Suixin. By an odd coincidence the maid given him in marriage was named Ruyi *(satisfy desire)*. It is evident from this coincidence that vengeance is now more likely than ever, for to the name Suixin has been added the portent of Ruyi.

CRITIQUE

One marvelous feature of this chapter is the way the straight-forward, rough-and-ready Honest Quan manages by devious, convoluted means to work his way inside the "iron door," thus reenacting the romantic exploit of Sima Xiangru.[71] And a second marvelous thing is the way Master Iron Door, who has worried over every possible contingency and taken every conceivable precaution, falls right into Honest Quan's trap like a latter-day Zhuo Wangsun. The thought and imagination that have gone into *The Carnal Prayer Mat* also deserve to be called convoluted in the ultimate degree!

---

71. Zhuo Wenjun eloped with the poet Sima Xiangru in a famous romance. Her father was Zhuo Wangsun.

CHAPTER *F*OURTEEN

When he shuts his door to talk of love, the walls have
  ears;
When she forbids anyone to watch her bathing, "there's
  no money here."[72]

Poem:
  A wanton woman loves to spy on man
  But gets indignant when on her he spies.
  Her indignation has a single purpose:
  That on her pretty pout he feast his eyes.

Let us explain that the story of how Honest Quan sold himself
lies in the future. Well before he entered the household, Mistress Jade Scent had fallen prey to a secret melancholy, which

---

72. This expression is based on a joke about a man who, wanting to
hide his money, buried it and put up a sign saying, "There's no money
here."

our brush has been too busy to describe but which we shall now address. Just at the height of her sexual enjoyment, her husband had been driven away by her monster of a father, a development that left her feeling like a drunkard who has just sworn off wine or a gourmet who has just given up meat. She couldn't even get through the next few days, let alone survive for years as a grass widow. Deprived of real pleasures, she was reduced to placing the erotic album in front of herself and trying to quench her thirst by looking at plums and satisfy her hunger by drawing a cake. To her dismay, however, she found that looking at plums increases rather than quenches one's thirst and that drawing a cake sharpens rather than satisfies one's hunger. The longer she looked at the album, the worse she felt, until at length she put it aside and brought out a few idle books instead, in the hope of relieving her distress and boredom.

Gentle reader, what kind of books ought she to have read, do you suppose, in order to relieve her distress and boredom? In my humble opinion, no play or novel would have been of any use whatever. Only the books her father taught her to read as a girl, such as *The Lives of Virtuous Women* and *The Girls' Classic of Filial Piety*, would have met her need. If only she had been willing to take them out and read them, they would have relieved her distress and boredom and also quenched her thirst and satisfied her hunger. She might then have been able to endure a real widowhood, to say nothing of the grass variety.

But Jade Scent took a different course and gave undue credence to the "Four Virtues for Girls" and the "Three Obediences for Women," which stipulate: "Before marriage obey your father, after marriage your husband." Accordingly she ignored her father's books and began to read her husband's, tipping out his entire stock of obscenity, such as *The Foolish Woman's Story, The Unofficial History of the Embroidered Couch*, and *The Life of the Lord of Perfect Satisfaction*, and going through them carefully and methodically. She noticed that these books invariably praised penises as either extremely large or exceptionally long, using expressions such as "a head the size of a snail," "a body like a skinned rabbit," and "strong enough to support a peck of grain without bending." She noticed also that men's thrusts were numbered in the thousands and tens of thousands rather than in the dozens and hundreds.

I simply don't believe there is any man as strong as that between Heaven and Earth, or anyone with so impressive an instrument either, she reflected. My husband's is less than two inches long and two fingers thick, and he cannot last more than a couple of hundred strokes before discharging. He has never reached a thousand! He told me himself that he was without equal among men, so surely there cannot be anyone *dozens* of times stronger than he is! As the old saying goes, "Better to have no books at all than to believe everything you read." These absurdities must have been concocted by the authors! Such marvels don't exist!

But her skepticism did not survive for long. "That's not true, either," she reflected. "It's a big world we live in, with vast numbers of men, among whom there must be all kinds of exceptional cases. How do I know that what the books say isn't true after all? If a woman were able to marry a man like that, her bedroom pleasure would be beyond description! She'd be loath to change places with the immortals in Heaven! But that's too much to hope for!" Thus, having gone from skepticism to faith, she reverted to skepticism.

Day after day she would get up and, neglecting her needlework, match herself against these idle books, trying to bring her sexual excitement to a fever pitch so that when her husband returned, they could relieve it together. But when time passed and no word came from him, she could not help feeling a certain resentment. I've noticed that there's not a single woman in any of these books who does not have several lovers, she thought. Evidently it is not at all unusual to take a lover. I must have misbehaved myself in my last existence to get such a beast for a husband. Only a month or two after our wedding, and he goes off and stays away for years! I very much doubt that anyone as highly sexed as he is will have held out this long without straying. And if *he* has strayed, it would hardly be wrong for me to have a backdoor affair of my own. The only pity is that we women are so strictly regulated that we never even *see* a man.

Then, having arrived at this stage in her thinking, she transferred her resentment from her husband to her father and looked forward eagerly to the latter's early demise so that she could bring a man into the house.

Thus when she first set eyes on Honest Quan, she was like a ravenous eagle spotting a chicken or a hungry cat coming upon a mouse—rough or smooth, good-looking or ugly, she wanted nothing better than to gobble him up. While he was still working his land, she could do nothing about her desires; firstly, because she had observed that he was a terribly prudish soul who would not even look at her as he passed by and would certainly not jump at an invitation; and secondly, because he came in the daytime and left at night, and even if he did accept, they would have had neither the time nor the place for sex. But when she heard he was selling himself as a bond-servant, her heart leaped and she resolved that on his very first night in the house he would not escape her.

As it happened, however, the one who was waiting anxiously to fulfill her desires *(suixin)* did not fulfill them, while someone else who was not expecting to satisfy hers *(ruyi)* did so. Jade Scent watched with a pang of jealousy as the bridal couple took their vows and entered the bedroom together. Waiting until her father was asleep, she then stole out of her room to eavesdrop on their lovemaking. Honest Quan's penis was by no means insignificant, and Ruyi, although in her twenties, was still a virgin because her highly principled master had never molested her. How could a space scarcely big enough to hold a finger endure a laundry beater stuffed inside it? Naturally she screamed and wailed fit to shake the heavens, until the eavesdropper herself began to feel pain on her behalf.

This maid is a few years older than I am, thought Jade Scent. On *my* wedding night I felt only a slight discomfort as my husband worked his way in. Why is she so helpless, making all this fuss over a little pain?

Quan saw that his wife couldn't bear it and hastily brought matters to a close. Jade Scent, after standing there a while, heard nothing more of interest to her and went back to bed. Returning to eavesdrop the next few nights, she heard more cries of pain but none of pleasure.

After the third night, however, Quan's prowess was destined to be revealed. On previous nights he had blown out the lamp before going to bed, but on this occasion, as if he knew someone was watching and wanted to show off his effects, he neither blew out the lamp nor let down the screen. Before entering Ruyi, he told her to fondle his penis, which was over eight inches long and too big to be grasped. By this time her well-reamed vagina was no longer too tight, and Quan extended all of his powers. The number of his thrusts compared well with what Jade Scent had read of in her books, for he refused to stop until he had given several thousand, by which time Ruyi had graduated from acute discomfort to the most acute pleasure. Her frantic actions and cries fairly shook the heavens, and the observer, who had previously felt pain on her account, now began to feel pleasure. In fact the fluid that resulted from her observing exceeded that of the sexual act itself, and not only were her trousers wet, even the top part of her stockings was damp.

Henceforth Jade Scent was obsessed with Quan. He, for his part, changed his tune the moment he entered the household, dropping his prudish ways completely. Whenever he met Jade

Scent, he stole glance after glance at her. If she smiled, he smiled, too, and if she looked sad, he responded with a sad look of his own.

One day she was taking a bath in her room, when he passed by and happened to cough. She realized who it was and, hoping to arouse his desires by getting him to look at her, called out, "I'm taking a bath in here! Whoever that is outside, don't come in!"

Quan knew she meant it in the sense of *there's no money here*. Not wishing to disappoint her, he moistened a tiny patch on the paper window and observed her from above.

Jade Scent saw there was someone outside the window and knew it must be Quan. Previously she had had her back to the window, but now she turned around until her breasts and vulva faced it directly, offering them for his inspection. Lest the most important part of all be half hidden underwater, she lay back and spread her legs, giving him a full frontal view. Then, after lying like that for a while, she sat up, cradled her vulva in both hands, looked at it, and heaved a deep sigh, as if to say she was longing for a chance to put it to use.

At this sight Quan's desires flared up until they could no longer be held in check. Moreover, he knew that her desire was at its height and that she felt bitterly frustrated. If he did not accept the invitation to her party, he would be blamed, and conversely, if he did accept it, he would never be turned away. He pushed the door open, burst in, and kneeling down in front of her, pleaded, "Your slave deserves to die!" Then, scrambling to his feet, he took her in his arms.

Jade Scent pretended to be shocked. "How *dare* you take such liberties!"

"Mistress, the only reason I sold myself was to get inside the household and be with you. I meant to declare my feelings when we were alone together and get your permission before I did anything rash. But today I happened to be passing by and saw how incredibly soft and delicate your precious person was, and I couldn't restrain myself any longer, but had to come in and inflict myself upon you. Spare my life, Mistress, I beg you!"

Jade Scent had a few more stock protestations ready, but she feared they might take too long to deliver and in the meantime someone might come upon them.

"Well, then," she asked, "what do you have in mind? This bath is hardly the place for anything."

"I realize this isn't the time or the place, but I do beseech you to let me wait on you tonight."

"But at night you sleep with Ruyi! She'll never let you come."

"She's a very sound sleeper. After we've had sex, she goes straight to sleep and sleeps until dawn, and even then I have to call her dozens of times before she awakens. She'll never know, if I deceive her and join you during the night."

"Very well, then, do as you suggest."

Now that he had received her consent, Quan caressed and kissed her and then started to leave. She called him back, worried that he might not keep his word.

"Are you really coming tonight? If you are, I'll leave my door open. If you're not sure, I'll lock it and go to sleep."

"Of course I'm coming! But I urge you to have a little patience. Don't be too anxious."

Their arrangements made, the pair separated.

By this time it was evening. Jade Scent dried herself, but did not dress or eat dinner. She lay on her bed, intending to take a nap and build up her strength for the night's encounter, but she could not get to sleep and lay there impatiently until the beginning of the second watch, when she heard the door creak and knew it must be Quan. "Brother Suixin," she whispered. "Is that you?"

"Yes, Mistress dearest, it's me," he whispered back.

Worried that Suixin might not be able to find his way to her bed in the dark, Jade Scent scrambled out and guided him in. She was worried, too, that in his ignorance of her proportions he might be too wild, so she gave him instructions: "Dearest, I've noticed that that thing of yours is different from other men's. I won't be able to bear it at first, so please go slow."

"I wouldn't dare offend your precious person. I know a very effective means of entry that will cause you no discomfort at all."

"I would be ever so grateful," murmured Jade Scent.

Despite his assurances, Quan suspected that her modesty was mere coyness. Her husband, after all, was an adulterer, and must be well endowed; surely he didn't cause pain to his own wife? Placing his penis against her vulva, Quan proceeded to offend her person anyway. The pain was too much for Jade Scent, who lost her temper. "Did you forget your promise the moment you made it? What's all this hurry, when I told you to go slow?"

Unable to gain entrance, Quan realized that her request was not false modestly and apologized: "Frankly, Mistress, this is the first time I've seen a beautiful young woman, and when I touched you, I got carried away and couldn't wait to enter. That's why I was too energetic and upset you. Let me make it up by taking things much more slowly." He raised his penis and rubbed it on both sides of the vulva. Afraid not only to enter the inner room but even to ascend the hall,[73] he thrust away between her thighs.

Why do you suppose he did this? He was employing the method known as Clearing Away the Rocks to Get the Spring

---

73. See D. C. Lau, trans., *The Analects* (London: Penguin Books, 1979), p. 108.

Flowing. The best lubricant in the world is vaginal fluid, a substance designed by Heaven and Earth to moisten the vulva and penis. Spit, although acceptable, is simply no match for this fluid. It is generally used when the man is too impatient to wait for the fluid and turns to what he has in his own mouth instead. But the water from another spring is never as good as one's own. The fluid is more convenient—and also more appropriate, because using it to moisten the vagina follows the same principle as using river water to cook a river fish; the flavor of the fish is not adulterated, and it slips easily into the mouth. Originally Quan had been ignorant of this method, but when first married to Fragrance he had found it difficult to enter her because of the size of his penis, and she had racked her brains to come up with this method, which made easy what had seemed impossible. Jade Scent's vagina now was about the same size as Fragrance's had been in those days, a circumstance that put Quan in mind of her. His old problem had come to mind, too, and with it his old solution. Placing his penis between her thighs, he gave her vulva such a massaging that the inside began to itch abominably and fluid naturally ran out, after which he felt like a heavily laden boat floated off a sand bar by the spring floods and swept hundreds of miles downstream.

Meanwhile, seeing that he had gone past the gate, Fragrance thought he had lost his way and was using the gap between her thighs as a vulva, and she began to giggle.

"What are you *doing* down there?" she asked.

"Making love. Surely you know *that*?"

"No, I'm afraid you're doing it wrong. *We* never used to do it that way."

"It's perfectly all right. You must have been doing it wrong. This will bring you pleasure, believe me."

After he had thrust for a while, the inside of her thighs began to feel slippery and Quan knew that the spring floods had arrived. Worried that the fluid would now make things so slippery that he would slide off somewhere else instead of entering her, he parted her legs, caught one of her hands, and put his penis into it.

"You're right," he said, "I was doing it all wrong before and now I can't find the right place. Please show me."

Jade Scent drew up her vulva and placed the glans directly over it. "Now it's in the right place. Give it a try, then I'll let go."

"Wait a moment," said Quan. "Hold on until it's inside the gate."

Jade Scent knew what she was about, and when he said this, she used the other hand as well, encircling his penis with both hands like an outer wall to make sure it entered. Quan thrust forward, beginning at the outer wall and then gradually penetrating a fraction further each time until, after twenty or more thrusts, that penis of his, over eight inches long and too large to be grasped in the hand, had entered all the way.

Observing that he was an expert in sexual technique, Jade Scent felt even more loving. Clasping him tightly, she asked, "Dearest one, how is it you're so sophisticated when you've had no experience with women? My husband had affairs and went to brothels all the time, and yet he was never as gentle and considerate as you are. Oh, I could love you to death!"

Receiving this accolade so soon after assuming his duties, Quan naturally redoubled his efforts. This was no time to rest on his laurels. He feared she would scorn him as weak if he thrust too slowly and as violent if he went too fast, so he proceeded neither too fiercely nor too gently, neither too slowly nor too fast, until she was totally incapable of uttering a word of praise, let alone an accolade—at which point he stopped. Jade Scent had never in her life experienced such a thrill. From then on nothing would do but that he come to her every night.

At first they kept Ruyi in ignorance, but then it occurred to them that they could not go on doing so forever and that they might as well tell her now and act openly. Fearing she might be jealous, Jade Scent went to great lengths to make up to her. In name they were mistress and maid, but in fact they were more like wife and concubine. Sometimes one of them slept with him all night and at other times they shared him, changing places at midnight. And there were even a few festive occasions when they all slept together, and Quan, unsure who was the mistress and who the maid, would cry out *darling* indiscriminately on reaching his climax.

His original motive had been revenge. He had hoped to seduce Jade Scent, sleep with her for a few months, and then leave. He could not afford to become captivated and waste his powers so badly with constant sex that she would be the one taking revenge. But it is always hard to free ourselves from a predestined enemy. He had slept several years with Fragrance without having any children, but the very first time he slept with Jade Scent, she became pregnant. She did not realize it at first, but after two or three months she began to suffer morning sickness and knew well enough. They tried desperately to find a medicine that would induce a miscarriage, but without success.

"My death will be on your head," sobbed Jade Scent. "You know the kind of man my father is. A word out of place, and he rants and raves. You surely don't imagine he'll let me get away with something as bad as this? When he finds out, I'll die anyway. Far better to die now and spare myself the agony." She tried to hang herself then and there, while Quan pleaded with her to stop.

"If you want me to go on living," she retorted, "you'll have to think of a plan to get me away from here to some distant place where we can escape all our troubles and live together as husband and wife. Furthermore the child I'm carrying, whether it's a boy or a girl, is your flesh and blood, too, and if we can get away, it won't have to be drowned at birth. You'll be saving two lives, not just one. Well, what do you say?"

Quan recognized the force of her argument and agreed. At first they were going to leave Ruyi in the dark, but they feared she might find out about their plans and reveal them, so they had to include her. They packed up their most necessary clothes, waited until Master Iron Door was asleep, and then opened the main gate and fled. But if you are wondering where they went and what became of them, you will have to read on until you come to Chapter Eighteen.

CRITIQUE

On finishing this chapter some readers will charge the author with bias, claiming that his retribution is inconsistent with respect to exhortation and admonition. Whereas Vesperus, as an adulterer, deserves to have a wanton for a wife, Master Iron Door, as a virtuous man, does not deserve a daughter who elopes. If the Lord of Heaven is going to admonish us against vice, surely he will also exhort us to virtue!

You are mistaken, say I. This type of requital does indeed demonstrate the Lord's infallibility. During the course of his life, Master Iron Door never makes a single friend, or even meets anyone—behavior that can only be described as misanthropic. And on top of that there is the evil of his stinginess. Take, for example, such harsh and mean-spirited actions as allowing his tenants only one year rent-free on new land, when custom dictates three years, and constantly calling his tenants in to do his household chores for no pay. How can he be allowed to escape ultimate retribution? That is why the man who holds himself aloof will not flourish in the long run. When carried to extremes, such aloofness results in an untold amount of misanthropic behavior and harsh, mean-spirited rule, which is why the man who holds himself aloof offends against Heavenly tranquillity and does not flourish. This is a matter to which the superior man should pay careful attention. If the author punishes vice, but does so too gently, how are people ever going to learn? The traditional advice on reading—that we consider a book in all its aspects, not just one—applies in this case.

CHAPTER FIFTEEN

Three allies gallantly discuss nocturnal revels,
And two sisters evenly divide a night of pleasure.

Lyric:

So swift, alas, the springtime night!
Of the lords of time I ask a boon.
I'll trade ten thousand white-jade suns
For a single, pearl-bright moon.

It hangs afar, like a flowered mirror,
And lights pink cheeks and raven hair.
If no one stirs, we'll lie here still,
And the pain of parting never bear.

The full story of Honest Quan's vengeance is not yet over, but
the greater part of it has been told, and the rest will be given

after a brief interval. Let us now take up again the merry tale of Vesperus's triumphs. We may as well let him carry his enjoyments to the limit before they come back to confound him.

That night, as he held Cloud in his arms, he learned that all three beauties were her relatives and that the two younger ones were particularly close to her. But the night was short and every moment precious because of their desire to make love, so he never did ask the women's names, their husbands' sobriquets, or where they lived. Not until his visit the next night did he make good the omission.

"The one I call Aunt," said Cloud, "was born on Flowers' Birthday and was given the name Floral Dawn. Because she is our aunt and older than we are, we can't very well use her personal name, so we call her Aunt Flora. When her husband died ten years ago, she wanted very much to remarry but was prevented from doing so by the birth of her husband's posthumous child, and so she has had to remain a widow.

"The ones I call sister are married to two brothers, nephews of Aunt Flora's. The elder girl is named Lucky Pearl, the younger one Lucky Jade. Lucky Pearl's husband is Scholar Cloud-Reposer, Lucky Jade's Scholar Cloud-Recliner. Although all three families live in separate houses, the houses are so interconnected it is as if they shared a common gateway, where they are constantly running into one another. I'm the only one who lives apart, but even I am only a few doors away. At least we all live on the same lane. When you and I met yesterday, I thought you must have moved here on their account and then waited a full six months before calling on me, which is why I got so angry with you. How was I to know you'd had nothing to do with them?"

At this news Vesperus became even more jubilant. He recalled the Knave's telling him about two sisters from a rich and distinguished family who were married to two brothers, and the brothers' sobriquets happened to match these. Obviously, a thief's eye is like a libertine's; it misses nothing.

"Yesterday you were so kind as to promise your sisters to me," he said. "I wonder when I'll be allowed to meet them?"

"It won't be long now. In three or four days I shall have to go over and explain matters, after which I'll take you to meet them. There's just one thing I should mention, though. Once I'm over there, I shan't be coming back here again. We'll not be making love in this bed anymore."

Vesperus was astonished. "Why is that? No sooner do I move in than you move out to avoid me!"

"There's a perfectly good reason for it. If I'm over there, you can come and see me anytime, and while visiting me you can visit them too. Two birds with one stone! You've nothing to worry about."

"I simply don't understand a word you're saying. Kindly explain."

"Well, my husband, as you know, is a tutor in their husbands' family, and both men are students of his. Their writing is poor, and they're afraid of the triennial examination they will have to face as licentiates, so they've bought places in the Academy, and are about to set off for the capital. Since they can't get along without their teacher, my husband has to go too. He's worried that I'll have no one to look after me while he's away and wants me to live with their families. I shall need to move within the next few days. That's why I won't be back again. We'll just have to meet over there."

At this news Vesperus's joy was redoubled. It was as if the Heavenly powers had put themselves out to please him, sending the three husbands off on a journey and bringing their three wives together in one place where he could indulge his every erotic desire with complete license.

In a few days, as Cloud had said, the teacher and his students departed, and she at once moved into the other house.

Her move came at the height of her affair with Vesperus, and she could not bear to be parted from him for long. She knew that somehow she would have to reveal her secret if she was to get her sisters' agreement to bring him over for sex. Her motivation was seventy percent self-interest, thirty percent altruism.

"Have you ever been back to the temple to burn incense?" she asked, after exchanging a few pleasantries with her sisters.

"No, we went there only once," said Lucky Jade. "Why would we want to burn incense all the time?"

"With such a handsome man kowtowing to you, a visit every few days would hardly be too much."

"We'd like to, but we have no fans to give him, and we wouldn't want to go empty-handed."

"Stop making fun of me, sister," said Cloud. "I got nothing in return for my fan, I know that. And although you may have gotten a few bows, I never saw any sign of him following you home. All he likes to do is perform a few meaningless kowtows and get you to fall in love with him."

"You never spoke a truer word," said Lucky Jade. "We were just talking about that incident, and there's one thing we still don't understand. Why did he fade away like that after such a brave beginning? From the crazy way he carried on, you got the impression he couldn't wait until the next day but would come over that very night. We waited and waited, but there was no sign of him. If he's so heartless, why did he bother to kowtow in the first place?"

"I've heard that he spends all his time longing for you, but is frustrated because he doesn't know where to find you."

"It may not be the two of us he's longing for. I suspect he's lovesick from looking at the fan and thinking of the one who gave it to him."

"He did feel lovesick over the fan, it's true. But fortunately the sickness was not deep-rooted and has yielded to treatment, and the account has now been settled. But as for his lovesickness over the kowtowing, that is a very serious matter indeed, and will take time to cure. If he dies of it, I'm afraid you two may have to answer with your lives."

This remark struck Lucky Pearl and Lucky Jade as highly suspicious, and they peered closely at Cloud to observe her expression. She did seem to have a supercilious air about her as she talked and laughed.

"You're looking so smug," they said in unison. "Don't say you caught him and settled accounts for the fan?"

"You're not far wrong. And I did it behind your backs."

At this the sisters resembled nothing so much as two failed candidates for the provincial examinations meeting a newly successful one—a mixture of humiliation and envy.

"Well, congratulations!" they said, forcing smiles to their faces. "You've given us a new brother-in-law to be proud of! But when do we celebrate?"

This last remark carried three distinct implications: jealousy, ridicule, and the suspicion that Cloud might not have caught him, after all, but be indulging in a little leg-pulling at their expense. If so, they thought, she would surely be disconcerted when they challenged her claim.

But Cloud was not in the least abashed; if anything, she was more smug than ever. "You may not have celebrated yet, but there will certainly be a wedding reception," she said. "One day I'll give a party and invite you both."

"In that case," said Lucky Jade, "where *is* our new brother-in-law? Would you permit us to see him?"

Cloud prevaricated. "You've already seen him once. You've even been kowtowed to! Why do you need to see him again?"

"He was a total stranger then, and although he did kowtow to us, we weren't able to respond. But now that he's related to us, why shouldn't we see him again? Let us return his bows, address him as brother-in-law, and show him a little affection, for your sake."

"There's no problem in meeting him," said Cloud. "I'll have him over any time it suits you. What worries me, though, is that when he sees you, he may go crazy the way he did before and offend you both with his bad behavior. For that reason it might be best if you didn't meet."

"On that occasion he had no one to keep him in check," replied Lucky Jade, "so he went wild. But now that he has a jealous woman like you in front of him, he won't dare let himself go."

Lucky Pearl turned to her sister. "You're wasting your breath," she said. "She can't bear to have anyone else meet her beloved. When we took our vow of sisterhood, although she promised to share and share alike, she doesn't keep her promises. She'll share her bad luck, yes, but not her good luck. You'll be doing well if you can get her not to act jealous and keep raking up that kowtowing business. It's no use hoping for anything more."

Cloud could see they were upset, so she dropped her bantering tone and became serious. "Now don't get upset. I'm not like that at all. If I'd wanted to keep him to myself, I could have stayed home and enjoyed myself day and night instead of moving in with you. Why move house just to get jealous? The very fact that I told you about him shows my good intentions. Provided we can arrive at some fair and impartial arrangement, so that we remain on good terms after the introduction, I'll bring him over to meet you."

"If you're willing to do that," said Lucky Jade, "it would really give some meaning to our vow. Let's ask you to set the rules and we'll abide by them. There's no need for any discussion."

"I was the first to meet him," said Cloud, "and also the first to sleep with him. By rights I ought to be in the position of a wife as compared with a concubine, or a senior as compared with a junior, and enjoy extra privileges, getting half his time while you two divide the rest. But we're such close friends that I'd be loath to take that line. We don't need to consider any other options, let's just go by seniority. Whether we're enjoying ourselves by day or by night, we'll proceed from senior to junior. We mustn't get in each other's way like the boy of Que Village who 'presumed to sit with his seniors and walk abreast of them.'[74] And in all we say and do, let's give each other a little grace. Someone younger mustn't be too bumptious and try to show up her elders with things she may be better at. The new friendships mustn't get so close as to weaken the old one, making me feel like the fish that got thrown back in the river. If we can stick to this rule, we'll get on well together without quarreling. Agreed?"

Lucky Pearl and Lucky Jade assented in unison: "Your reasoning is absolutely fair. The one thing that worried us was that you might not be willing to share him. Of course we agree."

"In that case get me some notepaper and I'll call him over."

The sisters were jubilant. One fetched the paper while the other ground up the ink. Cloud picked up the brush and wrote two lines:

The female companions of Mount Tiantai,
Are waiting for Liu, their pact complete.[75]

---

74. A reference to Confucius's bumptious messenger boy. See *The Analects*, p. 131.

75. The reference is to the "Tale of Immortals" (*Shenxian zhuan*); see the *Taiping guangji*, 61. This tale, which belongs to a common type, tells how two young men, Liu and Ruan, meet and fall in love with two divine maidens. It is a leitmotif that runs through Vesperus's encounter with the three young women and signals the fact that this part of the novel belongs

She then threw down the brush, folded the note several times, and placed it in the container.

"Why did you write only two lines?" asked Lucky Jade. "You haven't finished it either. What kind of poetry is that?"

"I know what she has in mind," said Lucky Pearl. "She can't bear to make him exert himself, so she saves him the trouble of writing a letter by giving him a couplet to complete." She turned to Cloud. "You're head over heels in love!"

Smiling, Cloud sealed the container, gave it to a maid, and told her to throw it through the gap in the wooden wall of her room and wait there for a reply. Once the maid had left, the three women resumed their discussion.

"Tell me," asked Lucky Pearl, "what method did you use to get him to your place? And how many nights did you sleep with him?"

Cloud told them that he lived next door, had removed part of the wooden wall, and would come over at night and not leave until dawn. She said that they had slept together several nights.

"Well, and what is his ability like, as compared with your husband's?" asked Lucky Jade.

"Speaking of that, well, it's simply adorable! You've seen only his looks, which are unequaled, true, but which an artist or sculptor might conceivably capture. But his endowment is a priceless treasure of a kind that no woman has ever heard of, let alone seen."

Pearl and Jade became more and more excited and bombarded her with questions, like candidates for an examination buttonholing a friend outside the hall and asking him about the paper: How large? How long? From the classics? Were

---

to a different order of reality. The reference to sesame in Vesperus's reply is from the same tale.

candles supplied?[76] They wanted answers to all these questions.

The meal was over, but the dishes had not been cleared away. Cloud felt she could never describe the object successfully without giving an illustration. When asked how long, she picked up an ivory chopstick and replied, "The length of this chopstick." When asked how thick, she picked up a teacup and replied, "The size of this teacup." When asked how hard, she pointed to a bowl of bean curd and replied, "As hard as that bean curd," a reply that sent her listeners into fits of laughter.

"In that case it's awfully soft," they said. "What's the use of its being so big if it's like bean curd?"

"You're wrong there," said Cloud. "There is nothing in the world that's harder then bean curd. It's harder than metal, for metal, hard as it is, melts on contact with fire, whereas bean curd gets harder and harder the longer it's exposed to heat. That object of his is the same, it gets harder with sex, not softer, which is why I compared it to bean curd."

"We don't believe such a treasure exists," said the sisters. "You're overdoing it."

"Far from it. I haven't even told you all of its strengths. It has two other marvelous qualities apart from those I have mentioned, but if I tried to describe them, you'd be even more skeptical. You'll just have to wait until you're having sex with him and can experience them yourselves."

"Do tell us," chorused the sisters. "Never mind whether we believe you."

But Cloud was not about to reveal his qualities so easily. She let the sisters become more and more agitated before

---

76. *Chu jing*, as well as meaning *come from the classics*, is a pun on *emit semen* and *put forth strength*. Candles presumably refer to Dousing the Candle.

finally giving them a systematic account of Vesperus's ability to get larger and hotter, an account that stirred up the sisters' passions and brought a flush to their cheeks and ears. They longed for him to walk in that very moment so that they could drag him off to bed without a word of greeting and put his extraordinary talents to the test. Unfortunately the maid had still not returned, although she had been gone a long time.

The reason for the delay was that Vesperus was not at home. The maid waited inside Cloud's room, where she was spotted by Satchel, who climbed through the gap in the wooden wall and had a long and heavy session with her. When Vesperus returned, she threw the letter over and received his reply, which she duly brought back.

The three women squeezed together to read it. They saw that he had understood Cloud's intention and, instead of writing a letter, had merely added a second couplet:

All prepared is the sesame food;
Restrain your hunger when we meet.

Now that their night's pleasure was assured, the sisters were eager to go in and arrange their beds, fold the covers, bathe and perfume themselves, and await his lovemaking. Cloud stopped them.

"Don't run away so quickly. Let's get tonight's order settled now, lest we make a spectacle of ourselves with a scramble at the last minute."

Lucky Pearl was well aware that Cloud, having slept with him several nights, ought to give up her place, in which case it would be her turn; this was no time to apply the seniority rule. Instead of saying this, however, she gave a calculated display of deference. "But you set the rules just now, from senior to junior, and it goes without saying that you'll be first. What is there left to discuss?"

"By rights we ought to do it like that," said Cloud, "but a different principle should apply tonight. As the saying goes, 'He who enters first is host, he who enters last is guest.' I've slept with him several nights already and would have to be considered the host. Let's use the host–guest principle tonight and switch to the seniority system after you've both slept with him. That's definitely the right solution, so let's have no false modesty. There's just one question still to be settled: with me out of consideration, he should naturally begin with Pearl. But are you going to take a whole night each or will you divide the night between you? Talk it over and let me know."

But the sisters just looked at one another and said nothing. "We're too embarrassed," said Lucky Pearl after some time. "You're the eldest, you decide."

"A whole night is more satisfying," said Cloud, "but it would be hard on the one who has to wait. It might be better if you took half the night each."

She offered this as a suggestion only, because she wanted them to accept it before she converted it into a ruling. To her surprise, each of them had reservations that she could not bring herself to express. Again neither said anything.

"I know what your silence means," said Cloud. "The one who goes first is afraid he won't put himself out for her but will reserve his strength for the second party, so she won't agree. And the one who goes last is afraid she'll get someone who has shot his bolt and lost his edge, so she won't agree. Let me put it to you straight: he is a match for several women."

She turned first to Lucky Pearl. "Even if you have him the whole night, you'll still get only half a night of the real thing. Well before midnight comes around I'm afraid you'll beg to be excused. You'll end up handing him on anyway."

Then she turned to Lucky Jade. " 'The wine affects the last guest to arrive just as much as the first,' as the saying goes. Moreover, his particular winepot tastes especially good toward the bottom. There's no need for you to be suspicious of each other, so let's do it that way."

Now that she had guessed their thoughts, the sisters resolved their doubts and agreed: "We'll do as you say."

The arrangements complete, Cloud told a maid to stand by the door. They hadn't long to wait before Vesperus was ushered in.

As he entered, the sisters affected a maidenly confusion and withdrew a step or two, leaving Cloud to receive him. Vesperus gave a deep bow in greeting her, then straightened up. "Please ask the young ladies to come forward and be introduced," he said. Cloud led them forward to meet him, gripping one girl's arm with each hand.

After the introductions Lucky Pearl called to the maid to bring tea. "There's no need to order tea," said Cloud. "He's been longing for you two so badly that he's quite bitter, so give him some of the nectar in your mouths instead of tea." As she spoke, she took the girls' hands and placed them in Vesperus's. Embracing both girls, Vesperus popped his tongue first into Lucky Pearl's mouth and let her suck it and then into Lucky Jade's and let her do the same. Then he brought all three mouths together to form the character *pin*,[77] after which he took both tongues into his own mouth and sucked them.

It was getting late and Lucky Jade was worried lest her time with him be delayed, so she hurried out to the kitchen and urged the maids to get supper on the table.

"Let's go to bed," said Vesperus. "It's late."

"But we haven't had our sesame food yet," said Lucky Pearl. "How can you talk of bed?"

"I drank your nectar just now. That will do nicely instead."

---

77. The character *pin* consists of three mouths in close conjunction.

They were still joking as the food was brought in. Vesperus sat in the place of honor, with Cloud opposite him and Pearl and Jade on either side. They had finished their supper and were about to clear the dishes away when Vesperus pulled Cloud aside.

"Tell me, what are the sleeping arrangements for tonight?" he asked.

"I've settled it all for you," she said. "The first half of the night you'll be with Pearl, the second with Jade."

"And what about yourself?"

"Oh, I'll take the middle half," said Cloud, dissembling. "That'll be fine, too."

"That *too* sounds a little odd. You're surely not implying that I'm being unfair, like someone who keeps the middle part of the fish for himself and leaves the head and tail to others, so that they complain of getting all the bones! In that case why not put all your energy into the first and last parts and cut back in the middle?"

"I wouldn't dream of it. What worries me is that my time will be frittered away running to and fro. Let me ask you your opinion: Wouldn't it be better if we all slept together?"

"I know what you have in mind! You're not worried about the toing and froing, you're simply too greedy to part with either of them. You want to do as you did just now when you kissed together, except that underneath the *pin* you want to draw a *chuan*.[78] I've no doubt we'll get around to that later, but this is your first meeting and you mustn't try it yet. I was having you on just now. I'm quite content to withdraw for the night and let them enjoy themselves. You're to keep to the order I mentioned and sleep with Pearl the first half of the

78. The character *chuan* consists of two circles bisected by a straight line.

night and with Jade the last half. You'll have to be on your mettle to live up to everything I've told them about you."

"No need to remind me. But it's going to be rather hard on you."

Cloud summoned a maid to bring a lantern and take Vesperus and Lucky Pearl to the latter's room. She herself was concerned that Lucky Jade might be upset, so she chatted with her a while before going to bed.

Vesperus and Lucky Pearl undressed each other, then climbed on to her ivory-inlaid bed and began their sport. It was difficult at first. Pearl found the pain too much to bear, but fortunately she knew from all the marvelous things she had heard that her subsequent pleasure would amply reward her for the pain she was feeling, and that in fact there was no way to get the pleasure except by suffering the pain. So she gritted her teeth and bore his onslaught. Wanting to put his priceless treasure to the test, she was constantly on the watch for it to swell and heat up and was thus far more aware of its size and temperature than another woman would have been. Eventually, as he worked, it did swell and heat up, like some enormous Mr. Horn filled with boiling water and jammed inside her. Even if he had not moved at all, simply left it there, she would have felt pleasure, but how infinitely more pleasurable it was with his rapid, lively movement! At last she realized that the account she had been given was not hyperbole and that the term priceless treasure was a fitting sobriquet for it.

Clasping Vesperus tightly, she gave him a couple of playful taps. "My dearest, your looks must have driven thousands of women to their deaths of unrequited love! How ever did you come to possess such a priceless treasure as well? Do you want to drive every woman in the world to her death?"

"Only by *doing* someone to death can you make her die of love. Dearest girl, are you willing to sacrifice your life and let me do you to death?"

"Now that I've met this fierce creature, do you think I want to go on living? But let me do it a few more times first, and then I'll die content. Don't dispatch me on the first occasion!"

"Tonight," said Vesperus, "my time is divided between you and your sister. So even if you die, you'll still be only half dead, and I don't suppose I shall be accused of murder. But who knows what tomorrow night or the night after will bring?"

With that he began a series of earthshaking thrusts. Although Pearl's vagina was deep, the heart of the flower was extremely shallow, and he needed to penetrate only an inch or two before touching and teasing it, so that every thrust hit the mark. After several hundred thrusts she was in a desperate state and kept crying out, "Dearest, I'm not just half dead, I'm completely dead! Have mercy!"

But Vesperus, who was intent on displaying his prowess, took no notice of her cries and thrust with undiminished vigor from the first watch to the second, by which time her arms and legs were limp and her breath had grown cold. Realizing she was not a strong opponent, he stopped, clasped her tightly in his arms, and slept.

Pearl awoke after a brief sleep. "Dear one, how is it you're so capable? If I die, my death will be on your head, I need hardly say. But you'd better go now; my sister is expecting you."

"It's pitch-dark outside," said Vesperus, "and I'll never be able to find my way. Dearest, won't you get up and take me over?"

"I'm so limp from your lovemaking that I can't even move. I'll get a maid to show you."

She called one of her maids out of bed to lead Vesperus over. The maid was a fourteen- or fifteen-year-old virgin who had been aroused to fever pitch by overhearing their earthshaking activity and had emitted a good deal of fluid in the process. Now, with Vesperus's hand in hers, and under cover of darkness, she was not going to let him escape. When they came to a secluded spot, she halted.

"How can you be so cruel," she said, "as not to let me taste any of those sweets you gave my mistress? As the saying goes, 'Passing by the paddy fields, you don't worry about drought.' Now that you're at *my* customs checkpoint, you surely wouldn't try to slip through without paying your dues?" Winding one arm around Vesperus, she took off her trousers with the other.

Vesperus, realizing that she was beside herself with passion, felt he could hardly deny her a turn. He told her to lie on a bench and, after opening her vagina, took out his penis and tried to enter without rubbing any spit on it. The maid, having never been with a man, assumed that his instrument would be a delicious sip of broth, which is why she had halted, her only fear being that he might not agree to her demand. Little did she realize that the delicious sip would prove to be a cupful of hard liquor. Someone who has never tasted mustard will start coughing and choking at the mere smell of it, and she began to scream as soon as she saw him about to thrust. Vesperus realized that her seal was still intact, and he rubbed a lot of spit on his penis before trying to drive it in. But she began screaming again. "It's no good," she said. "If it's like this, it will be no fun at all. But why should something that brings the mistress such pleasure bring me nothing but pain?"

Vesperus explained that it was necessary on the first occasion to break the skin and cause a little bleeding, but that after ten or twenty times she might expect to enjoy the experience. "My endowment is much too large for you," he said, trying to console her, "but I have a young page called Satchel, and his is still quite small. Why don't I bring him over tomorrow and let him do it with you a few times before I try again?"

The maid thanked him profusely, then got up, fastened her trousers, and took him the rest of the way.

Lucky Jade's quarters were brilliantly lit up. She was waiting for him and, on hearing footsteps outside, told a maid to open the door and show him in.

"Dearest," said Vesperus, approaching her bed, "I know I'm late. Please don't be cross."

"You might just as well have stayed there the whole night," she said. "Why put yourself to the trouble of coming over here?"

"I'm terribly upset as it is about our having only half the night together. How could I stand a whole night without you?"

By the time these words were out of his mouth, he had completely undressed. He opened the bedclothes, got into bed, and set to. At first, needless to say, Lucky Jade felt a moment's pain, just as Lucky Pearl had done, but when she reached the state of rapture, she gave an impression that was very different from Lucky Pearl's—one of utter desperation. It was a sight to make a man pity her but at the same time want to make love to her all over again. Why was that? She was three or four years younger than Lucky Pearl, and rather slight. There was nothing to compare with her skin for softness and delicacy, and her breasts were like two new-laid, soft-shelled eggs, which the mere weight of a man's body threatened to crush. As for the soft suppleness of her figure, the demure charm of her manner, when she stood outdoors, you feared lest the wind might blow her over, and even when she sat indoors, you felt she needed people beside her to hold her up. How could she endure the wear and tear of actual sex? After a few hundred strokes her eyes were half-closed, her lips were parted, and her heart was choked with things she was too weak to say. She feared that her constitution could not stand the strain and that if he went on much longer, her life would be in danger. Her only hope was that Vesperus would stop thrusting and let her revive.

Vesperus noticed the state she was in and was overcome with pity. "My sweet little darling, can't you bear it anymore?"

She nodded, unable to reply.

Vesperus slipped off to let her recover. He knew she could not endure it if he went on, but he loved her too much to stop. In the end all he could do was take her in his arms and draw her on top of him, in which manner, fitted snugly together, they slept until dawn.

Cloud and Lucky Pearl arose early and, with a view to working out a long-term plan with Vesperus, visited Lucky Jade's bedroom to urge him out of bed. On opening the screen, they found Lucky Jade sprawled on top of him and awoke them both.

"We won't need any candles when we light up tonight," they said mockingly.

"If the oil is all used up and there aren't any candles left, don't blame us!" said Lucky Pearl.

After a few more jokes they put their problem to Vesperus. "If you leave every morning and return every night, sooner or later someone is going to notice," they explained. "If you're gone every night, even your own concubine will suspect you of having an affair and try to find out about it. Can you think of any solution? It would be best if you could stay here a while and not return home even in the daytime. If we could be together, we wouldn't necessarily have to make love all the time. It would be fun to play chess, write poetry, tell jokes. Do you happen to have some brilliant scheme that would bring all this about?"

"Before I came over," said Vesperus, "I put the most marvelous plan into effect. I didn't leave everything until now."

"What is that?" they asked.

"My concubine is pregnant and can't sleep with me any-more. I spoke to her yesterday and suggested that since I've been away from home a long time, it might be a good idea if I made a return visit during her pregnancy. The whole journey need take only three months, which would bring me back in time for the delivery and free me from having to go home afterward, at a time when we could be enjoying our-selves. She said it made good sense to her. On my return to the house this time, I'll pack up and set off with one of my pages, making as if to return home but actually coming over here. During these next three months we'll not only write poems, play chess, and tell jokes, we'll even have time to put on [*chuan*] some plays."

The three women jumped for joy. "It's such a brilliant scheme, not even Chen Ping could have thought it up!"[79]

"There's one other thing I need to discuss with you. I have two pages, one a bit naive, the other rather smart. I'm going to leave the naive one at home and bring the smart one with me. But the trouble with this lad is that he has his master's ways about him—he's sex-crazy. If we don't let him have a piece of the pie, he'll get restless and want to go back, which will only lead to trouble. What can you suggest?"

"That's simple," said Lucky Pearl. "We have plenty of maids, and we'll just give him one at bedtime and let him enjoy himself. It will serve to tie him down and also stop up the maids' mouths and prevent them from tattling when our hus-bands get back."

"Good idea," said Vesperus. Their arrangements made, the women saw him off. That same evening he returned with his bags.

---

79. A famous strategist who aided in the founding of the Han dynasty.

From then on, not only did Vesperus lie down drunk amid the flowers and savor every erotic delight, even his page turned into a miniature version of Lin Bu, who was surrounded by his plum-blossom wives until he almost died of the accumulated scent.[80]

Alas, one day the beauties of spring will fade in the old garden and thoughts of the past will be too painful to bear.

CRITIQUE

Far from feeling jealous of her sworn sisters, Cloud was prepared to share the man she loved with her kindred spirits. Immoral as her conduct may have been, it has much to commend it as an act of friendship. If you look for comparable behavior among men, you won't find any. Nowadays the projects that sworn brothers embark on may not be entirely moral, either, but the spirit of envy is even stronger among them than among outsiders. What a lucky thing such men were not born as women! As women they would have gone to extremes and not rested until they had run the gamut of debauchery.

---

80. A reclusive poet (A.D. 967–1028). He never married, but grew plum trees and raised cranes, calling the plum trees his wives and the cranes his children. Note that one term for a maidservant is *meixiang*: *plum fragrance*.

CHAPTER *SIXTEEN*

Real enjoyment comes to grief at midpoint,
As a human erotic album is seized in its trunk.

Poem:
> Her suffering heart belies the spring,
> As she works the silk with another thread.
> The needle breaks at the lovebird scene—
> And the joy in her picture is also dead.

The women hid Vesperus in their house, and each of them slept
with him for one night, in order of seniority, after which the
rotation began again, all without discord. After several rota-
tions, Vesperus added a new rule entitled the "Thrice Alone
Once Together Coordinated System": after sleeping with him
individually for three nights, they were to sleep with him
collectively for a night before returning to the rotation.

Thanks to this new rule, they were able to experience the joys of togetherness.

Once the rule was established, they set up another, extrawide bed and made for it a five-foot-long pillow and a coverlet sewn from six widths of material. When they slept together, Vesperus would get the three sisters to lie side by side, while he himself rolled here and there from body to body, never touching the bed, but making love wherever he fancied as he worked his way from one side to the other. Luckily none of the women possessed a great deal of sexual stamina, and after thrusts ranging in number from one hundred to two hundred, they would want to spend. When the woman in the middle had spent, he would move to the one on the left, and when she had spent, he would turn to her neighbor on the right. A few hours sufficed to complete his main task. The rest of the time he liked to spend fondling their soft charms and savoring their fragrance. The bliss that was now his had been enjoyed in the past, even among emperors, by only a handful of epicures such as Xuanzong of the Tang, Yangdi of the Sui, and the Last Ruler of the Chen. Since all of the other, more straitlaced emperors had never enjoyed it, think how remote it was from the experience of some licentiate too poor to keep wife or concubine!

Shortly after Vesperus moved in, Cloud held a secret conclave with her sisters. "It's a marvelous piece of luck having this immortal, this treasure, here for our enjoyment," she said. "My only concern is that the best things in life always come to grief. At the height of success one ought to be constantly on guard against failure. We mustn't let any outsider know, or the news will spread. Then he'd have to leave, and that might be very awkward."

"This house is out of the way," said Lucky Pearl, "and we don't have any casual visitors, so what goes on in here will never be known outside. Even our own stewards have to wait beyond the inner gate, and we simply won't let them in. No, it's not men I'm worried about, it's a certain woman who lives nearby. If *she* ever finds out, the fun will be over."

"Who do you mean?" asked Lucky Jade.

"Someone with the same surname was ours. Don't you know?"

"Aunt Flora?"

"Who else? You know what an oversexed creature she is. She may be a widow, but men are constantly on her mind. What's more, she was with us that day at the temple, and when he kowtowed, she went crazy, too, as if she'd have liked to kneel down and kowtow along with him if only she weren't too embarrassed. What a performance she gave! When we got home, she praised his looks to the skies and said what a pity it was she didn't know his name, because if she did, she'd never let him get away. If someone as lusty as that learns we have him tucked away over here and are having such a good time with him, do you suppose she won't get envious and set a trap for us? Something awful is bound to happen—apart altogether from the fact that the fun will be over."

"You're absolutely right. She's terribly devious. We'll just have to take precautions."

"But what should we do?" asked Lucky Jade.

"I used to worry that the maids might leak the news," said Lucky Pearl, "but now that they have Satchel to keep them quiet, I doubt that they'll be inclined to gossip. So I'm not worried that she'll *hear* about Vesperus, only that she'll notice him. When she comes over, she'll suddenly sneak into the room without warning, her eyes darting about like a thieving rat's, as if we were up to something behind her back. The key thing in defending ourselves against her is to have the maids take turns keeping watch along the border between the houses. When they see her coming, they should give a secret signal, a cough, say, or a shout, to allow us time to hide our man.

The other thing we have to do is think of some hiding place where she won't find him."

"What would be the best place?" asked Lucky Jade.

The three women exchanged ideas. One suggested he hide behind the door; another suggested under the bed.

"No, neither place will do," said Lucky Pearl. "Those thief's eyes of hers are awfully sharp, and they'll spot someone behind a door or under a bed in a flash. In my opinion there's just one place you could put him where even an immortal would never think of looking."

"Where do you mean?" asked the other two.

Lucky Pearl pointed to a piece of furniture, a trunk used for storing old paintings. It was more than six feet long, two feet wide, and over three feet high and was covered in bamboo fabric stretched over thin wooden slats. "That would be ideal," she said, "not too long nor too wide, but just big enough for a man to lie down in. If we empty out all the paintings, we can hide him in there in an emergency and she'll never suspect a thing. My only concern is that he may suffocate, but if we knock out a couple of slats, he should be all right."

"Brilliant! Let's do that," said the others. They told the maids to take turns on lookout duty and then knocked a few slats out of the trunk. They also told Vesperus that anytime he saw a strange woman coming, he should lie down inside the trunk and keep absolutely quiet. After the plan was put into operation, their aunt made several visits, but the maids gave the secret signal, Vesperus disappeared inside the trunk, and she noticed nothing.

But there was trouble in store for the sisters. One day they found a notebook in Vesperus's cardcase and, on opening it, saw that it contained the names of a number of women who were classified into categories and evaluated in critical comments. The notebook was in Vesperus's handwriting.

"When did you see these women?" they asked. "And when

did you write this? And what was the point of it?"

"Oh, I did that while I was living in the temple," said Vesperus. "I made those notes as I observed the visitors to the temple. My idea was to compile a list from which I would select a few brilliant prospects for intensive cultivation."

"Well, and did you find your brilliant prospects?"

Vesperus folded his hands in salutation. "Behold, my three pupils."

They laughed. "We don't think we deserve *that* kind of evaluation. You just made that up on the spur of the moment."

"There's no need to be so suspicious," said Vesperus. "I have the poems to prove it." He looked up their rankings and evaluations and showed them. After a careful scrutiny, they began to swell with pride. The praise might be a little overdone, they allowed, but at least it was apt, not general criticism of the one-size-fits-all kind.

Only Cloud was less than joyful, because his comments on her were a little shorter than those on her sisters. Fortunately Vesperus had taken precautions. Fearing she might see the entry, he had added another circle to the two she already had, raising her from a *magna* to a *summa*. As a result, although her evaluation was less detailed than the others', Cloud was at least in the same class, and she was not too disappointed.

But when the sisters turned the page and found a Black Belle whose evaluation was every bit as high as Lucky Pearl's and Lucky Jade's and rather higher than Cloud's, they were astonished.

"Where does this beauty come from? What makes *her* so gorgeous?"

"She's the one who came to the temple with you," said Vesperus. "You remember."

Lucky Pearl burst into laughter. "You mean *that* old baggage! At her age and with her looks, it's sheer blind luck that she got a *summa*, too!"

"If that's the case," said Cloud, "our rankings are more of an insult than an honor, and who wants *that* kind of evaluation? Why don't we just cross them out?"

"There's no need to get upset," said Lucky Jade. "There must be a motive behind his method of selection. He must have heard the story of the old pupil who repaid his examiner's kindness over three generations,[81] so he examined only three candidates and gave us all *summas* without regard to what we wrote, in the hope that we'd repay the favor someday. That would account for you three, all right, but I am by far the youngest and ought to get the lowest class. How is it I have a *summa*, too? Kindly remove my name."

Vesperus wanted to make a clean breast of everything and persuade them that one person's luck rubs off on everyone present, but his three pupils were raising such a commotion that the examiner could not get a word in edgewise.

"Sister Jade, you are absolutely right," said Lucky Pearl, "but although you are the youngest, we're not exactly old, either. I say we remove all of our names and let the old pupil be the sole winner." She picked up the brush, crossed out their names and evaluations, and appended a note of her own:

Huaiyin was youthful, Jiang and Guan venerable.[82] The former would not presume to be ranked with the latter and must respectfully yield.

---

81. The story is Feng Menglong's "The Old Student Repays a Debt of Gratitude Over Three Generations."

82. The allusion is to the Han dynasty general Han Xin, who was "ashamed to be ranked with Jiang and Guan." Jiang was Zhou Bo (enfieffed as Marquis Jiang); Guan was Guan Ying. See Han Xin's biography (*Shi ji*, 92).

Then she turned to Vesperus. "Fortunately this brilliant prospect lives not far from here. You'll find her through that door over there. Do go and give her some cultivation. From now on we three won't be troubling you for any."

Confronted with this display of public indignation, Vesperus could do nothing more than hang his head meekly, acknowledging his bias. Let them drive him out if they wished, he would not say a word.

He waited until they had calmed down a little before trying to win them over with a confession. "In the first place, it was a natural extension of my love for you. Secondly, I wanted to find her and get her to introduce us, so that I could make love to you. That's how I overcame my scruples enough to write those flattering words; it was not an honest evaluation, by any means. I hope you ladies won't judge me too harshly."

At these words the women's indignation began to evaporate, and Vesperus took the opportunity to ingratiate himself further. Undressing first, he lay on the bed waiting for them to join him. They were about to do so, when all of a sudden the maid on guard duty gave an emphatic cough. Recognizing the secret signal, the women began pulling on their clothes again with lightning speed. As soon as they had dressed, Lucky Pearl and Lucky Jade rushed out to receive their visitor, leaving Cloud behind to hide Vesperus. Because he had undressed before the others, his clothes lay underneath theirs. At first he couldn't find them and then, by the time the women had dressed, it was too late for him to dress anyway. There was nothing for it but to climb into the trunk stark naked.

Let us tell now of Flora as she arrived in the main room to be greeted by Lucky Pearl and Lucky Jade. She noticed at once that they looked flustered and that they stood side by side as if barring her way into the bedroom, a fact that only added fuel to her suspicions. Concluding that they had been up to no good, she insisted on storming in to see for herself. But one person's guile is no match for two people's craft, and by the time she reached the bedroom, the live erotic album had been safely locked inside the picture trunk.

In the bedroom Flora made a point of praising her niece. "I've not been in here in quite some time. You've got the place looking nicer than ever." She went first to the head of the bed, then to its foot, and even inspected the cupboards, but she found no telltale signs anywhere and concluded that she must have been unduly suspicious and imagined things. She took a seat and began chatting.

By their quick action the nieces had reduced a potential disaster to a harmless incident, which was fortunate indeed. Little did they realize, however, that in their haste they had overlooked something, and that, one way or another, their secret would soon be out. Flustered by the maid's cough, they had had time only to get dressed and open the trunk. Since their overriding concern had been to stuff their prize inside the trunk, they had neglected a pocket-sized notebook lying on the desk. Only later, while chatting with their aunt, did one of them notice it. She was just reaching for it when Flora, with her sharp eyes, noticed it, too, and snatched it up first. Panic-stricken, the girls tried unsuccessfully to wrest it from her. Then Cloud, realizing they would never get it by force, let it go and affected indifference: "Oh well, it's only a tattered old book we found in the street anyway. Why not let Aunt have it? There's no sense in trying to get it away from her."

"Cloud is really so-o-o generous," said Flora. "A book the size of your hand—it can't be worth very much. So why do we need we to have this tug-of-war over it? Since Cloud has given it to me, let me open it up and see what kind of book it is."

Standing a full ten feet from her nieces, she opened the notebook. From its title, *Garner the Beauties of Spring from Far and Wide*, she assumed it was an erotic album and hastily leafed through it to enjoy the pictures first. To her surprise it contained not a single erotic picture, only a few columns of tiny characters, which she was forced to read. She had read several pages before she realized that the notebook was more interesting than any erotic album; it consisted of evaluations of beautiful women done by some amorous young man of talent. After carefully savoring the evaluations, she came in the end to one of a Black Belle, whose comment read exactly like a pen-portrait of herself, at which point she felt a certain titillation.

Could this have been written by that young man we met at the temple? she wondered. Turning back to the previous page, she saw a note before the names in the last entry that spoke of meeting three peerless beauties on a certain date. After puzzling for some time over the names Pale Rose Maid and Lotus Pink Beauty, Flora gave a sly smile and concluded that the young man was indeed the author. But when she came to the note

> Huaiyin was youthful, Jiang and Guan venerable. The former would not presume to be ranked with the latter and must respectfully yield,

she recognized Lucky Pearl's writing and stopped smiling. Tucking the notebook up her sleeve, she gave a calculated sigh. "What a genius Cang Jie was, to invent the character script for our use!"

"What makes you say that?" asked Cloud.

"There's not a single stroke in any of the characters he invented that does not have its meaning. For instance, the character *jian* in *jianyin (adultery)* is composed of three *nü (woman)* characters. Since you three are living together and committing adultery, you must surely appreciate the brilliance of the invention!"

"We may be living together," said Lucky Jade, "but we've

never done any such thing! How can you *say* that?"

"If you've never done any such thing, where did this notebook come from?"

"I found it in the street on my way over here," said Cloud.

"A two-year-old child wouldn't believe that!" said Flora. "I'll say no more, except to ask you where the man is who wrote this. Confess everything, and you'll hear no more about it. If you don't confess, I shall have to write to your husbands, enclosing this notebook, and summon them home for a little chat with you."

At this ugly tone, her nieces felt they could hardly remain defiant. "We really did find it in the street, and we have no idea of who the writer is or where he lives. What else can we tell you?" they replied meekly.

All the time she interrogated them, Flora was looking around the room. The only place I haven't looked is in that trunk, she thought. It's normally left open, so why is it locked all of a sudden? There must be a reason.

"Since you won't confess," she said to Lucky Pearl and Lucky Jade, "I'll have to suspend my investigation until a later date. But that trunk of yours contains several old paintings I've not seen yet. Would you mind opening it up for me?"

"We've mislaid the key," they replied together. "It hasn't been opened in ages. As soon as we find the key, we'll take out the paintings and send them over."

"That's no problem. I have tons of keys and can open any lock at all. Let me send for them." She gave an order to one of her maids, who returned in a few minutes with several hundred keys. As Flora tried them in the lock, her nieces resembled nothing so much as three corpses. They could not very well protest or prevent her from trying, but they were hoping against hope that the keys would not fit and that the trunk would stay shut.

But fortune favored the enemy. Flora did not need even

the second key, for the first one fit perfectly. Opening the lid and glancing inside, she discovered the smooth, snow-white body of a man across whose thighs lay a flesh-and-blood laundry beater that was woefully limp but still big enough to shock. She could only imagine what it might look like when stiff.

Confronted with such rare merchandise, Flora felt a natural impulse to monopolize it. Without disturbing anything in the trunk, she let down the lid, relocked it, and launched into a tirade. "A fine thing you've been up to, with your husbands away! When did you smuggle him in, I'd like to know? How many dozens of nights has he slept with each one of you? Come on, out with it!"

The women's faces turned ashen with fright, but they said nothing, no matter how she cross-examined them.

"Since you won't confess, I have no choice but to go to the authorities." She told the maids to inform the neighbors that she had caught an adulterer in broad daylight and wanted them to come and attest to the fact, after which the man would be taken to court inside the trunk.

Her nieces withdrew for consultation. "She's bluffing," they said, "but if we don't clear matters up at once, her bluff may turn into reality. We'll have to come to terms with her and give him up for general use. Surely she won't sentence us to death!"

They approached Flora and apologized. "We oughtn't to have carried on behind your back. We know we were wrong and won't try to quibble about it. We simply appeal to your generosity, Aunt, to let the man out of the trunk so that he can confess and ask for clemency."

"And just what form is his confession going to take? I should like to have that settled in advance."

"To be quite candid, Aunt," said Cloud, "we've been dividing his time into three equal shares. We'll be glad to cut you in. In fact, on account of your age we'll give you first place in the roster."

Flora burst into laughter. "A fine penance that is! You keep him hidden away in your house and sleep with him for I don't know how many nights and only now, after you're caught, do you offer me a share! By that logic, when the authorities catch a robber, they wouldn't need to beat or torture him, they could just stipulate that anything he steals in the future will be forfeit while all the things he has already stolen are his to keep."

"Aunt," said Lucky Pearl, "what *ought* we to do, in your opinion?"

"If you want to settle the matter privately," said Flora, "you'll have to let him come back and sleep with me for as long as I like, until I've made up all the arrears due to me, after which I'll hand him back and we'll resume the one-person-a-night rotation. Otherwise we can simply settle it in court, which would mean breaking the family ricepot and letting everybody go hungry. Well, what do you say?"

"If we do that," said Lucky Jade, "you'll have to specify a time limit, three nights or five nights, say, after which you'll release him. You surely don't expect to be given *carte blanche* to keep him for months or even years!"

"I can't specify a time," said Flora. "Let me take him back with me and question him as to how many nights you three have slept with him, and then I'll keep him the same number. After that I'll hand him back and we'll say no more about it."

Although the nieces said nothing, a possibility had occurred to them: Vesperus loves us dearly and may well under-report the number of nights to her. So they agreed. "Well, he's only been here a night or two. Take him off and question him. You'll see."

Now that an agreement had been reached, the nieces were about to open the trunk and let Vesperus out so that he could go back with Flora. She, however, was afraid he might run away, and hesitated. "If he goes over in broad daylight," she said, "the servants may see, and that would look bad. We shall have to think of some way of getting him over in secret."

"Why don't you go back now," her nieces suggested, "and we'll send him over when it gets dark?"

"Don't bother," she said. "I have a better idea. There's no need to unlock the trunk. We'll just pretend it's full of old paintings that belong to me and call in a few stewards to carry it over with the man inside. No problem."

Acting on her own initiative, she told the maids to summon some stewards. Within minutes four men arrived and, hoisting the trunk onto their shoulders, bore it swiftly away.

Pity the three sisters! Their grief was as keen as that of any widow who ever said farewell to a coffin and yet, unlike the widow, they were unable to express it. They couldn't bear to have this live erotic album stolen from them in its trunk, and they were afraid, too, that the man inside would be worked to death by the old bawd. There was a road that led over there, but no road back. Was it not a bad omen that the picture trunk was carried off on men's shoulders like a coffin?

CRITIQUE

After reading the chapter in which they met at the temple, one expected that Flora's pleasure would precede Lucky Pearl's and Lucky Jade's, and that Vesperus's comments on Flora would be the thread that strung the pearls together, the tile that drew the jade in response. Who would ever have imagined that the author's mind would so resemble the Creator's in disposing independently of people and events and confounding all our expectations? The author has taken the woman easiest to seduce and placed her after the ones hardest to seduce, which is remarkable and fantastic in the extreme! He has made the thread that was to have strung the pearls together and the tile that would have drawn the jade in response into the very reasons Pearl and Jade are cast aside. The tempest in the bed-chamber originates in a scene of noisy argument, which again is remarkable and fantastic in the extreme! How unpredictable is the authorial mind!

CHAPTER *SEVENTEEN*

Through others' deception she gains the advantage;
By her own arrogance she suffers abuse.

Poem:
    Let Experience not with Youth contend,
    For fear of arousing the youngsters' spleen.
    You elders will always lose in the end,
    So stand aside and observe the scene.

After the trunk arrived at her house and she had dismissed the
stewards, Flora did not open it immediately, but fetched a suit
of men's clothes from her own boxes, together with a well-
worn cap and a pair of shoes and socks, all of which had
belonged to her late husband, and laid them out. She then
unlocked the trunk and invited the paragon to step forth and

dress, after which they greeted each other and sat down for an intimate talk. As might have been expected, Vesperus's nimble tongue, so adept at deceiving women, invented a lie or two, such as, "After seeing you in the temple, I longed for you day and night, but not knowing your honorable name, had no means of finding you. Fortunately Heaven has vouchsafed me this chance to turn bad luck into good, and now at last I am able to gaze on your fair countenance!"

Having read his comments on her, Flora believed that he really did admire her and she took his lies for the truth and was full of gratitude. She told a maid to prepare lunch, after which they waited impatiently for evening and went to bed.

Although she could not be described as really fat, Flora was undeniably plump. Vesperus had mounted her but barely begun to move when she hugged him tightly, planted a kiss on his lips, and cried, "Dearest!" This was enough to set him tingling all over. He had slept with many women, but had never experienced such a reaction from a hug.

What was the reason? You must understand that there are two categories of women: those for looking at and those for practical purposes. The former are not necessarily suitable for practical purposes, just as the latter are not necessarily good-looking. In all recorded history, there has been just one woman, Yang Guifei, who has managed to combine both qualities.

In general, there are three desiderata of the good-looking woman:

1. Better to be thin than fat
2. Better to be short than tall
3. Better to be weak and delicate than strong and robust

This explains why the women you see in paintings have wisp-like waists and figures too slight to fill out their clothes, and why you never see any plump or robust ones among them: they are there for visual rather than practical purposes.

The practical women are a different species, but for them, too, there are three desiderata:

1. Better to be fat than thin
2. Better to be tall than short
3. Better to be strong and robust than weak and delicate

Why do they need these three qualities? In general when a man lies on top of a woman, the first requirement is that she be as soft as a cushion; the second is that she match his height; and the third is that she be able to bear his weight. A thin woman's figure is like a stone slab, and your whole body aches unbearably just from lying on top of her. A fat woman, by contrast, is soft and tender, and when lying on her, you don't even need to start moving before you feel your body tingling and your spirit in raptures. And she has another marvelous quality, too: she is warm in winter and cool in summer. All of which explains why it is better to be fat than thin.

When you sleep with a short woman, your body cannot meet hers at all points, for if the upper parts fit together nicely, the lower parts do not, and vice versa. Moreover, a body as slight as a child's will stir a man's pity rather than his passion. All of which explains why it is better to be tall than short.

A man may weigh anywhere from seventy or eighty catties to over a hundred, which is a weight that only a strong and robust woman can bear. If you lie on top of a weak and delicate woman, you are on tenterhooks all the time in case you crush her. Sexual enjoyment is entirely dependent on your peace of mind; it cannot survive if you feel nervous. All of which explains why it is better for a woman to be strong and robust than weak and delicate.

Thus good looks and practical usefulness are mutually exclusive. If a woman manages to combine both qualities, she need be only eighty percent beautiful to rate as one hundred and twenty percent, for in such a case how can one insist on perfection?

Although Flora was an older woman, she did combine both qualities. As soon as Vesperus got into bed, she automatically revealed her long suit by clasping his upper body in her soft arms and enveloping his lower body with her soft legs, wrapping him around like a downy quilt. Enjoyable, wouldn't you say? Moreover, her body matched his nicely, and she was also able to bear his weight. The women Vesperus had slept with before had all been on the small, weak, and delicate side and he had never known that this kind of pleasure existed, which is why he felt himself tingling all over before he even set to. Precisely because he found the sensation so delightful, that object down below swelled up to extraordinary proportions, getting longer without penetration and hotter without friction, as if it had thrust dozens of times already. Aligning itself with her vulva, it stabbed its way in.

Flora had already borne a child, and naturally her vagina was large, unlike those of the sisters, who had suffered considerable pain before gradually reaching a state of bliss. But after only ten strokes, she suddenly went into convulsions and, clutching Vesperus, cried out in great agitation, "Faster, darling, faster! I'm going to spend!" Vesperus thrust furiously for ten more strokes before she cried out, "Stop, darling! I'm spending!"

Vesperus placed the head of his penis against the heart of the flower and waited while she finished her orgasm, then resumed thrusting. As he did so, he asked her, "Dearest, why is your stamina so low? You spent after only twenty or thirty strokes. Your nieces lasted for two or three hundred, and I thought they were easy to dispatch. I never expected to meet anyone even easier."

Flora fixed him with a stern eye. "Now, look here! Don't you go thinking of me as easy. I'm the hardest woman of all to dispatch. It takes between one and two thousand strokes to get me to spend, and even then you have to put in a great deal of extra effort. You'll never succeed with *this* sort of thrusting."

Vesperus was surprised. "If you have that kind of stamina, why were you so easily dispatched just now? Surely you weren't faking?"

"No, I wasn't faking. There is a perfectly good reason for it. I've not been with a man in over ten years, and my passions are at their height. When I saw how handsome and well-endowed you were, my joy got the better of me, and my essence came of its own accord soon after you entered. It amounted to spending on my own and had nothing to do with your thrusting. If you don't believe me, just watch me next time. It will be very different, I assure you."

"I see. But there's something I still don't understand. You said that even with over a thousand strokes, it still took extra effort to get you to spend. That takes some effort to understand, I'm afraid. You mean something else in addition to the thrusting?"

"Simply this, that you have to put extra effort into arousing me, either by doing it audibly or else by saying lewd things. That brings my passions to life and I'm able to spend. If there's no sound from down below and nothing lewd from you, it would be like the deaf having sex with the dumb, and where's the fun in that? If you were to go on all night, I might get a pleasant sensation inside, but I'd still feel no joy at the bottom of my heart and the essence wouldn't come. But there is one thing I have to warn you about. I may be slow to spend, but the way I do it is different from other women; I actually pass out for a quarter of an hour before coming back to life again. I'm telling you this now, so that you won't panic when it happens."

"In that case only the strongest man could make you spend. My stamina may not be in the highest class, but at least it is well up in the second and, if I summon all my strength, perhaps I'll be able to cope. But what was your late husband's stamina like, I wonder? Was he able to satisfy you every night?"

"His stamina was not even in the second class," said Flora. "At first he was very highly sexed and an experienced seducer, and he did a great many immoral things. He used to say to me, 'Other women's are made of flesh, but yours is made of iron. I've tried everything I can think of, and I still can't get you to spend.' But then he thought up a number of ways of arousing my passions, and sex became a lot easier. Regardless of how many strokes it took, one thousand or two thousand, I'd feel joy at the bottom of my heart and would want to spend."

"In that case please tell me what his methods were. I 'may not have an old man ripe in judgment to guide me, but at least I shall have your statutes and laws.'[83] Let me copy his methods and perhaps save myself some effort."

"The methods are extremely simple, and great fun to try. There are just three of them, six words in all, which are self-explanatory. You'll understand as soon as I say them."

"What are they?"

Flora recited: "Erotic pictures, erotic books, lewd sounds."

"As for erotic pictures and books, I used both methods when I was newly married and they worked well, with one limitation. They aroused me the first time I looked at them, but by the second or third time I became bored. They can be used once in a while, but not as a regular standby."

"I imagine you had only a small supply at home and that you finished them up quickly and got bored. I have a large stock, several dozen albums and several hundred novels, and by the time you finish the last one, you've forgotten the first and can start all over again and get just as excited as before.

---

83. From the *Poetry Classic*. See *The Book of Songs*, p. 253.

"However, there is a right and a wrong time to use them. Erotic pictures should be looked at before sex, while the partners still have their clothes on and are behaving correctly. When looking at a picture and analyzing its subtleties, you should not do anything, even if your feelings happen to be aroused. If the penis stands up and the fluid starts to flow, you must ignore both developments until you've looked at several dozen pictures and can restrain yourselves no longer. That's the way to get the full effect of an erotic album.

"For erotic novels to be of any practical use, they should be read after you've begun but before you've finished. Place the book in front of you before you begin. Then, when you've done it for a while, one or other of you should open the book and read aloud from it. When you come to an exciting passage, start sex again. When you reach a less interesting stage in sex, start reading again. That's the way to get the full effect of an erotic novel."

"What a subtle observation!" said Vesperus. "Obviously I have neglected my studies and made no progress. As the adage says, one's education never ends. Without the benefit of your instruction, I might have gone on studying and practicing all my life and never learned this. I now understand the first two items, but not the last. Not only have I never written on that topic, I'm not even sure what it means. What do you mean by lewd sounds?"

"In my opinion," replied Flora, "there is nothing to surpass it among all the thrills and pleasures of sex. It means lying beside a pair of lovers and listening to the sounds they make—enough to drive you wild with delight. I've always taken a special pleasure in listening to other people in action. While my husband was alive, I used to get him to seduce a maid and do it as rapidly and noisily as possible, so that the girl was quite beside herself and began to cry out. That would bring me to

a fever pitch and I'd give a cough, at which he would fly into
my bed and pound away furiously. I'd make him ignore the
usual strategy and throw himself into a continuous, all-out
assault. Not only would I get a pleasant sensation inside, it
would spread to the bottom of my heart and I'd spend after
no more than seven or eight hundred strokes. As a method, it's
even more fun than erotic pictures and novels."

"An even more delightful disquisition!" said Vesperus.
"But there is just one point that puzzles me. You told me your
honorable husband's stamina was on the inadequate side. If so,
how did he manage to seduce a maid and then have sex with
her mistress straight afterward? Moreover with the maid he
had to do it as rapidly and as loudly as possible. I'd expect him
to be a spent force by the time he got to you, so how could
he hurl himself into an all-out assault? I'm afraid I'm not able
to credit that quite so easily."

"In the first stage I didn't ask him to do it himself, but to
use a stand-in. Only in the second stage, the all-out assault, did
I have to ask his help. He'd never have been able to manage
it all on his own."

"I think I know that stand-in. Is his name Mr. Horn, by
any chance?"

"Right. We have lots of them in the house. And as for
pretty maids, we have several of those too. I daresay that in
our first encounter today I won't have any difficulty spending,
but we must try that method tomorrow."

Vesperus was enthralled and felt as if he had just seduced
the maid, heard the cough, and rushed into Flora's bed. Heedless of strategy, he threw himself into a continuous, all-out
assault.

During their conversation he had not been idle but had
thrust steadily away, at least five hundred times in all. Now,
with this renewed assault, the pleasant sensation in her vagina

THE CARNAL PRAYER MAT

spread to the bottom of her heart and, just as if she were dying, her hands and feet grew cold, her eyes glazed over, and her mouth dropped open.

Had Flora not told him her secret in advance, Vesperus would have been alarmed. But after a few minutes, just as she had predicted, she revived and, clasping him to her, sighed in admiration: "What a fine, capable sweetheart you are, to make me spend without a stand-in. Judging by this performance, your stamina belongs in the *summa* class. How can you say it's only a *magna* plus?"

"I gave you a *summa* in my notebook and now you're doing the same thing for me! How quickly you've returned the compliment!"

"I was going to ask you," said Flora, "who crossed out those three names in your notebook and added that comment."

Vesperus was loath to tell her and pretended not to know.

"You may not want to say," said Flora, "but I can easily guess what happened. It was those three wenches, who think I'm old and have lost my looks and can't compare with them, so they liken themselves to Huaiyin and me to Jiang and Guan, as if to say they're ashamed to be ranked with me. Well, they may be a few years younger than I am and their skin a little softer, but I assure you that they're good for nothing but sitting there and letting you admire them. I doubt very much that they can equal this old lady when it comes to the real thing. On top of that, if you compared our vaginas, you'd find a similar difference in quality. I'll keep my feelings to myself for the present and not quarrel with them, but once we have some free time, I'll go over there and organize a contest. We'll all undress and have sex together in broad daylight. Each woman will show what she can do, and then we'll see whether youth or experience wins the day."

"You're right. They're young and untried and they do

need an experienced hand to guide them. You should arrange a contest."

"That's for later. We can discuss it some other time. Let's think how to enjoy ourselves now."

It was getting late, so they dressed. Flora told the maids to prepare a formal dinner of welcome for Vesperus. She had an excellent capacity for wine, fully equal to his, and the two of them played guess-fingers and drinking games until the second watch had passed. By that time their feelings were so stirred by the wine that they went back to bed and began again. That evening saw Flora's long period of enforced celibacy come to an end. Her essence flowed easily, and she had no need to resort to her special methods.

Next day she arose and brought out her erotic albums and novels, which she had not looked at in years, and placed them on the table in readiness. She had four personal maids, all attractive, two of whom were sixteen or seventeen and, having lost their maidenheads, could accommodate him. The others, being fourteen or fifteen and still virgins, were useless, and Vesperus suggested that Flora send them to Satchel and let him break them in for several days and nights, in preparation for their role in arousing their mistress.

From this time on, Vesperus and Flora pursued their pleasures by night and day with the aid of all three methods. After he met Flora, Vesperus's enjoyment was of a different order from what it had been, and his knowledge was also greatly enhanced.

Flora worried that her nieces would come and ask for their property back, so from the moment the trunk arrived, she kept the side door locked and refused to open it no matter how loudly they clamored. On the fifth day of unrest, however, Vesperus felt sorry for them and tactfully pleaded their case to Flora, who was obliged to settle the issue by promising to return him in two days' time. With a definite date set for his return, the nieces ceased banging on the door.

Early on the eighth day Vesperus went to take leave of Flora, but found her still hoping for a delay. Fortunately he could be very persuasive and at length managed to leave.

When he walked through the side door, the sisters reacted as joyfully as if the sun had dropped down from the sky. "How have you enjoyed yourself the last few nights?" they asked, after greeting him. "What's the old baggage keen on? Did you ever touch bottom or reach dry land?"

To avert their jealousy, Vesperus muted his praise, mentioning only Flora's three methods of arousal in the hope that her nieces might emulate her. He also mentioned her suggestion about the contest, to encourage them to do their best and not be deterred from "showing their superiority simply because they were a little younger."

"In that case," said Cloud, "she'll allow us to go first so that she can share in everyone else's pleasure and then enjoy hers all on her own. But let's not worry about *her* pleasure, let's go first ourselves and try something on. So long as we do it quietly, with no sound from down there or up here, she'll lose her advantage, fail to get aroused, and be caught in her own trap. What do you think?"

"In my opinion," said Lucky Jade, "we should not let her choose, but insist that, since she's our aunt, naturally she has to go first. Then, when she has had rather a poor time of it, it will be our turn and we'll make a point of crying out in order to get her worked up. By that time she won't be able to do it again or even to stand the sound of it, and she'll simply *die* of frustration! Nothing would give me greater pleasure!"

"There's a lot to be said for both ideas," said Lucky Pearl, "but I'm afraid she'll come up with some other trick and we won't be able to use them. I suggest we wait until the time comes and watch out for an opening."

"You're right," said the others.

Proceeding according to the established order, each of them slept one night with him and then, on the fourth night, just as they were looking forward to a combined event, a note arrived from Flora proposing the contest. She also sent along one tael as her share of the expenses, together with instructions for the party, which, she suggested, would be enjoyable only if there were wine on hand as well as sex.

"It's lucky she's coming today," said one, as they consulted together, "on one of our combination days! 'Adding another guest, but not killing another chicken,' as the saying goes. Let her come. It'll be hectic in bed and she'll get only a small share of the real thing. We'll be doing her a pretty useless favor."

We shall respectfully follow your instructions, they wrote in reply.

Since Flora was their senior, why did she go to her nieces' place rather than have them over to hers, you ask. You should realize that Flora had a nine-year-old son, who, for all his youth, was highly intelligent. When she entertained Vesperus in her house, the boy saw nothing, but if a man were to be carousing and cavorting there with four women, she could hardly hide the fact from him, and it would be embarrassing if he noticed. Her nieces had no children, so all they had to do was shut the door and no one would be any the wiser. That was why Flora sacrificed seniority to expediency and consented to join them.

Not long after they had sent their reply, she arrived for the party. Vesperus noticed a bulge in one of her sleeves as if she had something hidden there.

"What do you have up your sleeve?" he asked. "Not Mr. Horn, by any chance?"

Flora shook her head. "No, but something just as amusing. It's for looking at while drinking or having sex, so I brought it along in case we needed it." She took it out and showed them. It was a pack of erotic playing cards.

"Normally these things are just for amusement," said Vesperus, "but we do have a use for them in our contest today. Let's not look at them now, but wait until the wine takes effect. Then each of you must pick a card and act out with me whatever it shows."

"Exactly what I had in mind," remarked Flora.

"In that case," said Cloud, "let's look at them first. If we understand what they are, we'll be able to act them out better when the time comes."

"Very well," said Vesperus, placing them in front of Flora. His idea was to have the more experienced woman take the lead and offer her guidance to the others.

"I've seen them many times," said Flora, "and I'm quite familiar with their techniques. I'm no sudden convert, I assure you. I'll stand aside and let the girls take the test on their own."

The three young women laughed and, spreading out the cards, scrutinized them one by one. But when they came to a card that showed a young woman lying on an ornamental rock and raising her buttocks in anal sex with a man, they put their hands over their mouths and giggled.

"What*ever* is this position? Why would anyone go in for such dis*gust*ing behavior instead of doing it the wholesome way?"

"Which one is that?" asked Flora. "Let me see."

Cloud handed it to her. "This method is taken from literature," Flora announced after a glance. "Surely you know that?"

"Where is it from? We're not at all clear," said Cloud.

"From a work called *I Want to Get Married*. Have you read it?"

"No. Please tell us about it."

"There was once a beautiful girl who lived next door to a handsome student. The student fell sick because of his love for the girl and asked someone to go to her and give her the following message: 'If I could meet you just once, I'd die content. I wouldn't dream of doing anything improper.'

"The girl was so affected by his pathetic plea that she felt obliged to consent. When they met, she sat on his lap and let him hug, fondle, and kiss her to his heart's content; but she would not let him have sex. When he asked, she told him, 'I want to get married, so it's out of the question.' The student, who was by now in a state of intolerable frustration, knelt down and begged her, but she still refused, repeating the words, 'I want to get married,' and adding, 'The reason you wished to meet me was that I'm pretty and you wanted to fulfill your deepest desire by being close to me and touching me. Now that I'm sitting on your lap letting you fondle me all over, you can fulfill your desire. Why do you have to ruin me? I want to keep my maidenhead and become a bride one day. It may not matter now if I lose it, but when I get married, should my husband notice, I'll never be able to hold up my head again as long as I live. It's out of the question.'

" 'But when a man has intercourse with a woman,' said the student, 'this three-inch thing has to go in there for it to count as love. Otherwise they're nothing more than strangers. No matter how close our bodies are, no matter how we touch, my heart's desire will never be fulfilled.' This time he knelt down and refused to get up.

"Unable to withstand his pleas, the girl hung her head in thought and came up with a stopgap solution. 'I want to get married,' she said, 'and so I definitely cannot let you do this. But what would you say if I found something else for you?' 'What else *is* there, apart from this?' 'You'll have to try the back instead of the front and satisfy your heart's desire by putting your three-inch thing in there. That's my last word on the subject!'

"Daunted by her firm tone, the student could protest no more, but accepted the stopgap solution and began to copulate with her by treating the rear courtyard as if it were the front. This method is taken from that story. How can you be so ignorant, not to have read such a good book?"

Her nieces were upset by her supercilious tone and apprehensive lest she put on airs during the sex itself, so they dropped the cards and withdrew for consultation, united in their desire to take her down a peg.

The three days Flora had been parted from Vesperus seemed like nine years to her, and she could hardly wait for the others to withdraw before beginning to pet. They had embraced, and exchanged kisses and endearments before the other women returned and told the maids to set out the wine.

Vesperus sat at the head of the table, with Flora opposite him and the young women on either side. After several rounds of drinks, Flora had the cards brought in so that each of them could pick one and serve the wine accordingly. Her nieces objected: "After looking at the cards, we'll be so distracted by thoughts of sex that we won't be able to touch the wine. Let's play some other game now, drink until the wine takes effect, and then bring out the cards. There'll be nothing to stop us from both serving wine and having sex as shown on the cards."

"You're right," said Vesperus. Lucky Pearl passed over the dice box and called on Vesperus to start.

"It's too much effort playing dice," he said. "Why don't we play Prima guess-fingers,[84] to settle the order for the wine now and the sex later. What do you say, ladies?"

---

84. A variety of the guess-fingers game in which the winners are given the titles of the top examination graduates.

Flora, who knew her *Classic of Guess-fingers* by heart, beamed at this suggestion; she could hardly wait to be declared Prima in order to put them all in their places. The only thing that bothered her was the thought that if she won, she would have to have sex first, even though she was the one who needed to hear other people's cries. How could she bear to be in the vanguard? She was in a quandary.

"The order we do it in," she said to Vesperus at last, "need not be the order we finish in. Let it be up to the Prima to decide whether she goes first or last."

"Very well," said Vesperus.

That settled, they extended five snow-white fists and began to play, beginning with Vesperus and ending with Lucky Jade. Flora was indeed an expert and quickly won first place. As Prima, she did not wait to see who would become Secunda and Tertia, but immediately issued an order: "Since I am Prima, I will be Magister Ludi. Not only must the Old Scholar pass my test, even Secunda and Tertia must accept my rulings. Anyone who disobeys will have to drink a large cup as forfeit."

"In that case," said Vesperus, "may I ask that you post your rules well in advance, so that they are laid down once and for all and there is no room for any doubt or suspicion."

"With regard to the number of cups," said Flora, "we'll start with Prima and go as far as Tertia, increasing the amounts as we go. The Old Scholar will stand to one side and hold the winepot.[85] She is entitled to pour but not to drink. The order for sex will be exactly the opposite, running from Tertia to Prima, again increasing the amounts as we go. The Old Scholar will stand to one side and remain strictly neutral, permitted to wipe up but not take part."

---

85. The Old Scholar: the perennial failure.

"Those rules are all very fine," said Vesperus, "but you haven't thought them through. If by some chance your humble servant becomes the Old Scholar and cannot take part, none of you will be able to do a thing. What then? Won't you be falling foul of your own laws?"

"Of course, but I've already thought of that. You'll be exempt from the examination. I'm appointing you Overseer, for assignment later."

"But then I'll be able to take part in the sex and not in the drinking!"

"You will get more wine than ever," said Flora. "When Prima drinks, you'll drink with her, and when Secunda and Tertia drink, you'll drink with them. But you're not to put yourself out for the Old Scholar, who will be serving us, or it will mean a large forfeit."

"I'll have to push myself to the limit to keep up with all three of you! It doesn't bother me at all that the Old Scholar isn't competing. Let her suffer!" said Vesperus.

Although the sisters had given their aunt a wry look or two, they had allowed her to go on issuing orders without raising any objections. Fortunately they had foreseen the problem and held their conclave, at which they had come up with a brilliant plan. But they kept it to themselves, uncertain whether they would have a chance to apply it.

"You are the Overseer," they said to Vesperus. "You ought to make your presence felt when the Magister Ludi is being unfair and impeach her instead of toadying to the old tyrant. If she goes on like this, we shall make a big fuss and reject her authority altogether."

"If I'm acting unfairly," said Flora, "there's no need for the Overseer to impeach me. Just make the charges openly and, if they are sustained, I'll drink a forfeit."

Having set the rules, Flora exempted Vesperus and told the three girls to compete again, which they did, finishing, as if by supernatural means, in precisely the order of their seniority: Cloud as Secunda, Lucky Pearl as Tertia, and Lucky Jade, who was too delicate for vigorous sex anyway, as the Old Scholar. (She was the only candidate who hadn't passed, so it was appropriate that she humble herself and, as the youngest, take on the burden when there was work to be done.)[86]

When the game was over, Flora called upon Lucky Jade to serve the wine, one cup for her, two cups for Cloud, and three for Lucky Pearl, all of whom were accompanied in their drinking by Vesperus. Then, when they had drunk the wine, she ordered Lucky Jade to shuffle the cards and place them on the table, after which she was to stand to one side in a neutral position, ready to wipe up while the others had sex. Jade did not dare disobey, but did as she was told.

"With the first of us," Flora said to Vesperus, issuing her orders again, "you'll be restricted to one hundred strokes and with the second to two hundred. If you are one stroke over or under the count, you'll drink a forfeit accordingly. It's entirely their luck if they spend; you are not responsible for seeing to it. After that it will be my turn. The Magister Ludi is in a different position from the other players. No matter how many strokes it takes, you must go on until I spend. In the first two cases the score will be kept by the Old Scholar, and any discrepancy will be punished."

She turned to her nieces. "Pick up the top card and follow the method shown on it. Whether it's to your liking or not is all a matter of luck; you can't change cards. To pass, you need to imitate the model exactly. The slightest discrepancy will be punished with a wine forfeit as well as a reduction in the number of strokes."

"If we don't imitate the model, of course we'll drink a

---

86. See *The Analects*, p. 64.

forfeit," said Lucky Pearl. "But what happens if the Magister Ludi fails?"

"If she fails, she will have to drink three forfeit cups and repeat the test until she passes."

"In that case the top card is mine," said Lucky Pearl.

"Correct," said Flora.

The card Lucky Pearl picked up showed a woman lying on a bed with her legs apart but not raised in the air and a man's body some three feet away. He was supporting himself with his arms and facing her as he thrust—a position known as The Dragonfly Skims the Surface. Having offered the card in evidence, Lucky Pearl set to work to imitate it. Stripping off her trousers, she lay on the bed while Vesperus mounted her and played the dragonfly, skimming madly without pause. Lucky Pearl was intent on pleasing the Magister Ludi and getting her excited, so she did not wait to feel pleasure before crying out. For every skim she gave a cry, and then, after sixty or seventy, she began giving several cries to each skim, until Vesperus reached his quota and stopped.

"Now it's my turn," said Cloud, picking up the next card. It showed a woman lying on a lounge chair and a man standing in front of it with her feet over his shoulders. He was supporting himself with his arms on the chair and pushing vigorously—a position known as Pushing the Boat Downstream.

Placing the card in evidence, she lay on the lounge chair and imitated the position with Vesperus. Her cries were quite different from Pearl's, however. Since a boat is easy to push downstream, the water rushing past tends to produce sounds from under the bows that, swelling together with those from beneath the hull, are delightful to listen to, are they not?[87] And

---

87. *Lang sheng* (*sound of waves*) is a pun on *lewd sounds*.

if they were delightful to listen to, you may be sure that Cloud's expression was something to behold.

When Flora had eavesdropped on lewd cries before, the girl had been hidden from sight; she had never actually seen anyone's expression in the moment of rapture. Now she not only heard something she had never heard before, she also saw something she had never seen, and her sexual excitement was far more intense than on those occasions when she had signaled her readiness with a cough. She could wait not a moment longer.

As soon as Cloud had received her complement, Flora stood up. "Now it's the Magister Ludi's turn. Move aside and let me on stage."

As she picked up a card with one hand, her other hand was already at her trousers, undoing her belt. But when she looked at the card, her face blanched in fear and the hand with the card in it sagged limply to her side. "We can't use this one," she declared. "I'll have to change it."

Her nieces were up in arms. First they hid the rest of the cards, then they came and looked at the one she had chosen. What position did it show, do you suppose? None other than that of the story *I Want to Get Married*, the technique in which the woman raises her buttocks in the air and engages in anal sex with her partner.

How can such a coincidence be accounted for? Of all the cards, how was it that she picked this particular one? In fact the coincidence was the result of the young women's plan. They had assumed it would fall to one of them to shuffle the cards and had marked this one so that it could be dealt to their aunt. When Flora ruled that the Magister Ludi would go last, Lucky Jade, in shuffling the cards, had put this one third from the top, and Flora had duly picked it up. However, the coincidence may not have been entirely the result of human ingenuity. Excess of any kind is anathema to the Creator, and Flora's overweening arrogance may also have played a part in her downfall.

After inspecting the card, the three urged her to take off her trousers, but she adamantly refused. "I appeal to you to consider whether it is even feasible—especially with that object of his. Just think a moment."

"Out of the question!" they replied. "We're all in the same boat. If we'd picked up that card, would you have let us off? Moreover, you were the one who ruled that we were not to change cards. The methods on the cards were familiar to you and you alone; we were totally ignorant, remember? If you thought this method so impossible, why didn't you remove the card? Now that you've taken it, there's nothing more to be said. Come on, off with your trousers, or we'll shame you by pulling them off."

"A fine Overseer you are!" they said, turning to Vesperus. "Why don't you say or do something? Do we have to strip her and hand her over to you?"

"It's not that I'm playing favorites," said Vesperus. "The trouble is that her behind cannot take this thing of mine. We ought to allow her another means of reparation and let her drink a few extra cups of wine instead."

"Utter rot!" they retorted. "If wine can substitute for sex, we would have opted for it, too. None of us is so shameless as to *want* to undress and make a spectacle of herself."

Vesperus saw that the three sisters were adamant. Even Flora hung her head in despair, at a loss for words.

"There's nothing else for it," said Vesperus. "But let me ask you ladies to allow her a way out and not be too strict. Let her take down her trousers and give a token demonstration only."

But Cloud and Lucky Jade would allow no substitutions. They accepted no leniency and were still insisting on actual sex when Lucky Pearl gave them a broad wink. "All we need is a token demonstration," said Pearl. "We certainly won't insist on a strict application of the law."

"That's easily settled, then," said Vesperus, seizing Flora and trying to pull down her trousers. At first she stubbornly refused, but she could not hold out against his entreaties and at length grudgingly consented, removing her trousers and lying facedown on the lounge chair. He took out his penis, wiped a good deal of spit on it, and tapped it once on the outside of her anus. Flora began to squeal and tried to get up, refusing to let him proceed.

All this while the three wicked young women had been waiting there with their murderous hands at the ready. The words Lucky Pearl had accompanied with a wink had been designed to trick Flora into taking off her trousers, and now that she had done so and was lying on the chair, they came forward. One held her head down, while a second held her hands fast, preventing her not only from getting up and escaping but even from changing her position or twisting her buttocks to one side. And the third, the wickedest of all, hid behind Vesperus and chose the very moment when he was tapping at her anus to give him a mighty shove, driving his penis in to fully half its length, whereupon she wrapped her arms around his waist and pushed and pulled while Flora squealed like a slaughtered pig and cried over and over, "Spare me! Spare me!"

"It's no laughing matter when someone's life is at stake!" said Vesperus. "Have mercy!"

"She ruled that the Magister Ludi was in a different position from the rest of us. No matter how many strokes it took, you were to go on until she spent. Ask her if she's spent or not."

"I've spent! I've spent!" said Flora. Because she was so

obviously in distress, and because Vesperus kept imploring them, her nieces had to let her go.

When she got up, she looked like a corpse. Unable to speak and unsteady on her feet, she had to call a maid to come and help her home.

Later her anus swelled up, she had bouts of fever and shivering, and had to keep to her bed for three or four days, just as if she had suffered a major illness.

Afterward, although bitterly resentful, she was so eager to join in their activities that she could not afford to remain hostile. As the old saying goes, "If you want to be friends with someone, first take him to court." The aunt and her nieces had been at loggerheads, but following this quarrel they patched up their friendship and the one man and four women shared the same bed and enjoyed pleasures too numerous to recount.

Vesperus had arranged with Fragrance to stay away no more than three months so as to be back in time for the baby's birth. But he had been so preoccupied with sex that he had quite forgotten his promise, and by the time he recalled it, the three months had elapsed. He sent Satchel off to inquire and found that Fragrance had given birth to twin girls. Flora and the sisters contributed to a party in Vesperus's honor and celebrated with him for several days before sending him on his way.

Fragrance was afraid the babies would be a burden to her and prevent her from enjoying herself, so the moment they were born, she hired two wet nurses to look after them at home. As a result she was leading as carefree a life as if she had never given birth and, when Vesperus walked in one month later, she promptly called on him to draw up his forces and engage her in battle again. She was intent on collecting all of the accumulated debts she was owed. How could she have forseen that "the people were exhausted and the treasury was bare," and that he could not even raise an army?

What was the reason? For four or five months now Vesperus, a lone male, had been pitted against four women. What's more, he had indulged his debaucheries by day as well as by night. Even an iron penis would have been worn down by such an ordeal, even a river of semen would have been sucked dry. How could he be anything else but debilitated in body and mind? A few months away from her, and she was forced to look at him with an entirely different eye! From that moment forward Fragrance deeply regretted what she had done.

CRITIQUE

Some people criticize this chapter's descriptions for going too far, allowing the adulterous husband and his wanton women no grace at all. But without the extraordinary lechery of this chapter, there would be insufficient cause for the drastic retribution of the next. Indulging the characters really means tormenting them. When you read the passage in which Jade Scent, as the leading exponent of the most extraordinary wantonness of all, repays her husband's debts, you will finally realize that the previous few chapters have done well to go too far in their descriptions.

CHAPTER *E*IGHTEEN

His wife becomes a prostitute and publicly repays his
   debts,
While two brothers compete for a charmer and secretly
   collect their dues.

Lyric:
   Do not, I pray, take up a lecher's loan!
   The better the terms, the sooner it must be paid.
   Your wife will be the one to foot the bill
   For debts that, unlike you, she can't evade.

   A human lender may forgive your debt,
   But Heaven plays a far more ruthless part.
   What's to stop you selling her body?
   Your own you needn't sell, just your heart.
   (To the tune "Springtime in the Jade Bower")

Most of Vesperus's triumphs have now been told, but only a fraction of the disasters that were to befall him. We shall proceed step by step to repay in full those lecher's loans of his and then, after concluding this tale of retribution, put our brush and inkstone away.

His wife had run off with Honest Quan and the maid Ruyi. Jade Scent began having abdominal pains at the first place they stopped, and the fetus she was bearing, which could not be induced to miscarry before despite all their efforts, now miscarried of its own accord under the strain of the journey. If only it had done so a few days earlier, they would not have had to flee, but it was now too late to turn back. Jade Scent had eloped to no purpose whatever. Surely it was her husband's sins that had brought her to such a pass!

Quan's original motive had been vengeance rather than lust, and from the moment he abducted her, he had meant to sell her into prostitution. But she was carrying his child, its sex still unknown, and he could not bear the thought of his own flesh and blood being born in a brothel and growing up to shame him. He was in a quandary until the miscarriage, when he quickly decided on a course of action.

Taking both women with him on a nonstop journey to the capital, he lodged them at an inn while he looked about for a buyer. Now, when someone is trying to sell a woman of good family into prostitution, he has to employ deception. He will tell her he has a relative there who is trying to find them somewhere to live and by that means get a potential buyer in to see her. Only if the buyer likes what she sees is it possible to trick the woman into joining another "family."

There lived in the capital a certain celebrated madam named "Immortal Maid" Gu. One look at Jade Scent was enough to convince her that this was rare merchandise indeed, and she paid Quan the full price asked by the go-between. She also bought Ruyi, to continue serving Jade Scent as a maid.

Before the sale Quan had been too obsessed with the idea of revenge ever to question it. But immediately afterward he felt uneasy and gradually came to repent his actions, turning the following thoughts over and over in his mind: I've heard that, according to the Buddhist scriptures, if we want to know the karmic causation from our last existence, we should look at our fortunes in this life, and if we want to know the causation for our next life, we should look at our actions now. I failed to safeguard my women's quarters and allowed my wife to behave disgracefully. For all I know, in my last existence I may have seduced some other man's wife and am now being punished by having to give my wife up to someone else. I ought to have meekly accepted the humiliation and so canceled my karmic debt. Why did I have to go seducing someone else's wife and incur a sin for my next existence? Even though I felt the need for revenge, I ought to have slept with her for a few nights to purge my anger and let it go at that. Why did I have to sell her into prostitution and make one man's wife the wife of ten thousand? I may have a vendetta against the husband, but does that mean that everyone else has a vendetta against him, too? And if the sin of selling her into prostitution is so unbearable, why did I have to compound it by selling an innocent maidservant along with her? Jade Scent may have a husband I hate, but what husband does the maid have?

At this point in his reflections, he fell to beating his chest and stamping his feet in self-loathing. He knew perfectly well that wrongs once done cannot be undone and that his only recourse was to repent his sins for the rest of this life in preparation for the next. He gave the money that he had received from the sale to the poor and the handicapped, and he himself, after shearing off half his hair until he looked like a mendicant friar, traveled about in search of a truly eminent monk who would be willing to induct him into the monastic order. In due course he came to Mount Guacang, where he met Abbot Lone Peak and recognized in him a living buddha. After Lone Peak had accepted him into the order, Quan struggled to perfect himself for twenty years before attaining the fruits of enlightenment.

But these events still lie ahead of us. Let us speak now of Jade Scent's fall into prostitution. Having arrived in Immortal Maid's household, she and Ruyi took one glance at what was afoot and realized, needless to say, that this was no decent family they were joining, but that they had been duped by a scoundrel. A vulgar saying puts their reaction in a nutshell:

They knew this wasn't proper company,
But in a pinch they thought it best to join.

Even the most chaste of women, once she had crossed that triple threshold, could not have escaped. How unlikely it was that one who had already lost her virtue and was not exactly averse to men would even try! Jade Scent simply told Immortal Maid her story and contentedly resigned herself to the career of a courtesan.

Of course it was necessary for her, on entering a house of prostitution, to adopt a sobriquet for her clients' use. To avoid confusing the reader, however, the author will continue to use her original name, as he did in the case of Honest Quan.

A very rich client chose her the first evening. Next morning he was about to depart, when Immortal Maid noticed and begged him to stay. Although he insisted, he had some advice for her as he left: "That daughter of yours has a perfect face and figure. All she lacks are those three superlative skills of yours. A great general oughtn't to have any incompetents on his staff, you know; you really ought to pass your skills along. I'm leaving now, but after you've taught her, I'll be back for my lesson." And with that he was off.

Why did he say this? Because Immortal Maid had long possessed three superlative skills, none of which had been mastered by any other woman. As a girl she had been of only average looks and had shown little talent for verse, yet by now she had enjoyed over thirty years of celebrity. Moreover the men she slept with were all from the aristocracy or the gentry; no ordinary citizen could get in to see her. Even after she reached forty or fifty and became a madam herself, the rich and eminent continued to patronize her for the sake of her skills.

What were these superlative skills of hers? The first was Lowering the Yin to Join the Yang, the second was Raising the Yin to Meet the Yang, and the third was Sacrificing the Yin to Aid the Yang.[88] When having sex with a man, she did not expect him to move, but did the moving herself. First she asked him to oblige her by lying on his back. Then she mounted him, inserted his penis in her vagina, and raised herself and sheathed it, sank down and kneaded it, raised herself and sheathed it, sank down and kneaded it. If another woman had done this, her legs would have ached so abominably after the first few strokes that she'd have been unable to continue, but the Maid's knees seemed to be made of brass or iron, for the longer she worked, the stronger she became. And it was not just the man she pleased, she also pleased herself. "Having a man do the moving," she used to say, "is like asking someone to scratch an itch for you. You can be sure that half the time he'll miss the spot. But when you scratch yourself, it's simply heavenly, because you never miss." This is what was meant by Lowering the Yin to Join the Yang, the first of her skills.

At other times, when she lay underneath, she would not let the man exert himself alone, but would insist on arching her body to help him. When he thrust forward, she rose to meet

_____

88. This is a Taoist technique of male rejuvenation.

him; when he pulled back, she gave way. Not only did she save him half the effort, she also got fully half the benefit for herself, ensuring that her secret pass was under constant attack.

"The most delightful things in life," she was given to saying, "cannot be enjoyed on one's own. Yin must fit together with yang, yang must fit together with yin. When they happen to meet halfway, you'll naturally start enjoying yourself; that is what is meant by the reciprocity of yin and yang. If the woman doesn't respond to the man but just lets him thrust away, what's to stop him from getting a wood or plaster mannequin and drilling a deep hole in the middle of it? As long as he can enter, he'll be able to thrust back and forth, so what does he need a woman for? That is why famous courtesans have to grasp this principle if they are going to please their clients as well as themselves." This is what was known as Raising the Yin to Meet the Yang, the second of her skills.

As for Sacrificing the Yin to Aid the Yang, it was incomparably more profound. When having sex, she was most reluctant to let her finite supply of female essence leak out where it would do no good. So long as the man got the benefit, she had no regrets about spending; but otherwise she felt as downcast as if she had lost money or made a poor business deal, and afterward, when it was all over, she would be inconsolable.

What technique did she use to see that the man got the benefit? Whenever she was about to spend, she would tell him to place his glans against the heart of the flower and keep it there without moving. She knew how to maneuver the tiny orifice in the heart into precise alignment with the orifice in the glans. Since she took care to teach the man in advance how to ingest the essence, it was no sooner secreted than he ingested it into his penis and thence through his coccyx directly to the pubic region. For sheer efficacy, ginseng and aconite cannot compare with this substance, which is unsurpassed even by the elixir of immortality.

She learned this marvelous art at the age of fifteen. She was losing her virginity to a magician at the time, and he had inadvertently revealed it. Whenever she met a sympathetic client, she would instruct him in what to do, and he invariably benefited. After a few nights with her, not only would he become twice as vigorous, even his complexion would take on a new glow. People said she must be the incarnation of an immortal maid, which is how she acquired her name.

Once her clients had been taught the principle, they duly practiced it at home, where of course they had no need of her. Little did they realize, however, that people can be taught how to ingest the essence but not how to align the orifices. The key factor is the woman's skill in bringing them together, and Immortal Maid was the only one who knew the secret; others could not succeed no matter how hard they tried. The remarkable thing was that all other women were in the dark except for her, which is why it was known as a superlative skill.

When Jade Scent first arrived, it was not *her* reputation that drew the rich client but Immortal Maid's, as a formidable adversary. The client took it for granted that Jade Scent, as someone trained by the Maid, would be familiar with her tactics. What complicated matters was that he was grossly fat. When he climbed into bed and lay on her, he began puffing and wheezing after no more than forty or fifty strokes, so he quickly dismounted and held her on top of him while she did the work. But Jade Scent, accustomed as she was to a life of leisure, had never done anything half as strenuous as this in her whole life. She may have Doused the Candle a few times, but always with the man holding her by the hips and bouncing her up and down; nominally she was the active partner, but actually it was he. How could she make that slight, delicate frame of hers do anything as rough as this? After less than ten sheathings, her feet and legs ached so badly that she collapsed onto his stomach. The client realized that she had not mastered this skill, to say nothing of the others, and he hastily finished off and slept until dawn. But although he could not enjoy her, he was not prepared to give her up, which is why he offered his parting advice to the Maid.

The Maid assumed, as she showed him out, that Jade Scent had put on ladylike airs instead of trying to please him. How was she going to make any money by receiving such an important gentleman and then sending him away after just one night? The Maid armed herself with her rod and was about to start beating, when Jade Scent fell to her knees and begged for mercy. Because this was her first offense, the Maid forgave her, but scolded her severely and insisted she study the three arts by day and night. While the Maid was having sex with a client, she taught by practical example, making Jade Scent stand beside the bed and watch closely to see if she could master the techniques. And when Jade Scent was having sex, the Maid gave her an individual tutorial, sitting beside the bed and watching closely to see that her pupil was doing it right.

Where there's a will there's a way, as the proverb says. Jade Scent was forced to study hard, both from fear of the Maid's discipline and also because she wanted to make a name for herself. As a result, in no more than a month or two she had mastered the three skills. Her art was now fully equal to the Maid's, while her beauty and poetic talent were far superior, and it goes without saying that before long an endless stream of carriages was calling at her gate. Soon she was famous throughout the capital, and there was scarcely a wealthy gentlemen or young nobleman who did not come to sample her delights.

Among her clients were two gentlemen so eager to lavish their money on her that they promised her a dozen taels for a single night, a promise that made her especially solicitous. Who were they, do you suppose? None other than Lucky Pearl's and Lucky Jade's husbands, Scholars Cloud-Reposer and Cloud-Recliner. As students enrolled in the National Academy, they had heard of Jade Scent's towering reputation and vied with each other to be the first to visit her. Without telling his brother, Reposer slept with her several nights, after which Recliner, without telling Reposer, slept with her a few nights more. Each of them, in deceiving the other, had assumed that, although she was a prostitute, she would hardly be so ignorant of ethical principle as to receive one brother after already receiving the other. Little did they realize that it is money, rather than ethics, that motivates prostitutes. Not only were brothers and classmates regular visitors under her skirts, she also received grandfathers as well as grandsons, and fathers as well as sons, transforming this one small article of hers into an ancestral shrine for three generations and offering equal access to old and young, noble and base.

When the brothers eventually found out, they felt they might just as well invite her to their lodgings for the common enjoyment of all, for brothers and classmates—and for teacher and students. Because even Cloud's husband, Master Felix, would often make a superficial contribution to the proceedings. After a night or two with her he actually did feel a renewed vitality, which convinced him that Scent's vagina was a medicinal tonic and that if only he had married a wife like her, he would not have had to dodge his connubial duties.

After a year at the Academy the brothers began to feel homesick and decided to pay a return visit, lest their young wives become depressed and ill from pining for them. They asked the dean for a few months' leave, and the request was granted.

After saying goodbye to Jade Scent, they traveled back with Cloud's husband. Once home, needless to say, each was treated to a welcome-home party by his wife, and then asked how many courtesans and catamites he had been with and how he had enjoyed himself as compared with his experience at home. Each husband, of course, told of his liaison with Jade Scent and described her three superlative skills in glowing terms, inevitably saying more than he should have said.

Next morning, when the wives arose, they told one another what they had learned, and all of their stories tallied.

"We don't believe such a prodigy exists," said Lucky Pearl and Lucky Jade, "although if she does exist, she will render us passé. But we think that the whole story has been cooked up by our husbands to make us look like the only truly useless women in the world. The idea is to needle us into putting more effort into our lovemaking."

"Ah, but they won't be able to deceive the man we've been living with," said Cloud. "He has lots of experience, and if such a whore exists, he's bound to know of her. Let's ask him when next he comes over."

"Good idea," said the others.

During the Qingming festival their husbands went off to visit the family graves and were not expected back until the following day. The women promptly sent a maid to invite Vesperus over. After exchanging greetings, they asked about the woman.

"There are all kinds of things in the world," he said. "Perhaps there *is* such a prodigy of a prostitute somewhere. Anyway, if she's in the capital, I'll meet up with her one day. Just give me one night with her; and only if she's a match for me will she qualify as a prodigy. Those fellows wouldn't know a good woman if they saw one!"

After chatting for a while, they spent the night together. As Vesperus left the next day, he was still puzzled. It *must* be true, if all three husbands tell the same story, he thought, and since we have such a magician as that among us, why shouldn't I go and see her? I've been to bed with any number of beautiful women in my time, but I've never come across one who could do the work herself—it's a distinct gap in my experience.

Moreover, my blood and semen have been sadly depleted by these four, and I need to learn some tactics for building them up again. If that whore knows all these magical arts, it'll take me just one night with her to learn how to ingest the essence, after which I'll be able to enjoy myself for the rest of my life. If it's such a boon, why not try it?

He decided to return home to see his wife and then travel on to the capital to visit the famous courtesan.

His journey itself was of no importance, but it led to certain results:

> The fury in his heart could not have been vented by
> toppling Mount Tai,
> The shame on his face could not have been cleansed by
> scooping up the West River.

If you wish to learn the details, you will find them in the next chapter.

CRITIQUE

Vesperus's lechery and wickedness have now reached their climax. If his wife had been made to take a lover without becoming a prostitute, it would not have gladdened our hearts, any more than if she had become a prostitute without entertaining the three women's husbands. If, by the end of a lewd book, there is no character or event but has met with retribution, all those readers who have committed any sins of the flesh will find themselves bathed in a cold sweat. That is just the kind of lewd book we should read more of!

CHAPTER *N*INETEEN

The cup of his sins runs full, as two wives bring
*   disgrace;*
Buddhist mysteries are revealed, as sensuous pleasure
*   turns to emptiness.*

Poem:

How vivid the peonies, purple and gold!
Yet sense is empty, to Buddha's mind.
Just wait till all the peonies fall,
And Buddha's eyes won't seem so blind.

Before setting off, Vesperus paid a farewell call on the Knave
and asked him to watch over the family during his absence.

"Looking after someone's family is not something to be
taken on lightly," said the Knave. "Children are easy enough.
It's wives that are the problem. I'm a rough and ready sort of
fellow, and all I can see to are the daily necessities; I can't stand

guard over your women's quarters for you. If there's anything your wife needs in the line of food, firewood, or money, she has only to ask for it; but I can't give much of a guarantee about other matters. You'll have to go home and instruct her yourself."

"The daily necessities are my only concern," said Vesperus. "I've already spoken to her about the other matters. Anyway she's an experienced woman, quite different from when she was first married. A potential seducer with any practical qualifications would surely be no better endowed than Honest Quan, and she found him inadequate and married me instead. I doubt that there's another man like me anywhere, so there's really no cause for worry."

"You're right. Just so long as you can trust her. In that case I don't mind taking it on."

Vesperus took his leave, then wrote four love poems and sent them secretly to Flora and her nieces as a farewell message. Finally, after several nights of love with Fragrance, he set off.

Arriving in his hometown after days of travel, he made his way to Iron Door's house, where he knocked for a long time without response. He was rather pleased. So the household really is strictly run, he thought. I doubt that any outsider has been in; it wouldn't have mattered if I'd stayed away months longer.

After knocking until dark, he finally glimpsed someone peeping at him through the crack in the door. Vesperus realized it must be the Master and addressed him: "Father-in-law, open up. It's your son-in-law."

The Master hastily opened the door and let him in. Vesperus went through into the hall, greeted him formally, and then sat down and began asking after the family, first about his father-in-law's health and then about his wife's.

The Master heaved a sigh. "I keep fairly well myself, with

no ailments to speak of, but my daughter suffered a terrible misfortune. After you left, she came down with an illness that prevented her from either sleeping or eating. Finally she fell into a depression, and in less than a year she passed away." He began to sob bitterly.

"How could that happen!" exclaimed Vesperus, as he began to beat his chest, stamp his feet, and accompany the Master in his sobbing. "Where is her coffin? Has she been buried yet?" he asked, after sobbing awhile.

"It has been kept in the cloister. I wanted you to see it before the burial."

Vesperus had the cloister opened and, prostrating himself on the coffin, wept again before eventually composing himself.

Where do you suppose the coffin came from? When the Master found out that his daughter had run off with a lover, he could not bear to tell anyone, partly because he was afraid of the neighbors' ridicule, and partly because he feared the day his son-in-law came looking for her. His solution was to buy a coffin, seal it up, and give out that his daughter had died of an illness and that he was keeping her coffin at home for the time being. In this way he could stop the news getting out and also deter his son-in-law from trying to find her.

Since his father-in-law was normally the soul of honesty, Vesperus readily accepted the explanation. Moreover, his own departure had come right in the middle of his wife's sexual awakening, and it seemed entirely plausible that, with her torrid sexual desires suddenly denied an outlet, the resulting depression might have brought on an illness. Thus his suspicions were not in the least aroused. In fact quite the contrary; in a mood of bitter self-reproach, he called in priests to hold services for three days and nights to commend her soul to immediate rebirth, lest she resent his lechery from her place in

Hell and become so jealous as to emulate the dead wife who snatched Wang Kui from the living.[89]

After the services, on the pretext of seeking further education, he again took leave of the Master and set off for the capital to learn the technique of revitalization.

Arriving in the capital after a laborious journey, he deposited his luggage and went in search of the beautiful courtesan. He found out where she lived and went to see her, but as bad luck would have it, she had been invited out a few days before by a certain gentleman who was loath to let her return. The Maid reported as much to Vesperus, who departed crestfallen.

He waited another day or two in his lodgings before paying a second visit. "I had a note from her yesterday," said the Maid, "to say that she would not be back until this evening but that if there was a guest here, I could ask him to wait."

Delighted, Vesperus handed over a thirty-tael retainer, enough for a stay of several nights. He had also brought several private gifts that he planned to give her in person.

"It's still quite early," said the madam, taking charge of the retainer. "If you have other business, sir, by all means attend to it and come back later. If you have nothing better to do, of course you are most welcome to stay."

"I did not think a thousand *li* too far to come to see your daughter. No, I have no other business."

"In that case you may sit in my daughter's room and read a book or take a nap, as you wish, while you wait for her to join you. There are things I need to attend to and I'm afraid I'll not be able to keep you company."

---

89. In a famous story Wang was supported in his studies by Gui Ying and swore vows of eternal love. Then, after succeeding in the civil service examinations, he married someone else. After Gui Ying had killed herself, her ghost claimed Wang's life.

"Don't let me hold you up. Please feel free to go on with your work."

The Maid showed Vesperus into the room and told a young prostitute to burn incense and make tea and attend on him as he read. But Vesperus was interested only in building up his vital energies for his sexual encounter that night, so he lay down and rested from noon to dusk. At dusk he arose and, picking up an idle book, was leafing through it when he saw a strikingly beautiful woman peer in at him through the window and then rush off. The young prostitute was in the room at the time. "Who was that who looked in just now?" he asked.

"That was my elder sister," she replied.

From the beautiful courtesan's behavior, Vesperus was afraid that she meant to reject him, and he hurried out to intercept her before she could get inside.

Jade Scent had recognized her husband at first glance and leaped to the conclusion that he had come to have her arrested. Panic-stricken, she rushed in to ask the Maid for some way of escape, but before she had time to explain, she realized that Vesperus was coming after her. This alarmed her even more. She did not know what to do and just said, "This man is someone I cannot possibly meet. You mustn't let him see me," then dashed into the Maid's room, shut the door, and lay down trembling on the bed without another word. The Maid had no idea what Jade Scent meant, but simply assumed that she disliked the man and would refuse to come out and meet him.

"I've had another note from my daughter to say she has been kept on and won't be back today," she told Vesperus. "In fact not for another couple of days. I hardly know what to suggest."

"Your daughter's back already! Why are you telling me this? Is it because my retainer was too small and you want an increase?"

The Maid continued to dissemble. "She's not back, and that's all there is to it. I assure you I have no such thought in mind."

Vesperus's face hardened. "But I saw her just now, as clear as day, peering at me through the window and then darting off to avoid me. Why are you telling me these lies? It's only because my retainer wasn't big enough that she won't receive me! But, as the saying goes, 'Keep your reproaches to yourself.' What's the harm in meeting somebody? She can still take her leave of me with a few parting words. Why does she have to cut me off so cruelly? Does she think she'll make a big impression on me if I just see her once?"

The Maid stuck to her story, her jaw set firm.

"Look here, just now I saw a woman run into your bedroom and hide. Since your daughter isn't back, let me search the room. If she's not there, I'll leave just as I am, without a woman and without my money. What do you say?"

His words cut too close to the truth. The Maid thought it would be embarrassing if he found Jade Scent and brought her out, so she tried to disarm him. "To tell you the truth, sir, she *is* back. She's keeping out of sight because some vicious lout drained her energies for several nights in a row, and she's such a wreck she'll need a night or two to recover before receiving anyone else. But since you're so determined to see her, let me call her out. There's no need to search the room."

"Then let me ask her myself," said Vesperus, "so that she won't think me insincere and use that as an excuse for not seeing me." He followed hard on the Maid's heels as she went up to the door and began to plead.

"Child," called the Maid, "this gentlemen is absolutely determined to see you. Won't you come out and meet him?"

She repeated her request several times, but heard nothing in reply. "Try once more," said Vesperus, "and if she still won't open up, I shall have to use force."

Inside the room Jade Scent saw little hope for herself. Vesperus would surely insist on taking her to court, where she would be tortured and die, by one means or another. Far better to die now, before he saw her, and spare herself all the misery. She undid the silken cord from her waist, strung it over a low beam, and hanged herself.

When Vesperus forced his way into the room, she had already been dead for some time. His one thought, on seeing the tragedy he had caused, was to escape, and he had no time to look at her closely. He had turned and was about to flee, when the Maid saw that he had driven Jade Scent to her death and held him in a firm grip. "Where do you think you're going?" she screamed. "You and I have no feud from a previous life and there's no bad blood between us in this one, so why did you drive her to her death, the one person I had to depend on in my old age?"

At the height of the commotion, a number of customers came up. They were all young noblemen, clients of Jade Scent's who had been deprived of her company for the past few days and now, on learning of her return, had hurried to the house and chanced to arrive together. Hearing she had been driven to her death, they were even more distraught than if their own wives had been murdered. Bristling with fury and consumed with hatred for the murderer, they promptly ordered the house stewards to attack Vesperus. The stewards pinned him to the ground and rained hundreds of blows on him with their clubs, avoiding those places where a blow might have been fatal, but leaving the rest of his body black and blue. Then they put him in chains and locked him up beside the dead woman until the constables could make their inspection and take the next of kin to court to press charges.

Up to this point Vesperus had been so intent on escaping that he had not even glanced at the dead woman. But now, with his bones broken and his muscles torn, he could scarcely move and, shackled as he was, he abandoned all hope of getting away. There was nothing left to do but look at her and find out what nemesis this was that had done him such grievous harm. But when he approached the corpse and examined its face, he was aghast.

She's the image of my dead wife, he thought. How can there be any two faces so exactly alike?

He looked at her and pondered, and the more he looked and pondered, the more closely she resembled his wife, until finally it occurred to him that the story of her dying of an illness had been suspect from the beginning. Perhaps, he reflected, Jade Scent ran off with someone and my father-in-law was too embarrassed to tell me about it—even bought a coffin to deceive me? What's more, if this woman had nothing to be ashamed of, why would she try to hide from me? Finally, when she realized she couldn't hide, why else would she take her life?

At this stage in his thoughts he felt fairly certain, but the possibility nagged at him that it might still be a case of identical women. He needed to think of some unique feature of his wife's that would clinch the matter. Recalling that she had a cauterizing scar on the crown of her head where the hair had not grown back, he undid the dead woman's chignon and parted her hair. On her crown he found a patch of bare skin the size of a fingertip.

Just as he arrived at his conclusion, the constables burst into the room and began asking him about the cause of death for their report on the incident.

"The dead woman is my first wife," Vesperus told them, "who was abducted and sold to the Maid to entertain clients. I came here to visit the courtesan in complete ignorance of all this, and she hanged herself because she was too ashamed to meet me. It wasn't until I was locked in here with her that I looked at her closely and recognized her. I shall certainly protest this injustice to the authorities. I wish to be taken there at once so that I can be set free. I have nothing further to say."

The constables then questioned the Maid. In fact she knew nothing about it, but they suspected her of trying to lie her way out of trouble. "Who sold this woman to you?" they asked. "If it was a dealer, he must have brought several women along, not just this one. Since the dead woman can't tell us anything, we shall need to question the others."

"I bought her together with her maid, who is here now. Let me call her out."

But when she went to call her, Ruyi was nowhere to be found. The Maid assumed she had run away, but in fact she had merely hidden herself under the Maid's bed, where she was soon found. On seeing her former master, she had been terrified and had fled into the Maid's room together with Jade Scent. Then, when she saw her mistress hang herself and Vesperus force his way into the room, she knew there would be trouble and wriggled under the bed, where she had lain all this time, wondering what to do. To her surprise she was discovered and dragged out.

The constables asked if she knew Vesperus. Ruyi meant to deny it, but her face and voice gave her away. The constables understood and threatened her until she confessed. She told them in great detail how Jade Scent had committed adultery with someone at home and gotten pregnant, and then, for fear her father would condemn her to death when he found out, had been forced to elope, taking Ruyi along with her. Her lover, however, had betrayed her and sold her into prostitution.

Now that they were in possession of the facts, the constables urged the parties to settle the case out of court. Someone who drove his wife to her death would surely not have to answer for it with his life, they felt, and someone who bought a woman in good faith for the entertainment of her clients could hardly be convicted of kidnapping.

All that remained was the question of Ruyi's future. Did her former master want her or not? If he did, he should buy her back. If not, she should stay where she was. By this time Vesperus, who had given himself up for dead, no longer cared about his own life; in fact he wanted to die, and the sooner the better. What use did he have for a maidservant?

"By rights," he said, "I ought to take the case to court and request an investigation, if only to relieve my anger. But I'm afraid the story will get bandied about and give me an unsavory reputation. So I'll suppress my feelings and do as you gentlemen suggest. As for the maid, since she has been a prostitute, it would be awkward to take her back. Let her stay."

On hearing him speak so honestly, the Maid concluded she would have nothing to fear from him in the future and, at the constables' suggestion, she unlocked his chains, gave him back his retainer, and sent him on his way. Before he could get out, however, he was punched by the other clients and cursed as a cuckold. By the time he reached his lodgings, the pain of the beatings had intensified, and all he could do was lie on his bed and bemoan his fate.

I used to believe I had a right to sleep with other men's wives, he thought, but that my wife could never under any circumstances sleep with anyone else, so I spent all my time lusting after women and taking advantage of every woman I met. I never dreamed that the principle of retribution would work with such amazing speed. While I was down there sleeping with their wives, they were up here sleeping with my wife, but whereas my affair was secret, theirs was carried on in public, and while I took a man's wife and made her my concubine, someone took my wife and turned her into a prostitute. In the light of my experience, adultery is something to be avoided at all costs. I remember Abbot Lone Peak pleading with me three years ago to join the Buddhist order. When I kept refusing, he tried to persuade me by explaining in great detail what the retribution for adultery would be, but I continued to argue that not every adultery would necessarily be punished. I see now that every last one of those debts has to be paid. I doubt that the Lord of Heaven holds a special grudge and reserves all his harshness for me while letting everybody else off lightly!

He continued his self-examination: I also argued that a man's own wife and concubines are limited in number while there is an infinite supply of women in the world, so that if he seduces an infinite number of women and pays for it only with a wife or concubine, he is making a huge profit and certainly not taking a loss. But, by my calculations, I have slept with only five or six women in the course of my entire life, whereas my wife, after taking up this business, has slept with thousands or at least hundreds. Has any debt ever been repaid at a higher rate of interest?

Lone Peak also told me that since his words had failed to convince me, I would have to gain my enlightenment on the carnal prayer mat. I've spent enough time on that mat these past few years and tasted every drop of honey and gall it has to offer. If I am ever to see the light, now is the time! The humiliation I suffered today was more than just the beating and the cursing. Obviously it was Abbot Lone Peak working through others to administer a blow and a shout to force me to repent![90] Even if I don't repent, I shall never have the face to return home. Far better to beat a retreat and write a candid

90. A Buddhist notion, it denotes a salutary shock administered by a religious mentor.

letter to the Knave asking him to arrange a match for Fragrance and marry her off. The twins can go with her, if she wishes, or else stay with the Knave and be raised by him. I myself will go off on my own to Mount Guacang to look for Abbot Lone Peak and do penance for my sins with a hundred and twenty ringing kowtows. Then I'll beseech him to point out where I have gone astray and guide me back to the path of enlightenment. Capital!

Now that Vesperus had decided what to do, he sat down to write the letter to the Knave, but his hands had been so badly hurt in the beatings that he couldn't write. Only after a month of recuperation was he able to write again. By an odd coincidence, just when he was beginning his letter, a letter arrived from the Knave. On opening it, he learned of a crisis at home that required his immediate return, but he was not told its nature. "The only possibility is that my wife is ill or that something has happened to one of the children," he speculated. When questioned, the messenger at first said nothing; only when pressed did he reveal the truth—that Vesperus's second wife had taken a leaf out of his first wife's book and run off with a lover.

Vesperus asked who the man was. "I don't know," replied the messenger. "In fact, not even her maid knows. All she can say is that she heard the bed creaking every night before the mistress went off, but when she got up in the morning, there was never a trace of anyone there. After a dozen nights like that, she got up one morning to find the doors wide open and the mistress nowhere to be found. The head of the house set off to catch them and at the same time sent me here to urge you to return at once."

Vesperus sighed. This letter is just another blow and shout! Obviously, he thought, adulterous debts must never be incurred, for they need to be paid back a hundredfold. I realize now that my debts cannot be repaid and that, so long as there are any women left in my family, they will have to go on paying my debts off. In the light of this, I ought not to think too kindly even of those two mites of mine. How do I know that they're not potential redeemers themselves? But I can't worry about any of that. I'll wait until I have consulted Lone Peak about the future.

He ground up some ink and wrote a letter of farewell to the Knave:

> The elopement of my wanton concubine should come as no surprise, for what is ill gotten will be ill lost. This is a constant principle in life, and the recent events at home are just another illustration of it. I am well aware that the cup of my sins has run full and that I deserve this retribution. However, the day evil influences are exorcised is the same day that the spirit of penitence emerges. Instead of returning East of the River, I shall go home to the Pure Land of the West.[91] My sole regret is that the womb of disaster has not been destroyed, but that I continue to clasp these twin nemeses to my breast. Let me trouble my old friend to extend their lives for the moment. When I have seen the buddha, I shall borrow the sword of wisdom and dispatch them. In haste.

He sent off the letter and packed his bags for departure. He had intended to take Satchel with him, to serve him as a

---

91. *East of the River* was the base from which Xiang Yu, a contender for the empire during the decline of the Qin dynasty, launched his campaign. In defeat, he spurned the idea of returning and beginning all over again. The Pure Land is the Buddhist Western Paradise, which holds the hope of perfect happiness.

novice. But on reflection, he feared that having a catamite with him might only stimulate his lust again. Better not risk distraction by setting eyes on any object of desire. In the end he sent him back with the messenger and started off alone, an action that is summed up in the proverb "A man bitten by a snake will be frightened of an old rope for years thereafter."

CRITIQUE

In this chapter the author's main purpose has at last become clear. Readers of *The Carnal Prayer Mat* will qualify as competent readers of fiction if they read the other chapters once but this chapter and the next one three times each.

CHAPTER *TWENTY*

Through Leather Bag's generosity, satyr and rogue are
*   saved;*
On the broad Buddhist highway, enemy and creditor
*   are able to meet.*

Poem:
>   Though enemies fight to the bitter end,
>   With an eye for an eye, is the feud ever done?
>   So abandon the path where enemies meet,
>   And leave it to Wu and Yue to run.[92]

Let us tell how the priest Lone Peak had been continually
reproaching himself ever since he let Vesperus slip through his

------

92. In the Zhou dynasty, the states of Wu and Yue were legendary
enemies.

fingers. In the last resort my Buddhist powers were not strong enough nor my compassion deep enough, he said to himself. This demon of love and satyr of lust passed right in front of my eyes, and I was not able to capture him. All the blame for letting him pollute mankind and work his evil will on the fair sex belongs to me, not to him. Since I've failed at catching demons and satyrs, what earthly good is this leather bag?

He hung the bag from the top of a pine tree outside his door, then planed a piece of wood, wrote a message on it in small characters, and nailed it to the tree.

The notice read,

For as long as Vesperus stays away, I shall leave this leather bag here, and for as long as it endures, I shall not give up hope. My only wish is that I may soon be able to take it down and that he will not have to occupy the carnal prayer mat forever.

There was something distinctly odd about the bag, for from the time of Vesperus's departure, when it was hung on the tree, a full three years had passed, a thousand and several hundred days in all, and not only had it not deteriorated in the slightest, it had steadily become more durable.

Vesperus could see from a distance that there was something hanging from the tree. At first he supposed it to be a cassock hung out to air, and only when he got closer did he see that it was a leather bag. Then, on reading the notice, he began to weep and wail. There was no need to save his kowtows for his meeting with the priest; instead he treated the notice as if it were the priest's image and kowtowed dozens of times before it. He then climbed the tree, took down the bag, and went into the Buddha Hall wearing it on his head. As on his first visit, Lone Peak was engaged in meditation. Vesperus promptly knelt down and kowtowed nonstop, like

the disciple who bowed down before the Fifty-three Deities.[93]
He kowtowed from the beginning of the meditation period
right through to the end, some six hours in all, far exceeding
the one hundred and twenty kowtows he had set for himself.

At last Lone Peak arose from the prayer mat and helped
him up. "Worthy lay brother, your favoring me with another
visit is generosity enough. Why this elaborate ceremony? Do
come up!"

"Your pupil is a born fool!" said Vesperus. "I deeply
regret that I did not accept your teaching when last I came
here. Through wanton self-indulgence and folly I have done
all manner of things sufficient to condemn me to Hell. My
thisworldly retribution has already been received, but the
otherworldly variety still awaits me. I beseech you, reverend
master, take pity on me now and accept me as your pupil,
teaching me to repent my sins and turn to religion. Are you
willing to take me in?"

"You brought in my leather bag," said Lone Peak, "so you
must have seen the notice. After you left, I almost wore out
my eyes watching for your return, so how can I refuse you
now that you turn to Buddha? My one fear is that your
vocation may not be strong enough and that you will fall back
into the mundane world. But it was for your sake that I left
the bag at the mercy of the elements these past three years."

"I was in the depths of remorse," said Vesperus, "when
suddenly I felt the need to repent. I think of myself as having
escaped from Hell and would never dare go back. Of course
I'll never change my mind! I beseech you, master, take me in."

"Very well, I shall accept you."

Vesperus got to his feet and began to bow in greeting all

---

93. A reference to Sudhana, whose visits to religious luminaries
occupy much of the *Huayan Sutra*.

over again. This time Lone Peak stood there and received the bows, then chose an auspicious day for the tonsure. With Lone Peak's permission, Vesperus selected his own name in religion: Stubborn Stone. It signified regret over his slowness to repent, which showed the stubbornness of a stone, and also gratitude for Lone Peak's skillful preaching, which had persuaded a stubborn stone that hadn't nodded its head in three years to start nodding it again. In general, too, he wanted a name that would serve him as a reminder, lest he forget what he had done and start thinking evil thoughts once more.

From that time forth he took pride in his Zen meditation and devoted himself wholeheartedly to understanding doctrine. Lest a life of luxury stimulate his lust again, he neither dressed nor ate well, but preferred to develop his religious vocation by exposing himself to hunger and cold.

But any young man joining the order has certain problems he must face. However strongly he tries to rein in his lusts, however firmly he tries to extinguish his desires, prayer and scripture reading will get him through the day well enough, but in the wee hours of the morning that erect member of his will start bothering him of its own accord, making a nuisance of itself under the bedclothes, uncontrollable, irrepressible. His only solution is to find some form of appeasement, either by using his fingers for emergency relief or by discovering some young novice with whom to mediate a solution. (Both methods are regular standbys for the clergy.) Had Vesperus done so, no one who caught him at it would have been disposed to criticize. Even Guanyin herself would have forgiven him, if she had come to hear of it; she would hardly have had him consumed in the fires of his own lust![94]

Vesperus felt differently, however. He maintained that those who had joined the order ought to accept its command-

_____

94. The goddess of mercy.

ment against sexual desire as a cardinal rule, whether or not their standbys took the form of actual adultery. Even if the standbys broke no rules and brought no dishonor to those practicing them, they represented a failure to suppress desire just as surely as adultery itself. Moreover, the handgun led to intercourse, and homosexual relations to heterosexual. Sight of the make-believe causes us to yearn for the reality, and one act leads to another by an inexorable process that we must not allow to get started.

One night he dreamed that some women came to worship at the temple. On approaching them, he was astonished to find that they were all old friends of his. Flora was there, as were Cloud and her sisters, and also his two eloping wives, Jade Scent and Fragrance.

The sight of his wives infuriated Vesperus, and he called on Flora and her nieces to help him catch them. But in the twinkling of an eye the wives vanished, leaving only the four friends, who drew him into a priest's cell and proceeded to do with him what they had done so often before. They undressed and were about to begin another contest, with Vesperus's penis fitted into someone's vagina and ready to thrust, when all of a sudden he was awakened by a dog barking in a nearby wood and realized that he had been dreaming. That erect member of his, however, still assumed there was a treat in store for it, and it butted and burrowed here and there among the bedclothes looking for its old haunts. Stubborn Stone took it in his hand and was thinking of some way to appease it, when suddenly he stopped.

This is the root cause of all my sins, my nemesis, he thought. I don't have to take revenge on it, but I must not let it loose.

Having come to that conclusion, he banished the foolish idea from his mind and tried to get some sleep before it was time to rise and chant sutras again.

But he tossed and turned in bed and could not get back to sleep, tormented beyond endurance by the root of evil under his bedclothes. So long as this accursed thing is attached to me, he thought, I'll always be bothered by it. The best solution is to cut it off and eliminate all the trouble it's going to cause me. Moreover, dog's flesh is anathema to the Buddhists and I oughtn't to have it attached to me. If I don't cut it off, I can never be anything more than an animal. Even if I cultivate my behavior to perfection, the best I can hope for is to be reborn as a human being. How can I ever become a buddha?

Having arrived at this conclusion, he could not wait for daybreak. He lit the lamp, picked up a thin vegetable knife, and honed it a few times on the ewer. Then, taking his penis in one hand, he brought the knife down on it with all the force he could muster, slicing the organ right off.

Evidently he was destined to shed his animal fate and to be transformed, for the amputation did not feel terribly painful. From that time on, his desires ceased and his moral purpose gained in strength, and the perceptiveness shown in his religious studies grew steadily. By this time Lone Peak had numerous disciples, all men of some knowledge. They would gather to listen to his sermons and, of them all, Stubborn Stone was the one most apt to nod his head in understanding.

His first six months were devoted to a general training in moral conduct in readiness for ordination. When the training period was over, Stubborn Stone gathered together a dozen or more priests and asked Lone Peak to take the platform and expound the doctrine. All the priests were men who had committed themselves to accepting the commandments and living a life of meditation, with no thought of ever returning to their old lives.

Now, when monks are about to receive the commandments, their first step is to confess every sin they have committed in the course of their lives and then, having set forth the case against themselves, to kneel down before Buddha and beg an eminent priest to pray for their forgiveness. Any suppression of the facts is known as "cheating Heaven and deceiving Buddha" and infringes upon one of the cardinal tenets of the faith. No transgressor can ever hope to attain true enlightenment, even if he slaves away at moral cultivation for the rest of his life.

The priests invited Lone Peak to mount the platform, where he prayed and then set the order for their initiation. The priests sat in two rows on either side of him as he explained the commandments. After detailing what it meant to accept them, he ordered everyone to confess his sins, holding nothing back. Stubborn Stone, as the last to arrive, was sitting in last place and all he could do, until his turn came, was to listen to the others' confessions. Among them were murderers and arsonists, thieves and bandits, as well as some who, like Stubborn Stone himself, had undermined the moral law with their adulteries. All of them confessed, not daring to hold anything back. At length it was the turn of the priest sitting next to Stubborn Stone, a man who, despite a coarse appearance, seemed to have a certain spiritual air about him.

"In thirty-odd years," he confessed to Lone Peak, "your disciple has done only one evil thing: I indentured myself as a servant, seduced my master's daughter, and then abducted the daughter and her personal maid and sold them both into prostitution. It is a sin that cannot be expiated by death. I beg you, master, to intercede for my forgiveness."

"That is far too grievous a sin," replied Lone Peak. "I'm afraid it is beyond the reach of forgiveness. As the adage goes, 'Of all evils, adultery is worst.' Adultery on its own would be bad enough, how could you go and compound it with abduction? Both adultery and abduction are always extremely difficult to gain forgiveness for. Why did you sell her into prostitution and turn one man's wife into every man's mistress? She cannot be set free in this life, which means you cannot be set free either. Even if I pray for forgiveness, I'm afraid Buddha won't grant it. What can I do?"

"Master, I beg leave to explain. It was not by my own choice that I did this. I was forced into it. The woman's husband seduced my wife and then made me sell her, and I was powerless to resist. So I had to go outside the law and do these terrible things. But they were done under extenuating circumstances; I should not be compared to some lecher who is merely seeking to gratify his lust. I wonder, might you still be able to pray for my forgiveness?"

Stubborn Stone found himself strangely affected by the man's confession. "Let me ask you, worthy brother," he said to the priest, "what was the name of the woman you abducted? Whose wife and whose daughter was she? And where is she now?"

"She was the wife of Scholar Vesperus and the daughter of Master Iron Door. Her name is Jade Scent and her maid's name is Ruyi. She and the maid are in the capital now, entertaining clients. You don't happen to know her, by any chance?"

Stubborn Stone was thunderstruck. "Then you must be Honest Quan," he said. "How do you come to be here?"

"Let me ask, might you be Scholar Vesperus?"

"Yes, I am."

The two men left their prayer mats and begged each other's forgiveness. Then they revealed to Lone Peak all that had happened and each confessed his sins.

Lone Peak roared with laughter. "What a fine pair of enemies you are! You were bound to cross each other's paths sooner or later. Since you knew what the outcome would be, why didn't you pay heed at the outset? Luckily for you, Buddha's compassion has given you this broad highway on which enemies can pass without let or hindrance. If you'd met on any other path, you'd now be locked in endless struggle. In principle your sins are beyond forgiveness, but thanks to your virtuous wives' redeeming your debts for you, much of the burden has been lifted from your shoulders. Otherwise, even if you cultivated your conduct for ten lives, let alone one, you'd still be condemned to the cycle of birth and death, unable to escape your fate. I shall now pray for your forgiveness and beseech the Bodhisattva to extend her compassion and show you a measure of mercy for the sake of those wives of yours. Pity these poor women! Each of them was worthy of a memorial arch or tablet, but was forced by her husband's lechery to behave like a wanton and redeem his debts. And even after she has discharged his debts in this world, there will still be debts for her to discharge in the other. The men we needn't concern ourselves with, but oh, how they ill-use the women who redeem their debts, women unjustly condemned to lives of shame!" He told both men to kneel down in front of Buddha while he recited from the scriptures and prayed for their forgiveness.

"Master," Stubborn Stone asked him when the prayers were done, "I have a question for you. If, to give a hypothetical example, an adulterer were to have both a wife and a daughter, once the wife has redeemed his debts, can the baby daughter be spared, so that she doesn't have to redeem them, too?"

Lone Peak shook his head. "Quite impossible. The adulterer's only hope is to have no daughters at all. Any daughter he has will be a potential redeemer. How can she be forgiven?"

"To be frank with you, master," said Stubborn Stone, "your disciple has the misfortune to be the father of two potential redeemers, both of whom are at home. From what you say, they will definitely not be forgiven. Your disciple therefore wishes to return and eradicate these roots of evil with the sword of wisdom, as if they had been drowned at birth. That should not be too grave a sin."

"Amitabha Buddha!" exclaimed Lone Peak, placing his palms reverently together. "Such a wicked suggestion should never have left your lips or entered my ears! How can a priest who has accepted the commandment not to kill even think of such a thing? A layman is forbidden to kill, let alone a priest! They're still in swaddling clothes, they've done nothing wrong! What crime are you going to kill them for? And if you wait until they *have* done something wrong, it will be too late to reclaim the debts they'll have repaid. Your violence will all be in vain anyway. Far better to spare them!"

"But how can I settle this matter?"

"Those two are not your daughters," said Lone Peak. "They were sent by the Lord of Heaven to redeem your debts when he saw the intolerable evil you were doing. As the proverb says, 'One good deed cancels out a thousand evil deeds.' If you turn your mind steadfastly to goodness, the Lord of Heaven may change his decision and recall them. There's no need for any sword of wisdom!"

Stubborn Stone nodded. "You are perfectly right, master, and your disciple will do your bidding." From that day forward he ceased to worry about his family and turned his whole mind to the service of Buddha.

Another six months passed. One day, as Stubborn Stone was talking to Lone Peak in the hall, a great, strapping fellow whom he recognized as the Knave came rushing in. The newcomer paid homage to the image of Buddha, then bowed before Lone Peak.

"Master," explained Stubborn Stone, "this is my sworn brother, A Match for the Knave of Kunlun, whom I have often mentioned. He is the foremost gallant of the age, one who manages to do righteous deeds in the midst of evil."

"Am I to understand that you are that hero of a burglar with his Five Abstentions?" asked Lone Peak.

"He is," said Stubborn Stone.

"In that case you're a bodhisattva of a thief!" said Lone Peak. "Who am I to receive bows from a bodhisattva?" He was about to kneel down and return the bows, when the Knave reached out and stopped him.

"If the master is unwilling to receive a thief's bows," said the Knave, "I can only assume it is because you want to exclude me from the faith. Your disciple may be a thief, but I have a kinder heart than many who are not thieves. The reason I came to this treasure mountain was both to visit a friend of mine and also to pay my respects to a living buddha. If you refuse to accept my bows, you will be cutting off my path to goodness and strengthening my will to evil. It would seem as if we ought to hide the nature of our profession and become the sort of thieves who are clad in official robes rather than the sort who break and enter, and that would never do."

"In that case," said Lone Peak, "I shall not dare return your bows."

After greeting Stubborn Stone, the Knave sat down and exchanged a few polite remarks with Lone Peak, then drew the Stone aside for a private conversation.

"I have told the master everything," said the Stone. "Whatever the family secret, you can talk about it in front of him. Anyway, this living buddha knows the past as well as the future and cannot be deceived."

The Knave sat down again and told Stubborn Stone the news of his family, apologizing for failing in his responsibilities and breaking his promises to a friend. Not only was he unfit to entrust a wife to, he was also unfit to take care of children, and he was ashamed to face his friend.

"From what you are saying," said Stubborn Stone, "I gather something must have happened to the fruits of my sin?"

"Just so. I don't know why, but your daughters suddenly died, both at the same time. They weren't suffering from smallpox or convulsions, and they were sleeping peacefully when it happened. The night of their death the wet nurses heard a voice calling out in their dreams: 'His debts have been settled and there is no need for you anymore. Come back with me.' When the nurses awoke, they had no sooner touched the children than they realized it was too late. There is something terribly strange about the whole affair."

Stubborn Stone said nothing in response, but went and bowed several times in front of Buddha and again before Lone Peak. Then he told the Knave how he had been worried lest his daughters redeem his debts and how Lone Peak had told him that if he turned his mind steadfastly to goodness, the Lord of Heaven might change his decision and recall them. "It's a stroke of good fortune," he went on to say, "that these agents of retribution have been removed. You ought to be congratulating me, brother, rather than talking about a breach of trust."

At these words the Knave felt a chill run down his spine and paused a moment before continuing. "Apart from the bad news, I do have one piece of good news that should cheer you up."

"What is that?" asked Stubborn Stone.

"I felt terrible when that slut Fragrance ran away. I tried to catch her, but without success. It turned out she had been abducted by a priest, who kept her hidden in a cellar. Quite by chance I found her there and rid you of this root of evil. Doesn't that cheer you up?"

"A cellar would seem to be a safe enough place to hide," said Lone Peak. "How did you happen to find her?"

"The priest was living near a crossroads, where he used to

rob and murder passersby. I heard that he had a vast sum
stashed away in the cellar, so one night I went there to steal
it. Imagine my surprise when I found him in bed talking with
a woman who sounded exactly like Fragrance! I kept out of
sight and listened, and gradually the situation became clear to
me. I heard my name mentioned as well as yours. She said her
first husband was Honest Quan, who, although a little coarse,
was at least a one-woman husband, without any other wives
or concubines. To her surprise a certain person helped another
person to seduce her and force her into marriage, after which
the latter abandoned her and gave himself up to debauchery,
leaving her alone in an empty house. Eventually, physically
worn out, he was unable to cope with his domestic duties and
set off on a long journey to escape them, heedless as to whether
his wife and children lived or died. 'Why should I stay with
such a faithless wretch?' she said. At this point my anger could
no longer be restrained. Luckily I had a sword on me, so I flung
aside the curtain and cut them both in two with a single stroke,
then lit a torch and hunted for their booty. I found over two
thousand taels, which I brought back and donated as I saw fit
to countless poor people, doing numerous good deeds. Let me
ask you, master, was it right, in your opinion, to kill this
couple and take their money?"

"They deserved to die," said Lone Peak, "but it was for
Heaven to kill them, not you, worthy layman. And they
deserved to lose their money, but it was for the authorities to
take it, not you. Your action is deeply satisfying, to be sure,
but it doesn't quite square either with the Principle of Heaven
or with the law, and I'm afraid you will not be able to escape
retribution for it in this world or the next."

"But if our nature is in accord with the Principle of
Heaven," said the Knave, "so long as we feel an action to be
deeply satisfying, why shouldn't it square with the manifest
justice of the Principle? Your disciple has spent his entire life

as a thief without ever getting into any trouble. Are you telling me that I'm now going to fall foul of the law?"

"That's not the way to look at it, layman," said Lone Peak. "Both the Principle of Heaven and the law are absolutely watertight. No one who harms the Principle or breaks the law ever gets away with it. His retribution may come early, or it may come late. If it comes early, it will be less severe, but if it is long delayed, it will suddenly burst upon him with intolerable force. That priest had broken the commandment against lust and the woman the law against adultery, and of course the Lord of Heaven would have destroyed them. But does he not have the Thunder God to do it for him? Does he need to turn to a mere mortal for help in killing them? Even if he does, well, every mortal in the world has a pair of hands. Why should he turn to you in particular? Are your hands the only ones that can kill? The sovereign authority must not be lent, nor the sword of authority allowed to slip away. The Lord of Heaven cannot handle such a serious matter himself, so he sees that sinners are killed by other sinners. No one, absolutely no one, is left out! Thus your otherworldly retribution certainly cannot be avoided.

"Perhaps your action is less serious and will be judged a little less severely than if you had killed honest folk. But since you've followed this profession all your life, surely by now every official in the country knows your reputation. As the proverb says, 'A man fears fame as a pig fears to grow fat.' You may have done good by giving your money to the poor, but no one will ever believe it; people will always suspect that you have a secret cellar under your house where you've hidden the money, and sooner or later they'll come after you. If you really had the stolen money at home, you could use it to buy them off and so save your skin. But I'm afraid you'll find the money you gave to the poor impossible to recall at short notice, and your life will be in jeopardy. Thus your thisworldly retribution is inescapable too. And a delayed retribution may well prove worse than the sin itself."

The Knave had always been a violent man with a fiery temper that everyone feared, so he had never received any moral advice. Now, confronted with the priest's compelling arguments, he felt moved by a spirit of repentance. There was no need to pressure him further; he was committed to reforming himself.

"Admittedly," he said to Lone Peak, "the things I have done are not the actions of a good or superior man. But since rich men are unwilling to distribute their money themselves, it has been my practice to take a little from them and do a few good deeds in their behalf. In doing so, I am thinking of others, not myself. From what you say, however, I have done many evil things for which retribution is inescapable, both in this world and in the next. If I repent now, will you still be able to intercede for forgiveness?"

Lone Peak pointed to Stubborn Stone. "His sins were far worse than yours, but because he turned his mind to goodness, he moved Heaven into taking back the daughters who would have redeemed his debts. That is something you saw with your own eyes, not something I made up, so you already know whether you can be forgiven."

Stubborn Stone was delighted when he heard of the Knave's intention to turn his mind to goodness. He told how he himself had rejected the master's advice three years before and thrown himself into all kinds of debauchery, and how the retribution he suffered as a consequence had borne out the master's warnings to the letter. He urged the Knave to heed his example.

The Knave took his decision and made his bows to Lone Peak that very day, acknowledging him as his teacher. Receiving the tonsure, he embarked on a strict course of self-denial and in less than twenty years attained the fruits of enlightenment. He died sitting in the buddha position, like Lone Peak and Stubborn Stone.

Obviously there is no man who is unfit to become a buddha. It is only because we are so controlled by money and sex that we cannot avoid the path of error and reach salvation's shore. That is the reason why Heaven is so sparsely populated and Hell so densely crowded, why the Jade Emperor has nothing to occupy his time and King Yama is too busy to cope. In a more general sense it is all due to the meddling of the Sage who separated Heaven and Earth. He should never have created woman or instituted money, reducing man to his present sorry state. Let me now sum up the case against the Sage with a quotation from the *Four Books*: "Was it not the Sage himself who invented burial images?"[95]

CRITIQUE

Whereas at the beginning of the book he was grateful to the Sage, now, at its close, he berates him. That worthy cannot be feeling either too pleased or too vexed about it. This truly is a book that mocks *everything*! Let me come to the Sage's defense with yet another quotation from the *Four Books*: "Those who understand me will do so through *The Carnal Prayer Mat*; those who condemn me will also do so because of *The Carnal Prayer Mat*."[96]

---

95. The quotation is from *Mencius*. See D. C. Lau, trans., *Mencius*, p. 52. Confucius condemned the use of burial images because he thought they encouraged human sacrifice.

96. The quotation is adapted from *Mencius*, where Confucius is described as defending his composition of *The Spring and Autumn Annals*. See D. C. Lau, trans., *Mencius*, p. 114: "Those who understand me will do so through the *Spring and Autumn Annals*; those who condemn me will also do so because of the *Spring and Autumn Annals*."

ABOUT THE AUTHOR

Li Yu was a renowned essayist, novelist, short-story writer, playwright, and critic. *The Carnal Prayer Mat* was first published in 1657.

ABOUT THE TRANSLATOR

Educated in New Zealand and England, Patrick Hanan is a professor of Chinese literature at Harvard University. Among his books is a study of the author of *The Carnal Prayer Mat* entitled *The Invention of Li Yu* (Harvard University Press, 1988). Mr. Hanan is a Fellow of the American Academy of Arts and Sciences and has received numerous awards for his research and translation projects.

TITLES OF THE AVAILABLE PRESS in order of publication

*Available in a Ballantine Mass Market Edition.